<u>INVETIA</u>

By

John Greasby

First Printing: 2014

ISBN 978-1-291-83266-2

www.johngreasby@gmail.com

Ordering Information:
Contact to the above email address with the requirements of your order.

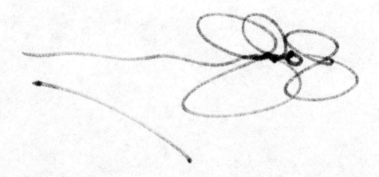

To Angela,

For the belief you have, the guidance you offer and the love you give.

You are my world.

CHAPTER

1

Sam Meredith gazed absentmindedly at the clock and wondered how there could still be a whole two hours to go before finishing time. The day was turning into a never ending onslaught of filing, typing and photocopying, he thought to himself darkly. He was sure that when he looked at the clock three hours ago there was only two hours left then! Today marked his three year anniversary of joining Simmonds & Co Solicitors as a junior receptionist, but this was not a reason for celebration. It was only ever meant to have been a temporary job, something to earn him extra money so that he could finally spread his wings and travel the world. He had his whole life mapped out three years ago. He would take this job and stay for just over a year until he had finally managed to save enough to travel the world. He would be gone for a whole year, maybe longer. He would see the best of what this planet had to offer, he would live and breathe the different cultures and experience the excitement of new challenges and new places. He would fill every waking moment with discovery and adventure and, once he had filled his life to the point that it could hold no more, he would then return wiser and worldlier, enriched and fulfilled. He would then buy a house, marry a beautiful girl and live everyday to the fullest. But now, three years on, there were no signs of any impending trips, his rent for his one bedroom flat used up most of his wage and he was now firmly embroiled in the 'working to survive' scenario that every adult eventually passes into. His plans as to how life would pan out for him that he had three years earlier had all but disappeared, now reduced to nothing more than dreams that floated further away from his grasp with each passing day. He had had urges to move on and yet he had stayed. Life had a way of doing all that it could to push you down a path, and unless you were prepared and brave enough to push back, you would eventually be too far down its road to turn-around. The problem was that 'you were always too far down when the eventual realisation of this was made clear to you', he thought. He had also stayed due to his lack of energy and interest to look for another job, and partly due to his secret desire for Jane Fielding on the third floor, although he wasn't even sure that she knew that he existed.

The last six months had seen two major milestones in his life, he had seen his twenty first birthday come and go, and had seen the death of his mother just last year. Having never known his father, the world now found him alone. He would tell himself that this meant that he was 'Master of his own future and free to do as he pleased,' but then he would ponder why he was still working as a receptionist in a solicitors office, after all, this was hardly the wondrous life he had once envisaged. He leant back in his chair and ran his fingers through his thick mop of blonde hair as he thought back on the missed opportunities that had passed him by.
'Strange,' he thought, that time was so generous with its passing when the bad times came and so miserly with the good times, however, the good times seemed so rare these days that he hardly noticed anymore.

'Still,' he thought, 'tomorrow was a new day and with it brought the possibility of new opportunities.' The other certainty about life was that you never knew what was waiting for you just around the corner.

His infatuation with the clock and his musings came to an abrupt halt as the phone on his desk let out its usual screech. With the minimum of excitement he pushed the button on his headset and answered the call.

"Good afternoon, Simmonds and Co, how can I help?"

The voice on the other end was that of a woman's, and one that he did not recognise.

"You can help me Sam by meeting with me at the Plaza at seven o'clock tonight," replied the unfamiliar voice. He thought for an instant that Jane had finally noticed his starring and unspoken desire, but that idea left him as quickly as it had come.

"I...I... am sorry," he stumbled over his words, so unexpected was her statement, "you are speaking to Sam, Sam Meredith, who is it you wish to speak with?"

There was a short silence before the caller continued,

"I know who you are and it is you that I wish to speak with Sam," the caller replied, "after all, I have been waiting to speak with you for a very long time. I understand that this may be somewhat strange and unexpected, but our meeting is not avoidable. Your future and mine depend on it."

As he listened to the caller's voice, he began to grow impatient and frustrated. This was obviously some kind of joke, and as he stared at the mountainous piles of ever increasing filing on his desk, it was clear that it was one that he did not have time to indulge in.

"Sam," the voice cut through his growing anger, "you must meet with me for I have a message of great importance for you. This message is for you alone so I ask that you bring no one and tell no one of our meeting, for to do so could be more dangerous than you could possibly imagine."

He couldn't hold his tongue any longer, his anger spilling out.

"Who are you? Do you seriously expect me to believe this? Expecting me to meet someone who I do not even know, and why is it that you can't simply give me this message over the telephone? In fact what is this message? Who is it from?" The voice cut him short,

"Sam, I will be happy to answer all of your questions, but not now, you must meet with me. I will find you; just ensure that you are there. I assure you my dear Sam this is not a joke, you must find it in yourself to trust my word. If you look hard enough you will see that there is no deceit in that which I speak. I have been, and will always be your friend." With that the line went dead.

It took Sam several minutes to get his head straight. He was sure that this must be a joke and he even had a prime suspect in mind, but if it was Anna playing her usual tricks then it would probably see the evening end up in a bar or in a club, and seeing as today was Friday, he would go along with her ruse, after all, he had nothing better to do.

He had known Anna since school. She was the type of person that made you feel good just by being around her. He had grown to love her as a brother would his sister. She was incredibly intelligent, but hid this behind her fun loving and quick witted persona. She wasn't classically attractive, but she had the most piercing dark brown eyes, jet-black shoulder length hair and a smile that was infectious to all. He would constantly tease her about being short, a teasing that usually ended up with him receiving a firm punch to the arm. She was very athletic and during her time at school had been an avid swimmer. He had often wondered why he had never felt anything more than friendship for her, but somehow he felt that this would have cheapened the relationship that they had, and he couldn't afford for that to happen, for after all, she was his only real friend.

His thoughts were suddenly interrupted,

"Sam Meredith, have you finished that filing yet?" Sam looked up to see Mr Adams standing in front of him, not looking at peace with the world.

"Nearly Mr Adams," he lied, "I have been inundated with calls," he lied again, "I will get it all done before five o'clock though," this was almost definitely a lie!

"Well ensure you do young man, I will be checking again at five o'clock." With that, Mr Adams turned and strode purposefully back down the corridor. Once again Sam wished that he had been more energetic with regards to his job hunting!

He glanced again at the clock, "Damn it," he thought, "where did all that time go?" The clock now read four thirty. His mysterious phone call and his absent musings had cost him over an hour.

'You wait till I see that Anna,' he thought lightly, 'she's in for it!'

The last half an hour, by contrast, seemed to go on forever, still, all his filing had been done, except for the files that he had hidden in his desk, and Mr Adams had returned bang on five to check his progress, although Sam had never doubted for one moment that he wouldn't. The weekend had arrived at last.
As he grabbed his jacket from the hook he found himself thinking again of the impending meet. He had decided that he would go, and he was convinced that he would find Anna laughing at his naivety. He was so wrapped up in his thoughts that he failed to notice Jane Fielding's look back at him as she left the building.

After the short walk home, Sam began to ready himself for the evening ahead. Believing that he was to be out for quite sometime, he thought that he would dispense with the usual frayed jeans and tee-shirt look and go with a more sophisticated look of non-frayed jeans and a shirt, this was about as sophisticated as he ever got. With that in mind he jumped into the shower, toothbrush in mouth, and began the grooming ritual. Once finished he dried himself off, had a quick shave, splashed on his favourite Paco Roban aftershave and dressed. Within an hour of getting home, he was locking the front door and heading for the Plaza.

As he made the short journey back into town, he allowed his mind to drift back to memories of his mother. She had been gone now for just six months however it seemed like a lifetime and he missed her everyday. She had been everything to him. As he had never grown up with a father, she had substituted for both parents and she had done a fine job in his opinion. She had ensured that he never went short and made sure that his life stayed on the right path. She had always got on well with Anna, as both of them were full of life and energy, and would laugh uncontrollably at anything remotely funny when in each other's company. Anna used to say that Maureen was more like a sister to her and he believed that Anna missed her almost as much as he did.

Before he knew it he was at the Plaza. He checked his watch; 'a quarter to seven' read the display. He allowed himself a grin of satisfaction; it was not often that he was early for anything. It was not until now that it dawned on him that he did not know where to meet Anna, or the mystery woman, he amended mentally to himself. He was at the Plaza as requested, but this place was a mass of shops and coffee bars, escalators and lifts, and it was busy with shoppers all anxious to grab a last minute bargain before the start of the weekend.

As he was early he decided to take a slow amble through the mall and headed for the furthest coffee bar, after all, if Anna was behind this then it was likely that the coffee bar would be his best bet.

He started to stare at the various window displays as he walked, each one trying to sell a compelling reason for shoppers to enter and make an impulse purchase for something that they never even knew that they wanted or indeed needed. He was also sure to be keeping an eye out for the elusive Anna as he did so.

Eventually he arrived at the coffee house. He scanned the area; no one he recognised sprang into view, so he went inside and ordered himself a tall Latte and an Apple Danish and found himself a table in the seating area outside of the shop. Halfway through his Latte he glanced again at his watch, a quarter past seven, typically Anna was late. It wasn't until his watch showed seven-thirty that Sam began to get a little edgy. Anna, whilst not the most punctual, would have usually called by now if she was going to be this late, unless of course this was part of the ruse. It was however becoming less funny, Friday nights were valuable, and sitting around in a coffee bar was not his idea of a great evening. He tried to call her several times on her mobile phone but had just reached her answer phone, and despite leaving a rather terse message, he had still had no reply. He continued to watch the mass of people, as he drained the last remnants of coffee from his glass, as they rushed all around him with arms loaded with bags and bags of 'stuff.' Despite his darkening mood, he inwardly smiled at the fact that we put so much importance on things that really didn't matter, material possessions and other peoples business, and yet, most barely gave a passing thought to life's real values such as sharing time with those you loved or giving time to those that needed it most.

He looked around again for the umpteenth time for Anna before deciding that he would order one more Latte and if she had not appeared by the time he had finished, then he would head for home and try and salvage what remained of the evening.

Upon returning from collecting his coffee, he was further annoyed to find that his table had been taken by a small girl with a large milkshake. He began to look for another table to sit at, when he heard his name called. It was not shouted nor was it whispered, it just seemed to be carried to him like a leaf on the wind.

He turned around but found no one to be looking his way. In fact he turned in a complete circle but no one caught his eye. Slightly confused he renewed his hunt for a table. "Sam," the voice sounded again, this time more urgent, but still he was unable to see where it had emanated from. He spun around this time, determined to catch the trickster. He was greeted by the stare of the young girl sitting at his former table.

"Please come and join me Sam," came her voice. The only way he knew it to be from the girl was that she indicated to the seat opposite her with her eyes, no sound came from her mouth. "Do not be afraid, I am your friend." He stood there lost for words, blankly staring at the girl.

"How could this be? It was not possible was it?" he thought. He then began to feel the blood drain from his face as he suddenly realised that this was not Anna's doing.

Although by now he was shaking, he found himself strangely drawn towards the girl and the soothing sound of her voice. Before he had time to stop and think about what he was doing, he found himself seated opposite her.

Sam sat there unblinking, unable to take his eyes off the girl. Now he was closer he saw that she was indeed young, but not as young as he had originally thought. She seemed almost ethereal in appearance. She had a perfect unblemished complexion and her hair was as golden as the sun's rays, and although she was sitting in front of him it seemed that, should the faintest breeze touch her, she would simply blow away. He sat facing her for what seemed like an eternity. She did not show any signs of emotion, she simply sat and returned his gaze until finally she spoke.

"My name is Ruern, I have been waiting to speak to you for many years." Sam didn't speak he simply sat staring at the girl desperately trying to think of something to say.

"I have been sent by my elders to find you and watch over you, a task that I have been undertaking for the past three years."

"Three years!" Sam blurted out, "That's not possible, I mean I have never seen you before, this is ridiculous, who put you up to this, where is Anna?" Sam stopped, quickly aware that people were now staring at him. He felt his face redden from the foolishness that he now felt. He took a while to compose himself, and then, in a more controlled manner began again.

"You cannot expect me to believe what you are saying," he kept his voice low and composed as he leant in closer to the girl opposite, "I mean don't you think that I would have noticed you over my shoulder for the past three years? I have never seen you nor heard your name before, and why should you be so interested with me?" He felt himself getting angry again so was mindful to keep his composure.

"Now look, I can take a joke but this is going too far. Tell me where Anna is, as I don't find this funny anymore." He stared at Ruern awaiting her response. She simply stared back at him, her face almost saddened as she held his gaze. After a short while she spoke again.

"My dear Sam," she replied, "so anxious for answers, so sure of your life's path. You are however in mortal danger Sam and because of this you will be leaving with me in two days. This is not something that you or I can change as this is your destiny and it has already been written, nothing you can do or say will change the path that stretches out before you. I understand your mistrust, I understand your anger, but look deep within yourself Sam and you will see that I speak the truth. Your entire life has been leading up to this event and, whether you choose to acknowledge this or not is of no importance, for it is the inescapable inevitability of fate; I will be your guide and I have been entrusted to keep you safe on the journey that awaits you. But I must warn you that the steps that you must take are but the first of many, the future that awaits you is not a safe one, but a future that is yours to fulfil."

Sam sat open mouthed. He wanted to ask a thousand questions, he wanted to scream and shout, he wanted to laugh out loud at the ridiculousness of the situation, but he didn't, he couldn't, his body felt heavy and tiredness coursed through his veins.

" Go now my dear Sam," Ruern continued, " pack provisions for the road ahead, but remember that speed is required so be sure to choose wisely. Tell no one of this meeting, remember, danger surrounds you and you can no longer trust anyone."

He didn't argue, he simply smiled at Ruern and nodded his agreement as his body began to feel light and the colours of the world began to meld into one. As he began to drift into the world of dreams, he managed one final question,

"Who sent you to me Ruern?" and as he finally gave into sleeps call, he heard Ruern softly reply, "Your father."

CHAPTER
2

He had no recollection as to how he got home that evening. He couldn't remember the walk to his flat or getting into his bed nor did he remember the storm that raged for the majority of the night. Sam slept a deep dreamless sleep. A sleep that was to leave him feeling refreshed, alive and full of life, but unbeknown to him, it was a sleep that was to be his last for sometime.

He came awake to the ringing of his phone. It took him several moments to get his bearings. Still half asleep, he reached out and lifted the receiver.

"Hello," Sam mumbled.

"Sam, is that you? I've been trying to reach you for half the night, where have you been?" asked the caller.

"Ruern, is that you?" Sam blurted out

"Ruern? Who the hell is Ruern, its Anna, you remember me, dark hair, attractive, short," she said sarcastically. "Last night must have been good, you didn't return my calls and you can't

14

even remember whom I am, charming," she continued. "Where did you go anyway I thought that we usually met on a Friday night, I was quite put out?"

Sam hesitated, the warning that Ruern had given him sounded in his head like an alarm *"Don't trust anyone."* But this was Anna. Still he resisted the urge to reveal his previous evening's encounter.

"Sorry Anna, I got stuck at work and by the time I had finished all I wanted to do was go to bed." He didn't even convince himself and was sure that Anna didn't buy it, so he changed the subject as quick as possible.

"Anyway what are we doing tonight?" he enquired eager to get back into Anna's good books. Anna immediately launched into a well-planned itinerary for the evening ahead. As she continued to narrate the evening's plans, Sam's thoughts remained fixed on last night's events. He could remember everything up until his departure with complete clarity, and yet he still found the whole experience more like a dream, although the crumpled receipt for one Latte and an Apple Danish that rested on his bedside table ruled that out almost immediately. As Anna continued with her plans, Sam's thoughts returned to Ruern. There was something not right about her but he couldn't put his finger on it. She was definitely young but he couldn't hazard a guess as to her age. She seemed to be almost unreal. And what was this journey that he was supposed to make, and how could she have been watching him for three years. He began to feel his head start to spin with the hundreds of questions that seemed to rush into his mind. Anna's voice interrupted the maelstrom of questions.

"Well are you gonna answer me or what?"

"Sorry Anna what were you saying?" he replied rather sheepishly.

"Bloody hell Sam, have you been listening to a word I've been saying? I was asking what time do you want to meet?"

"Whatever, I don't mind, what's best for you?" He replied, happy to have been able to stall for a little time as he tried to regain his concentration on Anna's questions.

"I was going to suggest seven-thirty if that's ok with you oh master," she said in her usual sarcastic style. Despite his turmoil, he chuckled to himself, "Good old Anna," he thought, "always there with a quick answer."

"Yes seven-thirty would be fine me lady." He tried to match her sarcasm but he knew that she would always win that particular battle.

They arranged to meet at 'Henry's', which was their local bar in town.

If Sam was totally honest with himself he would have preferred to stay in tonight but he thought that it would do him good to unwind with a pint, and to be in Anna's company would be the tonic that he required.

By the time he had finished on the telephone with Anna, it was still only midday.

He took his time readying himself for the day ahead. He had decided to put Ruern and all the events of the past evening to the back of his mind. So he allowed himself a long soak in the bath, followed by some lunch and then a few hours reading the paper and watching the television. He smiled to himself "Half past five in the afternoon and still in my dressing gown, this is how a day off should be spent". After a further hour of doing nothing, he set about getting ready for the night out. By seven o'clock he was dressed, out the door and heading for Henry's.

It was a warm night, and he enjoyed the walk to town, albeit that he was still keeping an eye out for Ruern, despite his previous promise to himself that he would put the thought of her out of his head. He felt better as he reached the Bar, he seemed to be exposed on his walk, but now he was among the usual bustle of a busy pub on a Saturday night and he was no longer looking over his shoulder after every other step.

As he entered the building he scanned the area to locate Anna but, as he expected, she didn't seem to have yet arrived. He ordered a beer from the bar and found himself a table. He sat for a while and watched the people drifting in, he watched couples dance, and others argue, he watched the bar staff run

16

around in thousand different directions at once all trying to satisfy the thirsty crowd that surrounded them. He found it interesting to 'people watch'. People were all so different in normal life and yet get them in a pub and they all start acting the same.

"Sam." Came the familiar cry. He looked towards the door and saw Anna and Ben at the entrance.

Ben was Anna's brother. He was three years her elder and was the sensible part of the duo. He was much taller than Anna, but shared many of her characteristics. He was fit and of athletic build. He possessed the same penetrating brown eyes and the same black hair. The main difference was that he was very much a thinker. Whereas Anna would think nothing of jumping into the unknown with both feet, Ben would always look to take the most pragmatic approach, and only after he had weighed up all of the available options. He was quiet in contrast, but had a wonderful dry sense of humour and he often employed this to counter his sister's sarcasm, although she usually won. Sam often thought that it was unusual that Brother and Sister should get on as well as they did. This is not to say they never argued, they did, often, and yet there was always an element of control on both sides to ensure that neither went too far. They shared a mutual respect for each other, and would always be there for the other should they be needed. Sam would sometimes wish that he had a brother or sister to share his worries and excitements with, but he was more than happy that he had Anna and Ben to fill that role.

"So you are here," Anna stated as she strode up to where he was seated, "I half expected you to let us down again!" Sam smiled inwardly she never missed an opportunity to get the first attack in.

"Yes, but I only came because I knew Ben was coming," he replied. She smiled her usual infectious smile and seated herself next to him.

"C'mon Ben, get the drinks in," she ordered

"Hiya Sam, what you drinking?" Ben asked as he reached the table. Sam bid him hello, placed his ordered, and watched as Ben dutifully made his way to the bar.

17

"I don't know how he puts up with you," he said to Anna smiling.

"He loves it, makes him feel useful," she replied. "So, what you been up to?"

Sam thought momentarily of relaying the events of last night to Anna in full, but quickly dispelled the idea, as she was sure to think him a fool. So he told her about his uneventful week at work, about Jane Feilding's continuous lack of interest in him and about his lack of filing skills. As he was finishing, Ben reappeared with a handful of drinks and a bag of dry roasted peanuts clenched between his teeth. Anna looked at him with an air of distain. "What?" he replied to her look, "I'm hungry!"

The evening continued at a steady pace. Each of the three were by now fully relaxed and enjoying the evening. Ale flowed steadily and they talked of times past and present and their hopes for the future. Sam made them both laugh uncontrollably by announcing that he would probably leave his job within the next six months and do something with his life. Unbeknown to him Ben had bet Anna before they entered the pub that Sam would say this before nine o'clock and he had been proved right.

"You've been saying that since you started there!" Ben interjected.

Sam laughed loudly in response, "Nothing was as good as a Saturday night with friends," he thought to himself.

It wasn't until just before ten o'clock that Sam noticed her. He was in the middle of listening to Anna and Ben arguing as to whose turn it was to go to the bar next, when he looked up. There sitting at a table on the other side of the pub was Ruern. He stared at her, not willing to believe his eyes at first. She simply returned his gaze. She was transfixed on him. Her stare seemed to cut deep into his very being. Her face showed no signs of emotion just as before. Sam felt himself begin to panic. He had managed to avoid thinking about Ruern for most of the day and it was beginning to feel like their meeting was a dream or at best a mistake, but seeing her so unexpectedly, watching his every movement, was unsettling to say the least.

"Calm down, deep breaths," he told himself. He broke of his gaze as he tried to regain his composure. He stared at his drink trying to think what to do next.

"Sam, will you tell Ben that it's his turn, I got them last time." Anna stated in a childish voice. What Sam did next surprised even him, "I'll get them," he stated, and without looking up he made his way to the bar.

He half expected to find that Ruern had disappeared when he looked up again to find her, but when he did he found that she remained seated as before. He walked past the bar and over to the table to where his watcher sat. Even before he had reached her table he heard her words "Sit down with me Sam." It was spoken so softly and yet her voice transcended the noise of the room with ease. It reached out to him and pulled him gently to her. He felt strangely excited to hear that voice again, and felt no resistance this time to join her.

"Ruern, why are you here?" he asked. "Why do you follow me?" He was not angry; his voice was one of concern rather than annoyance. She smiled at him,

"Sam, I have already told you that I have been with you for many years now, it is just that you now choose to see me. I trust that you have not told Anna of our meeting?"

The question caught him by surprise, "She knew Anna?" As if by reading his thoughts she went on. "I know everything about you Sam, that includes who you're friends are. I trust that you have begun to make provisions for our journey? I will come for you tomorrow night and you must be ready." Her voice seemed to grow anxious, "There is no time to waste, and you must be ready to leave when I come for you next."

"Why must I go with you Ruern? And why the urgency? I do not understand any of what you have said to me although I have thought of nothing else. None of what you speak makes any sense at all."

"All will be revealed when the time is right my dear Sam, and that time is not yet upon us," came Ruern's reply. Sam knew that there was little point in pursuing this line of conversation, he glanced back, aware that Anna and Ben would be wondering as to what was taking him so long, however it appeared that they were deep in discussion about something or other and didn't yet seen to notice his prolonged absence. "Ruern, I want to ask you something." He waited for some confirmation that she had heard him; however, she sat impassive as ever and returned his stare. He continued anyway, "When we met yesterday you called me although I didn't see you speak my name, it was as if your voice called to me from within, almost as if I sensed you call me rather than heard you, how was that possible?" Ruern seemed to consider his question then gave him a slight smile. "You still doubt all that I have told you. There is much for you to learn on the journey ahead. I am a Sario. I am not of your world Sam; I have crossed worlds to find you." She said it so matter of factly, and although he tried, Sam could not keep the astonishment from showing on his face.

"Am I now being asked to believe that you are from another planet?" His words were laced with incredulity. Ruern continued to smile "Not exactly another planet as you put it Sam," she replied, "think of me as an imprint in time. I come from a time very different from yours and yet, in many ways, a world and time that is not unknown to you, although you have ceased to believe in its existence." Sam was even more confused than before and still not believing any of what he was being told. He was rapidly drawing to the conclusion that Ruern could quite possible be completely mad and yet he could not shake the feeling that he would be proved wrong.

"Listen Ruern," his voice now hushed and composed, "I have to be going, my friends are waiting for me to return, but answer me one last question, where are we going on this journey that you have continuously spoken of, what is its purpose?" Ruern remained silent for a moment as if considering her reply, finally she spoke,

"Your life as you know it is about to change Sam, and no amount of guessing as to how will bring you closer to the truth. To give you all the answers to your questions would place you in a greater danger than already exists, but take some comfort from the knowledge that this journey, that is yours to take, is

20

unavoidable. It will ask questions of you that have no right to be asked, and will answer questions that you have yet to consider. The journey will be long and I do not pretend that danger will not be ever present. As to where and how this journey will be undertaken, I ask that you remain patient, as time will provide the answers that you seek. Go now to Anna and speak not of our meeting, I will come to you in one sunrise time. You must be ready to leave with me, for failure to do so will close your life's chapter before it has been written." Ruern appeared to change, Sam noticed, albeit slight. She took on a dark appearance. The once passive and youthful face seemed to pass into shadow and she appeared older and almost imposing. "Strip away your doubts Sam and allow your mind to be opened to the truth you know dwells within. Do not take my words as futile, for if you should, you will rue that decision forever." Sam took a step back; he would have run at this point if he were able, but as before, he felt compelled to stay, even though her words seemed to cut at him like knives. Ruern held his a gaze for a moment longer then smiled her face again placid and serene.

"Be strong Sam, I will let no harm come to you for you are my charge, you are my hope." With that Ruern stood and walked away.

Sam turned and made his way to the bar, collected the drinks order, and returned to Anna and Ben. Once again his head was spinning from his encounter with Ruern.

"What the hell's wrong with you?" Anna admonished on his return. "You look as white as snowfall." Sam tried to smile through his now rescinding confusion.

"I am fine," he managed, "but I think I'll make this my last," he nodded at the ale that he held before him.

"Now I've heard everything," Anna replied, "Sam Meredith knowing his limit and actually daring to go home on the right side of midnight on a Saturday night!"

"Anna just drop it will you! I am allowed to make my own decisions," he snapped, and then almost immediately regretted his outburst. "I am sorry Anna, I didn't mean to snap. I'm just not feeling all that good." Anna smiled, "I'm sorry too Sam, sometimes I let my mouth run off before my brain's caught up, look we can go now if you would prefer?" Sam began to laugh. "I may not feel well, but I have never left a drink before and I don't intend to do so now, I'll go after this one." The three sat and finished their drinks. They talked of their week ahead and of that awful Monday feeling you always got on a Sunday evening. Sam had that feeling already and it was still only Saturday. He laughed inwardly he would probably be at work just the same. Monday, although promised excitement from Ruern, would prove to be just another day of work and boredom, of this he was *almost* convinced.

Once they had drained their glasses they left Henry's. Anna and Ben said goodnight and headed for the taxi rank, Sam set off in the opposite direction preferring to walk. He did so slowly, taking in the noises of the town and the people as he went. Couples passed him hand in hand, some rushed to their destinations, and some simply stood as if waiting for something to happen. Which one was he, he wondered? Was he rushing to his destination or was he waiting for it to find him? As he walked he began to think again of his most recent meeting with Ruern. *"It will answer questions that you have yet to consider."* What the hell did that mean? He asked himself. After all, it was true that he had always wondered as to where his life was taking him, but doesn't everybody at some stage? It was then that he thought back to her closing statement on their first encounter. She had said that his father had sent her! It was only now that he had considered this. Why had he not asked this evening to explain? The truth was that he had simply forgotten, but the more he thought of it the more it annoyed him. "Stupid fool," he thought darkly. "Surely this was the most important question to have asked, after all, his father had died before his second birthday, how could Ruern of defended that!" He continued his slow walk home. It was turning into a cold evening so he pulled his jacket tight about himself and stuffed his hands into his pockets in an attempt to ward off the nights chill. His thoughts switched to Anna then. He was wrong to have snapped at her. She was his best friend, possibly his only true friend in the real sense of the word. Sure he had other pals

22

one of which was Ben, but that was mainly through acquaintance with Anna. He had no secrets from her, until now, he thought. He could tell her anything and everything and she would always be honest with him, sometimes brutally, but honest nevertheless. What's more is whether right or wrong she would always stand by him. She was his council on most things and he respected her opinion. Likewise, he was the only person to know her true persona. She would not even let Ben in too far. He knew that she was tough and would never back down from an argument, but she was also insecure. He could see beneath the protective shell that she hid behind. She did mind what people thought of her, she did need to feel loved and she definitely needed Sam when things got too much. It was only ever Sam that she fully confided in and he felt almost honoured to be placed in such a position of trust. She was very special to him and he felt bad about the way that he had spoken to her. "I ring in the morning to apologise," he thought.

As he rounded the corner to his home, he saw that he would not have to wait that long, for there in his lobby stood Anna.

"C'mon Sam, hurry up, it's bloody cold out here and I need a coffee," she shouted across to him. Despite his dark mood and scattered thoughts he smiled, she could always make him smile.

"I thought you'd gone home with that brother of yours," he stated as he turned the key in the lock.

"Wasn't ready for bed just yet, and besides, I got the impression that you might need a chat." She cocked her head knowingly to one side.

"Smart arse!" He replied with a smile.

They entered his flat and Anna immediately made herself comfortable on the sofa while Sam attended to the coffee. Once made, he brought it into the lounge and settled down next to her. "Do you want the TV on?" He ventured.

"Not particularly," came her reply

"Music then, what do you fancy?" He tried again.

"Sam!" I know you to well and have known you for too long, if you don't want to talk well then call me a taxi, if you do, I am here for you, what's it going to be?" *"Brutal as ever"* he thought.

Although he had absolutely no intention of telling her of the last twenty four hours, even though he had been determined to keep it all to himself, after twenty minutes he had narrated the whole tale. He had left nothing out and had laid it all bare on the table for her sift though. As soon as he had finished he wished he hadn't, but he also felt better for doing so.

Nevertheless, as he spoke the words he realised just how crazy it all sounded. After he had finished, he sat back and waited for a response.

He waited for what seemed an eternity. Anna simply sat and mulled over his every word. This was most unusual for Anna, in fact he had rarely seen her this slow to respond. Eventually her head came up from her hands and met his gaze square on. "I'm going with you," she said in a hushed voice. This was the last response that he had expected and he failed to mask the look of astonishment that had gripped his face.

"What the hell do you mean, you're going with me? You don't honestly believe any of what I have told you to have the slightest chance of being the truth do you?"

Sam was flabbergasted, of all the people he knew; he would have expected Anna to be the most pragmatic. But here she was, sitting in his lounge and fully believing what amounted to little more than fairytale, and a bad one at that! She sat there and stared at him for a while, her face totally impassive. "Sam, as I have previously said," she started, "I have known you for too long for you to be able to hide things from me. This Ruern has troubled you now for a whole day with her words and warnings. This is not the response that I would have expected from you unless you believed there to be more to her claims than you are admitting to. I have therefore reached the conclusion that, no matter how much you deny it to yourself, you believe some, if not all, of what you have been told, or at least want to believe," she amended. "Ever since I have known you, you have been unsettled with your life. Since your mother's death you have been searching for a meaning to it all. Now it would appear that you have been presented with a thread of possibility to grasp at. Most would think you mad for reaching for it; however I am willing to wager that you cannot shake the feeling that some of it might just be true no matter how crazy it sounds." Sam listened silently as she continued with her reasoning, still confused by her apparent acceptance of the possibilities that faced him. "Ask yourself just one question Sam, what if; what if it was true? Couldn't this be the something that you have been so desperate to find?"

He could hear the words that were coming from her, and yet he still could not believe what he was hearing. This was not the Anna that he thought he knew so well.

"Anna," he was unsure how his next words would be received, but nevertheless, he had to try them on for size, "why are you so willing to believe this..," he couldn't think of the right word to use, "story," he eventually managed. "I mean it's not everyday that someone tells you that they have been approached by a stranger, who can communicate telepathically and has apparently been stalking you for three years although you have never seen or heard of them before," He was getting animated again, "and informs you that you are to undertake a long perilous journey, and no matter what I choose I am in some kind of mortal danger. If I didn't know better I would have thought that you knew more about this than I do."

The moment the last sentence left his lips he regretted it. He was suggesting that Anna was somehow connected with all of this.

"I'm sorry Anna, that was a stupid thing to say, I don't know what's wrong with me lately, I didn't mean to…"

"I might know something Sam," she cut in. She was no longer holding his gaze but her eyes were transfixed on the pattern on his carpet. Her voice was now little more than a whisper. "I mean how could you…" Her words then hit him like a train.

"What did you say?" The look on his face was now one of horror.

"Sam," Anna pressed on, still unable to meet his stare, not bearing to look upon the lines of mistrust that were mirrored on Sam's face. "Just before Maureen's death, three days before to be exact, I spoke with her at her request. She was so ill Sam and her conversation was vague at best." Sam envisaged his mother then, too weak to rise from her bed, some days to weak to even speak. She had known that her life was near completion and had refused to be admitted to hospital. She had argued that she would rather die amongst friends as opposed to strangers. Her will was the last thing to break.

"But she called me too her, she gave me a specific message. At the time I thought the message to be part of her illness; I thought her confused and believed her to be rambling. She told me that shortly after she was gone you would be visited." Sam felt the blood drain from his face. "She didn't say by whom or to what purpose, but that you would be going away, that you would undertake a journey, a journey that had been arranged on the day that you were born. At the end of this passage you would discover your purpose." Anna was crying now, unable to cope with the raw emotions that coursed through her, each word now laced with tears and she was having difficulty speaking them. "She charged me Sam with ensuring that you undertook this flight, she made me promise that I would do all I could to make sure it happened when the time came." She wiped angrily at the tears that rolled down her face. "I agreed Sam, I thought her lost to a world of half truths and dreams. She was so ill Sam I just wanted her to be at peace, had I have known she spoke the truth I would have told you. Please Sam you must believe me..." With that she began to sob uncontrollably and buried her head in her hands.

Sam pulled her close and hugged her. He was not angry or hurt anymore, in fact he felt almost numb. "Of course I believe you, of course I do." He was close to tears, images of his mother filled his mind and he missed her so much.

They sat for a long while, holding each other fearing that should one let go they would be lost. Eventually it was Anna that broke the embrace.

"Great way to spend a Saturday night," she whispered as she wiped away the remaining tears from her face. Sam smiled a sad smile in response. "What the hell do we do now?" It was more of a statement than a question, but Anna couldn't help but notice that Sam had said 'we' as opposed to 'I.'

They sat for a long time after that talking about Sam's mother, his childhood and the appearance of Ruern. It seemed impossible to Sam that his mother could have known of Ruern's arrival and yet it was beyond doubt that this was just coincidence. He was still struggling with all the truths that lay scattered about him.

"I think we should wait for this Ruern to reappear and demand that she tell us what's going on," Anna ventured, "after all you still are no closer to knowing the truth. But first I would suggest that we pack some provisions just in case this journey or whatever proves to be unavoidable and get a good night's sleep," she added. It appeared to Sam that Anna had not waited for an invite to join this nightmare, she was coming and that was that. He was suddenly aware that he was indeed tired, not that he had the right to be after the long sleep and restful day that he had enjoyed; still it was two in the morning and sleep sounded like a good idea. After all, his mind had been pulled in every possible direction and he didn't have the energy to think anymore about anything.

He insisted that Anna take his bed, it was too late for her to go home and he felt reassured to know that she was close. He fetched spare blankets from the airing cupboard and settled himself down on the sofa. Despite his lassitude it became apparent that sleep would not find him as easily as it should have done. He lay awake, his mind still turning over the last two days events. "It was the stuff of a fiction novel and not that of real life," he thought. Although it was correct that he had not been happy with the direction that his life was taking, he couldn't have thought for a moment that this could have been a possible outcome. In the deepest part of his mind there lived the possibility that it was all still a mistake, but this was rapidly becoming an outside bet. He heard the light switch flick on in his bedroom; obviously Anna had not yet found sleeps embrace either.

After a further half an hour of tossing and turning he gave up. He was too awake for sleep to come. He got up and made his way to the kitchen. "A glass of milk and a piece of toast might do the trick," he thought. As he pushed the door open, he was greeted by Ruern standing in the middle of his kitchen.

He froze. He wanted to run, scream, anything but he couldn't. "It is time Sam." Ruern gave him a reassuring smile. His mind went into overdrive. "It wasn't Monday, Christ, it was only just Sunday, and she shouldn't be here yet!" He panicked, and as if reading his mind she spoke again.

"The situation has changed, we must leave very soon, trust me Sam we need to be on our way."

"I haven't packed!" was the only response he could manage.

"There is no longer time, what little we had has slipped away." Ruern's voice remained calm and soft. Sam's, by contrast, was not so composed.

"What about Anna? We just can't just leave her!" He screamed.

"You're not leaving me anywhere!" came Anna's voice from the hallway. Sam spun around to see Anna pushing her way through the kitchen door carrying a holdall.

"I took the liberty of packing you some clothes," she said as she followed his gaze down to the bag. Anna seemed neither phased nor surprised to see Ruern; she simply took it in her stride.

"It would appear that our little group has grown to three," Ruern whispered, "let us be gone."

"Yes lets." Anna replied defiantly, eyes locked on Ruern. Sam suddenly felt rather incidental to the whole thing.

CHAPTER

3

They left just before dawn. Anna had taken a moment to grab some bread and cheese from the refrigerator and fill an empty bottle with water. Then the company of three left Sam's home and stepped into the night. Ruern took the lead and immediately led them away from the dim lights of the town. She had still not given any indication of the destination or as to how long it would take to reach. They walked in silence, no one felt much like talking. Ruern strode purposefully on, never checking her stride, never looking back to ensure her silent companions were keeping pace. Sam followed, his mind still turning over the overwhelming events of the past few days, still not fully believing that he could be part of this madness, and Anna brought up the rear, silent in her resolve, confident that she would not falter, no matter what. Everything else around them was still. No birdsong, no sounds of life from the houses they passed, even the wind seemed to be holding its breath.

As they continued on, eventually, all signs of life disappeared completely. They passed no more houses and were now walking towards open farmland and rolling hills, the town now left far behind. Sam wondered how long it would be before he would see it again, whilst quietly praying that it would be 'when' as opposed to 'if'. Still they continued onwards. The moon was beginning to give up its dark watch as the sun was preparing to start its vigil. However dark clouds and gloom had enveloped the land thus ensuring that the sun would not be taking over just yet.

A few times Sam had asked Ruern if they were nearing their destination, but was greeted each time with silence. It was as if she was in deep concentration and either didn't hear him, or chose to ignore him, he thought it was probably the latter. He watched her as they walked; both Anna and he were sweating and were finding the going difficult. The ground was heavy and slippery underfoot from the early morning dew that glistened in the half-light, and crossing fields in the near dark made it twice as hard, but Ruern moved onwards with an effortless grace over the earth. She traversed with fluidity, never losing her step or pausing to find the easiest path. Both Anna and Sam were having trouble keeping up. She obviously knew where she was going, and never once did she seem to doubt her way.

'Perhaps she had made this journey before,' Sam wondered. 'After all she had been waiting for this moment for three years by her own admission. Perhaps this is how she had managed to find the quickest route to wherever it was they were heading, perhaps a million things,' Sam thought wearily. He didn't have any answers to the thousands of questions that squeezed his mind so he gave up thinking and concentrated on putting one foot in front of the other.

The moon had long since disappeared but the gloom continued to hold the sun at bay. Still there were no sounds other than the ones made by their passing. All was still. Anna had noticed it the moment they had passed the last few houses; she had initially put it down to the earliness of the hour but was now not so sure. She didn't know what time it was for she had left her watch on Sam's bedside cabinet and Sam never wore one. She thought though that they must have been travelling for several hours and surely Nature, if not people would be awake. But nothing moved and all was still as if waiting for something or someone she considered.

After a while Ruern turned and offered them time to rest. Both Anna and Sam jumped at the chance. Both kept in shape, especially Anna who was a regular swimmer and often-spent evenings at the gym with Sam but they were both grateful for the break. Ruern, in contrast, seemed to be as fresh as when they first set out.

Neither Anna nor Sam had known how long they had been walking but Ruern advised them that they had been going two hours. Sam had suggested that she must be mistaken as it felt as if it had been ten! But she gave no response.

It seemed to Sam as if they had just stopped before Ruern had them on their feet again. She had said that danger was ever present and that they could not afford to rest for too long. She showed none of the serenity that she possessed when they first met. She appeared to have undergone a change since their departure. She was now more distant, almost as if she was pre-occupied with other matters. He had also noticed that she seemed, almost frightened. He couldn't put his finger on what made him feel this, but her whole manner had changed. She didn't seem as at peace now as she did when they had first set out just a few hours ago.

For the short time that they rested, she had stood with her back to them and starred back at the way of their recent passing as if looking for something. What's more she seemed to expect to find it. 'Was someone else supposed to meet her?' Sam wondered.' 'What if,' Sam suddenly thought, 'what if she was looking for a pursuer, was someone or something hunting them? Was this the danger that she had so often spoken of?' Just the thought of this made him shiver. It was bad enough to be out here in the near dark, cold, wet and aching, let alone to potentially have something following you. It was then that he

made a promise to himself, he would never moan about
Sunday's being boring again. He glanced at Anna, gave her a
reassuring smile, and then set off after Ruern.

They resumed their march through the gloom; every direction
mirrored the same landscape, fields and grassland. He decided
that he would approach Ruern again to find out as to where
they were heading, after all how long would he go on without
knowing where he was going? He had to draw the line at
somewhere and he was fast approaching it.
He ran to catch up to her shoulder; her cowl was now pulled
over her head to fend off the morning cold.
"Ruern, where are we going?" His voice laced with sternness,
no longer deciding to be patient. "We have been walking for
hours, we are in the middle of nowhere with no end in sight,
you must give me something or we're going back." He hadn't
bothered checking Anna's thoughts on this he assumed she
would back him up.
Ruern slowed then stopped, her head bowed. Sam stood a few
steps behind waiting for her answer. By now Anna had caught
them up and was looking at Sam with questioning eyes,
anxious to find out what was happening. She was about to ask
when Ruern spoke.
"We travel to the forest." An arm stretched out from her wrap
to point the way. "We will reach it within two hours if we do
not continue to stop" she stated. "If we do not reach it within
the time allowed it is likely that we will not reach it at all for
my time is nearly upon me." Sam shot Anna a look, not fully
understanding Ruern's reply, but she had failed to notice, her
eyes remained firmly locked on Ruern.
Sam turned back to Ruern to ask for her to explain. She now
stood facing him. He jumped back in horror; she was old, very
old. He nearly bolted such was the shock but found Anna's
reassuring arm for support around him. Her once unblemished
skin that seemed to radiate light now hung loose of the clearly
visible framework of her skull that housed her now sunken
eyes. The golden hair now turned brittle and dirty white. Her
teeth, once gleaming, now yellowed and tarnished.

"Do not be afraid my dear Sam," she spoke, her voice soft and soothing, "as I have said to you before, this is but your journey and I cannot make it for you. I will show you the path but it is your path, and your path alone to tread. I will keep you from harms touch until we arrive, for that is my charge, but once we reach the crossover I will have fulfilled my life's duty."

Sam suddenly realised that he was crying, he didn't know why or when he had started, but the tears flowed freely down his dirt-streaked face.

"Do not cry for me Sam for the part I play in your life is the greatest honour that I could have been given."

With the ending of these words she turned away and began to walk anew. Sam hesitated unsure as to what he should do next. He felt Anna draw up beside him. He felt foolish and angrily wiped at the tears that had formed on his face.

"C'mon," she whispered, "let's get this over with." She leaned forward and kissed him on the cheek then turned and started after Ruern.

They continued to walk for a long while after that. The forest that was once a distant shadow on the horizon now began to take shape. It loomed before them; great Oak trees stood tightly packed together, their branches twisted into each other as if doing battle for the feel of the sun's touch. They rose before them like massive sentries guarding some lost and forgotten tomb. Sam was beginning to feel quite uneasy about the whole situation once again.

Still a mile from the imposing wall of trees, Ruern rested them again. They ate a little bread and cheese and took some water, all except Ruern, she neither ate nor drank. She remained statuesque, staring back at the way of their passing. She never turned nor spoke; she simply stood and watched over the rolling grasslands. Sam was convinced that she was looking for something, but he never saw nor heard anything. Conversation was kept to a minimum between Anna and Sam. Both were cold, wet and weary from the long march. The sun had failed to break through the gloom and everything remained locked in shadow and grey.

33

After a while Ruern turned to him and spoke. Sam noticed how she kept the cowl pulled close about her this time. He couldn't make out the features of her face from within; although he felt her penetrating eyes lock onto him from within the dark.

"Soon we will be within the forest," she whispered, "it will be drier underfoot but dark and choked with roots and bush."

"Fantastic, I cannot wait." Anna interrupted in her usual sarcastic manner. Ruern paid her no heed and continued, "Traversing it will be difficult, as soon as we enter we will be made known to that which hunts us, so speed and stealth are required."

Sam felt a shiver run down his spine. This was the first time that Ruern had implied that something was indeed hunting them. He shot a quick glance at Anna, but her eyes, once again, remained transfixed on Ruern.

"Our destination lies to the west, we will make our way to the Fallen, once there we will await our escort."

Little of this made any sense to Sam; apart from the fact that it would appear that someone else would be joining them. "A guide perhaps" he thought, but as to where he was, he was still none the wiser.

They departed again shortly after that. Ruern had offered no further information and both Sam and Anna felt it would prove fruitless to ask for her to expand on her conversation as it had always been to no avail. They continued onwards, each step brought them closer to the forbidding shadow of the forest. Sam's feeling of uneasiness remained unabated, even Ruern seemed to have shrunk further into herself. She never turned to check that her companions were keeping pace with her. Her head remained bowed during their walk, never once looking up at their destination. Anna, by contrast, seemed almost hypnotised by the wall of trees that now drew close. Never once did she break her gaze at the formidable wave of oaks that stood to greet them. It had the look of a dead place, each tree stripped of greenery, standing skeletal against the iron-grey sky, silent sentries that watched their approach.

Something frightened Sam about the forest. It didn't help to know that something was keeping watch for them, but that was not all, it was as if the giant oaks were calling him in to their domain, watching him, waiting for him. He had felt it a while back but dismissed it as paranoia, but as he grew close to the forest the feeling grew to an almost unbearable level. He was sweating profusely, not from the long trek, but from the fear that was welling inside and yet he was unsure as to what he was afraid of. The forest, whilst indeed formidable, suggested nothing of danger, but he was convinced that Ruern was keeping something from him, he felt as if death waited for him from within the shadows and there was nothing he could do to avoid its touch. Slowly he began to let the fear swell inside. He began to hear noises that weren't really there; he began to see monsters that were nothing more than shadows on the ground. He began to feel afraid that should he cross into the forest he would never leave. As he began to slip further and further into the pool of fear. Then, Ruern spoke to him from within. Her voice cut through the cacophony of voices that sounded in his head, reaching out to him and pulling him away from the chasm's edge that he teetered on.

"Do not be afraid my dear Sam. Those that seek to harm will not be permitted. I am with you and will guide and protect you. Trust in me Sam and all will be well, for be stayed in the knowledge that the hunter fear's its prey more than you can ever know. Keep Anna by your side, she will need your strength when the time comes. Keep close to me, hear my voice. Do not let the fear consume you, for if you do, you will be lost to me. We will reach the Fallen, it has been foretold. Walk with me this one last time and let your destiny begin. You have always been my charge, and never will I fail you." Never once did she look back at him nor slow her step. She seemed to walk taller now, no longer staring at the ground but her head rose defiantly as she broke through the first line of trees. Sam stopped to find Anna's hand, took in a deep breath and started forward. Instantly the darkness of the forest rushed to greet him.

It took him several minutes for his eyes to adjust to the blackness within. What little sunlight there was outside failed to permeate through the canopy of twisted branches that hung overhead. It was suffocating within, clammy, almost warm, and deathly still. He instinctively tightened his grip on Anna's now sweating hand. She gave a reassuring squeeze back, but he could feel her shaking, or was it him? He pulled Anna forward and stumbled forward to Ruern's side.

"Stay close to me now," she hissed. "You will not be stolen from me!"

She made this statement neither to Sam nor Anna but to the forest that stretched away before them. She pulled her cowl from her head; the young girl from the coffee bar now looked directly into his eyes. No longer was she old, but now radiant. She smiled at him the way a mother would smile at her child. He stood and returned her stare, open mouthed in awe at her beauty and brilliance.

"This forest is ancient and part of both worlds Sam," she said in answer to his unspoken question, "magic laces the air we breathe; we are almost home!" He immediately noticed the sense of relief that entwined her words. With that, she turned and began the journey in.

They walked at a quicker pace, anxious to reach their destination. Ruern walked with confidence, guiding them through the maze of tree trunks with ease. Sam and Anna followed close behind; still they held each other's hand, not daring to let go. Occasionally one would stumble over the tangle of roots that covered the forest base, but each time the other was there to stop their fall.

Still they ventured deeper, entrusting Ruern to guide them safely. The forest grew more humid the deeper they went. Sam felt the sweater he wore stick to his back. No wind, light nor rain got in this far. Sam was amazed as to how anything could grow in this cauldron of black.

The march continued unabated, never did they hear nor see anything that suggested that any life, other than their own, existed within. However, after a while, Sam began to feel more at ease within the confines of the forest. The initial fear of entering had since passed and he was growing accustomed to the feel of the woodland around him. Occasionally he would glance at Anna and was just able to make out her features in the gloom. Each time she would smile reassuringly at him. After almost an hour of walking through the forest without incident, Sam felt safe enough to talk in whispers with Anna.

"Are you ok?" he asked.

"Yeah, you?" Anna replied without taking her eyes of Ruern's dark form in the distance.

"How far do you think this Fallen is? Do you have any idea what it could be?" Sam asked.

"No idea, but I hope we are getting near I want out of this place, I feel like we are being watched and its giving me the creeps. I haven't got the first clue as to what this Fallen is, perhaps a fallen tree or something, all this way to find some rotting tree trunk that would be about right!" she replied with hint of sarcasm and a shrug of her shoulders. Sam was inwardly pleased that she hadn't lost her sense of humour and was about to answer her, when he suddenly realised that Ruern had stopped.

"Get down, no talking!" her voice commanded. Sam instantly went down pulling Anna with him. He could feel his heart pounding; the sound of his blood rushing through his veins filled his ears. He held his breath. Ruern lay by his side. He almost hadn't seen her. She seemed to have become part of the forest floor. He looked at her from the corner of his eye and saw that she was starring intensely at a patch of ground not more than thirty feet ahead. She neither moved nor breathed; she starred unblinking into the distance. They lay for what seemed an eternity to Sam. He felt Anna's heart pounding as she lay by his side. Each breath he took seemed to shatter the unnatural quiet of the forest. Ruern remained unmoving; she was as if turned to stone.

"Ruern," he whispered, "What's going on?"

To his surprise she turned and looked directly at him, her eyes wide and glazed. She was afraid, Sam immediately thought, her

37

eyes betrayed her feelings, no not afraid he amended, she was terrified!

"Look and see what hunts us, see what they have sent to greet us," came her voice in response. Sam immediately felt sick; something in the distance awaited his arrival, something that could fill even Ruern with fear. He lay motionless, not convinced that he could move even if he wanted to, so great was the fright that had gripped him. His gaze remained locked on Ruern. He felt her eyes burn into him.

"You must look Sam, you must see the danger of which I speak." He felt her words wrap around him; he felt them seek out his fear and carry it away. She smiled a sad smile to him, and then returned her gaze to forest ahead. Slowly Sam shifted his stare to the distance. He searched in the half-light for the danger that Ruern had warned of, but saw nothing.

Had she been mistaken? He thought momentarily, but dismissed that thought almost immediately. After looking for several more minutes he had still neither seen, nor heard anything. He was about to give up when Ruern's words again cut into his mind. "Seek out the treetop that is where you will find what you are looking for."

He hadn't considered looking skyward. With a deliberately slow motion, he cast his eyes towards the roof of the forest. He saw nothing at first, just the grey gnarled branches that reached up to a sunless sky. Again he was about to give up his search, when something caught his eye. To the side of a particularly large branch, the gloom, which encased the whole forest, seemed darker, much darker. He continued to scan the outline of the shape. It was solid black from top to bottom except for two splashes of crimson near its top. At first he thought it to be part of the forest surround, but it was then with horror that he realised that it was not the forest colouring he was seeing, they were eyes. He saw them clearer now, two lidless blood red slits starred back at him unblinking. He felt his terror return anew, welling up inside him, almost to the point where it would surely explode from him. He would have run then, no longer did he care about the hunter that lay in wait, no matter as to the safety of Anna or Ruern, he just wanted to escape to anywhere

38

rather than here. Had it not been for the calming touch of Ruern's hand against his face, he would have bolted.

"Do not be afraid Sam, I am here, I will keep you safe," came her soothing words, words that slowly began to push the fear from his mind. They coloured his darkest thoughts in a blanket of light and stole away his fright. Never once did he break his stare with the blackness above.

He began to see more of it then. It was a misshapen thing, its body a mass of sinew and bone. Thick black Bristles thrust out from its body in ugly clumps and blackness coated its ruined form utterly

He couldn't see its face, so deep was the murk that surrounded it, but he noticed two massive horns that split out from its malformed head. But it was the eyes that frightened Sam the most, never blinking, never moving, dead eyes that looked as if they could stare into your soul and rip it apart.

He was then aware that Anna had crept closer to him. He had been so transfixed and terrified by the beast ahead he had completely forgotten about Anna. He turned to look at her with a slow and steady movement. She did not return his look, she was mesmerised by the creature ahead. Never once did she look his way.

It was then he decided that he had to speak with Ruern, after all, what now? As much as he didn't dare move, they couldn't stay here forever, although he feared that the beast ahead would stay as long as was required.

After several minutes of summoning the courage, he turned to speak with her.

Ruern was nowhere to be found!

Panic gripped him once more. Without Ruern they were lost, for she was the only person that might be able to offer some protection against the Demon that waited ahead. Only she knew where they would find the fallen. Without her, they were surely as good as dead. He scanned the area ahead as quickly as he could, still mindful not to make any sudden moves but she remained lost to him. He felt Anna press her body even closer to his own; he felt her trembling and heard her breath both short and fast. He turned to face her trying to mask the desperation that had taken hold of him. Her face was ashen; her eyes wide from the terror that gripped her like a vice. Sam was about to speak, anything would do, just to try and break the hold that encapsulated her, when suddenly the Demon's voice exploded forth.

"DO YOU THINK YOU CAN HIDE FROM ME?" The sound boomed throughout the forest, shattering the silence that had held it for so long. Sam felt the blood drain from his face. Every part of him was shaking uncontrollably. He felt as if he were in some dream, nothing seemed real, not the Demon, the forest nor Anna. Not even Ruern, she seemed a distant memory.

"Ruern," he suddenly thought, "How could she have left him now when they needed her most? It was her fault; all of this mess was because of her," he thought darkly. "Everything was alright before she showed up!" He began to feel the fear that had shackled him for so long fall away and be replaced by anger. Not towards the Demon as it surely should have been, but towards Ruern.

"She was the catalyst for everything, she had brought him here to be killed – her betrayal would cost him everything. Why had he come? How had he allowed himself to be tricked by her?" He was falling deeper into the blackness of rage that was threatening to engulf him. "Perhaps it was the demon that was his ally? Perhaps Ruern was the enemy, perhaps, perhaps…" He knew deep down that he was making no sense but he couldn't stop the thoughts from rushing into his mind. The Demons voice seemed to have planted a thousand doubts within him, he no longer knew what to think, what to do. His head was spinning with a multitude of questions each one screaming to be answered, each one more confusing than the last. He was being dragged in different directions at the same time and it was threatening to rip him apart.

"COME AND FACE YOUR DESTINY" The Demon rasped again. The words rushed towards him like a hundred daggers being thrown, each one burning him as they plunged deep into his mind.

He was screaming now, clawing at his head, desperately trying to rid his brain of the turmoil that resided. Anna pulled him close, she herself was crying, calling his name, trying to bring him back from the precipice edge. But it was Ruern that he heard first.

Her voice transcended all the voices that called him. Her voice swept them away and left but hers. It cut into his mind with such ferocity that it caused him to wince.

"Sam Meredith, hear my voice and mine alone," she commanded. "Do not allow yourself to be lost to your fear. Quiet the Demons words; you have the power to do so. It tries to trick you, concentrate on me. Rise up Sam, hide no more, and show yourself to the shadow that waits for you. It cannot harm you Sam, it fears you!"

He heard her words clear and firm. The Demons sounds were fading, just fragments remained, but it was hers that demanded his attention.

"Stand and face the dark, I am here, I will keep you safe for you are my charge."

Sam began to feel a new sensation rush through his body. He felt it course through his veins like cold spring water, dampening the flames of fear that had raged within that had held him captive. He felt neither frightened nor angry. The voices had quietened. No longer did he hear the Demons questions, nor Ruern's commands, he felt almost tranquil. He knew it not to be rationale but did not fight the feeling. He let it wash over him, cleansing him as it went. He was aware of someone crying, he turned to find Anna pressed close. He looked at her face streaked with dirt and tears.

"It's ok Anna," he whispered "It's ok." He leant over and kissed her on the forehead.

Before he knew it he was standing.

"Walk to my voice" Ruern beckoned. She did not command nor berate. Her voice was as soft and warm as the first time she had spoken with him. He began to walk toward the clearing, he knew the demon waited but it no longer concerned him.

Something had been done to him, magic perhaps, but he still offered no resistance. He was tired and confused, the serenity

41

he felt simply took these feelings away; something he was grateful for. He continued onwards.

The Demon watched him approach from its place of concealment. Its twisted maw, oozing with thick black bile as it anticipated the kill.

"Just a few more steps and it would be over," it thought darkly. As it shifted its massive frame, to make ready for its leap at the figure below, it caught sight of something to its left moving swiftly through the trees. As it spun its huge head around to seek out the cause, it caught sight of it again, this time to its right; a streak of white darted passed. Confused and enraged it lashed out, but found nothing but air. It was then it realised that it had been tricked!

With a burst of rage it let out an earth-shattering scream and swung down from the branches to which it had been clinging, desperate to claim its quarry before the trap could be sprung. It landed not more than ten feet in front of the stooped figure of Sam with a crash that shook the forest base

"LOOK AT ME AND LET YOUR DESTINY BE FULFILLED," it screamed at the advancing figure. Sam stopped, head bent low and waited.

The Demon raised itself to its full height. Nine feet of sinew and muscle, blackness and scales, and teeth and claw stood before the small defenceless figure. The Demon allowed itself a wicked grin, "This will be quick!"

Before the thought had left its head the boy raised his face to meet the Demons crimson stare.

"YOU!" the demon spat forth.

Sam's face did not stare back at the demon; it was Ruern's! Before it could react, silver fire smashed into its chest from the outstretched fingers of the Sario. It sent the Demon thundering back into the forest's growth and smashing into a large Oak tree. Ruern advanced; silver bolts arced from her outstretched hands again, this time catching the Demon on its right arm spinning it further into the forest gloom. Relentlessly she continued to advance.

Sam watched from his place of concealment on the forest floor. It was all happening so fast. One moment he was so scared he was ready to bolt, and then he had filled with rage after believing that Ruern had trapped then deserted him. The next moment he had seen her striding out into the clearing to face the demon. She had somehow disguised herself as him. To anybody else looking on it was he who stood in the clearing ahead. "Was this the magic that she had spoken of when they first crossed the forbidding wall of Oaks?" He had tried to scream but the sound would not come, he had tried to run but his limbs were heavy and unmovable, all he could do was watch the events unfold and hold onto Anna tightly, as Ruern had previously requested.

She continued to send forth the burning silver fire. Each time the forest flared into near daylight. Sam caught quick glimpses of her face during each burst, streaked with sweat and dirt, her eyes burning with determination and concentration. With each flash of fire she seemed to age, as if the fire she summoned was stealing her life away.

The Demon screamed in rage and pain. The smell and smoke of burnt flesh filled the air. Several small bushes blazed from the touch of the silver light, but still the fight raged. Ruern's fire slammed into the demon again and again but it would not go down. Smoke rose from its body and yet it would not slow. It made a lunge for Ruern, she quickly sidestepped the charge, when she turned to unleash the silver fire once more, the Demon had disappeared.

Immediately Ruern began to search for the Demon, frantically trying to find it before it struck. She sent the white fire in all directions in the hope that it would find its mark, but no sound or attack came.

She stood in the middle of the clearing, hands lowered and head bowed as if in deep concentration. She listened for it now, desperately trying to discover its hiding place. Smoke rose from the forest floor, which was scarred, and blackened by the battle, nothing sounded, all was still.

Sam looked all around but saw nothing. Anna too was scanning the clearing whilst remaining flattened against the dirt, but nothing. Just as Sam was beginning to consider that the Demon had fled, a burst of red fire arced down from the forest roof. Sam immediately pulled Anna close and covered his head. Ruern turned just as the wall of flame closed in on her. It caught her square in the chest and she went down in an explosion of red. Sam screamed at the sight of Ruern going down. He tried to run to her aid but whatever magic held him pinned to the floor continued to do so. He tried desperately to see through the dust and smoke that was covering the clearing but to no avail.

The Demon leapt down from the branches of a massive Oak that stood nearby. It seemed to have forgotten its search for Sam for the time being, as it began to approach the place where Ruern had gone down. Wicked red flames licked lovingly at its clawed hands, ready to burst forward at any given moment. As Sam watched it advance into the swirls of smoke and dust he noticed for the first time two massive wings that folded down its back. Vicious talons dug into the ground as it walked toward its target. With each step it took, the smoke and dirt swirled away enabling Sam to see further into the clearing. Despite his frantic search, he could not see Ruern. His heart skipped "She must have got out," he thought with relief and joy, "She would launch a surprise attack on the shadow Demon just as it had done to her" he surmised.

He continued to watch, his fear twinged with excitement and expectancy.

The Demon continued its slow approach; more and more smoke dispersed as it moved cautiously forward. Suddenly Anna gave out a sharp cry, for there in the clearing lay Ruern, lifeless and broken.

Sam felt his heart sink, he cried out to her but she did not move. He battled against the invisible chains that held him, but he could not break free. Anna too seemed to be struggling to raise herself of the forest floor, but it appeared that the magic that held Sam held her also. All they could do was watch.

"YOU SHOULD NOT HAVE CHALLENGED ME SARIO" the Demon boomed.

"YOU WERE NEVER A WORTHY OPPONENT, YOU HAVE LOST, THE BOY WILL DIE AND THE CIRCLE WILL CLOSE FOREVER FOR THERE ARE NO MORE KRELYN'S LEFT, HE WAS THE LAST." The Demon gave out a shrill cry, and continued to advance on the lifeless form of the Sario.

Sam could see clearer now, her left arm and shoulder were missing, her right leg was twisted at an impossible angle and her head bled profusely from a deep cut that ran the entire length of her forehead. He felt as if part of him had died with her. Anna's sobs were the only sound to break the hush of the forest that had once again been reclaimed by silences grasp. Strangely Sam did not cry. She had told him before they entered the forest not to cry for her, he would honour her request.

The shadowed Demon had reached her now. It prodded her with its blackened talons to check for any response…there was none. It bent its massive frame down and dragged the lifeless Sario up by her hair so her head was level with his.

"Time for my trophy," it hissed. Its gaping maw widened in readiness. Sam realised in horror that it was going to decapitate her! He tried to look away but found he was unable to. He felt Anna bury her head into his chest. She was crying freely now, he found he could offer no comfort.

"The boys next!" The Demon whispered to the ruined form of Ruern. With its mouth inches away from Ruern's head, she suddenly lurched upwards.

"I think not!" she screamed and plunged her good arm into the Demons gaping jaws and sent the white fire deep into its stomach. Instantly the demon burst into a thousand pieces of flesh, completely blown apart by her silver magic.

Ruern fell back to the ground in a crumpled heap. Her body and face smattered with the creature's fouled blood.

As soon as she hit the ground the chains that had held him fell away from Sam. He immediately began running to her screaming her name. He reached her in a matter of seconds with Anna close behind. He fell to her side "You did it Ruern,

45

you did it." It was then he saw the extent of her injuries. Her clothes were burnt to nothing and no part of her body was untouched from the damage of battle.

"Lay still Ruern, we will get help, just keep awake." He broke his promise then and started to cry.

"Sam," Ruern whispered in a barely audible voice. So frail were her words that Sam thought they would break before they could reach him. "Do not mourn for me Sam; it has happened as was foretold. I have completed my journey you must now begin yours." She began to cough. Sam carefully wiped away the blood that flowed from her mouth.

"When I have gone Sam the path you must tread will become clear to you. Remember, Anna is your charge now, do not fail her, be strong for each other."

Sam nodded in response, "Ruern," he whispered, "What shall I do? Who will come for me? Where will they take me? I am scared Ruern how can I keep you with me? Please tell me, I cannot find my without you, I can't even find this Fallen you speak of, please Ruern stay with me." He was holding her hand now and gently stroking her hair. She had returned to the young girl that he had met in the coffee shop not so long ago, although that now seemed like a lifetime ago.

"Sam," she replied her voice thick with blood, "You need not look for the Fallen as you have found it, you are standing by it. I told you Sam that it had been foretold, I am the Fallen that we sought, and you are already here!" Sam was shocked that she had known all this time of her impending death and yet never spoke of it.

Anna knelt by her side and continued to wipe the blood from her face and mouth. Ruern spoke to Anna next. "You have known of my coming longer than any other, I am glad that you chose to come along, keep Sam safe, he is very important, he will need you when no other can help, be there to answer his cries when they come, for only you carry the answers to his unspoken questions." Anna nodded in agreement although she wasn't sure that she understood what she had been told.

"Sam," Ruern tightened her grip on his hand, "My time approaches fast now, you must know one further secret." He dropped his head close to hers in order to hear, so fragile were her words. "I told you at our first meeting that I had been sent by your father to find you. I ensured that you could not ask me again of this until I chose to tell you, I have chosen now Sam." Sam listened intently not wanting to interrupt; her breathing had slowed and become even more laced with blood that crackled in her throat as she drew breath.

"I spoke the truth Sam, he waits for you and will look for you after 'crossover', but he will not be as you would expect, do not reject him Sam, embrace him for he is the key to your journey. Keep well my dear Sam and remember my warning to you... trust no one."

With a final heave of her chest Ruern died in his arms at the Fallen.

Sam and Anna buried her in a simple grave directly underneath a massive Oak tree. It took them several hours to dig as they carried no tools but neither complained. They didn't mark her resting place as they felt there was less chance of anybody disturbing the grave. After they had finished they ate some bread and cheese and took a little water. They talked infrequently, each going over the recent events in their minds. Sam didn't feel much like eating, but it was Anna's insistence that finally won through. He hadn't realised how hungry he had become.

By the time they had finished and cleaned up it was getting dark and turning colder. They huddled together under the warmth of their coats and waited. Neither knew exactly what they waited for. Ruern had said that the path would become clear to them once she had gone, but so far they had found no path nor seen anything that would indicate in which direction they must travel.

Sam looked down to ask Anna as to what she thought they should do but found her to be asleep in his arms.

"Goodnight," he whispered, "I'll keep you safe tonight. I bet you wished you stayed at home," he smiled, "personally I'm glad you didn't." He kissed the top of her head and settled

himself down for the long watch. Within ten minutes he was
fast asleep too.

He wasn't sure as to how long he slept for but it was still dark
when he came awake.
It was Anna that had woken him. He found her to be sitting
bolt upright starring into the gloom. He reached out and
touched her arm; she jumped in response.
"Look Sam, look at what has happened, I can't believe it, I
mean where did it come from? I think I'm going mad, what's
going on Sam? What is happening?"
He still had no idea as to what she was talking about. He
considered that she was just sleep talking, but she seemed too
lucid for this to be a possibility.
"Anna, it's ok, I am here, what's the matter? What's
happened?"
"Look Sam, look at her grave Sam."
Sam gingerly rose to his feet. What could have happened to
cause Anna to be in such a state? Suddenly he thought that
perhaps the Demon had returned, or another arrived to finish
them off. With a sense of dread he knelt by Anna's still rigid
form.
"Anna, has it returned? Has the Demon come back? We must
hide quickly, we can't let it find us, quickly Anna follow me
we will hide in....."
"SAM," Anna shouted her interruption, "Come Sam, come and
see." She took his hand and slowly raised herself to her feet.
"Don't be afraid Sam; I have seen nothing to suggest that
danger has returned."
She began to lead him into the trees to where they had buried
Ruern just a few hours before. "You are not going to believe
this," she continued, "I know we have seen some pretty wild
things but this takes the biscuit... look." She pointed ahead just
as they rounded a particularly large oak tree.
His eyes followed her outstretched arm to a thick wall of
hickory bushes. He remembered them from a few hours ago.
Ruern's grave stood just the other side.

He looked at Anna quizzically. "Go and see Sam, go and see what I mean." She gave him a nod ahead and released his hand. He started forward; with each step he felt the fear grow anew within him. Several times he turned back to Anna; she simply waved him forward. Nervously he continued onwards, rounded the wall of hickories and nearly walked straight into a white marble wall that jutted out from the rear of the forest growth. He stood opened mouthed, for there, before him stood a ten-foot high structure. It was encased from top to bottom in bright white marble. He reached out and gingerly touched the marble; to his shock it was warm! Still not fully believing what he was seeing, he began to walk around the building, allowing his hand to brush the walls as he went. Soon he was standing at what he assumed to be the entrance, although no door could be found.

Solid white walls lifted skyward. Ornate carvings adorned each corner of the structure. It was quite possibly the most beautiful thing he had ever seen. But what the hell was it doing here? It certainly wasn't here a few hours ago. As he stood looking in awe at the edifice, Anna came up to his side.

"Well, do you see what I mean? What is going on Sam?" She asked.

"I don't know Anna, I just don't know"

"Have you seen the inscriptions? They are written in some foreign language that I cannot understand, what do you think they could mean?"

Anna walked up to the building and brushed away some of the growth at its base to reveal the words she had spoken of.

"See what I mean, I can't read a word of it, don't even recognise the language, what about you Sam?"

Sam came forward and knelt by Anna's side. He had also never seen any language like it, but to his astonishment he understood every word.

"It says," he began,

HERE LIES THE LAST SARIO. FELLED BY THE FORCES OF DARKNESS, YET, HER LIGHT BURNS BRIGHT FOR ALL TO SEE. THE GIFT SHE GAVE WILL NEVER BE

MATCHED, HER SACRIFICE NEVER SURPASSED, AND HER DEVOTION NEVER BETTERED. LET HER NAME BE SHOUTED AND NEVER WHISPERED, AND THOUGH SHE HAS BEEN RECLAIMED BY THE EARTH THAT GAVE HER LIFE; STILL WE WILL ALWAYS REMEMBER HER…….RUERN – GIVER OF HOPE.

"You read Elvish well," an unfamiliar voice sounded from behind them. Both Sam and Anna spun around to find seven riders on white mounts. Sam noticed that three carried standards, a great oak tree above a crown with a rising sun behind. Two more flanked the group, both wore white lose fitting garments with brown boots and chain mail that fitted tightly over their clothing. Large swords hung from their waistband and both wore massive ash bows strapped to their backs. The final two rode in the midst of the others. White clothing and chain mail adorned both and yet they appeared to carry no weapons.

All had striking golden hair, piercing blue eyes and a lean appearance. Both Sam and Anna stared bemused at the sight before them, although they felt no fear.

The rider at the centre dismounted and walked towards them. Instinctively Sam placed himself between Anna and the approaching stranger.

"Who are you?" Sam asked bravely, not making any attempt to mask the distrust that was evident in his voice.

"Be at peace Master Sam, we have been expecting you for a long time, my name is Evaine; we are your escort, we are your friends. Welcome home."

Both Anna and Sam stared at the sight before them in disbelief. Immediately hundreds of questions raced through Sam's mind, but he found he was unable to get any words out. "I must ask that you come with us for danger is all around" Evaine continued.

Without any further words the riders moved around to flank both Anna and Sam and began to move slowly forward with the two bemused companions in their midst.

50

CHAPTER

4

The party headed westward, through the maze of trees that stretched out in all directions. The forest, however, was now quite different to what both Anna and Sam had become accustom to. All the trees were now covered in lush greenery, and it was alive with the sounds of insects chirping and birds calling, plus a few other sounds that Sam didn't recognise. But perhaps the most notable change was the warmth and light of the sun that broke through the forest canopy. It felt warm and vibrant, not clammy and suffocating as it had done before, but almost soothing. Everything felt different, looked different even smelt different. As they passed deeper into the west, Sam noticed the array of colours that grew sporadically throughout. Bright flowers of yellows and blues shimmered and swayed in the gentle breeze. Berry's grew on large bushes that edged the path on which they travelled, not the normal sight of

Blackberries or Raspberries that Sam was use to seeing, but berries of all colours and size. Oranges and Pinks, Silver and Gold coloured fruits grew throughout the greenery. Some as small as his finger nail, some bigger than his fist. The smell was both fragrant and fresh, and it filled the air and made the day seem warmer and brighter than it actually was.

Occasionally Sam would gaze over at Anna as they walked together. Each time though he found her to be equally mesmerised by their surroundings. He studied her for a while. She seemed both relaxed and happy. This was in stark contrast to just a few hours ago. Everything then was dark and grey and it had felt as if the forest were watching them, waiting to snare and consume them.

His thoughts drifted back to Ruern. So young and fragile she had seemed at their first meeting and now, barely two nights later, she lay broken, bloodied and dead in his arms. Strangely it seemed a long time ago now, even unreal, almost as if it had been some distant dream. But he knew it was real, it had happened. He still wore the clothes stained with her blood. He could see her face starring up at him, and heard her voice speak his name, but she was gone, gone because of him. What the hell was happening, he thought to himself, he had to have some answers. With that thought in mind, he quickened his stride and caught up to Evaine's side.

As he drew alongside, Sam looked at him properly now for the first time. He was a tall man of slender build. Golden hair tumbled past his shoulders. Blue eyes stared out from an unblemished face. A massive ash bow was now strapped to his back and a quiver of arrows hung loosely from his side. He wore a forest cloak draped over a glistening coat of chain mail that covered his top half. White trousers tucked into brown boots completed the ensemble. He wore a ring on his right hand that mirrored the banners that some of the riders carried, a crown beneath an oak tree with a sun setting in the distance. He had since dismounted from his steed, preferring to walk. He seemed to glide over the ground, so graceful were his movements. Sam was finding the heat of the day and the speed of travel hard work and was breathing heavily from the exertion, and yet Evaine neither breathed heavily nor perspired. "You have many questions that you wish to ask of me young Sam?" He suddenly spoke,

"I ask for just a little more time, and then I promise I will answer all that I can." He had offered this without waiting for a response. He turned to meet Sam's stare and gave a reassuring smile. For an instant Sam thought he was looking into Ruern's face.

"I will tell you this much my young friend," he continued, "the forest that we are within is called Dunbar, and where we walk is dangerous for it is often patrolled by Gnome units. To the west lays Silverdale, and beyond, the great city of Varon. It is Silverdale that awaits our return. We should arrive in two hours if all goes well. A warm bath, fresh clothes and hot food await our return, but until we have reached its confines we must remain guarded and quick. Stay close young Sam and all will be well."

"Young Sam indeed, you're barely older than I am!" Sam muttered under his breath, not even aware that he had said the words aloud.

"Suffice to say my young friend that I have been waiting for your arrival for three-hundred years!" Evaine replied.

A smile crept into Evaine's face as he left Sam's side and went on ahead. Sam couldn't hide the surprise in his eyes and rather sheepishly dropped back and rejoined Anna's side.

He hadn't really spoken with Anna since the arrival of the Elven patrol. He shot her a quick glance and smiled to himself. Her hair was matted from the dust and dirt of the journey. Streaks of dirt ran down her face and her clothing was damp and stuck to her from the sweat of her body. "You look gorgeous," he whispered sarcastically to her.

"Well you look like crap," she replied, once again winning the verbal battle.

She smiled at him "What the hell must we look like eh?" she said, "We are like a couple of vagrants, smelly, dirty and without the first idea as to where we are or what we are doing.

My life was quiet before you," she continued, "now look at me; my life as I knew it has gone and has been replaced with madness. Magic is real, monsters are real and I am walking with bloody Elves!" She looked at Sam and began to laugh. Sam felt that this was probably not the best time to mention that he had learned of the existence of Gnomes as well!

It was funny that he had accepted Evaine's revelation that Gnome patrols watched this forest so easily; in fact he hadn't batted an eyelid at the prospect. Was he becoming accustomed to the madness so quickly? Although he would have laughed at anyone who had said this a few days ago, he found that now he felt it to be almost... normal. Ruern had said that he was going home after all. Could it be that this is where he belonged?

Anna's voice cut into his thoughts

"Well I guess we will both be sacked when we get home, I mean I can't put this down on my sickness form can I!" Sam briefly thought that Anna should have said, "If I get home," as oppose to "when." He looked at her for a short while, and then burst out into a loud long laugh. The Elven riders looked at them quizzically, and then returned their gaze to the forest ahead.

"Seriously, what is going on Sam?" Anna continued once the laughter had died down. "Do you have any idea? I have tried to ask old pointy ears over there," she cocked her head to one side to indicate the rider to her left, "But he says nothing. If you pinch me am I gonna wake up?"

Sam smiled at Anna, despite all that had happened she could still make him smile. He took her hand as they walked and recounted everything that Evaine had told him, even the part about the Gnomes, to which she also batted no eyelid to either. "Apart from that I know no more than you," he concluded, "but as long as this Evaine is true to his word, we will find out a lot more soon once we get out of this damn forest."

Anna was about to reply, when she noticed that the Elven soldier ahead of her had stopped. Almost immediately the soldiers that flanked them closed in about them tightly. Anna looked up at the closest to her to find him pressing his finger to his lips indicating for Sam and her to remain silent. All stood statuesque, not even the horses made any sound or movement. Anna squeezed Sam's hand tighter. Her guard had dismounted with speed and complete silence and was standing by her side with his bow loaded with an arrow. He was facing towards the undergrowth that grew on the side of the path that they traversed. She turned to see that Sam's guard had followed suit. They seemed to remain still for an age, and she was on the verge of whispering to Sam, when suddenly the Elven guard released their arrows into the foliage with a sharp snap. Two muted cries rang out from the forest, then a crashing as if something was running towards them through the bushes. Almost immediately a gnarled yellow body rolled out from the undergrowth and on to the trail not more than ten feet from where Anna and Sam stood. Anna starred at the crumpled heap before her. It was smallish and gaunt. Tough yellowed skin covered it from head to toe. Its head was disproportionately large in comparison to its otherwise small frame, and large yellowed eyes remained transfixed and open. Two white arrows were embedded into the creature's neck and thick brownish blood ran freely from the gaping wound. It was clearly dead.

Evaine walked up to the body to make sure, once satisfied, he turned and walked back towards Anna and Sam.

"That was Gnome tracker. He has been following us since we met with you," he offered, "but unfortunately for him he got a little too close. No doubt you heard him too?" Evaine said with a slight smile on his face. Both Sam and Anna stared blankly in response.

"You have much to learn my dear friends, the first lesson is never whisper in the company of an Elf, for they will hear you, isn't that right….pointy ears!" Evaine was looking at the guard that Anna had referred to earlier. This time it was the Elves who led the laughter and for the first time Sam saw Anna lost for words.

Before Anna had a chance to think of a reply the patrol had remounted and was moving forwards.

"Not just quick with their bows are they!" Sam quipped at Anna. She didn't bother responding.

They took one last look at the crumpled body of the Gnome as they passed.

"Evil looking thing!" Anna muttered, and then continued down the trail.

Conversation was sparse between Sam and Anna for the remainder of the journey to Silverdale. Each wrapped up in their own thoughts and both still battling with the fact that they were not caught up in some crazy dream. The forest continued to pass them by and the Sun continued to warm the land, although neither Sam nor Anna needed warming. Both were growing tired from the trek and were once again finding the going quite tough. Each of the Elven guard had offered them their horses to ride if they so wished, but both Sam and Anna had declined, the last thing they wanted was to be sat atop a giant horse and become an obvious target for one of those Gnomes' that roamed the forest. Whilst the rest would have been welcomed, the security offered by walking in the midst of armed Elven soldiers was preferable.

It was another hour before Evaine rode up beside them. He didn't dismount, but simply acknowledged them with a slight bow of his head and quick smile. For the first time Anna noticed the look of devilment that twinkled in his eyes. It was a look that a child would give to their parents when they were about to do something they shouldn't. Anna rarely trusted anyone she didn't fully know, but Evaine was different, she trusted him implicitly. It worried her that this should be so, after all, she had spent her whole life being cautious towards people, and it had always served her well to question peoples motives, and yet here she was, in god knows where, trusting a man she had met barely a half day ago. Evaine's voice broke through her thoughts,

"We will arrive at Silverdale shortly," he started, "Once there, a hot bath, fresh clothes and food will be afforded to you. Once we reach its outer walls I will be leaving you for a short while as I have other urgent business to attend to." Anna felt a very slight twinge at the thought of Evaine's departure.

"However," he continued, "I will be leaving you in the safe hands of Tamar."

Evaine inclined his head in the direction of one of the mounted Elven soldiers that rode with the group to indicate who Tamar was.

"Tamar," Evaine continued, "is Captain of the Elven guard at Silverdale; he will ensure that you are well catered for. I will endeavour to keep my business short, and I will rejoin you as soon as I possibly can." Evaine looked directly at Sam now "I will then be able to answer as many questions as I can, for I know that you must be both confused and frustrated. I ask for a little more of your patience."

Evaine waited for no response, he simply turned his stead around and headed back towards Tamar. After a few minutes of conversation, Evaine and one of the Elven guard rode off at considerable pace. Both Sam and Anna watched, as they grew more and more distant, until finally disappearing behind the wall of trees of the forest.

Tamar shouted commands to the remaining riders and then the group set off once again towards Silverdale.

They had travelled for barely ten minutes before Silverdale came into sight. It was not, however, how Sam had expected it to be. He had imagined great walls, towering castle turrets and splendour; it was none of these. In fact it needed Tamar to point out to him that they had in fact arrived at the perimeter of the town before Sam even noticed it.

The outer wall looked no different than rest of the forest that Silverdale sat within, for the 'wall' was simply a row of tall Hickory bushes that stretched out into the distance. Sam heard no sounds that implied that a town existed beyond, nor saw any other evidence that people lived within. Tamar, having noticed Sam's expression of confusion, rode up to his side and dismounted.

"Not what you expected is it?" Sam simply shook his head in response.

"Would you be surprised to know that Silverdale is one of the most protected places on this Earth?" Tamar continued, "In fact

Silverdale is one of the few places that exist that has never been breached by an enemy force, never has it been lost in battle and never has its walls been scaled by a hostile army." Sam simply nodded his head to indicate that he had heard Tamar's words, but was less than convinced that Tamar's words were true. After all, he thought, it wasn't exactly an awe-inspiring defence wall was it; it was a big bush!

As if reading Sam's thoughts, Tamar continued.

"You doubt my words I see, trust me, you are not the first. Here, take this and throw it over the wall." Tamar placed a small stone into Sam's hand.

"If you succeed, you will be the first that has done so."

Tamar laughed as he spoke the words. Sam, however, was not impressed. He took a quick look at the stone, looked at the wall of Hickory's and then launched the stone as high and as hard as he could. He couldn't help but grin as he watched the stone fly into the air and begin to arc over the defence. He watched it reach halfway over, and then, to his astonishment, it simply dropped from the sky and landed close to where he had thrown it. His reaction was one of confusion, which quickly turned to one of embarrassment. Loud laughter rang out from the group, mainly from the Elves, although Anna couldn't help but laugh at his helplessness.

"As Evaine mentioned earlier," Tamar laughed, "there is much you have to learn my young friend. You surely didn't think that the Elves would fail to protect their most sacred place did you?" Sam shot him an inquisitive look.

Tamar laughed again "Much to learn," he repeated. He gave Sam a friendly slap on the back and walked back to his horse. Sam rejoined Anna's side, still smarting from the whole incident.

"Well done Sam," Anna intoned, "you didn't look that stupid, honest." For a split second he thought that she was actually being sincere.

"Come now," Tamar interrupted, "we will enter a little further down." The Elven riders assumed their usual flanking position, and the party began to move off.

Tamar took them a little further down the row of Hickory, then stopped and dismounted. He waited for Sam and Anna to reach his side before speaking.

"It is here that we will cross into Silverdale, but before we do so there are a few things you should be aware of." His voiced was hushed and both Sam and Anna came in closer to hear his words.

"Silverdale is an ancient city, even by Elven standards. No one knows exactly how long it has been here, but in every history book we have it is listed and some of those books are over seventy thousand years old. It is believed that the very first council of Elves was formed here, and it is the most sacred place for all Elves. Evaine will tell you more of the history I am sure, but for now you must understand what I am about to tell you. Silverdale has been shut away from the rest of the world. It has only ever been home to Elves and visitors are extremely rare, for as you have seen, unless you are invited, it is impossible to get in. Silverdale has also been home to the Kings of the Elves throughout history, and whenever there is need for meetings and discussions that concern the Elven nation and the other races of Invetia, it is too Silverdale that all come. As for the King, you will be meeting him soon enough once he learns of our return and your safe arrival."

Sam felt a mix of excitement and concern course through his body at hearing these words; Anna simply maintained her steady eye contact with Tamar.

"Do not be concerned," Tamar continued, "if you are viewed as something of a novelty when we pass through. Many of the Elves that work within these walls have never seen the outside world, and as I have said, visitors are extremely rare. But rest assured that they wish no harm, they are aware of your imminent arrival and I am sure that there will be much excitement."

Anna shot Sam a quick glance. It seemed to her that everybody knew of their arrival and purpose, everybody except them she quickly corrected.

"It is with this in mind," Tamar continued, "that I require you to ride for the rest of the way. My duty is to get you to your place of rest as quickly as possible; this will be accomplished more easily if you do not walk." Both Sam and Anna nodded in agreement.

"I must tell you one thing more before we go in," Tamar added, "never leave my side once we enter. Silverdale is laced with an ancient magic, it is this magic that protects those that dwell within, but it is a magic born of Elves, for the Elves. It can be dangerous for others that venture into its embrace alone."

Sam felt a cold shiver run down his spine. Why, he thought, was there always a downside? Both Anna and Sam mounted the two white horses that were brought to their side and waited. Tamar sat atop his horse and faced the wall of Hickory that rose up before him. He raised his arms skyward and spoke a few words that Sam could not hear, and then returned to the group. Anna shuffled in her saddle uncomfortably, nothing seemed to be happening; they just sat and waited. She was getting restless and was about to turn and speak with Sam, when suddenly she noticed a faint glow emanate from the Hickory. She watched in puzzlement as the glow grew bigger and brighter. It was as if the bush had caught fire. It continued to grow as large as the horse she rode, then flashed and died away. In its place was a sizeable hole in the Hickory wall; this was the entrance to Silverdale.

The party wasted no time. As soon as the gap had appeared, two of the Elven guard went through and disappeared from sight. Tamar turned and indicated for Sam and Anna to follow suit. Both of their horses made for the gap without encouragement from either rider. As Sam grew closer to the entrance he noticed that no light permeated through. It was as black as night inside and he immediately felt uneasy about passing through.

"Go on Sam, all is well, all is how it should be," came the reassuring voice of Tamar.

Before he knew it his horse had carried him through the gate. Immediately he was greeted by the blackness as it rushed to greet him.

He was unable to see or hear anything around him. It was cold, very cold and he became disorientated very quickly. He moved forward and held his horse tightly around its neck. This was the only security he had in this nightmare of dark. He felt the horse's movements as it continued forward at a steady pace, it never faltered or slowed. Then Sam began to hear sounds, ethereal voices, calling him, begging him to come to them. He hugged the horse even tighter. The voices grew louder and more compelling, urging him to let go and join them in the gloom. Sam felt himself start to slip, as if being pulled from his horse by many invisible hands. He didn't struggle; their touch seemed calming and warm. He would have fallen then if not for the strong arm of Tamar that found him in the dark and held him fast. Tamar's touch brought Sam to his senses and he increased his grip on the horse's neck. He clamped his eyes shut and concentrated on hanging on.

Before he knew it he was through. Although his eyes remained firmly shut, he felt the warmth of the day return to his face and the sound of birdsong fill his ears. Slowly he opened his eyes. It took him a little while to adjust to the light after his journey through the blackness of the gate. Slowly he began to see the landscape around him. A valley of rolling green hills lay before him. Gone was the forest trees and covered canopy of branches, here it was open and fresh, blue sky covered the whole valley and the sun shone bright and hot. He stared, open mouthed, as he surveyed the sight before him. It was simply beautiful. Silver coloured trees grew in clumps dotted around the valleys edge and lush green grass swayed gently in the soft breeze. Birds flew overhead and insects chirped their calling song. A small river ran from his left, a river of crystal clear water. He followed its path with his eyes down towards the valley floor until it ended in a large pool of blue sparkling water. It was then he noticed the heart of Silverdale. In the middle of the valley were stone built houses dotted around gardens of unimaginable beauty. As he gazed harder into the distance he saw more and more of them, until eventually they lead into what he assumed to be the centre of Silverdale. Here stood a much bigger building than anything he had seen so far, but even from this distance he could see the white marble stones that made up its structure. It shone out as the sun's rays danced merrily of its walls, and was a sight to behold.

"That is the palace of King Thealine, king of the Elven nation," Tamar stated as if reading his mind once again. "All that surrounds it is Silverdale, unchanged since it was born, welcome to my homeland Master Sam Meredith."

Suddenly Anna came galloping out from the surrounding trees and skidded to a halt by his side.

"Bloody hell it was dark in there!" she said, "but this is lovely, at last a place that looks half decent, I was beginning to think that I would never see anything but trees and dark."

"Welcome to Silverdale Anna," Tamar offered.

"Thanks, glad I could make it." She replied whilst taking in the beauty of the land before her.

"Tamar," Sam spoke, "what happened back there in the dark, I heard my name being called over and over and something was calling me to join them. I know it's crazy, but had it not been for you I think I would have done, what was it? What was going on?"

"I did not expect it either" Tamar offered, "Some say that the walls of Silverdale are inhabited by the spirits of the dead kings of the land, some have even said that they have been spoken to by these spirits, although I have travelled the walls hundreds of times and have never heard nor seen anything – until today that is," he amended. "I am afraid that I have no answer for you, it may be something that Evaine will be able to answer."

"Typical," Sam thought, "yet more unanswered questions."

"Come now, we must be on our way, the King awaits our return, but remember what I have told you," Tamar spoke to Sam and Anna only now, "stay close to me until we reach our destination." With that Tamar wheeled his horse around and set off towards the valley floor.

The company began their slow descent towards the heart of Silverdale. The sun continued to warm everything with its touch, and the fragrant smells of the country filled the air. Sam and Anna rode side by side and drank in the beauty of their surroundings with every step. It was the first real time that Sam had felt at peace since starting out just a few days ago. He had felt relaxed the minute he had broke free of the blackness of the wall. He sat loosely upon his horse, happy to let it guide him towards the valley floor. He was exhausted, but even so, he found that he was unable to stop looking in all directions at this new landscape. Birds flew overhead and the once slate grey sky was now a vibrant sea of blue. Rich green grass swayed gently in the breeze beneath his horse's feet and the whole land seemed to be at peace.

Anna too was enjoying this welcomed change in their surroundings. By contrast to Sam, she sat bolt upright in her saddle and retained a firm grip on the reigns. Even in this pool of tranquillity, she remained alert and cautious.

Further down the valley's walls they descended, until finally their route began to level off as they reached the floor. The buildings that lay ahead were still some way off so the trek continued, although Sam did not mind. He began to feel as if he may drift off to sleep so restful was the journey. If sleep came, he thought, it would find no argument from him. A few times he would notice Anna looking his way, but he didn't acknowledge her, to do so might have broken the feeling of serenity that he basked within, and he wasn't about to risk losing it.

Onwards they went. Each step brought them closer to their destination of Silverdale's heart. Sam ceased hearing the conversations between the Elven guards that went on around him; he failed to hear even Anna's words as he drifted further into himself. It was so restful here, so restful, he thought. He began hearing his name being called, not shouted but soft and calming. It was carried to him on the soft breeze that brushed at his face. At first he paid it no heed, but it became more persistent the more he ignored it.

"Sam, welcome home, welcome back to us, you must never leave again. Welcome home Sam. Welcome"

Although he had no idea as to where the voices emanated from, it didn't seem strange to him to hear them calling him. They were almost comforting and gave him a feeling of security and serenity.

"Welcome home Sam, welcome back to your rightful place," the voices continued their call. With each word Sam grew even more tired and further lost within his thoughts. His eyes began to close as the voices continued to grow louder in his head. Many voices were all speaking at once, all calling him, welcoming him back to Silverdale. They began to swirl in his head as a whirlpool of noise, never giving up their relentless call, never stopping to wait for a reply. Sam, although confused by the cacophony of sound, felt more and more relaxed with each passing moment. He felt no danger from the voices, only genuine pleasure at his presence. So many now were the voices that he no longer heard individual calls, just a continuous wall of sound that soothed and relaxed him. No longer did he feel the aches of his journey, he felt as if he were floating on a cloud of silk. He couldn't remember if he had closed his eyes, but he no longer saw the path ahead, everything just blended into a pleasing blur. He was lost to the voices completely; it therefore came as shock to Sam when they suddenly stopped. Without warning they ceased their relentless call. Immediately Sam felt lost and exposed. So comforting and reassuring had the voices been that he felt vulnerable without them. Blindly he searched for them, desperate to get them to once again call him, but to no avail.

His body remained heavy with fatigue, and his eyes refused to open, but still no voices came. He was beginning to feel desperate; anxiously waiting to hear the calls return, but still no sound could be heard. He felt his body twist and turn in an effort to find the comfort that had now departed him, when suddenly a single voice spoke his name. He felt himself physically jump at the unexpected sound. It was not like the others that had relentlessly called him; this one was clear and steady.

"Sam, my dearest Sam, welcome to Silverdale." It was Ruern's voice that he heard!

"Hear my voice and mine alone," she continued. "You have reached the first part of your journey as was foretold. The voices you hear are echoes in time that have waited for this moment for many years. The voices belong to the rulers of great Elven kingdoms that have since fallen during the passage of time. They welcome you to their homeland, but also want you to join them in the mists where they now dwell. They wish you no harm, but harm would be caused should you fail to resist their call, as no mortal spirit can survive for long within the mists of Echenor. Hear only my voice and I will shield you from their cries."

Sam was unable to speak such was his shock at hearing Ruern's voice once more. The image of her broken form flashed through his mind and he winced at the pain the memory caused.

"Do not feel sadness for me," Ruern continued as if she had seen the image also.

"I have done as was required and I accepted the honour, even knowing my outcome, I was ready to undertake my charge. All has happened as I had foreseen. But it is now that I can see no more; I am blind to what the future will bring for you now my dear Sam." Sam felt the cold chill return to him as she spoke these words. Even though he had not been aware of her presence before, it seemed that she was once again leaving him, but this time for good.

"You will be joined on your journey Sam," she continued, "Many will help you achieve your destiny, but not all will be obvious to you. Alas, there are many that will attempt to prevent you reaching journeys end, these too will not be obvious to you. Choose your words carefully Sam, and remember be mindful of whom you choose to trust. My work is almost complete. You should go now and speak with King Thealine, for there is much for you to be told."

Sam felt her slipping further and further away from him with each passing word. Her voice was becoming more distant and frail and was almost lost to him.

"There is one further request that I need you to complete Sam," Ruern's voice was barely audible now, but Sam listened with intent, "Seek out Amador, for he will be your guide and protector on this quest…"

65

Ruern's voice faded into air and Sam heard her voice no more; he was once again alone.

"Sam, Sam!" came the faint sound of Anna's voice as it bridged the void of silence that surrounded Sam's thoughts. Slowly he began to drift from the world of unseen voices, and back to the madness of reality.

He began to feel the heaviness fall away from his eyes and gradually they began to open. Immediately the brightness of the day filled his vision and blinded his view. After several minutes of squinting, Sam was eventually able to make out the image of Anna's face that stared at him with a quizzical look.

"Sam, we've been calling you for ages, what happened, are you ok?"

"Yeah, I'm fine, just daydreaming I guess." His response surprised him. He didn't have any intention of lying; he just blurted it out. Anna shot him a disbelieving look, and was about to challenge his response, but before she could voice her opinion she was interrupted by the calls of Tamar beckoning them to rejoin the group.

"We'll talk about this later," Anna muttered to Sam as they trotted back to the waiting Tamar. Sam simply nodded in response.

Slowly, they began to get closer to their destination of Silverdale's heart. They began to pass the first of the houses that stood on the furthest outskirts of the centre. Anna noted that they all looked the same. All were constructed of a white wood that shone in the afternoon sun. All were immaculately clean and orderly. Well-kept gardens fronted the majority of dwellings, filled to the brim with flowers of every colour and size. The whole village smelt fresh and welcoming. A soothing calm seemed to blow in the soft breeze that toyed with Anna's hair. Everything was serene and at peace. With each step forward that they took, the feeling grew anew; Anna liked it here.

It was then that she began noticing the faces that stared out from the doorways and windows as they passed. Every one bore the characteristics of their guides. Lean features,

66

unblemished white skin and golden hair that was worn at shoulder length. As she returned their gaze she found that each new face portrayed a grace and an innocence that she had never seen before. She instinctively knew that these were good people, noble proud people, and she found a comfort just by being in their presence. As Anna continued to take in her hosts, she realised that although she had seen young Elven children and young adults, she had seen no older Elves within the confines of Silverdale. The eldest she had observed appeared to have been no older than her. It was then that she was reminded of the earlier encounter with Evaine, when he had informed Sam that he had been waiting over three hundred years for their arrival. Did all Elves live to a great age and yet cease to appear old? Just another question requiring an answer she thought to herself ruefully. She had also noticed that whilst she had attracted fleeting glances from their hosts, it was Sam that they were transfixed upon. Once they had caught sight of him that is where their eyes stayed, locked on his every move. She had turned to catch his eye a couple of times and he had returned her look with an almost nervous half smile, he had obviously also noticed the attention that he was generating.

They were drawing close to the heart of Silverdale now and the homes became more commonplace. All still identical in construction and beauty and all filled with inquisitive faces. No one came to greet them, in fact the fields and gardens were empty of anyone except for their little group.

"Look," came a whisper in Anna's ear. She turned to find Sam gazing ahead and she turned to look in the direction of his fascination. The gleaming white building that they had seen from the valley rim now stood not more than one hundred yards ahead of them. Built from the same white timber as the houses, it rose up above them in regal splendour. They continued forward at a slower pace, unable to break their stare with the beauty that stood before them. Pure white steps led up to a plateau that was adorned with banners bearing the familiar symbol of a great oak, with crown beneath, in front of a rising sun. Two massive oak doors marked the entrance to the building, each ornately carved with scrolls and more of the

Elvish writing that Sam and Anna had observed on the tomb of Ruern. Massive golden handles shaped as duelling dragons glistened in the sunlight that danced merrily of the polished metal.

"Even now, even after all these years, I still marvel at its beauty." Tamar whispered to no one in particular.

"What is this place?" Sam replied.

"You stand before the great hall of Ichbaru, home to the Elven Kings, the birthplace of freedom, the light that protects Silverdale. The King awaits your arrival within, there is much to discuss, much to arrange, let us keep the King waiting no longer master Sam and Mistress Anna," Tamar replied.

Anna was surprised that she had been included in Tamar's response. Each time previously it had always been Sam that was referred to meeting the King or coming home, she had never been mentioned. She gave Tamar a quick smile in response.

As they set foot on the first of the steps that led to the entrance, the massive doors swung silently open and two lines of Elven guard marched purposefully out towards them. Each line took up position on either side of the plateau and stopped. Sam jumped inwardly at the sight of these soldiers. They were dressed in different attire to the Elves that had been their escort. Black leather armour clad each guard. Massive ash bows were strapped to each of the men's backs and gold hilted swords hung from each of their waistbands. Sam felt a slight twinge of anxiety at the sight of these soldiers. These seemed ready for battle and none showed any sign of welcoming the party that slowly ascended the steps.

"Do not be afraid Master Sam," Tamar spoke, "these are the guards of Ichbaru, the Kings Personnel guardians. They are the elite division of the Elven army, and any guest greeted by their salute is a worthy guest indeed." Tamar gave a short laugh and placed his hand reassuringly on Sam's shoulder, "Lets us continue," he added.

Anna had noticed that the other soldiers that had accompanied them to Silverdale had gone from their side; just Sam, Tamar and she remained. Slowly they continued their ascension of the steps. As they reached the plateau, the Ichbaru turned to face them and placed their right arm across their chest in salute in complete synchrony, almost as if some silent order had been given. Tamar returned the salute and continued forward with Sam and Anna close behind. One solitary cloaked figure stood with head bowed in the massive doorway that marked the entrance to the great hall. Slowly they passed through the statuesque Ichbaru guard, until they stood not more than five yards in front of the figure.

"Welcome charges of Ruern," the individual spoke, and to Sam's surprise it was a women's voice that bid them welcome. "My name is Elay." As she spoke her name, she removed the cowl that covered her head. She was more beautiful than Sam thought possible. Deep wide blue eyes fixed on Sam. Golden hair tumbled past her waist and her face was as if stolen from an angel. Sam had noticed that Tamar had bowed his head in greeting to this Elay, and he was about to follow suit when Elay reached out to stop him.

"I am a daughter of a King, but I am not worthy of your reverence Master Sam. I greet you in the name of King Thealine and bid you welcome. I will show you to your quarters where you may rest and bathe. Once rested, a warm meal will be readied. Please follow me as there is much to attend too." With that, Elay turned and began walking back though the entrance. Sam felt Anna's hand slide into his.

"It is here that I will take my leave of you." Tamar's voice broke the silence.

"I will no doubt see you very soon, but for now I will leave you both to rest for rest is what you will need before you…" Tamar stopped short of finishing his sentence, gave them both a quick smile and a bow, and headed back through the lines of the Ichbaru guard.

Sam and Anna watched as Tamar descended the steps before heading off to follow after Elay as instructed. They stood in a long narrow hallway that was lit by burning torches that hung on the walls. Ahead of them stood a further set of great oak doors, framed by two of the Ichbaru guard who stood silent and unmoving in the half-light. To their left was a stone cut staircase that rose to the upper levels of the structure. Elay was standing halfway up and turned to indicate for them to follow, which they both dutifully did. Once they had reached the crest of the stairway they were greeted by a another corridor, not unlike the one they had just left except this one was much longer, and stretched away into the dark. At regular intervals on both sides of the corridor there were single oak doors. Sam surmised that this is where his room was to be found. Elay continued pass several doors before stopping and turning to meet Sam's gaze.

"You will find the promised rest and bath within," she indicated to the door that stood to her left with a tilt of her head, "I am sure you will both be comfortable."

Anna shot Sam a quick glance upon hearing that they would be sharing a room, but Sam did not respond. "Once rested and cleansed," Elay continued, "you will find fresh clothes and boots for your use. Should you require anything else you simply need to ask the guard that will be placed outside your door. I bid you fare dreams children of Ruern, I will seek you again when ready." Elay did not wait for a response from the bemused pair that now stood and watched her departure down the corridor until gone from their view.

"Well just the two of us again I suppose," Anna quipped. "Do you think the Hotel guest book shows as Mr and Mrs Meredith?" Sam smiled at her, "Well don't expect me to carry you over the threshold, I am too damn tired." Now it was Anna's turn to smile.

"Well let's see if we got the honeymoon suite," she whispered, then turned the handle and stepped into the room with Sam close behind. The sight that greeted them was welcome indeed. The room was dominated by a huge four-poster bed that stood at its centre. Several chests of drawers lined the walls, and a large shuttered window that rose from ceiling to floor sat in a bay that overlooked the blue lake that they had seen from the valley's rim. The room was decorated in subtle woodland colours and exposed dark wooden beams ran the length of the ceiling. Anna noticed that, as promised, there were fresh clothes lying on the bed. Cloth trousers and shirts, a pair of warm cloaks, belts, broaches and boots completed the ensemble. Off to one side of the room was an open doorway that housed the bathroom, or as Anna described it, 'a small room with a small metal basin and a not much bigger bath.'

"Well bang goes the honeymoon suite theory," Anna muttered. "As long as the bed is warm and comfortable and the water hot, I couldn't care less," Sam responded as he allowed himself to fall onto the bed.

He was asleep almost as soon as his body touched the soft coverings, and only stirred briefly once to kick off his shoes. When he did so he found Anna nestled close next to him. 'Mr and Mrs Meredith indeed,' he thought, just before sleep pulled him back to her embrace.

CHAPTER

5

Sam awoke to find himself bathed in the sunlight that streamed through the windows of the room. He lay still for a while and gazed at the massive Oak beams that ran the length of the ceiling. As he lay he listened to the sounds of birds calling too each other with song, whilst allowing the aches and cramps of his sleep to leave. So sure he had been that the last few days had been a dream he was expecting to wake and find himself back in his home. It took him several moments to accept that nothing had changed from yesterday, and that the dream was very real. To his surprise, part of him was pleased.

"At last!" Came a familiar voice. Sam jumped at the sound to a sitting position to find Anna at the foot of his bed, fully attired in the clothing that had been left for her to wear.

"You certainly can snore," she continued, "the Elves took some convincing that you weren't dying!" She smiled one of her dazzling smiles, and despite Sam's bemused state, he couldn't help but smile back.

"How long have I been asleep, what time is it?" he mumbled as he rubbed the remaining sleep from his eyes. Anna drew a deep breath,

"You've been asleep for almost two days, and it's about mid-day although I am not sure what day it is as I don't think they have names for different days here, it's just today. But I do know that it is time that you got up as no one will tell me anything until you are with me, so c'mon get these on." Anna tossed him the pile of clothes that had been left for Sam. "And let's get something to eat because I am starving."

Two days, was that possible? Sam thought to himself. It had only seemed a short while ago that they had arrived. No matter he decided, he was getting used to surprises and nothing making sense anymore, besides, he had woken feeling hungry and eating sounded a good idea to him. He threw off his bed covers and swung his legs out of bed only to discover that someone had undressed him during his time asleep. In an effort to save his blushes, Anna threw the discarded covers back over him and turned her back. Hurriedly he dressed. Once finished he took a quick moment to admire himself in the mirror that hung by his bed then slapped Anna on the back, "C'mon lets go get food and you can tell me everything that you have learnt whilst I've been sleeping." Anna turned and smiled,

"I've learnt where your birth-mark is!" she replied. Laughing she headed for the door with a rather embarrassed Sam close behind.

Anna led Sam out of the bright bedroom and into the dimly lit corridor. Outside of the door stood two Elven sentries that Sam assumed to be the personal guard of the king, the Ichbaru as Tamar had told them. Instead of turning left down the corridor, in the direction that they had come into the building, Anna took him right, and headed for the far end of the passageway. Halfway down there appeared another set of stairs cut into the wall. Anna led him down the winding staircase, which seemed to go on for much longer than the one that had led him to their bedroom when they initially arrived. Eventually the staircase ended and led into cavernous hall that seemed to run the entire

73

length of the building. A great open fire burned brightly at the far end, and a massive oak table with high back chairs sat in the centre of the room. Rich coloured tapestries adorned the walls and the now familiar crest of an Oak tree with Crown and Sun was carved into the stone on the opposite wall. Although huge, the room was warm and had a welcoming feel.

Anna boldly strode across the room and seated herself in one of the chairs that surrounded the table and beckoned for Sam to join her. With a certain amount of trepidation, Sam sat next to her whilst still surveying his surroundings.

"This is the King's council room," Anna told him, "and there are nineteen chairs that represent the founding nineteen members of the council. We are in the lower level council room, and there are a further six meeting rooms that are used depending on the number of attending members. According to Tamar, it has been over sixty-years since all nineteen have met together." Sam starred at her in bemusement.

"You sound like a tour guide," he admonished.

"Well you said you wanted to know what I have learnt since you have been asleep, that's about the depth of it. As I said, no one would tell me much without you being here. Tamar has filled me in on a few details when I have managed to catch his attention but I have seen neither Evaine nor the elusive King at all. I did see that Elay a few times but I think she has been avoiding me! It seems that I have only been told odd bits and pieces, just to keep me quiet I suspect." Sam momentarily thought about making a comment about Anna being quiet, but decided against it and let the moment pass. "I know that the council is made up of three representatives from the six dominant races", she continued, "but as to what these races are I am not sure. I did ask about the one chair left over but was told that it would become clear in time. This is a phrase that I am getting used too!"

"Well perhaps after tonight you will hear it spoken no more," came a familiar voice from behind them. Sam and Anna spun around to find Tamar standing at the foot of the staircase.

"Well rested I assume Master Sam?" Tamar enquired. Sam simply nodded in response. "Not that I doubted you wouldn't be, after all, you have had more sleep than the dead!" Tamar chuckled loudly to himself.

"What's happening tonight that's so important then?" Anna ventured.

"Always questions, questions, questions with you Mistress Anna," Tamar responded in a light hearted manner, "Tonight, history will be written for there will be a gathering at this very table. The gathering will comprise of three Elves, three Dwarves, three Men and three Trolls. Four of the original races will be represented for the first time in over forty years. Unfortunately the Gnomes and Goblins that made up the original six declined the offer, but seeing as they have been in a state of perpetual war with everybody for the past twenty years this is hardly unexpected news. There will however be fifteen chairs filled, two of which will be taken by you." Sam looked at Anna then back again at Tamar.

"And the final chair?" He enquired

"Even I do not know the answer to that question Master Sam, but time will give us the answers, of that I am sure."

"Why?" Sam pressed, "What is the purpose of this historic meeting?"

"You are." Tamar responded with a smile and a flash of devilment in his eyes.

After a lunch of cold meats, bread and cheese, all washed down with a few glasses of ale, Anna took Sam on a tour of the palace. It was a limited tour as Anna had yet to see a lot of the building herself, but Sam nonetheless enjoyed the break in the monotony of the day. Tamar had departed shortly after their food had been served and they had seen nothing of him since. The same could be said for both Evaine and Elay, in fact they had seen only the palace retainers go about their daily chores and the ever-present Ichbaru guard that oversaw their every footstep from a distance. Anna relayed all that she had learnt during Sam's extended sleep, about their situation and their hosts, however it was virtually a repeat of what Tamar had offered during their journey to Silverdale. Sam however didn't

75

mind, in fact he was happy just to listen to Anna's narration that was perpetually edged with a heavy dose of sarcasm. They walked for a long while both inside and outside of the palace, although it was clear from the presence of the Elven guard at almost every turn as to where they were permitted to go and where they were not. The day was bright and the gardens that surrounded the palace were full of colour and fragrance and Sam found that he felt strangely at ease in the unfamiliar surroundings.

It was after about an hour of walking that Anna asked the question that had been on her mind for several hours. It came so out of the blue that it took Sam some time to respond.

"Do you think the fifteenth chair is for your father Sam?" She asked it in her usual matter of fact way, there were never any deviations to Anna's thoughts, just straight to the point. The same question had been on Sam's mind since Tamar's statement, but he had felt unsure as to how the words would sound spoken aloud. But once again Anna had taken the bull by the horns.

"I...I'm not sure, I had been thinking the same thing but thought it better to keep it to myself, however, as you obviously don't, I can't say that I know anything about anything anymore," he replied in a hushed voice.

"But what if it is?" She pressed, "how do you feel, don't you think it a bit scary, a bit exciting? How are you going to react if it is?"

"I haven't given it much thought to be honest, after all, I'm not sure that I am used to the idea yet that I may have a father. It was only a few days ago that I believed my father to be long dead, and now I am being told that during my whole life I have been lied to." Sam kicked absent-mindedly at the pebbles that lined the path of the garden where they walked. "I suppose, if I am honest, it scares the hell out of me if it is true, I mean, what else in my life has been a lie? What if the whole of my life has been some kind of dreamt up story? I think I am happier believing myself to have no father, I think that knowing the truth is something that comes with a high price." He stopped and starred up at the blue cloudless sky that hung above.

"Perhaps it is a price that I cannot afford." He looked down to find Anna meeting his gaze. She gave him a short smile, placed her hand in his and they continued their walk through the colours of the palace gardens.

After a further hour of walking the palace grounds, they headed back to their room. The day was still bright and retained much of its midday warmth; however, Sam had seen enough of the gardens and the walls of palace. He was beginning to get the now familiar feeling of uneasiness in the pit of his stomach as the day marched onwards towards the impending arranged meeting. The Elven guard remained in their silent watch at his door and offered the slightest nod of acknowledgement as they passed through. Once inside, Anna took herself off for a long soak in the bath whilst Sam threw himself onto the bed and found himself once again staring at the ceiling.

After a short while there came a knock on the door. Anna was still busy soaking, so Sam, with considerable effort, hauled himself off the bed to answer the call. He released the latch and pulled it open. The smiling face of Evaine greeted him.

"Greetings Master Sam, I trust you are well rested and refreshed?" Before Sam could respond, Evaine had passed him and stood in the centre of the room.

"Are you going to stand there all day with the door open? Or would you like me to try and answer some of those questions that you have?" Evaine chuckled. Sam immediately pushed the door closed and made his way to where Evaine stood.

"Firstly," Evaine continued, "I must offer my apologies for not finding you sooner, I am afraid that at present there are many who require my time, however, I understand from Tamar that you have been asleep for most of your duration here so you haven't missed me that much I suspect." Evaine again chuckled. Sam found that he was unable to think of anything to respond with and shuffled uncomfortably from foot to foot.

"Still no matter, I am here now. Let us sit by the window as we talk." Evaine gestured towards the leather bound chairs that sat in the bay of the room and, without waiting for a response, promptly walked over and sat. Sam followed like an obedient child and sat in the chair opposite, still unable to find the right words to say. For a while they sat in silence. Evaine closed his eyes and seemed to be enjoying the warming touch of the sun on his face. Sam, by contrast, sat and scowled at Evaine. He felt rather insignificant in his presence, and had done since their first meeting and it was not a feeling that Sam was particularly comfortable with.

"Well, what do you think of Silverdale?" Evaine suddenly spoke without opening his eyes.

"It's..., erm..., lovely?" Sam responded, not entirely sure as to how he should answer the question. "But I'm more interested as to why I am here." Sam ventured. Evaine's eyes snapped open, "I am sure you are" he grinned, "This will become clearer as you listen to what I am about to tell you. Some of which will be hard to bear, but I ask that you listen and hold any questions until I have finished. Most of which I would hope, will be answered in my narrative." Evaine's face had taken on a more serious guise, different to the jovial one of just a few moments passed. "What I am about to tell you my friend is known by very few, but it is imperative that you know before you join the gathering tonight. I am acting on the instructions of the King himself to tell you all the truths that you require, to hold nothing back, no matter how hard they are for you to hear". Sam didn't like the sound of that and was beginning to regret asking so many questions.

"Shall I begin?" Evaine offered. Sam was about to respond when suddenly Anna rushed into the room and jumped onto the bed. Her clothes clung to her wet body as she had obviously dispensed with the need to get herself dry in the rush to hear what was going on.

"Ok, you can start now." she puffed as she got herself into a comfortable position. Evaine gave Sam a quick look, who simply shrugged.

"She will make me tell her once you have left anyway, so you might as well carry on," he replied to the unasked question. With the smile now returned to Evaine's face he began.

"As I have already said, some of what you are about to hear will be hard for you to accept," Evaine's eyes remained locked on Sam as he spoke in a hushed tone, "I ask again that you listen and let me finish before asking further questions of me." The room went quiet in anticipation as Evaine drew breath. "I firstly need to take you back to the days of the founding of the council, the very same council that you will take your place within tonight. The council was formed over five thousand years ago following the end of a forty-year war that had raged throughout the land. It was made up of the wisest and most respected members of the six main races. Elves, Men, Dwarves, Trolls, Gnomes and Goblins were all represented. The other races that inhabited the earth were either not interested in the councils aims or were content for others to speak on their behalf. The main purpose of the council was to ensure that all enjoyed a maintainable peace and equitable existence, and to undertake the rebuilding of that which had been destroyed in the war. They drew on each of the races particular skills to work together in order to achieve that, which could not be achieved alone. There was much to be done for the world had been decimated by a conflict that had lasted for so many years, however, trust was the first thing that needed to be rebuilt. Trust between the races." Sam continued to hold Evaine's gaze, anxious to understand as to what relevance any of this had on him, however he remembered Evaine's request and held his tongue. "As I have already stated, the council members were selected by each represented race. It was the finest collection of visionaries, philosophers, mages and craftsmen that the land could muster. These gathered eighteen were the founding fathers of the land that we now know as Invetia, an Elven word from ancient times that meant 'Undivided People', which seemed most appropriate as this was the principle vision that the council stood for." Anna seized the quick break in Evaine's narration to get into a more comfortable position; Sam however, remained impassive and unmoving. Once Anna had settled Evaine continued. "Time passed slowly onwards and the work the council had set out for itself began to take shape. Communities were rebuilt, crops harvested and education of the people began. On the surface all was progressing as had been hoped and promised, but within the council there were cracks beginning to form. Whilst it was true that they had indeed achieved much, it was the mistrust between them that could not be so easily healed. Great rifts began to form between the races. Men wanted overall control on how the land was governed, the Dwarves wanted bigger cities, and the Gnomes and Goblins wanted both these things and more besides. Eventually after sixty years of relative progress the council disbanded. The Trolls retreated back to their communities in the mountains to the west, the Gnomes and Goblins dissipated into fragmented tribes that were scattered throughout the land, the race of Men built fortified cities and claimed most of the Southland for their own, the Dwarves returned to their Eastland kingdoms and the Elves remained where we are today". Evaine paused in his narration to take breath. As he did he averted his eyes from Sam's continued stare and looked out of the window from where he sat, as if to gather his thoughts for the next part of the tale. Sam continued to keep his eyes locked on the Elf. He was feeling that Evaine's tale was building to a crescendo that somehow linked Sam and Anna's presence to the land of Invetia, and he was feeling a little uneasy at the prospect. Once again Anna grabbed the opportunity to reposition her aching body and shuffled into position, ready for the next instalment. Neither was prepared for what Evaine said next.

Evaine remained starring out of the window as he began anew with his tale. "After several years following the split of the Races, your father came to Silverdale, Sam." It was said in such a matter of fact way that Sam nearly missed it, but Anna didn't, "Here we go," she muttered to Sam, "Here comes the juicy bits!" Sam neither spoke nor moved, but he felt his mouth go dry and his legs start to shake.
Evaine did not wait for a response to this statement, he simply forged ahead with his tale, but his eyes had now returned to meet Sam's incessant gaze.

"His arrival was unexpected and unplanned and yet it proved to be the most pivotal moment in the history of the Elven nation. His name was Ceriphan." Sam was now sitting as close to the edge of his seat as he could. He was bent forward to ensure that he missed nothing of Evaine's tale. He felt his stomach turning and his legs continue to shake, but was eager to hear more about his father. It seemed strange to him that he was accepting this tale as easily as he was, never once did he consider any of what he had heard to be untruthful; it simply felt right.

"Many years before the forty-year war, there had been rumours of a great Elven mage that walked the land," Evaine continued, "no-one was sure as to where he had come from or to what purpose he worked towards, although it was widely accepted that he worked for the powers of light and was a friend to the people of Invetia. Many had heard his name mentioned in stories of old but few had met or spoken with him. Over time he had become a legend of the world and most believed him to be an enigma that never really existed. It was therefore a great surprise for the then Elven king to find this Ceriphan at his door requesting council."

"Are you telling us that Sam's father was an Elf?" Anna interjected, despite Evaine's earlier request that he should be permitted to finish before taking questions. Nevertheless, he answered her question.

"As I stated at the outset Mistress Anna, much will be difficult to believe or accept, but you have accepted me as being real and Silverdale and Invetia have you not? I ask that you apply the same acceptance to this tale." Anna slumped back on to the bed in a funk. Sam neither looked her way nor acknowledged her question; he simply remained impassive and concentrated on Evaine. "Shall I continue Sam, or would you like a moment?" Evaine enquired.

"Please continue Evaine," Sam whispered, "please finish the tale." Evaine drew breath then continued anew. "Ceriphan brought grave news to the King. He came to advise him of an Elven mage named Molgoran. Molgoran was once friend and ally of Ceriphan, and they had studied together during their youth. Whilst Ceriphan had always been mindful of the

uncontrollability of magic, Molgoran had not. He had
developed an appetite for power, an appetite that could not be
suppressed. Ceriphan had warned his friend of the dangers, but
to no avail. Eventually Ceriphan left Molgoran and started out
alone. Many years passed and Molgoran remained locked in his
domain at the foot of the mountains of Varek. Strange fires and
flashes were reported from the area by passing tradesmen and
all kept clear. Over time vast numbers of Trolls and Goblins
were seen to be gathering at Varek. The sounds of construction
were heard throughout the land. For many years the sound of
rock being split and metal being ground could be heard night or
day. Until eventually a mighty fortress was visible rising out of
the smoke and dust, a fortress that had been built into the
mountainside. A fortress as black as the storm clouds that
perpetually hung overhead. Not even the sunlight ventured into
that place, and over time, the land died and nothing grew.
Ceriphan, by contrast, had spent his time travelling the lands.
Very few even saw his passing as he travelled from village to
village. None could even describe his features, as he remained
permanently hooded and mysterious. Seventy-years after
leaving Molgoran, Ceriphan arrived at Silverdale."
"What about the defences of the wall?" Anna once again
interrupted, "How did he get in if not invited?"
"A good question," Evaine replied. "To this day he remains the
only one to have gained entry to Silverdale without the help of
the Ichbaru or King. The history books record that Ceriphan in
fact helped strengthened the magic that kept Silverdale safe
from the outside world, and even hints that he was responsible
for the creation of the Mists of Echenor, but no one knows for
sure."
"You said that this Ceriphan brought grave news to the King
Evaine? Please continue," Sam ventured. Evaine's attention
was brought back on Sam and he continued with the tale.
"Ceriphan had practised his art for thousands of years. He was
learned beyond all living men and was a very powerful mage
indeed. However, as I previously mentioned, he learnt with a
respect for the magic and was always mindful of its
unpredictability if it were not kept in control. He therefore only

practiced that which had a positive effect on the land and its people. Ceriphan despised the damage that Molgoran's domain had caused at Varek, but he was also aware that for light to exist there must also be dark, so he chose to ignore it, a decision that he was to later rue. As time passed the strange happenings at Varek continued, more Trolls, Gnomes and Goblins came daily to live in its shadow. The Westland began to empty and the sporadic groups of Gnomes and Goblins that once roamed the lands began to unite under one banner, under one rule, the rule of Molgoran. He was amassing an army of great power and great numbers, but as to why no one was sure. Great furnaces burned constantly for many years as weapons were forged and armour was hammered. Thick acrid smoke clung to the mountain side and the land grew darker still. The many streams that ran from the foot of Varek and fed the land of Invetia began to foul and become stagnant and the darkness crept ever further into Invetia." Evaine broke his gaze with Sam and turned to look out of the window. "The Elves were foolish; they failed to see the danger that was building in the very heart of Invetia. They turned a blind eye to the darkness and destruction that was threatening their very existence. They took comfort in the fact that they led unnaturally long lives, they would survive this period of history locked within the confines of Silverdale and after all, they owed the other races no allegiance, it was not the Elves that broke the council. Ceriphan came to open their eyes to the danger they were in, he came to ask for old alliances to be re-forged, and he came to prepare them for war." Evaine drew breath and returned his attention to Sam and Anna. "To cut a long story short, he succeeded, not only with the Elves but he had been to see the Dwarf lords and the Kings of Men. He had brought them all together to face this threat from the darkness of Molgoran's army. After one-hundred years of relative peace the land was again plunged into war. This was to be the most ferocious battle that Invetia had seen in its history. Elves allied with Men and Dwarves fought against the hoards of Troll's, Goblin's, Gnome's, Kobold's and nameless other creatures that crawled from the pitch of Varek. The war raged for one hundred and twenty years. The race of Elves was nearly made extinct and the land so badly scared that, to this day it still recovers. Eventually it was Ceriphan that ended the conflict. Cloaked in his magic he was able to pass through the blackness of Varek and seek out Molgoran. The battle between them lasted eighteen days, but eventually Ceriphan threw down Molgoran and stole his magic away, forever to be safeguarded. The shade of Molgoran that remained was banished to the mists of the Echenor, from which there would be no escape. Without the controlling hand of Molgoran the dark army fell apart and fled back from whence they came. The war was over, the battle won but at terrible cost." Evaine paused to gain his breath such was his vigour in narrating the tale. Once composed he continued, both Sam and Anna remained eager to hear more of the story.

"Ceriphan was not seen for four years following the defeat of Molgoran. Most assumed that he had died in his efforts to rid the land of Molgoran, however, after the passing of the years, he returned once again at Silverdale and requested the King's audience. He was barely recognizable from the Ceriphan that led the battle cry all those years before. He was old and bent; he walked with the aid of a staff and with great difficulty. He barely seemed able to raise his head aloft and his speech was quiet and slow. King Eaine, the then Elven King, was struck by the fact that whilst Ceriphan had the guise of a beggar, his eyes still burned ice fire blue and sparkled with the intensity of their first meeting all those years before." Evaine shifted nervously in his seat. Sam felt that the story was again building to release a further secret and began to feel his stomach turn at the prospect.

"Ceriphan brought further news to the King, news of his imminent departure from the world of Invetia. Ceriphan had done all that could have been done to restore balance to the land following the torrid years of war. There was no more that he could do to help in the recovery of Invetia; it was now up to its people to safeguard its future prosperity. But Ceriphan came with a warning, a warning that would once again threaten to consume and destroy all of Invetia if not heeded. Ceriphan had foreseen the rebirth of the ancient magic, an evil that had given life and power to Molgoran all those years ago, would once again cover Invetia in shadow if not thwarted. The problem was that this evil would be unreachable for nearly five thousand years. None could reach it, find it or destroy it, not even the mighty Ceriphan; it would just grow untouched and unchallenged until it was ready to show its guise to the world of Invetia." Once again Evaine paused to draw breath. Sam shot Anna an uneasy glance then returned his determined gaze to Evaine.

"Now Ceriphan knew that he would no longer be alive to meet the challenge of this new peril, and he also knew that it could not be found or harmed during the time he had left, so he came to the heart of the Elven nation to give them hope for the years ahead. He would bear a child, an heir to his dynasty of protector, an heir blessed with the learning's of his lifetime and the power to thwart any future threat to Invetia and its people."

"Oh crap!" Sam whispered. Evaine continued unabated, eager it seemed now to get the words out.

"Ceriphan knew that none of his lineage would be safe within the realm, as they would surely be hunted down and destroyed before any defence could be mounted. He would have to find a time and a place far from the reach of evil to bring this heir into the world. So it came to pass that Ceriphan entrusted this task to the Sario. They were chosen to carry the seed of his creation until the time came to give it life. The race of the Sario were a natural choice, they were blessed with long life and the ability to navigate the mists of Echenor and cross worlds as and when they pleased, no other life force within Invetia could do this. The race of the Sario were but one-hundred in numbers but lived to protect and aid each other." Evaine paused to look upon the now ashen face of Sam.

"Would you like me to stop for a bit?" he offered, but Sam simply shook his head in response.

"The years passed by, the land changed, Kings were born and died. The races of Invetia grew further apart and the evil grew unchecked and hidden. The knowledge of its existence rested solely with the Elves. Each ruling house knew of it, the tomes of the old age passed down throughout their bloodline and each King secretly prayed that it would not come to pass in their time of rule. All this time the Sario carried the seed of hope, never faltering, never growing tired of the waiting, only anxious to act when the time came. Ceriphan, following his visit to Silverdale, was never seen or heard of again within the world of Invetia. He must have died a solitary death, having fulfilled his obligation to the land," Evaine surmised. He looked up to see a tear run down Anna's pale face, Sam, however sat impassive and lost within the words of the tale.

"It was about forty years ago that the first signs of the evil that had been forewarned began to show itself. Strange sightings were being reported by townsfolk, dark shadows that walked the earth in the depths of night. No one was able to describe what they had seen, just a shadow darker than any other passing on the breeze. The most alarming sign however, was that the race of Sario were slowly disappearing from the earth. Their numbers were mysteriously reducing. Nothing the Sario's did could seem to stop their number dying unexpectedly. It seemed as if an unseen assassin was stalking them and systematically wiping them out one by one. At the dawn of each new day another would be found dead within the mists of Echenor. Some lay drained and lifeless, some ripped apart and left scattered across the floor of the mists. It was at this point that the gift of Ceriphan found its way into the hands of a young Sario named Ruern." Sam's head suddenly snapped up as he remembered that fateful night in the forest, he closed his eyes against the torrent of images that crowded his mind of Ruern lying lifeless and broken within the Dunbar and winced silently at the pain that the image brought. Evaine did not slow with his narration.

"So it was that Ruern passed from the world of Invetia in search of a place of concealment for her precious charge. No one knew where she went or who she found to nurture the seed, but I guess Sam, that you know this part better than anyone." Sam didn't respond; he felt his head grow heavy and felt the now familiar sting of tears roll down his face. He felt tired, confused, angry, sad and a hundred other emotions all at once. His worst fears had been realised, his whole life had in fact been a lie.

"The remaining Sario's built a monument to Ruern at the place where she left Invetia," Evaine pressed on, "as her fate had also been foreseen, the same monument you both saw when you arrived. Shortly after its completion the last of the remaining Sario was found dead at its steps, no more lived, all but Ruern were slain."

A silence hung over the room. Evaine had finished his narration and sat upright in his chair, again staring out of the bay window into the now dimming light of the day. Anna sat on the bed frozen as if a statue, her eyes transfixed on Sam, whilst Sam sat with his head hung low and kept his eyes screwed tightly shut.

No one spoke for what seemed an eternity, but eventually it was Evaine who broke the silence. "You see Master Sam, your importance to the Elven nation and the land of Invetia is vast. We believe you to be the descendant of the great Ceriphan and saviour of our land. You are born of Invetia and its people, you are the hope that we have been waiting for all our lives. I do not know what it is you are meant to do, I do not know what magic flows within your veins, but you are special, you are the one that will offer salvation to your people whether you would wish it or not. I can offer no further answers for I have told all that I know, but what I can offer is my life into your service. Whatever your destiny demands I will stand by you every step of the way. You are not alone Master Sam, you are amongst friends, and you have come home."

Evaine stood and placed a comforting hand on the slumped shoulders of Sam, then turned and headed for the door. "The gathering will begin in two hours," he spoke without turning, "I suggest you rest as best you can for you will need your strength more than ever now I fear." With that he opened the door and stepped into the darkness of the corridor.

Neither Sam nor Anna moved for some considerable time after Evaine's departure. Each sat lost in their own thoughts. Time continued to march toward the impending gathering and Sam could do nothing to halt it. All he wanted to do was to curl up in a ball and go to sleep for a very long time, but he knew that this was not an option. With considerable effort, he broke the silence. "Best get ready I suppose," he stated, unable to hide the dread from his voice, "might as well get this part over and done with, after all, it can't be any worse than the last couple of hours." He tried to sound humorous, but failed. Anna looked at him from her position on the bed, "What now?" she asked, "Where do we go from here?" Sam looked at her from across the room,
"I guess we do what we have done since arriving, exactly what we are told to do. Who knows, this meeting may prove to be fun!" Anna shot him a quick glance, and then smiled her dazzling smile, "Ever the optimist heh?"

The time passed surprisingly quickly for Sam as he readied himself for the evening gathering. He decided that he would give no more thought to the words that Evaine had spoken. Despite his long sleep he was exhausted from the experience and he was not able to think straight, so he decided that it was best not to think at all. He allowed himself a long soak in the bath, much to Anna's irritation, and tried to let the day's events wash away from his troubled mind. Afterwards, he got dressed in some fresh clothes that had been left for him to wear and seated himself in the bay and watched the sun finally drop from the sky and the first touch of night slip over the land. Anna, by contrast, rushed around in her usual hurried way. Frantically combing her hair and readjusting her clothing constantly until finally even she slumped in the chair opposite Sam with a groan. "Hope dinners been laid on," Anna stated, "I am starving again."
"You are always starving!" Sam replied with a smile. Anna was about to respond when a knock sounded on the door signalling that it was time to go.

The Ichbaru led Sam and Anna down the now familiar corridors of the great hall, now ensconced in half-light, down the rock hewn staircase, and eventually into the great hall itself. Both the guards then assumed a flanking position at the foot of the stairs and remained unmoving. The room stood empty before them. The fire burned with intensity at the far end and the great table laid prepared for the impending meeting, but all the chairs remained unfilled. Unlike before, Sam noticed, there were now just fifteen chairs that sat around the great table. All would be filled tonight he, recalled from Tamar's speech, two of which would be filled by Anna and himself.

"I trust that you are as prepared as one can be for this evening's event?" A gruff voice sounded from behind them. Sam turned to find Tamar standing at the foot of the stairs. He was clothed in plate armour, golden in colour and highly polished. Strapped to his waist was a row of daggers and on his back rested a great Ash bow.

Sam smiled dutifully at Tamar. "As prepared as I could ever be I suppose." He shrugged with an air of indifference; however his insides were doing cartwheels at the thought of the events that lay ahead. Anna said nothing; she simply took in the surroundings of the room that she now stood within. She was naturally untrusting and nothing that had happened in Invetia since their arrival gave her cause to feel any different. She was still not sure that everything that had been relayed to them by Evaine during the course of the day was strictly accurate, she couldn't put her finger on what exactly was wrong, she had however decided to keep her feelings of mistrust from Sam, after all he had more than enough to contend with at present, but she fully intended to keep her wits about her during this meeting.

She was about to go and take a seat at the table when she heard voices approaching. Not from the direction of the staircase that they had descended but from the opposite wall on which the now familiar crest was to be found. She turned to question Tamar and Sam but they too were listening at the approaching sound. She again turned to face the wall ahead just as a slim panel swung inwards to reveal a second set of steps that ascended into darkness. As the party watched, figures came into sight as they descended the exposed steps. A familiar face came into view, it was Elay. She was closely followed by Evaine. Both were adorned in ceremonial dress. Sam stood staring at the figure of Elay as she entered. She was even more beautiful than he remembered. A long flowing white dress dragged on the floor behind her as she walked to the centre of the room. White flowers were embroidered into the fabric and a sliver necklace hung around her neck that glimmered as the light from the fire reflected off it. She was every inch a Princess in Sam's eyes. Her golden hair was tightly bunched against her head now and white flowers adorned the headdress that she wore. Her blue eyes burned with the same intensity that had greeted him at the steps of the Great Hall. For a split moment her eyes met his, and then she averted her gaze to Tamar, who in turn bowed with respect.

"Welcome my friends," Evaine spoke, "It is good to see you both again. Please, let me show you to your seats." He held out his arm and indicated for Sam to be seated around the great table. Sam followed his instruction and was seated near the end of the side row. Anna followed and pulled the chair out next to Sam and prepared to be seated. "No Mistress Anna, you are to be seated over here." Evaine was indicating to a chair opposite from Sam. "You are to be seated next to me for the duration of tonight's gathering."

"Fantastic," Anna quipped in the most sarcastic voice that she could muster. Evaine didn't respond, either not hearing or choosing to ignore her, Sam speculated that it was probably the latter.

With both Anna and Sam now seated, Evaine, as promised, pulled out the seat next to Anna and sat down. To Sam's surprise, it was Elay that sat next to him on his left. He felt butterflies start to fly around his stomach and squirmed uncomfortably to try and control his feelings. He noticed that his side of the table had been set for seven, and Anna's side six. One chair sat at each end of the great table. He assumed that one would be for the King and surmised that the other was for the enigma that would be joining the evening's events.

"I will take my leave now my lord," Tamar announced. "I will await your call." With that, Tamar turned and ascended the staircase. Sam watched him until he was out of sight. He shot Evaine questioning glance.

"The Captain of the guard has other duties to carry out this night Master Sam." Evaine answered the unasked question. "Tonight's business is but for those chosen to attend."

Evaine gave him a broad smile, but this did little for Sam's confidence. An uncomfortable silence hung over the four seated figures. No one spoke. The only sound was the occasional crackling of the fire at the far end of the Great Hall. Anna fiddled nervously with the cutlery set out before her, pretending to admire the craftsmanship of the pieces, but secretly just grateful for something to do. It was therefore with great embarrassment when she dropped one of the knives on to the hard marbled floor. It made such a noise when it struck the ground that everybody jumped in spite of themselves. She immediately felt herself begin to blush as she reached down to retrieve the errant piece of tableware. Sam tutted loudly, Evaine smiled and to his surprise Elay giggled despite her efforts to stop herself. Sam turned to look at Elay. It was the first time that he had seen the girl show any emotion at all. She wrinkled her nose as she laughed, she seemed, for that split moment, vulnerable and innocent, losing the aloofness that she had portrayed on every other meeting. It lasted just a moment then it was gone and her expression returned to that which Sam had been greeted with each time they had met.

He was about to comment on Anna's table manners when further voices were heard descending the concealed staircase. Deep booming voices sounded above the scrapping of heavy footsteps. Sam gave Anna a quick glance, then Evaine.

"It would appear that our guests have begun to arrive," Evaine spoke to Elay.

Before anything more could be added, the concealed door swung inwards and three short stocky figures stepped into the light of the room. They stood at the opening for a short while, studying their surroundings. Sam observed that all were heavily armoured in brown cracked leather chest plates, pants and boots. All three stood no taller than five feet and all sported long tangled beards that hung to their belt buckles. Although they carried no apparent weapons, Sam quickly decided that they had seen plenty of battles. This was partly due to the amount of scarring that covered their exposed arms and faces.

Evaine rose to his feet, "Sam, Anna, I present Bannock, Lord of the Dwarves." The tallest of the three stepped forward and bowed his head in response. He had distinctive red hair that fell about his shoulders in an unkempt fashion. He looked neither at Sam nor Anna, but met Evaine's gaze with a determination. Undeterred, Evaine continued the introduction, "May I also present Greston, son of Bannock and General of the Dwarvian armies." The Dwarf on Bannock's left stepped forward and nodded in response to Evaine's words. He was of slighter build than his father, and despite his beard and scarred features appeared quite young. "Finally, may I introduce Rotrim, Commander of the elite fighting corps and protector to the Lords of the Dwarvian lands." He was the heaviest set of all three men. White lines of battle criss-crossed every exposed part of his body. He neither advanced nor gave any recognition to his introduction; he simply locked his eyes onto Sam. Sam felt extremely uncomfortable about Rotrim and averted his stare.

"Well, it's been many years since I have set foot within this room," Bannock boomed. "Where is Thealine? I expected more than his son and daughter to meet us!"

'Son?' Sam wondered, then it suddenly dawned on him, he was referring to Evaine! He gave Anna a quick glance. The comment had not passed her by either; she sat starring at Evaine with surprise etched on her face. Evaine exchanged a quick glance with Sam and Anna, "The King will be here very shortly Bannock, and we will try and make you comfortable until his arrival. Our other guests will also be arriving shortly; can I get you and your party a drink whilst we wait?"

"Ale and lots of it!" Bannock stated gruffly. Almost as soon as the words had left his mouth, three of the palace's retainers appeared at the foot of the stairs carrying pitchers filled with the requested ale. Evaine motioned for the Dwarvian party to be seated. As before they had their places indicated to them by the Elven prince. Sam was less than pleased when it was Bannock that was ushered into the seat next to him. The Dwarf muttered a comment about wanting to choose where he sat, but the comment was ignored by the Elf. Rotrim was duly seated next to the Dwarvian Lord, and Greston was seated next to Anna, opposite Bannock. As soon as the Dwarves had been seated they started to make light work of the pitchers that had been placed on the table. It appeared to Sam that no sooner had they all been seated there came more footsteps in the hidden stairway. Once again the door swung open and in walked three further figures. Sam nearly fell on the floor. In complete contrast to the Dwarves, these three were at least seven feet tall. The one that took the lead must have stood closer to eight! As with the Dwarves, all were clad in thick leather armour blacker than the darkest night. They had a bark like skin and were all muscle and sinew. Each had expressionless faces and large unblinking black eyes.

"Greetings, Commander Kelphus." Evaine spoke to the largest of the three. There was no acknowledgement from the giant that he had heard the words, he simply stood and surveyed each individual that was seated around the table.

"Long ways from your lands aren't you Troll?" Bannock spat. The Troll didn't even look in his direction.

"Sam, may I also introduce Ki," Evaine indicated with a slight tilt of his head to the Troll on Kelphus's right, "Ki is the Commanders personal guard"

"Assassin more like!" Rotrim voiced as he wiped his beard dry of spilt ale. Once again the comment was met with silence.

"And finally", Evaine continued, "Kalt, the Commanders son and Captain of the Troll armies." Kalt placed his arm across his chest in response and moved to the Commander's side.

Once again it was up to Evaine to show the new arrivals to their places at the table. Kelphus was seated next to Rotrim, much to Rotrim's disgust, Ki sat next to his commander, Kalt was seated next to Greston which met with the same reaction from Greston as had been voiced by Rotrim. None of the Troll party spoke, they just sat impassively. Sam felt the tension in the room grow with every passing second. He was feeling very out of place and vulnerable. He looked over to Anna; she was making no attempt to hide her stares at the assembled party. "You find something about me interesting girl?" Greston rumbled.

"I doubt that anything about you is interesting!" Anna replied curtly. Sam could have sworn that he saw Evaine smile.

"Brave, I'll give you that girl." Rotrim laughed, Greston however scowled his displeasure.

"Evaine, how does this evening find you old friend?" A new voice from the far end of the hall rang out. All, except the Trolls, swung round to see who had spoken. Advancing from the stairs were three Men.

"Well this looks like a great party, nothing like a bunch of Trolls and Dwarves to get the conversation going, just as well we arrived when we did." The nearest Man spoke.

"For those of you that do not know me," he looked at Sam and Anna, "my name is Oldair and I am King of Varon, the mightiest city in Invetia." The Dwarves again muttered words of disagreement. Sam liked him immediately. He was tall and well built, brown hair streaked with grey sat at shoulder length and green alert eyes flashed with devilment. Like the rest of the assembled party, he wore armour, chain-mail in this instance that had a light blue glimmer.

"Forgive my rudeness," Oldair continued, "this is Kyle, my army's Captain and my advisor on all things." He slapped Kyle on the back as he took his place by Oldair's side. He too was tall but of slighter build. Like the Dwarves before him, his face was streaked with scars, which, to Sam, indicated a violent past. "And finally I give you Teon, my son and heir." Anna's eyes lit up at Teon's introduction. He was slightly shorter than his companions but was much younger. He was a handsome man with jet black short hair a rugged, but pleasing complexion and the deepest blue eyes that Anna had ever seen.

94

Sam stretched out his leg under the table and kicked Anna to get her attention.

"You're staring with your mouth open!" he mouthed. Evaine moved to seat the new guests.

"No need Evaine, I think I know where we are to be seated." Oldair announced.

He seated himself next to the impassive Ki. Teon seated himself next to Kalt and Kyle sat on Teon's left. More retainers appeared carrying more pitchers filled with ale. Sam decided to steer clear of the refreshment; he wanted to be fully alert for the remainder of the evening's events. He quietly asked one of the servers if he could have some water. Obviously his request was louder than he had intended and Bannock made some comment about having a 'mans' drink. Sam smiled politely at Bannock but held his tongue. Civil conversation between Oldair and Evaine continued, the Dwarves talked among themselves in a language unknown to Sam and the Trolls remained silent. It seemed an eternity had passed before faint footsteps were heard from the stairwell. Evaine and Elay instinctively stood, all the others remained seated, as the Elven King entered the hall. The room fell silent.

He was younger than Sam had imagined, although after Evaine's revelation about his age earlier it was impossible to judge. He wore silver chain-mail over a pure white tunic. An amulet hung from his neck depicting the crest of the Elven household and a plain gold band sat atop his head. His hair was purest white and tied at the back. He seemed almost ethereal in appearance as he glided across the floor towards the table. He met none of the stares from Oldair, Ki. Kelphus, Rotrim or Bannock as he passed behind them. He stopped at Sam and placed his hand on his shoulder.

"Welcome my young friend," he whispered as he passed. His eyes found Anna's and bowed his head in gentle greeting. He seated himself at the end of the table between Elay and Evaine and placed both hands palms up in front of him.

"I know that each of you have made numerous sacrifices to attend this evening, some more than others and I thank you for your patience and trust. Bannock, Kelphus and Oldair; I am grateful for your attendance, I know, only to well, that the pressures of leadership steal most of the spare moments you have, you are most welcome." Thealine's eyes came to rest upon Sam and Anna, and he smiled.

"Anna and Sam," he looked at each individually, "you have both undergone the greatest flight to be here tonight, I know the strains and requests that have been made of you, I know that your confusion must be great and your demand for answers must be greater. I hope that my son has gone some way in explaining some of the madness to you, and I hope to be able to fill in any gaps tonight." He smiled kindly at them. "I think we should eat before discussions commence."

"I'll drink to that!" Greston shouted his approval. With that, several palace retainers appeared at the foot of the stairs carrying silver trays loaded with meats, vegetables, fruit and nuts. There seemed to Sam to be enough for forty people let alone fourteen.

"Let us eat," Thealine announced.

As the gathered began to fill their plates and the room filled once more with conversation and laughter, Sam could not take his eyes off of the one remaining empty chair.

CHAPTER

6

Sam picked through the fine foods that had been set out for the evening's meal. He was not at all hungry and didn't feel like eating much. Anna, by contrast, was eating enough for both of them twice over. Conversation was sparse. The Dwarves continued to converse in their strange language, the Trolls remained unspeaking and impervious to all around them, the group of Men seemed to be enjoying the hospitality, but as the Dwarves did, kept conversation between themselves. Thealine spoke to only Evaine and only once in hushed tones. To his credit Evaine did periodically check to ensure that both Anna and he were alright, and asked if the food was to their liking. Both were polite and courteous in their responses and no further conversation ensued. Elay said nothing; she simply picked at her meal and kept her gaze firmly on the table top. Once most of the fare been eaten, Thealine summoned the retainers to clear the plates signifying the end of the meal. Sam was relieved, at least we can start now even if this scared him even more, he thought. He felt like he did when he went to the Dentist. He didn't want to go but once there he just wanted it to be over and done with. The table had been cleared and new glasses and wine had been delivered. A hush settled over the gathering. Thealine stood. "I propose the moment is now right to begin the meeting, the reason why we have all assembled tonight." All eyes now stared at the Elven king. "It has been in excess of forty years since this hall was last used for a council of Invetia to meet, we are without two of the founding races but it is no small achievement to have brought those gathered tonight under one roof, around one table, uniting in one voice. We are united because we are all affected by Invetia's problem. The land is dying; the waters are fouling and the livestock sickening. We will all suffer from the blight that has touched this land, eventually; we will all perish if the disease is left untreated. The irony is that we have the cure to this illness; we have the power to heal the land, to bring back the light and to feed the weak. We have the power to defeat the evil that dwells within our realm. We have the one weapon no force of evil can sustain; we have the son of Ceriphan." There was sharp intake of breath from the gathered. They obviously hadn't been told the whole story Sam quickly surmised.

"What?" Bannock roared, "You told us nothing of this before, you simply stated that this boy and girl would aid the Dwarvian nation, you mentioned nothing about the son of Ceriphan." He was outraged. His face had turned a deep crimson as he fought a losing battle to control his temper. Others started shouting; Oldair was on his feet, and thumping his fists on the table fighting to be heard above the growls and curses of the Dwarves. Evaine and Elay were also on their feet; standing protectively by their father's side, ready to counter any threat that may be aimed at the king. Sam noticed the Ichbaru guards had doubled in numbers and stood at both entrances to the room, ready to pounce if the need arose. Sam put his hands to his ears, it was as if all hell had just broken loose and he was apparently the catalyst. It was only the Trolls that remained seated, they showed no emotion; they simply sat and waited for the maelstrom of noise to cease. Four of the lands mightiest leaders sat around the same table arguing, shouting and cursing and yet it was a girl that brought these mighty warriors to silence. Anna stood on her chair,

"SHUUUT UPPPP!!!" came a shrill cry. So shocked were the gathered party that they did exactly that, the room went silent in an instant. Elay stared at Anna and smiled.

"Thank you! Now I trust that you have all finished your childish bickering, perhaps we can get back to the reason for us all being here, I want to hear what we are doing here a damn site more than you lot do, so I suggest that you keep your mouths shut, and your ears open that way you might just learn something!"

It was Rotrim that broke the silence that ensued, "Brave indeed little girl, brave indeed"

He gave out a laugh so deep that it threatened to bring the walls down.

"I will continue if permitted to do so," Thealine resumed.

"As you are all aware, the Elven libraries have plotted the history of Invetia since its inception. Contained in the great halls of knowledge is a parchment. Nowhere is it written how this parchment came to be in the possession of the Elves, or how it found its way into Silverdale. It speaks of the legend of Ceriphan and of the forming of the Council. Upon reading further into the ancient text, our scholars have found reference to the arrival of the heir of Ceriphan."

Sam edged forward in his seat, eager not to miss any detail that may explain his part in all of this.

"Well, what is this heir supposed to do?" asked a frustrated Bannock.

"I do not know," came the unexpected reply from Thealine, "the text simply states that upon the arrival of his heir, clarity would be gained."

A murmur of discontent rumbled around the room. "It would appear Thealine", Oldair spoke, "that we do not know as much as we should, and that you are asking for our trust when there appears little reason to give it, wouldn't you say?"

Thealine clasped his hands together and laid them in front of him. "It does sound like that I suppose" surmised the Elven King, "However the parchment also went on to predict the return of the Lord Molgoran." All eyes were now fixed on Thealine. "The sickening of our lands and the recent sightings of what have been described as 'Storm Wraiths' would seem to indicate there is sufficient reason to believe in the predictions of the parchment." Thealine added. It was Oldair that spoke first in response. "I have neither heard nor seen anything to indicate to me that the Dark Wizard has returned to the realm of Invetia. It is true that my scouts have reported on the massing of Gnome, Goblin, Hobgoblin and every other worthless creature that Invetia had created in the east, but they pose no threat to Men, Dwarf, Troll or Elf, in fact they are little more than a disorganised, leaderless rabble. I am a patient man Thealine and I believe that your intentions are well placed, however, if I am correct in my assumption, I believe that you are leading up to ask for the race of man to stand with the Elves in war, if it comes. Unification of the races under one banner, fighting for the good of all is a noble and admirable dream my Elven friend but a dream nonetheless I feel. Bannock's people are secure in their holes," Bannock gave a loud grunt of disapproval, "and Kelphus and his armies live a solitary life by choice and as for the Elves, they remained shut away from the world behind the wall of magic that encapsulates Silverdale. We are all different in more ways than we are alike Thealine, except for the fact that we neither entirely trust each other nor need each other to survive. I see no reason that these events should change that viewpoint."

Again the room was stilled. Thealine sat impassively as he considered his response.

"May I say something?" Anna ventured, all eyes turned in her direction.

"We all have an equal voice hear tonight Mistress Anna." Evaine spoke as he shot her a quick reassuring smile.

"When Sam and I travelled to Invetia we came across a Demon. It was this Demon that eventually claimed the life of

100

our guide, Ruern. This thing told us that Sam possessed a magic, it said that it would not save him. Ruern herself told Sam that the Demon feared Sam more than he feared it. I believe that we have been called to this place for a reason; I believe that the reason could be to avert this war that you talk of. Furthermore I believe the words of Thealine. Trust me when I say that of all the people gathered here tonight, it is Sam and I that have the most right, and the biggest cause to doubt any of this. A few days ago I lived in a place where they would lock someone up who said that they believed in Goblins, Dwarves and whatnots! But here we are, sitting at this table in this place called Invetia. Sometimes even the hardest things to believe can come true. I don't understand how your land is governed, nor do I understand what a Troll or an Elf believe in, all I know is that when I feel threatened or scared it is my mother that I rely on for strength and understanding. Half the time I argue with her each time we speak, this is not because we are different, it's because we are too alike! Sam was sent to you for a reason, I don't understand it, but I do believe it." Evaine stared at Anna, his face reflecting the pride that he felt within. Once more the room fell still as the gathered pondered the words of Anna. It was then Sam's words that broke the stillness, he spoke without the intention of speaking, he was simply thinking it in his head and before he had realised he had spoken it out loud to the group, "Who is Amador?"

Again, the now familiar silence that seemed to follow every one of Sam's comments deepened. To Sam's surprise it was Kelphus that responded, in a low guttural tone.
"How does one so small and fragile know of the name Amador?" Sam felt all eyes rest on him. He felt exposed and insignificant. "Ruern's voice told me." He blurted out feeling immediately stupid with this response. "She told me that he would be my protector and guide in the quest that lay ahead," he quickly added. Sam began to feel his face redden as he averted his gaze from the gathered. Kelphus exchanged words with his companions in hushed whispers, then rose to his full seven feet in height and placed his right hand across his chest.

101

"Amador is a legend as much as Ceriphan ever was," he spoke, "Amador is believed to have been unequalled in combat and strategies of warfare, Amador is said to have led the races in the Great War to victory. He is said to have been a great many things to many people, a man with no allegiance to any flag, but an ally that all would desire. He is revered in our history as a warrior with no equal, skilled in not only combat but as a tracker and healer. He is said to move as silently as the sky and as swift as the wind, seen by few but sacred to all." Kelphus stood unspeaking for a brief moment, then seated himself at the table and resumed his gaze into nowhere. "Indeed, what Kelphus says is accurate," Thealine confirmed, "I find it strange however, that Ruern should speak of Amador, to my knowledge his name has never come up in conversation before, tell me young Sam could it be that you mistook Ruern's words and have since assumed that you heard the name of Amador as you may have heard it uttered elsewhere?" Sam looked quizzically at Thealine, "I have never heard the name before coming into Invetia and never since my lord" Sam responded. "The boy was not mistaken my lord Thealine" An unknown voice broke the silence that had ensued. All jerked their heads in the direction of this new sound. To their astonishment the fifteenth chair had been filled by a cloaked figure.

For the second time that evening it appeared to Sam that all hell had broke loose. Ichbaru guards rushed from their positions towards the uninvited figure, Rotrim stood up with such force that his chair was sent crashing to the ground, yelling and screaming undistinguishable words, Kyle leapt to his lord Oldair's side. Once again it was the Troll's that remained impassive and barely moving. It was Thealine that brought order to the maelstrom that had ensued. Bright blue light shot forth from his outstretched fingers and encapsulated the ceiling above, everyone momentarily froze. "State your name stranger, if you are, as foretold, the promised fifteenth guest."
Sam's heart jumped, could this be Ceriphan? Could this be his father? Had he somehow returned as Anna and he had

surmised? He gave a quick glance to Anna, but she also was transfixed by the cloaked form at the end of the room. The Ichbaru guard had fallen back to their posts on the silent order given by Evaine. It was as if the room held its breath awaiting the stranger to speak.

The stranger rose. Sam could see that he equalled the Trolls in height standing at least seven feet tall, maybe more. His cowl pulled closely over his head; he was nothing more than a black shadow that loomed over the assembled party. The cowl turned to the direction of Sam. He felt a shiver of cold run down his spine as he returned the gaze of the stranger, struggling to see past the blackness that fell across the others face, trying to distinguish any features, he could not.

"I am of who you speak," the stranger almost whispered, "I am Amador."

Sam felt his heart drop; it was not Ceriphan, not his father that had joined the meeting as he had hoped. "Not quite who you were expecting Sam Meredith? Or should I say Sam Krelyn?"

Sam was shocked; no one had called him by his second name since arriving and was of the belief that no one except Anna even knew it. But to be referred to as Sam Krelyn, he had been called that by the demon in the forest just before Ruern's death.

"I know what you are thinking Sam, I know these names because I was there, and I have always been there for you throughout your life. There has not been a day that I was not your silent protector and watch. I too watched over Ruern and kept her safe until the time for her to leave us had arrived. You did not believe that the son of Ceriphan would be left with just the Sario as a protector would you? You would have been dead a long time ago had I not been sent to ensure your safe passage. I have been waiting for this meeting for a very long time."

Sam sat in silence, trying to take in the mass of information that had been delivered by Amador.

"We must leave tomorrow Sam" Amador pressed, "Tomorrow we start to walk the path of your destiny." It was Bannock that spoke next,

"Amador indeed!" he shouted with incredulity, "We have been told nothing but half truths and lies from the moment that we arrived at this pointless and ill fated meeting, why should I believe you now, why should I believe that you are the Amador of legend? What proof do you offer? Speak now or I'll cut you in half!" Bannock had reached the very short limits of his patience. The dark stranger didn't even turn to look at Bannock, he remained sat in his chair much to Bannock's further annoyance.

"Three questions Lord Bannock and I shall give you three answers." Amador responded in a hushed voice.

"You will never believe me until the truth smacks you in the face, for you are a Dwarf, therefore by nature you are a mistrusting fool" Bannock growled in response. "Your second question of my claim to be Amador, I believe I have also answered in my first response." Although slightly confused, Bannock rose to his feet enraged.

"In response to your third and final question, I believe this should be proof enough."

With that Amador reached into his cloak and produced a dimly glowing egg shape object. He held it aloft between forefinger and thumb for all to see.

"What is that?" Bannock demanded. Amador paused before responding, gazing into the small orb that glowed before him. "The seed of Ceriphan," he responded, "and threaten me again Dwarf lord and you will be dead before you finish your sentence." He turned his shadowed face towards the now seated and quieted Bannock.

"This seed," Amador continued, "contains the very essence of Ceriphan, it will enable victory over the Shadow Master Molgoran, however, only one may undertake the journey to give rebirth to Ceriphan, only his heir may carry the seed, only his heir can give life back."

Sam felt the weight of the world come crashing down upon him. He knew that this was the climax of the meeting, he knew that this was the point of proceedings that he would learn what was expected of him, and he also knew that now was the moment he should be listening most intently. Unfortunately Sam was unable to hear much of what followed. The words that others spoke seemed to jumble into a morass of noise that made no sense. His head span either from the maelstrom of noise or the wine, and he had reached a point of acceptance, irrespective as to what he would be accepting. He wanted to sleep; he wanted to go home back to the drudgery of Simmonds & Co. He wanted his mother. The last he remembered of the evening was Amador's final warning, "Many will go upon this journey but few will return."

He woke to find himself back in the room that he had been allocated when first arriving at Silverdale. The long drapes remained open and it was still dark outside. He quickly scanned the room but Anna was not present. He didn't know how long he had slept, but felt better for it. He lay and stared at the ceiling for a long while, trying to recall the events of the meeting.

"Feeling better I trust?" came a voice from the darkened room. Sam sat bolt upright in surprise. He watched as the dark figure detached itself from the shadow. For brief moment he thought of the Demon in the forest, but as the form stepped into the half light he saw that it was Amador.

"I did not mean to startle you, but now that you are awake we will talk."

It was not a request for a conversation but almost an order that Sam would adhere too.

Amador crossed the room and seated himself in one of the high backed leather chairs that stood in the bay of the window.

"Well I am not going to shout at you from across the room," he stated, and motioned with his head for Sam to take the other chair. Sam rose from his bed to find that he was still fully dressed from the earlier meeting and made his way slowly over to the chair.

"Where is Anna?" Sam asked suddenly. She had been with him since his arrival in Silverdale and he felt exposed without her.

"She is resting, and does not need to be disturbed just yet," Amador replied in a hushed tone. Sam reached his chair and sat down slowly, never once breaking his gaze with the shadow that was Amador. He still remained cloaked and had not lowered his cowl to reveal anything more of himself. Both sat in silence for what seemed like an eternity for Sam, until eventually Amador spoke.

"Much was discussed after you had been carried from the room." 'Carried?' Sam thought, he didn't remember that? "You apparently fainted." Amador replied clearly reading the confusion on Sam's face. Sam felt his cheeks burn; he had never fainted before, what an idiot they must all take me for he thought darkly. Amador continued, "I believe that Evaine has imparted much of the history of Invetia and Ceriphan to you already, so I will not bore you with further detail. What I will do however is tell you what happens now, what you will do and how you will do it. But first, let me introduce myself properly." Amador reached up and pulled the cowl from his head. Piercing green eyes immediately met Sam's stare. Shoulder length black hair tumbled from the hood that had concealed his features, and the sharp angles of his face came into full view.

To Sam's surprise Amador appeared much younger than he had imagined, but remembered that in Invetia things rarely appeared as he believed they should.

"I am known by many names to many races," he spoke, "but Amador is the one I like best. I choose to be seen when I wish, and I bear no allegiance to any banner or cause. I have few friends, but am loyal to those few that I have, dead or alive." This statement didn't do anything to alleviate Sam's tension. "Your father was my friend, perhaps the only true friend I have ever had, and it is because of him that I choose to be seen by you now. You're father is dead and has been for a long time Sam Krelyn." Sam winced at this statement, so boldly made and without feeling. Albeit it was a statement he had been brought up all his life knowing, it took away the glimmer of hope that Sam had felt once he had arrived in Silverdale that perhaps he would meet his father.

"But his magic lives!" Amador hissed. He withdrew from his cloak the egg shaped orb that he had held aloft earlier at the gathering.

"Within the depths of this seed, lay Ceriphan's knowledge, skill, memories and magic. It contains everything that made him the man he was." Sam watched as the Orb pulsed with amber light in the shadows of the room.

"No one knows," Amador continued, "what needs to be done to release the essence of Ceriphan, for no instruction was ever left. It was simply told that an heir would arise and it would be their birthright to release the spirit that dwells within. This task therefore befalls you my young friend." Amador's gaze settled on Sam. A long moment of silence passed. Sam allowed the words to rush over him and he began to accept that his fate was sealed. He would have to take the Orb to wherever it was that it needed to go. He would have to do it as he was the only one that could do it. It was not a quest that he wanted, it was not a journey that he would have offered to take, but he had no options left, it was time to face his responsibility; no matter how bizarre or foreboding, it was his path to follow.

"I understand Amador that the task ahead has fallen to me," Sam spoke, "and I know that I am the one that must make this journey. No matter how scared or how much I wish it to be otherwise, it still rests upon my shoulders to undertake." He held Amador's gaze and kept his voice low and steady. He was scared and did so wish that this had befallen someone else to undertake, but in that moment, Sam felt something change within him. All his life he had played it safe; all his life he had had someone else to rely on and look out for him. Either Anna or Ben or his mother had always been there to fight his battles and keep him from harm. This was to an even greater extent since discovering the watchful eyes of Ruern and Amador had been his silent guardians in his life. This was the moment that he stood up and accepted the responsibility that he had avoided all of his life in everything that he had ever done. It was then Sam realised the change he felt within, he was finally growing up, and didn't feel quite as bad as he thought it would.

"Tell me what I must do?" he said defiantly. At that moment he could have sworn that Amador's eyes flickered with pride.

"All that I know from the conversations that I held with your father is that we must travel north to a place known as the Vale, a vast dark wood that is permanently embroiled in mist and the stench of decay. No one other than the foolhardy enter the Vale, for it has an inhabitant. Her name is Graflon and she is a Witch. A very powerful being that has lived within the Vale for as long as the histories record. She was in Invetia long before Man or even Elf inhabited its land. Legend says that Graflon was part of the creation of Invetia. Within her domain, there are few that can stand against her, within the confines of the Vale, she is queen."

Sam listened with intent. It unnerved him that a man such as Amador could be so obviously wary of another. It was still unclear as to what this Graflon had to do with him. Amador continued,

"I have never encountered her, I have never had the need, and you don't seek out Graflon unless you must, but those I know that have had the need, are now all dead or missing. I know of only one man that survived his meet with the witch of the Vale, Ceriphan. Your father visited her several times in his life, both were linked by the magic that bound the land and, although he rarely spoke of her, I felt that there was a mutual respect that existed for each other's mastery of the magic. His last visit to her was one week before his death, and although I know not what was discussed, or the purpose of his visit, it would appear that he told her something about you. It would seem that he left some instruction for her to pass to you. This is where we must start our journey; this is where I believe we will get the next part of the puzzle."

The thought of visiting such a being as described by Amador did nothing to help alleviate Sam's fears. "Why would my father leave such important information with such a dangerous person such as Graflon?" Sam asked. "Why would he put us all in potential danger by having us visit this witch?"

Amador seemed to ponder the question for a while, his eyebrows furrowed in thought.

"This is the very question that I first had," he eventually responded. "The only reason I can come up with is that this witch is beyond the touch of all mortal men. She cannot be challenged by almost any of Invetia's inhabitants when residing within the Vale, and there are only a few Demons strong enough to potentially pose a threat to her and these have no interest in the Vale and are weary of her. The only one potential threat to her is Molgoran, and this is where Ceriphan and Graflon are linked, each had a common enemy in him. A secret, or an item, left with Graflon would be secure from virtually all would be enemies. I can think of no safer place within the land. The trick here will be to get her to give it to us. Fate, my young friend is like dust in the breeze, it goes where it wants and clings to those it chooses. I am sure that it will reveal an answer on how we traverse the Vale safely once we begin our journey." Sam only wished he could share in Amador's apparent faith.

Amador rose to his feet, "We will leave at morning sunrise," he announced, "we will be a party of eight plus a unit of the Ichbaru will accompany us until we are out of Silverdale's borders. As is custom, we will be joined by the son and heirs of each of the Kings of Invetia. Tamar will also join as he is charged with the safety of Evaine and I have agreed that your companion, Anna, can also join as I find her to be spirited and a good support for you."

It was more likely that Anna had insisted to Amador that she come along and simply wore him down, Sam thought.

"You may have a few more hours rest until sunrise master Sam, but be sure to be ready when I come for you." Amador started for the door, then turned, "Before I take my leave, I want you to know that my loyalty and sword are with you Sam, but you are more accomplished than you think. You are the son of the greatest mage that Invetia has ever seen, do not think yourself as the weak link here. You are more powerful than the entire group combined. When the moment demands it you will discover this to be true."

With that, Amador spun around and was out of the door before Sam could ask him what he meant.

The next few hours passed slowly for Sam. Try as he might, sleep would not come. His head was ablaze with a million thoughts that all fought for space and attention. A few days ago he would have wished to wake and find all had been a dream, he thought, safely back in his flat and the security of his familiar surroundings, happy with his dead end job, and happy with getting by. All of his life was a low risk scenario. Nothing had ever stretched him physically or mentally, and life was safe and comfortable. But he was now not so sure if waking from this dream would be good, he was not so sure that the cosseted life that he had left behind was right for him. Life was passing him by and he was doing nothing, nothing to grab the opportunities that presented themselves or the chance to experience the wonders of the world. He had to admit that the situation that he now found himself in was a little drastic and extreme, but it was a second chance, a chance to make something of himself, a chance to grab that opportunity, a chance to feel alive. He feared for Anna though, she had a life, a family and a reason to get home. People would be missing her. Whilst the world would not have even noticed his disappearance, the world would miss her. It was at this moment that he came to a sudden and unexpected decision. If they were to see this through and come out the other end, he would rather like to stay within Invetia. It was such a revelation that it took him by complete surprise. He lay, staring at the ceiling feeling the idea wash over him. It felt right and it filled him with excitement and almost relief, he would have that second chance. It was now even more important than ever that he kept Anna safe and well, for she would return, back to the world that had missed her, back to her family and her life. He smiled, the likelihood was that he would not live another day, let alone settle in a mystical world of Elves and Trolls, but not even this thought made him crave his old life back.

As he lay on his bed and considered his future, the door to his room suddenly swung open with a crash. Sam, startled, leapt to his feet in an instance. The familiar dark and forbidding cloaked figure of Amador stood in the doorway.

"We must go now," he hissed, "I will explain on the way, now follow me." Without waiting for Sam to respond, Amador wheeled around and was out of the door in a flash.

Sam rushed for the door just in time to see the cloaked form turn left off of the corridor and down the stairs to the great hall.

110

Sam was running to catch him, his breath coming in short sharp gasps. A mixture of fear and excitement coursed through his body. As he reached the top of the stairway, Amador was already at the bottom and striding into the hall. Sam took the stairs as fast as he could and arrived in a rush at the bottom.

All the signs from the earlier meal had gone from the great hall. The table and chairs that had been assembled were gone, the food cleared and the blazing fire was reduced to a smouldering black. Standing in the place now was a heavily armoured unit of the Ichbaru. Sam guessed at about 30 Elves. They stood like sentinels, in perfect rows. Their black leather armour, that Sam had been so used to seeing them dressed in, had now been replaced by silver chain mail that covered them from head to toe. It glistened almost blue in the dim light of the torches that lit the room. The insignia of the Oak tree, Crown and rising Sun adorned white, loose cloaks that each wore. Some carried massive bows strapped to their backs, others had huge swords that hung from their waist, and all wore gleaming silver helmets that only just permitted a glimpse of the faces beneath. It was not hard to realise that these Elves were not dressed for any ceremonial reason, they were dressed for battle. Sam ventured forward, past the lines of the Ichbaru towards the rear of the hall.

Evaine and Tamar stood just behind, deep in conversation with each other. Both dressed in similar attire to the battle ready Ichbaru, except Evaine's chain mail was gold in colour. In contrast to Sam's first meeting with Evaine, he now carried a huge, gold handled sword that hung from his waistband. Tamar also was also dangerously armed, with a sword strapped to his back and a brace of vicious looking daggers strapped to his waist. Further behind stood the heirs of Invetia, Teon, Greston and Kalt. Teon wore a gold breastplate with chain mail beneath. In contrast, both Greston and Kalt wore black leather armour that gave greater mobility. As he stood staring at the bizarre gathering of armour and weapons, a familiar voice broke through his thoughts.

"Sam, Sam, over here," the voice bellowed. Sam turned to find Anna sprinting in his direction, her cloak billowing behind her as she ran. Sam was relieved to see a friendly face, although he couldn't help but notice, Anna too carried a long hunting knife that hung loosely from her waist. Anna reached Sam in an instant, her face flushed from the sudden exertion.

"Look at this," she shouted, "they have given me a bloody sword! I wasn't even trusted with a steak knife at home, but here I get a sword." Sam looked on in amazement, not at the sword that Anna was so obviously proud of, but the complete lack of fear that she seemed to show. She was excited at the situation as oppose to Sam who was totally scared senseless. She stood in front of him with her arms outstretched; allowing him to observe the tan leather skirt and top that she now wore. Tan boots and a black belt, with a huge buckle completed the ensemble.

"Give us a twirl then," he managed. Anna obliged without any further encouragement.

"Isn't it great, something is actually happening at last!" she stated, her voice laced with an unmistakeable excitement. "I overheard Evaine and that Amador speaking; they said that Molgoran's forces were almost amassed and ready to move, they said that the journey for the Vale would have to start now." She was talking really fast in an effort to be the first to impart the news to Sam. "I heard them mention Goblin Lords and Gnome Scouts, and all manner of things that sound bloody terrible, but I have no idea what they are, they mentioned that they...." "Thank you Mistress Anna," a low voice cut over hers. Anna's voice fell quite almost immediately. Sam turned to see Amador approaching. His cowl pulled closely over his head masking the man beneath, and his black cloak wrapped tightly around his massive frame. "Please save me something to impart." Anna took a step back in spite of herself. Her face reflected anger and embarrassment at the rebuke.

"Things change fast in Invetia Sam," Amador continued, "and today is no different. Our scouts have seen that Molgoran's assembled army is preparing to move west. Reports indicate that Silverdale and the Plains of Varon are the likely

112

destinations. We have dispatched warning to Varon, and Silverdale is being secured, but we need to move quickly. It is seven days march from the Bleaklands to Silverdale, nine before Varon can be reached, but scouting parties will be near already and we are out of time if we are to keep our journey secret. The first step of our passage starts now Master Sam; now begins the prophecy as was foretold."

CHAPTER
7

It was still dark when they left the warmth of the great hall.
The sun was showing no signs of beginning its daily vigil, and
the ground was damp from the early dew that still clung to the
earth. A company of ten Ichbaru guards headed the party,
followed by Evaine and Tamar. Greston and Teon followed
close with Sam and Anna behind. The imposing figures of
Amador and Kalt followed further back. Another unit of ten
Ichbaru followed at the rear of the formation with a flank of
five further guards on each side of the party. Evaine had noted
to Sam before they had set off that this diamond formation
provided the best possible defensive and offensive positioning.
Sam had smiled politely but this did little to reassure him for
the journey that lay ahead.

Amador had informed them all before leaving that the march to
the Vale would be three days if all went well. Provisions were
packed for five days, in case of delay. The decision was also
taken not to bring horses. They could travel with greater stealth

on foot, Amador had surmised, despite this adding a day to the journey time.

The homes of Silverdale stood silent as they passed. No lights shone from within and no sounds greeted them as they passed. Only the soft crunching of the gravel underfoot gave out any sound. They walked in silence, heads bowed to ward off the morning chill and an air of tension surrounded the group. It was not until they had long passed the last home in Silverdale and was into the rolling hills that surrounded the city that anyone spoke.

"How are you feeling Master Sam? came the now familiar voice of Amador. Sam turned to find that he had fallen in step alongside him. Before he could answer, Amador continued. "I have something that is yours to carry." With that Amador reached into his cloak and produced the Orb that he had seen earlier. It pulsated lightly in the half light of the morning. "It's called the Orloc," Amador stated as he closed Sam's hand around it." It's an old Elvish word meaning redemption." Sam was surprised to find it warm to the touch. It was no bigger than an egg and just as light. Sam opened his hand to examine the Orloc. It seem to contain an amber mist that swirled around inside. He could see no outer shell, but gently traced the egg shape with his fingers. "Keep this safe," Amador whispered, "for this is the seed of Ceriphan, this is your reason for being here." Amador watched as Sam carefully lowered the Orloc into his pocket. Once satisfied it was safe, Amador fell back in line with Kalt and the march continued in silence.

After several hours of walking, Sam began to see the outline of the massive hedge that encapsulated Silverdale. He knew, despite leaving from a different direction from when they entered, that within lay the mists and then the Dunbar forest. He inwardly shuddered at the thought of having to pass through those mists. He remembered the voices that had called to him so vividly the first time he entered Silverdale. Persuading him to let go and join them, welcoming him home and reaching for him with an icy touch. He remembered Ruern's voice that had

115

also called to him, telling him to seek out Amador and that he would be Sam's protector in the journey ahead. He remembered losing himself to the sway of their voice and song. He did not relish a further encounter with the ghosts of the Echenor.

As they marched towards the ever nearing border of Silverdale, the dark of early morning began to be replaced by a blanket of grey. The sun had risen, but was not able to penetrate the low cloud that covered the sky. Gone were the bright colours and warmth that had greeted Sam and Anna on their first encounter with Silverdale, everything now seemed dull and lifeless, and to make matters worse, light rain began to fall.

"Should have brought my coat!" he heard Anna remark in her familiar sarcastic manner, "They might have magic, but I had waterproofs at home." Sam smiled to himself; it was reassuring to have Anna by his side. Evaine turned around from hearing Anna's moans, "Come and walk with me a little Sam," he called.

Sam caught up with Evaine and fell into line beside the Elf. "Tamar told me of the voices in the Echenor that you heard when you first entered Silverdale," Evaine began.

"Do not be afraid, Sam, whilst it is almost unheard of for the spirits that dwell within to speak to anyone direct, we will keep you safe on your passage out. What concerns me more," Evaine continued, "is this meeting with the Vale Witch." Evaine lowered his voice and bent closer to Sam in order that his words were not overheard. "You know that you will have to face her alone, don't you?"

This was such a startling statement that Sam initially thought that he had misheard the Elven prince. Evaine saw the confusion on Sam's face and pressed on. "Graflon is from the ancient world, little is known of her and most keep far away from her. But those who have reason to travel to the Vale or stumbled in by mistake have only ever been permitted to enter unaccompanied. It seems that strong magic protects the Vale and passage to anymore than one is blocked." Sam felt his heart sink. All this protection and show of force, all the words spoken of allegiance and sacrifice, and yet the most dangerous part of the journey was to be faced by him alone, he thought. He bit his lip, "Then I will face her alone", he stated bravely. It was now Evaine who thought he had misheard.

As Sam fell back into line beside Anna, he felt strangely bigger than before, he had accepted at the outset of this journey that he would need to accept responsibility and expectation; he just didn't know that he would do so, so readily. He turned to Anna, expecting the usual insistence that he tell her everything of the conversation that had just ensued, despite it being quite obvious that it was for his ears only. Her eyes though did not meet his; they were transfixed on his cloak. Sam looked down at himself, only to see that it was as if he was on fire! Bright amber light emanated from within his clothing, though he felt no heat. He immediately threw his cloak open to reveal the source of the light. Carefully he removed the Orloc from within his pocket. It pulsated in his hand and was just warm, not hot, as he had expected. The bright amber light engulfed his hand and he felt his skin tingle in response. He realised that the group had stopped and all eyes were now transfixed on him. As he shuffled nervously, holding the Orloc at arm's length, he noticed that it pulsated brighter as he turned towards the Echenor mists, that were now just ahead, and dimmer when he turned away.

"It warns of magic and danger," Amador voiced, "the Orloc senses the Faerie creatures and the dead that dwell within. It will guard you against harm, for it is a powerful magic that you now own, you just need to learn how to control it, as magic can be a giver and a taker in equal measure." Sam wasn't sure that he understood Amador's words, but felt exhilarated by the Orloc's touch. He took one more look at the amber mist that swirled from within its invisible structure, then, carefully he placed it back within his tunic pocket. Immediately the Orloc's glow disappeared and was as it was before. Sam looked at his hand as he felt the remnants of the tingle disappear; all was as it should be.

After a brief delay, Evaine gave the order for the group to move ahead. Within ten minutes they stood at the border of

117

Silverdale. Massive Hickory bushes stood as silent sentinels in the grey half light. So thick were they that no clue was given as to what lay beyond. Sam felt Anna's hand slide into his. She gave him a reassuring smile as she gently removed the sword, which hung from her waist, from its sheath.

"This time we will be ready." she said to Sam with a knowing smile.

"Swords will not help you within the Echenor mistress Anna," Evaine spoke, "you cannot kill shades and shadows with a sword"

"That may be so, but I will keep it out just in case." she answered defiantly.

"Ha, what a load of superstitious rubbish," Greston roared, "nothing in there except rats and spiders, never seen a Shade and never met an enemy that couldn't be killed." Greston continued whilst shifting the weight of his great battle axe from hand to hand in front of him.

"Master Dwarf," Amador called, "it would appear that you have never seen a bar of soap, but I assure you that soap exists!" Anna laughed at Amador's rebuke, but was quickly silenced by Greston's growl of disapproval at her.

"We stay close and together as we pass through," Tamar voiced. He produced a long piece of thin white rope from his pack. "Tie this around your waist and pass it back to the next man." He passed the rope to Teon, who immediately began to secure the rope around him. "Once we are all secured, we will pass through with the Ichbaru in the lead. We will stay in our formation and watch for each other. If you get in trouble, tug the rope hard and help will come. The boy and girl are our charges here and will have Prince Evaine and Amador ahead and behind. Kalt and the rest of my men will watch our backs, whilst Teon and Greston will watch the front. I will flank our group with the Ichbaru." To Sam's surprise no one complained or questioned the Elf captain. Each man secured the rope, as requested, around their waist and passed it back to the next until all were secured. The Ichbaru fell silently into formation and all were ready.

One by one, Sam watched the Ichbaru disappear into the Echenor. As each entered, the rope pulled tighter. Before Sam knew it, it was he that stood at the edge of the wall of grey; it was his time to enter.

"Do not be afraid Sam, I am right behind you," came the reassuring voice of Amador. He took a deep breath and plunged into the gloom ahead.

Immediately he felt the damp cold mist envelope him. It was as if a bag had been pulled over his head, he could not see and everything was muffled and unclear. He stood for a while, trying to get his senses back, when he felt Anna push into his back. He heard her tell him to keep moving forward and stumbled onwards in response. As he pushed further on his head began to clear and he was just able to make out the lean form of Evaine ahead. The mists began to fill the silence with a rushing whine as it raced through the gloom at a pace."Keep moving forward" a shout came from ahead and the group responded. With heads bowed against the torrent of wind they plunged deeper into the mists, deeper into the gloom. Sam kept his gaze firmly transfixed on the earthen floor in an attempt to keep his concentration and to shut out the cacophony of noise that surrounded him. He had experienced already the shades of the mists and did not want to repeat that. As he pushed onwards he began to hear their call.

It started quietly at first. His name being called that seemed to echo around his head. "Sam, Sam you have returned" it called, relentless and steady. Voices of different pitch and tone cut through the howl of the wind so all could be heard.
'You must stay with us,' they continued, 'You must remain within the Echenor'
Sam bent his head lower so his chin was pressing into his chest, trying to keep the voices from his head. He felt the reassuring tug of the rope, aware that the others of the party continued to press ahead, all trying to make the passage as quick as possible through the Echenor mists. In response, the voices seemed to rise louder and more insistent.

119

'You belong in the mists of the faerie, you belong to us son of Ceriphan.' Louder and more desperate came their calls, almost screaming in a madness that he did not understand. He felt a sudden urge to go to them, to return their call and break from the rope that guided him, but each time he felt he was surely lost to their cries the rope tugged him forward and back to his senses. Cold, unseen hands reached out from all sides and tugged at his clothing, formless wisps' coiled around his legs trying to claim him. They were desperate to claim him, desperate to pull him deeper into the Echenor, but he resisted with every ounce of strength he could muster. He was barely walking now; he was being dragged through by the rope that remained tightly secured around his waist, pulling him to safety with each tug. Then, without warning, the rope fell limp. Desperately he checked its fastenings and found it still tied securely around his waist. He pulled frantically at the rope that hung in front of him, but there was nothing, just rope. He turned and grabbed the rope that trailed behind him, desperate to find Anna at the other end, but this too just hung limp, he was on his own. He felt his body shake impulsively, the worst possible thing that could have happened had happened and he was alone in the mist of the faerie.

He could not see more than five paces ahead, and even less behind. The mists had become an impenetrable blanket that left him virtually blind. He stood, frozen by fear and indecision, unable to think what to do. He screamed the names of his companions to come to his aid but the wind rose up and carried his cries away. The voices grew louder 'Sam, you must stay with us, you must join with the mists,' they called on, frantically begging him to stay. He felt his clothing being pulled in all directions as shapes began to take form in the half light. Childlike faces flashed before him as the ethereal shapes appeared and disappeared before him.
'We wish you no harm son of Ceriphan, we will keep you safe from all that threaten' they implored. He began to lose himself to the voices, he began to feel his resolve falling away and,

slowly but surely, he was losing himself to the Echenor. He closed his eyes and awaited his fate.

Then, as he stood on the precipice of no return, the voices ceased, the wind stilled and mists fell deathly silent. It was as if time itself had stopped and he now stood in the eye of the storm. Sam waited a moment to ensure his battered thoughts were not playing tricks, and then slowly opened his tightly closed eyes to an amber light that seemed to have burned away the greyness of the Echenor. The light engulfed him from head to toe and he felt free from the tiredness and aches of his ordeal. He felt refreshed in a way that he didn't believe possible. Every inch of his body tingled with warmth and he felt vibrant and alive. His mind had cleared and he felt serine. He stood and waited for his eyes to adjust to the brightness of his surroundings, he then began to see that the mists in fact remain; however, they seemed to have receded from him. No longer did they wrap around his body, no longer did the shapes claw and tug at his clothing or coil around his legs. He was enveloped in the protective amber light that seemed to keep the mists, and all that dwelled within, away. He could see that the storm still raged, and the forms of the faerie creatures still twisted and turned all about him, but he heard not a sound nor felt any touch. Sam stood for several minutes, trying to understand what had happened, and then he noticed that the amber light emanated from his pocket. Slowly he reached in and brought forth the Orloc. It shone a blazing golden hue that spread out in all directions and it pulsated warmth in a rhythmic throb, like a heartbeat. It was then he remembered Amador's words 'The Orloc will keep you safe.' It now that appeared this is what was happening.

Sam quickly regained his senses and began forward, slowly at first, to gain his escape from the Echenor mists. There was no sign of his companions and he surmised that they had gained safe passage and awaited him on the other side. He walked with renewed determination and ever increasing speed, watching the mist rescind from his every step as he went. Outside of Sam's protective shell the Faerie creatures howled

121

in anguish as their prize slipped away. Several tried to hurl themselves at the amber glow to get to the boy, but they simply burnt to ash the moment they got too close. They watched in anger and despair as the son of Ceriphan walked right through their midst and out of the Echenor.

As Sam raced through the swirling grey of the mists he began to see the light ahead. He knew he was almost through and a sense of relief washed over him. He was running now, sweating and flushed, scared and lost, but alive. The amber light continued to encase him as he ran; flaring now and again as faceless shapes appeared then disappeared. Finally he burst through the prison of the Echenor into the blaze of the sun, which caused him to clamp his eyes shut, such was the intensity of the light in contrast to the blackness of the mists. He stuffed the Orloc back into his pocket as he threw himself on the ground, gasping for breath and exhausted from his flight. He lay face down for several minutes, regaining control over his breathing and allowing his body to cool. He would have lain there for longer had it not been for a voice that startled him into consciousness.

'Do you still live Sam Meredith?' the voice spoke. So unexpected was the sound that Sam jumped to a kneeling position, only to be greeted by the beauty of Elay, Princess of Silverdale.

He stared at Elay, the confusion evident in his expression, she simply smiled back. He was still unsure if he were awake, unsure if he was seeing what was real and not still being held captive within the mists. Instinctively he reached down to his pocket and felt the now familiar outline of the Orloc. He pulled it free and held it before him. It glowed its now familiar dull amber hue, and was warm to the touch, but it no longer pulsed or flared as it had done moments earlier in his flight through the Echenor. All was still and back to normal, whatever normal was. Quickly he regained his senses.

"Where are the others?" He asked, suddenly aware that just Elay stood in sight. "They were in front of me, then the rope went slack and I lost them, did they make it through?"

"I have not seen them Sam, I have only found you and that is only because I knew where you would be." Sam stared at the Elven Princess in confusion.

"How did you know where to find me Elay? How did you even get here? We have been walking for hours, how could you have caught us up so quickly? I must find the others; I cannot find my way to the Vale without them." He was beginning to feel the panic take hold and he fought to keep his voice steady and controlled. Elay simple stood and listened.

"Elay, I need to find Anna, she is my responsibility. I need to get to the Vale and need Amador, Evaine and the others to protect me. Without them I cannot get to the Witch, without them I cannot do what I have promised to do." He stood facing Elay, awaiting her response. When it came it was not what he had expected. Elay burst into laughter. Her face lit up in a way that Sam knew that she was still the most beautiful thing he had ever seen, and for that moment he was lost in his reverence for the Elven Princess.

"So many questions you ask at once," she eventually stated, "patience is not a strong trait in your world I would assume. Eventually the answers will come; you just need to discover them for yourself." She reached out her hand and stroked his cheek. He blushed immediately in response.

"I do not have answers to all that you ask, I can however answer some," she continued, "since my birth I have been blessed with an insight into what has come to pass and what is yet to come to pass. Sometimes these insights are as clear as the day, sometimes they are clouded and I only see outlines. I had a vision of you Sam, many years ago, and centuries before your birth. It was based on my vision that Ruern was sent to your world to watch over you. It was based on my insight that I knew where you would exit the mists and where I could find you. I left Silverdale shortly after your group departed. I left with only my father, Thealine, knowing where I travelled and why. Secrecy has become ever more important and none were to know of my purpose. I cannot see every event, just flashes that need piecing together. This is how I knew where you would be waiting, but I was not shown the fate of the others."

Sam listened intently, frustrated that no news could be gained of his companions, but grateful at least that he was not alone. "I know that you travel to Graflon,' Elay continued, "I also know that you have been told that you must face the Witch alone, however, I will be with you until we reach the Vale. I cannot enter without bringing danger to our mission, but I will guide you to where we need to be."

"In that case," Sam interjected, "we must start looking for the others immediately, they cannot have got far and I need to make sure......" He noticed that Elay's expression had changed; she averted his stare and looked almost sad. "We are not going to look for them are we?" It was more of a statement than a question, and he already knew the response before it was given. "No Sam, we must follow our own path and do so with speed. The others have the protection of my brother, not to mention Amador. They are well protected from those that hunt us, I am sure that Anna will be quiet safe within their company. We must however get to the Vale as soon as we can for that is the only place where we will gain answers to our questions. We must leave now."

Sam stood, and brushed off the dust and began to straighten his clothing, deliberately taking his time to allow the words of Elay to be fully considered. As he continued the charade he thought his argument through. He would argue that they could spare an hour to track back along the Mist's edge to see for any sign of their passing. He would argue that without the protection of Amador's magic or the Ichbaru's strength of arms that it would be even more dangerous to proceed with just an Elven Princess and a man that had no understanding of what he was to do or what dangers awaited. Sure he had the Orloc, but he had no idea how to use it to protect them from the dangers that existed, at what seemed every step of their journey. But most of all he needed Anna. It was because of him that she had ended up in the mess, because of him that she had come to this world where magic was real, Elves were real and anything else you may read in a fairy tale seemed to exist as if it had always been. He was then hit with a sudden thought, what if Anna had been separated from Amador and the group, what if she walked lost alone in the Mists. Even if she had managed to get out, if alone, she would have no protection or direction. He had to find her, he had to try.

After a considerable time, he turned to Elay, now fully prepared to argue the case for looking for his companions. He never got the chance. Elay suddenly gave a shrill cry that seemed to shatter the quiet that had descended over the clearing. It was a cry of warning and defiance. She ran at Sam and launched into him sending him tumbling into the long grasses. Elay sat atop him, her arms outstretched and her face screwed up in concentration as her fingers twisted and clicked at lightning speed. Before Sam could react, blue fire exploded from Elay's fingers and blue dome of crackling haze surrounded them both. As soon as it had formed a rush of red lightning smashed into the protective dome. They scrambled to their feet. Elay's head bent forward in complete concentration, sweat now forming on her brow from the exertion of the magic she commanded. Another bolt of red thundered into the dome, that Elay fought to maintain, and shook the ground as it again failed to penetrate the blue magic of the Elven Princess. Sam's hand immediately went to his pocket for the Orloc. It was burning with an intensity that almost blinded him. Its amber glow had been replaced with a bright, white hot glow but, as before did not burn to touch. Another bolt shattered into the magic and Elay screamed in response.

"I cannot hold out much longer," she screamed, "you must use the Orloc Sam, quickly!" He panicked; he didn't know how this was meant to work. The Orloc was not in his control. It had protected him before but not his command, what if it failed. He didn't even see what was threatening to turn them into ash. The blue shield of Elay obscured all from outside. "Sam!" Elay screamed louder, more desperate this time, "my magic fails; you must use the Orloc Sam. Now!" With that a massive bolt of flame and electricity smashed into the weakening shield that Elay fought to maintain. It came with such ferocity that the ground shook so violently they both fell to their knees. Elay's shield crackled one last time then faded into nothingness. Elay had collapsed next to Sam, her breathing

125

fast and uneven. Sam scrambled to his feet, he still held the Orloc tight in his hand, the white light seeping through his fingers as if his hand were on fire. He spun around searching for his attacker. He found it all too quickly. Fifty yards to his left stood a thing from nightmares. It was as black as the night and a mass of sinew and muscle. It stood on all fours but still towered above six foot. It was bristling with spines that covered its back as it crouched as if ready to leap. Yellow eyes burned through the shadow that it cast and crimson mucus dripped from a mass of teeth, blackened and wicked looking. Its gaze never left Sam for a moment. Time seemed to stand still in that instance as both faced off in the now charred and smouldering clearing. It snarled and howled at Sam as it began to circle its prey. Sam was terrified by what he saw, and yet he did not flinch, he did not run, the panic that had gripped him moments before had fallen away and his thinking was strangely clear, he knew what he must do. Elay still lay on the ground by his feet, she was trying to get up but invisible chains seem to weigh her down. He felt the rage and hatred well inside of him. Slowly brought up his arm and held forth the Orloc. It pulsed so hard that he thought it would shatter. The Demon screamed and reared up in response. Sam saw the flickering of Red fire building in one its massive clawed hands '*I must act now*' he thought. He brought his arm up to chest level, pointed it directly at the Demon and closed his eyes, willing the magic to hammer into his foe, calling upon the Orloc to end this wretched nightmare's life. To his astonishment nothing happened!

The Orloc pulsed harder and the stone burned with intensity, but nothing more. He began to feel his resolve break apart. He gathered his thoughts and in an instant was summoning again the magic, again nothing happened. The Demon screamed louder in delight. Its maw split wide apart displaying its second row of blackened razor sharp teeth as it advanced. Red, wicked looking fire crackled and hissed within its clawed hand. Sam shrieked in panic, he was going to die, Elay would die. The others would never find him again and the Orloc would be lost.

126

He tried again in desperation to summon the magic, his hand so tightly enclosed on the Orloc that it cut into him, willing the fire to rise up and destroy his foe, but as before, there was no fire, no magic, nothing happened.

He stood froze to the spot, helpless to do anything other than to watch the Demon creep ever closer. Its massive clawed hand was now totally engulfed with the red flame that coiled up its blackened outstretched arm. So close it was now that Sam could feel the heat of the fire and hear the rasp of the Demons breath. He stared again at the Orloc, its white intensity continued to burn but no magic stirred within. The Demon raised its arm higher and began to scream its command to send the Red fire smashing into the defenceless form of Sam and Elay. Sam closed his eyes and awaited his fate.

In that instant he heard another sound, a cry, a cry of defiance that rose above the clamour of the Demon. Sam eyes snapped open; he knew that voice, it was Tamar!

Sam turned to the direction of this new sound. 'FOR SILVERDALE AND THE KING!' the cry boomed out. Tamar was bolting across the clearing in a blur. The Demon hesitated, its eyes transfixed on the charging Elf, suddenly aware of this new threat. It shifted its considerable bulk to meet the challenge head on, but it was too slow. Before it could fully turn to face the charging Elf, two white arrows were embedded in its neck. The Demon screamed in pain and surprise. It sent its Red fire arcing towards Tamar, but the Elf was too quick, and changed direction in the blink of an eye. The Red fire hammered into a nearby tree and sent it crashing to the ground in an explosion of flame. Already the fire was forming a new in the Demons claws, but again Tamar was far quicker. He had reached the Demon and sent his now drawn Broadsword sweeping into the exposed hide of the monster. It screamed in agony as the sword found its mark and left a crimson streak across its flank. Sam watched as the Demon sent its fire lancing in all directions, but the Elf continued to skip and dodge the onslaught. Each time slashing at the Demon and finding his mark. The

Demon was weakening from the damage being inflicted, but Tamar was also weakening, nearing exhaustion from the continued attack. No matter how much damage he inflicted on the beast, it would not go down and would not stop. Again Tamar made another pass, this time feigning to hit the Demon low, then at the last moment arcing his bloodstained sword upwards. The sword smashed into the exposed throat of the demon and red mist flew in all directions from the gaping wound that was left. The Demon tried to scream but choked on the blood that now filled its throat. It thrashed about grasping its wound trying to hold the rendered flesh together. Finally it sank to its knees, gasping for breath. Tamar turned again and brought forth the massive ash bow that he carried on his back. He let forth a volley of arrows. His bow snapped and cracked as arrow after arrow was fired at the incapacitated hulk of the monster, each one finding its mark and embedding deeply into the Demons hide. Sam counted at least ten arrows fired; each one was met with silence as they struck their target. The demon neither cried nor moved, other than its breathing that was laboured and slow. He watched as Tamar replaced the bow across his back and drew his sword to finish the Demon once and for all. Slowly and with caution he edged towards his foe. The beast lay on its stomach and showed no signs of resistance. Tamar stood over the fallen Demon with sword held aloft, and then, with his remaining strength brought the sword crashing down to finish the beast. As the blade arced downwards towards the head of the Demon, one of its massive clawed hands jerked upwards to meet the blade halfway. Sam heard the crash as the steel of the blade met the flesh and bone of the monster. The blade shattered into a thousand pieces that fell to the ground like stardust. The clawed hand continued its thrust and caught Tamar squarely in the chest ripping him in two. A fountain of red spewed in all directions as Tamar fell to the ground, his body severed from the chest.

Sam watched in horror as the Demon slowly began to rise. Propping itself up on its elbows, it began to stand again. Blood flowed quickly from the open wounds that had resulted from its battle with the Elf. Now fully erect it began to advance upon Sam and Elay. Not quick and agile as before, it now lumbered forward, slowed from the considerable damage that had been inflicted upon it.

Sam watched as it edged ever closer. No signs of the red fire it commanded before could be seen, as it clearly intended to rip its prey apart as it had Tamar. Sam stood his ground, his legs threatened to buckle underneath him so great was his fear, but he would not allow it to consume him this time, he would not allow anything to stand in his way. If he were to die, then he would die fighting to protect Elay. He wasn't sure where this new determination had come from, but he accepted freely the task that he had been given. The Demon was no more than twenty feet in front him now, it's rasping filling the quiet of the clearing. He felt Elay stand behind him, now risen. She grabbed his arm and he could feel her shaking through his tunic.

"Use the Orloc Sam," he heard her whisper, "the magic is yours to use, yours to command. Do not fear it and let it come to you."

Slowly he raised his hand in which the Orloc was contained. Its dull amber glow broke through his tightly clenched fist. He raised it in front of him and closed his eyes. The Demon was now less than ten feet away, it smiled its crooked smile as it faced the boy. A few more steps were all it would need before it could rip him apart. It knew that it was going to die, but the desire to see the boy destroyed kept it alive for as long as would be necessary.

Sam inwardly willed the magic to be called forth from the Orloc. He opened his eyes to see the Demon standing before him, the Orloc now burning brighter than ever. He opened his fist and allowed the Orb to lie in his outstretched palm.

The Demon screamed a blood choked howl, Elay tightened her grip on his arm and, to his amazement the Orloc burst into life. A pulse of amber light shot from his hand. It made no sound as it hit the advancing Demon. No sound as the white hot light burned the monster. There was no time for the Demon to scream in response, it simply ceased to exist. In an instant the light was gone and the Demon was nothing more than a smouldering pile of ash that now blew away on the morning breeze.

They buried Tamar in the clearing. No words were exchanged between the two, they simply used whatever they could find to dig a shallow grave and lay Tamar to rest within. They marked his resting place with a single stone. Once buried Elay spoke some words that Sam did not understand. Sam said "Thank you."

Once finished they sat next to the grave and ate some of the bread and cheese that they carried. Streaked in sweat, dust and blood their bodies ached from the efforts of burying Tamar and the battle with the demon, but there could be no rest, the Vale had to be reached as soon as they could. The encounter with the Demon had only confirmed that they would be hunted at every turn and that their pursuers would always be close to hand.

Wearily they packed away their belongings, stood, and began walking away. A few strides later, Sam felt Elay's small hand slip into his, and for the first time in a long while, Sam felt himself smile.

CHAPTER
8

From the very moment that Anna stepped forward into the mists, she could see nothing but the greyness that rushed to envelope her. The rush of the wind battered her senses as it filled her ears with its shrill cry and battered her exposed face. She stumbled forward and immediately walked into the figure ahead of her. She called for Sam to keep moving and felt the rope pull tight. Head lowered, she inched her way forward, looking left and right for any signs of attack, she saw nothing past the wall of grey. She shifted her drawn blade from hand to hand, reassured by its presence. She walked for what seemed an eternity, pausing occasionally for the rope to pull tight, and then following its lead. She could not hear any of her companions above the roar of the wind, but she was aware of their presence as she continued forward. Despite not being able to see further than her outstretched hand, she began to see a light in the distance, the group pushing forward to its glow. She felt a rush of exhilaration as the light signified the end of the ordeal. Her face was burning from the onslaught of the wind, but other than that, the journey had been easier than she had expected and she was pleased that it was nearing its end. She could now make out the outline of Sam ahead of her, silhouetted by the now ever brighter light. She saw as the figures ahead of her began to step into the light and disappear from view until she was standing before the light having seen Sam's hazy form pass out of the mists. She felt a sense of relief that all had passed without incident. As she stepped out into the light of the day, she realised that she had been very much mistaken. It was not Sam that she could see ahead but instead it was the form of the Elven prince, Sam was nowhere to be seen! Panic gripped her immediately. Frantically she began searching the assembled party for Sam. The moments passed quickly and each emerging figure from the mists brought hope that this was Sam, but each time she was disappointed. People began to shout in the confusion, orders being barked and the Ichbaru sent off running in all directions, but each time they returned alone. Some guards were sent back into the mists to look for him, they never returned. Seconds turned to minutes and it was becoming clear that Sam was lost to them.

"He was in front of me the whole time," she heard herself scream, "I never took my eyes off of him, how he can he not be here?" She was panicking now, she had allowed the one thing that the entire assembled group had sworn to protect against to happen. Sam was lost or worse and she felt the burden of the blame.

It was an hour before the remainder of the group reassembled in the long grasses outside of the mists. All looked forlorn; many had sought shelter and rest under a big Willow tree. Tired and disenchanted they slumped against the ancient bark, breathing heavily. Amador was in talks with Evaine away from the party and out of earshot, although the tension and concern between the two was palpable. Anna stayed apart, not wanting to engage in any conversation. Angrily she kicked at the grasses and cursed with every kick. She spent a long time pacing and kicking, before slumping to the ground in exhaustion. It was only when she sat quietly she overheard the remaining guards talking that she realised that Tamar was also unaccounted for. Her feeling of guilt passed quickly for not missing Tamar and she returned to her own thoughts of how they would find Sam.

As she sat she counted the remaining men from the party that had departed Silverdale. They had lost twelve of the Ichbaru guards along with Tamar and Sam. Thirty-eight had started and at the very first obstacle their party had been reduced to just twenty-four!

After for what seemed an eternity, Evaine came to advise her that they would be making camp for the night. Of course she objected, but Evaine remained calm and unmoved by her remonstrations. He had explained that night was not far off and tracking Sam and Tamar would not be possible. He also stressed that he would lose no more men on this night. Reluctantly she agreed, although the matter was never really up for debate. She ate alone, a meal of dried meats, bread and cheese with the now warm ale that had been packed before leaving Silverdale. She was hungrier than she had thought and finished her offerings in no time.

She had watched with disinterest as the plans were drawn up for the first watch. The ever loyal Ichbaru would take the brunt of the duties; however, Amador and Kalt would also take vigil. Night fell swiftly and the land lay still, but for Anna, sleep would not come quickly.

She spent that first night alone. She was tired, cold and for the first time, scared. Although she would have never admitted this to anyone, here, alone with her thoughts she could simply be Anna. There was no one to put on an act to, no one to impress with her bravery and quick wit, just her and her demons. "He had been right in front of her," she thought for the thousandth time, "the rope was taught and never faltered so, how the hell could he have just gone?" She let the tears roll down her dirty face and made no attempt this time to hide them. "He could be lying dead within those mists," she thought suddenly, but banished this thought as quickly as it had come. No, Sam was alive and he needed her now more than ever and in the morning she was going to find him, with or without the help of the others. With this thought she drifted into a deep sleep.

The night passed without incident and it was Teon that gently shook her awake. It was still early as the mist still hugged the land and had not yet been burned off by the slowly rising sun. Breakfast consisted of some dry fruits and some water that had been sourced from a stream that flowed nearby. Anna was neither hungry nor thirsty but Teon had advised her that the day would be long and that her strength would be tested, so food and water were not negotiable. Whilst her nature would have been to argue, she was slightly infatuated with Teon and accepted it without further discussion.

After breakfast was completed, Amador assembled the remainder of the group and informed them of the plan. Greston and Teon would take ten of the remaining Ichbaru guards and scout the surrounding countryside for signs of Sam and Tamar's passing. All being well they will locate their missing comrades and will then continue north until they reach the lip of the Vale and wait for Evaine's group to arrive. Evaine would be taking the remaining Ichbaru guard along with Kalt and Anna. They would travel directly to the Vale as this would be where Tamar would lead Sam too. Amador was going off alone. He said that he would attempt to contact Graflon prior to the group's arrival and would have to be alone to do so, but Anna suspected that perhaps this was not his only intention. Unusually for Anna she accepted what she had been told without an argument. She accepted that she knew nothing about tracking or the land in which she was in and therefore she would only be a hindrance to Greston and Teon and she would not jeopardize the safe return of Sam due to her stubbornness. As much as she would have preferred to have spent the next few days in the company of Teon, she would be well protected with Evaine and the massive Troll, Kalt, as her guides and protectors.

So it was that a little after daybreak the three parties said their goodbyes and headed off in search of Sam and answers.

134

Evaine started them off at quite a pace. It was a good three days march to the Vale and whilst Greston and Teon had a slower journey, both knew the countryside well and would take shortcuts wherever possible. It was a warm day and despite the earliness of the hour the land was warm and alive with birdsong and the irritation of insects that buzzed constantly around their heads. Anna however kept pace with the group, determined to be as strong and sure as any of her travel companions. Evaine had taken the lead, followed by three of the Ichbaru, Anna followed with Kalt close behind. The remaining five Ichbaru guarded the rear. Anna attempted conversation a few times with Kalt but either he did not understand her or chose to ignore her, she thought the later. Her mind wandered back to Sam as they walked. "I am going to punch him right on the nose when I see him for causing me all this concern" she thought. Then allowed herself a wry smile as she knew she wouldn't, even if he did deserve it. They walked until midday when Evaine brought them to a stop in a shaded grove so that they could take on water and food. Anna noticed that Kalt did neither, in fact she could not remember the Troll ever eating or drinking. She made a note to ask Evaine later about it when the quiet of the day was shattered by a piercing scream. Immediately the Ichbaru were on their feet surrounding Evaine, swords and bows drawn and at the ready. Anna jumped up at lightning speed but Kalt was already at her side in a flash. She had neither seen nor heard him but there he stood. He wielded an enormous Axe. It must have been as big as her, double sided and glinting menacingly in the afternoon sun. All stood statuesque, awaiting the next sound. They didn't have to wait long. Out of the row of bushes to their left a figure came crashing through. It was a man as far as Anna could make out, running at top speed. The group tensed and arrows drew back in readiness, but Evaine immediately called for bows to be lowered. It was one of the Ichbaru guards that had left with Greston and Teon. He was streaked with blood and his right arm was missing from below the elbow. As he burst into the clearing he stopped, clearly confused and unsure as to what to do. All he could manage was to scream "Run," before a bolt

135

of red flame shot from the forest behind and ripped him into pieces that landed with sound of wet tissue as they hit the ground. Anna instinctively went to move closer to Kalt but he had disappeared. In fact it was Evaine that had reached through the formed rank of Ichbaru and pulled her to his chest. He placed a finger to his lips then held her to him with one hand whilst holding his outstretched sword in the other. They waited as the clearing fell quiet. The only sound was the heavy breathing from the Ichbaru as they waited for orders. Anna slowly drew the hunting knife that hung from her waist and she stood ready to fight should she need to.

The minutes slipped slowly by, no one moving and no sign of the attacker that had destroyed the guard. Anna knew it was out there, watching them. She had seen it before, on that occasion it was Ruern that had been torn apart. She grimaced at the memory but surprisingly she felt no fear this time, in fact what she felt was anger. After several minutes Evaine silently summoned a guard and ushered instructions in hush tones. Anna could not understand what was being said, but the guard silently left the gathered group and headed towards the remains of the body of the Ichbaru that had been torn apart. Anna watched as he silently traversed the short distance and began scouting the surrounding area. No sooner as he had reached the hedge line, an ear piercing shrill cry was released and a black mass tore out of the bracken. So fast was the charge that the remaining guards could not even release their already drawn arrows in time before the blackness crashed into the helpless Ichbaru. There was a crunching of bone and tearing of flesh then an eruption of red as the guard was torn clean in two. Then the blackness was gone as quickly as it had arrived.

Evaine now shouted orders, the time for stealth and quite had long since passed. He thrust Anna behind him as five of the remaining guards raced into the direction of where the blackness had gone. They moved swiftly and silently intent on killing the thing that had so easily dispatched two of their number, Anna did not hold out much hope. The three remaining guards positioned themselves at the side of Evaine and Anna. Once again silence fell on the clearing. With all eyes frantically scanning the surrounding area they waited and listened...nothing, nothing could be seen or heard. Had they not been so intent in watching where the black form had disappeared to, they may have noticed the black shape that dropped silently from an old Pine tree that stood not 20 yards behind them. Had they not have been so focussed on the foreground they would have noticed the wolf like characteristics as it crept ever closer, never making a sound, never taking its yellowed eyes off its unsuspecting prey. It got within ten feet before Evaine wheeled around to meet the Demons advance. In an instance it leapt forward, its rows of teeth glinting as it closed in on the Elven prince's exposed throat. Evaine gave a cry of warning and drew up his sword to meet the lunging nightmare, but just as outstretched claws of Demon reached the tip of Evaine's sword another massive black form appeared from the side of the Elven prince. Anna just caught sight of a massive axe arcing towards the head of the Demon wolf. The sound of the mighty weapon catching the wolf right between its eyes sent the birds from the trees. A huge sound of splintering skull and bone echoed in the clearing. Black tar spewed from the Demons head as it fell lifeless to the floor. Kalt walked up to the unmoving beast and with one final swing of his monstrous axe cleaved its head cleanly from its body. Kalt wiped the blades of his axe and replaced it on the strapping on his back. He turned and gave the slightest of nods to Evaine and then walked off twenty yards and seated himself in the clearing with his back to the party.

The Ichbaru guards emerged in a rush from the hunt for the demon, breathing heavily and streaked in dirt, they immediately took their place by Evaine's side, however he ordered them away and to take on water.
"Are you alright Mistress Anna?" Evaine asked.
"I am fine, but thank god for Trolls eh?" she retorted.
"Indeed, Kalt is a mighty warrior and I now owe him my life as well as my gratitude. He will accept no thanks but I will be

there for him when the time arrives, as I am sure that it will before our journey finally ends."

Evaine stood pondering his statement for a moment in silence and then abruptly gave the order that they were to be leaving as soon as the dead had been buried. The Demon, he commanded, would be left where it fell. "Let it rot" Evaine had ordered. Anna took a moment, whilst the Ichbaru dug the graves for the fallen, to look at the monster that had so nearly ended their lives. On closer inspection it was not as large as the Demon that had threatened Sam and Anna previously. She noted its razor sharp claws and teeth that had made it so devastating when it fought. Its body was lithe and heavily muscled which accounted for the speed in which it was able to attack. "No match for a Troll's axe!" Anna thought almost with a smile.

Within half an hour the sombre task of the burials had been completed. Evaine gave an Elven prayer of thanks for the departed and the group began again its journey towards the Vale. No one said anything but Anna could not help wondering what had befallen Greston and Teon's group. The guard that had been killed was part of their troupe. She inwardly prayed that all were still alive, especially Teon.

Greston watched the party headed by Evaine set off before giving the command for the tracking party to depart. He had sent three of the Elven guard off ahead to see if a trail could be found and followed. Teon, the remaining guards and himself would then follow the forward party until both met. He explained that that way they would be sure not to miss anything, should there be anything to miss. He had discussed with Teon just before setting off that he felt the mission to be futile and that those that disappeared in the mists remained lost forever. Teon commented that Sam had the protection of the Orloc, however Greston was quick to point out that this was a magic that had never been tested or one that Sam was not entirely sure that he could summon. Never the less, both were

138

duty bound to this task and both would ensure that if Sam were alive and could be found, they would find him.

The morning hours slipped by slowly, as they continued their advance northwards towards the domain of the Witch. Conversation was sparse as they all concentrated on watching the landscape for any sign of Sam's passing. They had fanned out in a line to cover more ground as they walked, cautious to not miss anything, no matter how small. Teon and the Ichbaru walked silently and with ease through the high grasses and rutted slops of the wild country, Greston, by contrast, breathed heavily and loudly, constantly muttering about the annoyance he felt in having to be out here at all. Teon smiled to himself. He found it amusing to listen to Greston's constant grumbling. 'Dwarves,' he thought, 'I will never understand them.'

Towards mid morning they stopped to eat and drink before resuming their search. The forward party that Teon had sent on ahead had not yet been caught up with but they knew they were on the right path as Teon had picked up their tracks many miles back. Teon could track most things. It was a skill that he had developed over countless forays with his father into the hills and forests of Varon. He wondered, as he took a long pull on his ale skin, what his father would now do following the meeting of the council and the growing threat from the massing armies at Varek. His father was no fool, he would have the army of men readied for battle, but he also knew that his father would not put the lives of his countrymen at risk until he was sure that no other option existed. His thoughts then turned to Sam and the girl. He had to think to remember her name, 'Anna' it came to him. He instinctively liked them. Sam seemed vulnerable but there was also a determination to him that sat quietly under the surface. Anna on the other hand was brash and strong minded. He liked that. He found himself smiling as he recalled how she had brought a room of Kings to silence with a shout. His father had called her an 'impetuous child', he, by contrast thought her dazzling.

139

He began to stow away the contents of his pack when the familiar huffing sound of Greston approached.

"Clouds are rolling in lad, need to up the pace, I am not being out here in the lashing rain." He didn't wait for answer, he simply turned and strode away to await Teon to join him.

To Teon's surprise it was Greston that started conversation with him as they resumed their walk. Dwarves by nature were quite guarded and deliberately ignorant of the other inhabitants of Invetia and very much preferred to keep themselves to themselves.

"Tell me of Varon young Prince," he said gruffly, "tell me of the world of Men."

Teon told him all there was to know, grateful of the diversion that conversation brought. He told his companion of the sprawling walled city that was his home, of the people, the smells and the trades that they employed. He gave Greston an overview of how the land was governed and the accomplishments that the race of Men had achieved. He was honest on his appraisal and did not shy away from also highlighting the shortfalls of mankind. The infighting and constant struggles with the other major cities such as Fenham further to the south. He gave Greston a brief lesson in the history of Men and how they once possessed magic that the Elves used freely today and also how, over time, most was lost to them. He concluded that the race of Man had the biggest armies, the best government system and the most skilled tradesmen then any of the other races. They just needed to learn how they could better coexist with others. He mentioned that perhaps that when all of this was over they could work closer with the Dwarves and share knowledge and learning's. Greston huffed.

"So, now that I have given you a history of Men, I would very much like to hear about your people" Teon proposed. "Tell me about the Dwarves Greston."

"Like Men, just stronger, just better" came the curt reply. Teon waited a moment to see if there was anymore that the Dwarf was going to add but it became obvious that that's all he had to say on the matter. Teon stared at the Dwarf then burst into laughter. "Dwarves," he said, "I still will never understand them"

His laughter was cut short as, somewhere in the distance, a piercing scream sounded to shatter the stillness of morning. Immediately they were running towards the direction of the sound, no longer looking for tracks to follow, or a sign of Sam's passing, just desperate to reach its origin. Teon's heart was thumping hard. Thin branches of overhanging trees whipped at his face as he ran, but he did not falter or slow his speed. He feared that the scream was Sam's and that he was in trouble. They raced through the trees, the Elven guard of the Ichbaru were faster and lighter on their feet than either Teon or Greston and they ran ahead, swords drawn and bows held, ready to meet any challenge that they should encounter. Teon zigzagged through a cluster of trees and came to skidded halt in a small clearing. Ahead lay a mass of blood and bone. Trees covered with the red spray from something living that had been ripped apart. Greston joined him at his side, panting heavily from the sudden dash. His axe held menacingly before him. The Ichbaru stood and stared at the bloody mess ahead. Teon immediately thought that this would be journeys end if this was Sam and Tamar. He began frantically trying to identify anything that would indicate who the victims were. It was impossible to identify how many bodies lay in the clearing, they had been so totally ruined and destroyed, but as he stared at the scene his eyes came to rest on the blood-soaked cloaks that lay in tatters on the ground. He caught a glimpse of an oak tree and crown and knew this was scouting party of Elves that he had sent ahead. Relief rushed through him despite the tragedy of the massacre that he gazed upon. He studied the ground for a while, desperately trying not to vomit. The scouts had been attacked from behind by two assailants that walked on four legs. The tracks of the assailants were not as deep set further back which indicated that they had stalked their prey and crept up on them. 'The Elves had no chance' he thought.

A single set of Elven prints led away from the scene of the ambush and one of the attackers had given chase, the other

141

beast had headed in the opposite direction, the same direction that they were heading. He cautiously followed the set of Elven prints that led away from the carnage for a short distance and came across an arm! The Elf had obviously turned to fight its attacker here as he was pursued, but had come off worse. The trail of blood and footprints continued ahead deeper into the heavy forest growth closely followed by the attacker.

He returned to the others that stood in the clearing. Greston was roaring for the attackers to show themselves and fight, the Ichbaru stood impassive but clearly shaken by the sight of their fallen comrades. He relayed his findings to the group. He had advised them that there was little point in going to aid the Elf that had fled, he was in a bad way and most probably dead, besides, stalking into deeper forest would only give the attacker more places to spring an ambush. Teon was more concerned with the thought that the second attacker had gone further ahead to lay a similar trap for them. They would be wary and prepared should this happen, but nothing must stop them from completing the task that they had been given. Even more so now was the urgency to find Sam and Tamar.

"I do not care which way we go," Greston spat "as long as we find this beast and I can spill his guts. We have wasted enough time and need to move now!" he demanded.

The Ichbaru guards would clearly have preferred to follow and aid their lost comrade; however, they would follow Teon's orders dutifully as they had been charged to do so by their King.

The decision was made to leave the remains of the Ichbaru in the clearing. They would normally bury the Elves but they had no time. The remaining guards offered words of solace to the deceased and then they were on their way. A renewed vigour seemed to have gripped Greston as he had ceased his incessant moaning and was moving with purpose and determination. Teon could tell that it was rage that drove him mainly. He knew that what was required, now more than ever with a potential ambush around every corner, was a clear head and thought to keep a close eye on the Dwarf. Rage and anger could get you killed in an instant.

The progress marginally slowed by Teon having to continually check for signs of the beasts passing, but, fortunately he was able to see the path the attacker had taken quite quickly. It would appear that it had made no attempt to hide its tracks. Either it believed that it would not be followed or that it considered their group to be of such little threat that it saw no purpose in doing so. Its course remained arrow like towards the Vale of the Witch, never pausing or deviating. From the marks it left Teon estimated it to be over five feet tall to its shoulder and that was when on all fours and it was travelling much faster than they were. He guessed it to already be half a day's march ahead of them.

It then began to rain. The impending storm that Greston had talked about earlier had arrived with ferocity. The heavens darkened, the wind howled and the rain sheeted down and soaked them in an instant. They pushed forward as best they could but eventually Teon brought them to a halt.

"It's no good; I cannot see the tracks any more, not in this weather. We will have to stop and allow the storm to pass" he shouted above the maelstrom of noise.

"No," Greston snapped angrily, "that animal gets away every time we stop; we have to find it and kill it quickly. We have no time to waste. We know where it is heading, you said so yourself, so let's be done with tracking it and head for the Vale. We can deal with it there!" Greston was clearly not about to debate this, his mind was set.

"If I cannot see where it has gone," Teon shouted," then I cannot tell if it waits concealed ahead. Come to your senses Dwarf, it's too dangerous, we have to stop and wait out the storm." They glared at each other through the sheets of rain that came in torrents. "Let it come for me," Greston yelled, "my axe will meet its neck!"

Teon held his tongue, he wanted to scream at the stubborn headed Dwarf to think about how stupid he was being, but he knew that would accomplish nothing.

143

"Look," Teon said, "over there, that Willow tree. Let us take shelter for a few hours to see if the storm passes. If it does after that we will continue on as you suggest if it stops sooner we will be on our way as soon as the last raindrop falls. Give me two hours Greston that is all I ask."

The Dwarf snarled an unintelligible response and stormed towards the Willow, Teon and the Ichbaru followed.

They all slumped down under the branches of the tree. Soaked through and exhausted as they watched the wind batter the exposed landscape. Thunder boomed overhead and lighting lit the sky in silver streaks as it crackled above them. They didn't even bother attempting to start a fire, the wind was too unrelenting for that, they settled for a cold meal and some water. The Ichbaru organised pairs to take watch duty and the rest rolled into their blankets and tried to get some short respite before their turn to take watch came around. Teon thought about offering but the Elves had it arranged, Greston, by contrast, threw his blanket around his shoulders and, despite the screaming of the wind, rain and thunder, was snoring in moments. Teon sat with his back against the tree and watched the storm rage. He knew that this storm would not be over in the two hours he had asked for and even it was it would be dark by then and he would still not be able to track the beast, but he had to get Greston to agree. They were tired and needed the rest. It would not be any use to be suffering exhaustion when they caught up with the monster they tracked. He began to think as to how long they had left before they reached the Vale, but before he could give it much thought his head drooped and he was asleep.

He was awoken by the Elven watch. "My lord, the Dwarf has gone." He was on his feet in an instance. "That impetuous fool," he thought angrily. It appeared that Greston had left in the midst of the storm. The noise of the wind and thunder had masked his departure. Teon was angry, not with the Ichbaru for failing to notice that he had left, but with himself for falling asleep so quickly. He should have suspected that the Dwarf may have tried something like that, "Pig-headed fool" he cursed.

It was nearing dawn before the small group was ready to move out. They had slept for far longer than he had wanted, but he felt refreshed nevertheless from the rest, the storm had at least abated and left behind a slow drizzle that fashioned the world in a blurred haze. There was sufficient light to be able to track their quarry, although Teon now had to contend with finding Greston's tracks in order that they may locate the errant Dwarf. To his surprise the Dwarfs prints seem to follow the shallow imprints left by the beast. Perhaps Greston was more skilled as a tracker than he had let on, or maybe he was just lucky. Either way it made Teon's job a lot easier and quicker. The morning passed without incident, the rain had finally given up its occupation but the land remained grey and gloomy. A few times Teon needed to retrace his steps to keep track with Greston. The Dwarf seemed to be changing direction quite often; clearly he was having difficulty in following the beast's signs of passing. The route though was still on a direct path to the Vale. He began to wonder if the beast had caught up with the other group headed by Evaine, but he never had time to consider the answer, for there, not fifty feet ahead on the path they followed, was Greston, or what was left of Greston.

He had been bitten in half at the waist. The lower part of his body was missing. His insides lay scattered across the grassland. His axe still strapped to his back. It had not long happened either as fresh blood still oozed from his open torso. Teon and the Elven guard approached with weapons drawn, furtively looking in all directions to ensure no surprise attack was mounted. It watched them from the concealment of the bracken as they edged forward with weapons drawn. It had considered stealth, but it believed surprise was the better option. With its mind made up, it leapt at them through the undergrowth. There was a crash of branches and bracken as it rushed them, breaking from the cover of the forest with immense speed. Before they knew what had happened, two Ichbaru lay dead; their life blood flowing freely from gaping

145

claw marks across their chests and a third was missing all together. The beast had run right through them and disappeared back into the concealment of the forest. Teon shouted instructions for the remaining guards to gather to him. They would be better protected if they defended with their backs to each other, every angle could be covered for the next inevitable attack. The five men stood and listened, breathing heavy and weapons glinting in the daylight, they stood hunched together waiting. They did not have to wait long; the guard with his back to Teon gave a cry of warning as the beast lumbered through the trees at them. They turned to face the attacker head on, better prepared this time but still facing overwhelming odds. Teon could see it now. It was wolf like in appearance, but was the size of a Bull. Its muzzle drawn back to show rows of razor sharp teeth that gnashed and snapped as it ran. Its body heavily muscled and covered in black short fur. Its lidless eyes burned crimson. It bore down on them with speed and strength. It reached the closest Elven guard and tossed him aside with ease. The group of men broke formation as the beast careered through the middle of the formed defensive line. Each man hacking and slashing as it ran past. Teon brought his massive sword down on the beast as it ran past, it barely left a mark. The wolf ran straight through and into the forest surround on the opposite side and disappeared from view.

The men reformed, and waited anew. The Ichbaru guard that had been tossed aside lay ten feet away, his neck bent at an impossible angle, his eyes wide and staring.
"At the next pass", Teon panted the words out "Every one of us must focus our attack on its forelegs. We cannot bring it down quick enough by trying to kill it outright, we must disable it."
He barely got the last word out as the beast emerged again. The men drew ranks. Back it came, barrelling towards them with hatred in it eyes. As it got within five feet of them, the remaining four broke formation and swung their swords as hard they could at the wolfs legs, two of the guards missed and the force of their swing sent them to their knees, the wolf stooped and locked its jaws on the closest head and bit clean

through, the second was raked with its massive claws which spilled out his innards. Both Teon's and the remaining guard's swing's however found their mark; both sent their swords smashing into the wolf's foreleg as it disposed of the other two Ichbaru. The sound of bone splintering and the wolf screaming filled the air. Its momentum carried it forward for twenty yards before it crashed to the floor writhing in agony. Teon and the Ichbaru did not wait; they were on it in an instant. As they ran towards their prey the Elf sent a volley of arrows from his now drawn bow into the ruined leg of the wolf. It screamed in response. "For Varon and the King." Teon yelled as he closed in on the stricken beast, sword raised above his head. He sent the sword crashing into the animals exposed skull with such force that his arms shuddered and went numb from the impact. The wolf's head split wide open as it slumped to the ground and was still.

Both men collapsed in heap on the ground, each gasping to catch their breath, dizzy from the battle. "What is your name my Elven friend?" Teon asked in between gulps of breath. "Neria," the other wearily replied.

"You fought well Neria and you have my eternal gratitude." Neria's arm had been injured in the fight from a cut that ran bone deep from the claws of the wolf, but he insisted he was alright. Teon tore a sleeve from his shirt and tightly bound the others arm to control the bleeding. Teon felt himself gingerly for damage. He had escaped the worst of it. His breastplate was bent and ripped in places, but it had saved him from certain death. He knew he had broken few ribs as his chest throbbed in pain with each breath, and he suspected his left arm to be broken, but other than that he was in one piece. Whilst his body throbbed with pain it was bearable, he was just thankful to still be alive.

They spent the next few hours at the place of the battle. Neither one of them able to dig graves to bury the dead due their injuries, however, they collected their comrades and burned their bodies. It would not been right to leave them for the scavengers of the forest to feast upon. They had taken

147

Greston's axe from his body. It was decided that Neria would return to Silverdale. He of course objected but Teon was insistent. He would report to the King as to the events that had transpired and arrange for Bannock to be informed about the fate of his son and the returning of Greston's axe.

They ate a little of the dried meat and some fruit that they carried and took on water. Teon made sure that the Elf was very clear as to the message that needed to be relayed to Thealine, if demon wolves were scouting out here then the armies of Molgoran must be on the move. Scouts must be sent to investigate, if they had not been already, and the armies of Men and Dwarves must be readied. War was coming, of that there was no doubt.

The men embraced and Teon stood and watched as Neria disappeared into the distance. "Safe journey friend" he whispered, and then turned to resume his solitary walk to the Vale.

CHAPTER
9

They could see the Vale from several miles off. Thick smog seemed to hang over great swathes of sky in the distance. Elay told him that it was called "Skrill" by the locals. An old Elven word that meant Decay.

The land seemed to take on a darker hue as they edged ever closer. The once vibrant greens of the meadows now took on a dirty brown colour as plants struggled for the light to breathe. No birdsong broke the silence and it appeared that not a thing lived in the shadow of the Skrill. Both Sam and Elay's gaze remained locked upon the shadowed Vale ahead. Neither spoke, they just remained lost to their own thoughts about what would happen when they reached their destination. Elay still gripped tightly onto Sam's hand and he felt her tremble slightly as they walked. Next to hit them was the stench that arose from the steaming pit. It was a fetid smell of dead, decaying, damp wood and vegetation. It was a heavy smell that no wind would move. Sam began to try and breathe through his mouth more as the smell was soon unbearable. Everything was quiet and still, nothing moved. They were close now, about five-hundred yards to its edge, when Elay stopped and pulled her hand away from Sam's.

"You must go on alone now Sam," she spoke in a hushed tone, "I am not permitted to venture any further with you although I wish that I could, however, to do so would endanger you even more and I cannot allow that." He stood facing her now, watching her as she spoke. He realised again just how beautiful she was. He also realised that he was desperately in love with her.

"I will wait for you for three days," she continued, "I will wait by that Ash tree," she indicated to a huge tree off to the left, "should three days come and go and you have not returned, I will go and seek help." Sam shuddered inwardly at the thought of being in that morass of death and stench for three minutes let alone three days.

"Sam," she continued, "Graflon is a being of the ancient world; she cannot be trusted for a moment. She will try and trick you, scare you or claim you. You must be wary of everything and believe only what your heart tells you to be true. I do not know what you will find inside, nor do I know what it is that you are looking for but I am sure that you will know it when the time comes." Sam went to speak but Elay continued as if she would not get a chance to speak the words again. "Take this." She reached into her pocket and handed him a small opaque stone. He looked at it quizzically. "It is Elven magic," she responded to his look, "when three days have passed the stone will glow blue. You will have no idea of time once inside the Vale. It is the only way you will know how long you have been gone." He took the stone from her outstretched hand and placed it in his pocket.

"Go now Sam and watch for everything. I will keep you in my prayers." She leant forward and touched him on his cheek. He felt her hand trembling, and then she kissed him on his lips. A soft kiss as light as the winds touch, then turned and walked towards the Ash. She never turned back to look at Sam, for if she had he would have seen the tears that now streamed down her face.

He stood for a while and watched until Elay reached the trunk of the tree. He watched as she pulled her blanket over her shoulders and slumped down to sit with her back against its bark. She never looked up. He took a moment to gather his senses and steady his breathing, and then he turned and continued his walk to the Vale's edge. As he neared the lip of the pit the steam and smog grew thicker. He coughed against its harsh abrasiveness on his throat. He turned one last time to look for Elay, but the mist now obscured everything. It reminded him of the Echenor, and his stomach turned at the memories of that place. Instinctively he pulled his cloak around him to ward off the chill that had now developed and with a final deep breath ventured into the gloom.

He didn't go far. The blackness was so enveloping that he could see nothing. He had to stop and allow his eyes to acclimatise to the darkness that now stretched out in all directions. Although just a few paces in, he was disorientated, unable to discern left or right, up or down. It was a most uncomfortable feeling that made him feel unsteady on his feet. As he stood waiting for some vision to return, he could feel the damp cold of the ground seeping through his boots. "This was not going to be pleasant" he thought to himself.

After what seemed like an age, but was more than likely just a few minutes, he was able to make out shapes and trees that stretched before him. Not far, but sufficient to resume his walk into the Vale. Everything was reliant on assumption he suddenly thought. He had no idea as to where he was walking to and was working on the premise that he should head for what he believed to be the middle of the Hollow. He had no idea if Graflon was to be found within; after all it had been many years since her last reported sighting. For all he knew she could have moved on or have died years ago and no one would have been the wiser. He could quite easily imagine that he could spend the rest of his life walking in this gloom and never find his way out. Elay had said that she would wait for three days before getting help but his rations would not last another day let alone three, and he didn't imagine that he would be able to find much to eat along the way. As much as it scared him, the best option would be that he finds the Witch quickly and gets whatever has to be done, done. Strange, he thought, that the best option was the one that he would normally want to avoid at all costs. Meeting Graflon was terrifying him the most and yet this was his best chance of survival.

With the weight of doubt pushing down on him he continued forward as best he could. It was slow going. Every few steps that he took he needed to stop and try to make out where his next step should be. He stumbled often, cursing each trip and fall. Despite the penetrating cold of the ground he soon found that his shirt was sticking to him from the sweat of his body. There was no path to follow, no obvious signs that anyone had ever been here before and it was draining his energy with every step taken. He stopped often to take on water. The mist and smog, whilst less dense within, tore at his dry throat and made him constantly thirsty but still he ventured forward. He tried to remain positive that he was making progress, but he was less than half an hour into what could be a very, very long search.

He began to think of his old life as he walked through the damp gloom of the Skrill, as it was a welcome diversion that took his mind off of the misery that stretched out before him. He wondered who would be missing him. He knew that Ben and Anna's family would be desperate with worry, but, other than Mr Adams, who would be missing the filing being done, he doubted that anybody else really even noticed that he was gone. He wondered on the fact that his life had been mapped out from the day of his birth and on the meeting between his mother and Ruern. She had kept that secret from him all his life and even at the end of her days still did not disclose what had transpired. When he had first been presented with the idea he found that he was angry at the secrecy and subterfuge that his mother had extolled upon him. Angry that, to all intense and purposes, his life had been a charade that he had been unwittingly the key protagonist in. But he found now that he felt none of those initial emotions. He now felt an admiration for his mother in keeping this secret from him. He liked to think that it was her unyielding love for him that wanted to protect him to the end. Maybe a part of her never actually thought any of this would come to pass and that it would be better left alone until, if at all, the time came. Even Anna had an insight into the events to come albeit towards the end of his mother's life, and that he had been the only one kept in eternal darkness. In fact, he thought, this was probably the first time in his whole existence that no one was watching over him, guiding him and keeping him safe. This here and now was the time that he had to step up to the expectation that had been placed upon him and take control. It was not meant to be like this of course, Amador was sent as his protector and Evaine and the entire Elven nation appeared to be willing to lay down their lives to see his safe passage, but none were here now, he was alone and treading the path of destiny that Ruern told him was his to tread. He wondered if they had all managed to escape the Echenor, he worried mostly for Anna. He missed her company and counsel; he even missed her sarcasm and wit. Maybe he should have spent longer looking for her, maybe he should have insisted that they returned to Silverdale and sought help, maybe a thousand things he thought darkly. Life had a way of forcing you down a path without the time to pause for hindsight. He would have to live with the choices made and accept that these really were never choices that had alternatives. Lost to his thoughts and tired from the exertion of the journey, he failed to notice the knot of tree roots in front of him and went down with an audible thud and the gloom of the Skrill turned pitch black.

He didn't know how long he had been unconscious, but awoke to find his head throbbing. He tried to open his eyes but found he that couldn't. Something else was wrong to, try as he might, he couldn't move his arms or legs. He was as if paralysed! Panic set about him. No one would find him in the Skrill. He knew that he still lay on the ground as he felt the coldness radiate through his right side. He could lay here until either a wandering beast took him for its dinner or he simply starved to death and decayed. He felt the fear well inside him, slowly creeping up and threatening to take over him completely. He had to fight it, fear would not resolve his situation, and he needed to regain his senses fast. After allowing the fear to hold him for a little longer he began to gain control, he slowed his breathing and concentrated on clearing his mind of the thoughts that jostled for attention. Slowly he began to calm himself by concentrating on the sounds of his breathes. He began to try to establish what was wrong with him. He clearly wasn't paralysed as he could feel the cold of the Hollows floor. He could feel the sharpness of the roots that dug into his legs and the dampness of the mud on his hands, he just couldn't move. He tried again to open his eyes but they would not respond to his urges. He tried then to call out, he was not sure to whom as no one would hear, but to his further despair no sound would come from his lips. Try as he might he couldn't make any noise to alert anyone to his presence.

"Little fly, why do you struggle so when the web is clearly unbreakable?" came a soft voice from behind him. Sam immediately stopped his efforts to shout, stopped his attempts to open his eyes. He went still, but he knew immediately who spoke the words, he knew that he had found Graflon.

Elay awoke to find the same grey clad landscape as she had seen the day before, and the day before that. For two days now she had waited as promised, for Sam's return under the drooping branches of the Ash tree. She stretched away the sleep from her body and set about fixing breakfast. Her provisions were almost depleted and her meal consisted of no more than a little water and some dried meat and cheese. She wondered if Sam had found the Witch and worried for him in case he had. She had grown close to him in a short space of time. It intrigued her why she felt such a bond with Sam; it also scared her a little as she had not felt such feelings before. Was this what being in love felt like? The admission that she was falling in love scared her even more. She remembered the story of the 'Stranger Returned' as her father called it from when she was young. All Elves were familiar with the tale as it was constant in the teachings of their heritage and past, but only she knew and a select few knew the true impact of such a return. She was a Princess after all and it was her need to know of the sacrifice that the Elven nation must endure when the stranger returned. If Sam was the stranger prophesised, she could not allow herself to fall in love with him. She never fully understood why the Elves were the ones to carry the burden of Invetia. Men constantly warred amongst themselves, Dwarves remained largely hostile to all that were not Dwarves and as for the Trolls, Goblins, Gnomes and other tribal factions they stripped the land of what they could use and then moved on to repeat the cycle. It was only the Elves that cared and nurtured the earth. Only the Elves that gave back what they took out, only the Elves that kept some of the magic of the old world alive and yet it was the Elves that always had to pay the highest price when anything needed doing.

Still, as her father had often told her, 'You judge your actions on what is right and not what others do wrong', that was the way of the world and no bemoaning would ever change that. Her thoughts then turned back to Sam and his relationship with Anna. She did not know the girl as well as she would have liked. Did he have feelings for her? Was she the one that had his heart? She kicked angrily at the ground. Being in love, if that was what she was, took over your whole being, every thought and feeling. Everything she seemed to think about was in some way connected to Sam. She had never experienced anything like it before. She decided she would ask Anna as to her feelings towards Sam if they should ever reunite. "Damn," she chided herself, "concentrate on the now" she told herself aloud.

She spent the next few hours scouting the area for anything that she could collect for food. Her provisions would not last another day and she did not know how quickly she would find aid if Sam had not returned by tomorrow. In fact, now she gave it thought, she did not know where she would even start to look for help. Silverdale was several days travel away even if she travelled fast and unhindered and this would be too long. She did not know where Evaine, Amador and the rest of the party were and her father did not know that she was with Sam. She felt bad that she had lied to Sam earlier and said that her father knew she was with him, also she had mislead her father by telling him that she was going to visit the towns on the outskirts of Silverdale to help deliver medicines for the sick. He would never had permitted her to go with Sam and therefore she saved the time, trouble and inevitable arguments that asking would have brought. She was now realising that she was alone in this and no one would come to her aid if needed. She was a Princess of Silverdale and 'should have really thought this through a little more', she silently admonished. She had had no further visions since setting out to find Sam emerging from the mists and therefore it stood to reason that it was safe to be his guide and companion, however, it troubled her that she had only just sensed the Demon in time when they were attacked and that her senses were only just quick enough. She dismissed the thought as quick as it had come and continued her forage. After finding nothing more than a few edible roots and a fouled stream she returned to her now familiar spot under the branches of the Ash. The day had taken on a darker colour and it was only a matter of time before a storm rolled in she surmised. She pulled her cloak tight around her shoulders and settled down under the sparse protection of the tree and waited. She was just drifting off to sleep when she heard the rustle of footsteps approaching from behind. Immediately she was on her feet, it could be Evaine she considered, but best to make sure first. Snatching up her belongings she ran swiftly and silently to where the vegetation was thickest and flattened herself against the ground. She thought of summoning the magic that had protected them from the Demon attack, but she did not want to alert whoever may be out there to her presence. She decided to wait and see, but knew protection was there should she need it. She lay directly opposite from her earlier spot under the tree in a thick growth of grasses. She could see anything that approached from the front. She went as still as she could and waited, nothing stirred. She tried to see further into the gloom, looking for any sign of movement, but all was still and deathly hushed.

"You will catch a nasty chill lying in the damp grass," a sudden voice came from behind her. Elay instinctively brought her magic to bear and the blue protective light covered her in an instant. She remained where she lay, 'How had they gotten behind her without her seeing or hearing them' she thought. "Ah, you have use of magic," the voice continued, "how delightful." The voice was soft and non- threatening but it was mocking her. It seemed to be playing a game with her, and not at all surprised of the Elven Princesses defences.
"You are lucky that I am not offended easily, after all it could be considered rude to block me out," it continued, "never mind, I guess one cannot be too careful in times such as these. I will ignore this indiscretion if you would be kind enough to tell me your name and state what business you have to be in such a dreadful place?"

With her protective barrier in place, Elay climbed to her knees and turned to the direction of the voice. No one was there. She felt her breath quicken as she tried to see who was speaking, she was shaking despite her protection of magic.
"There there," the voice continued, "you have no need to be afraid of me, just answer my question and I will be on my way. Greater threats to you lay within the Vale and yet you seem to

be oblivious to that which lurks within, I am merely concerned as to the safety of a young Elven Princess so close to permanent harm." She instantly froze, the voice knew who she was, it could therefore see her and yet she still saw nothing.

"Show yourself" she managed to shout, trying to keep her voice from cracking from the fear that she now felt. "I will as and when I chose to be seen," came the response. Again the voice was soft and steady but Elay felt it laced with malice. "I will ask but one more time, who are you and what are you doing near the Skrill?"

"Why do you ask of my name when you clearly know who I am?" she responded.

"Because when I ask a question I expect the courtesy of a reply, whether I know the answer is irrelevant, I expect to be answered." This time the voice sounded edged with danger.

"My name is Elay, daughter of King Thealine." She could not entirely hide the cracking to her voice, "I am on my way back to Silverdale on order from the King and was not aware that I was so close to the Vale." She thought it better to be as nice as she could manage. "You startled me, I meant no offence in raising my defence and apologise if I have caused any." She was trying to think as to the best direction to run. She had never been a good liar and knew that the stranger would see through her misdirection. There was a long period of silence before the voice spoke again.

"If you meant no offence Elay, daughter of Thealine, why do you still call forth the magic?" it probed. "I am close to being offended and that is not a nice thing to do to someone who is just looking out for your wellbeing." She felt her body go cold with the fear that was welling inside of her. She was losing control of the situation and she was running out of options.

"Lower your magic so that we may talk a while, until I am satisfied that you are in no danger. After all I cannot leave a Princess unprotected can I? What if anything should happen to you and I just walked by, that would be unforgivable." Her mind was racing. She felt sure that if she made a run for it she would fail. She had to assume that the magic protecting her would defend any attack otherwise they would have just attacked and not asked her to lower it. She decided the best thing to do would be to stall for time and hope an opportunity arose very quickly to change her predicament.

"I am afraid that I am forbidden by the King himself to lower any magic until I can confirm that I am in no danger," she started, "and whilst I am sure that you mean me no harm, it would be easier to feel fully assured if I could see you. Can you not show yourself to me?" She asked.

Another long pause ensued before the voice responded. "Then you are lucky my young Princess that the King is not here to see your indiscretion as you **will** lower your magic for me.....or I will lower it for you."

Nothing was working, she was scared now. Although she could not see her tormenter, her senses screamed to her that they were not bluffing, she sensed power and magic that far outweighed anything she could muster. Maybe it would be appeased by her retracting her magic, either way she was defenceless if it could overcome her protection, but she was not ready to be a willing sacrifice, if it wanted her magic gone then it would have to destroy it. If she were to die then she would die fighting.

She climbed back to her feet now, still encased in the protective Blue shield. It snapped and crackled as she moved, the sound giving her some small amount of reassurance of its protective purpose. She looked up; ready to do whatever it took to extend her life, when she saw the stooped figure standing not more than twenty yards in front of her. It made her jump in spite of herself. The figure was unmoving. It wore a cloak that was hooded with the cowl pulled over its face so she could not see what lay underneath. She could not even tell if it was male or female, but from the voice she surmised it was a man. It stood crooked, its weight resting on a short staff that a gnarled old hand held for stability. For all intense and purposes it looked like any other old man that she would pass on the street without concern, but she knew this not to be true of this one.

Both the man and Elay stood in a silent stand off as they faced one another. She thought about slowly retreating, she thought of making it to the tree line and then seeking a place to hide, but she knew that despite the old man's appearance he would be quicker than the impression he gave. So they stood and waited.

After several minutes had passed it was the old man that made the first move. Slowly he reached up and pulled the cowl from his head. Anna immediately drew her short sword and crouched defensively. He moved slowly and with purpose as he allowed the hood to fall back. He was old, grey hair tumbled out of the hood and down to his shoulders. His face was lined with age and his skin bronzed and toughened from the exposure to the elements for many years. He smiled a crooked smile at her, his black unblinking eyes now fixed on hers. She held his gaze, not willing to look away for a moment. She concentrated on maintaining her magic that surrounded her and on the figure that stood before her.

"It does not have to be like this my child," the old man spoke eventually; "you must sense that I am more than my appearance suggests?" She chose not to respond, she just continued to hold his gaze. "This place reeks of ancient magic, it permeates everywhere, can you not smell it?" He did not wait for a reply. "This is a most dangerous place for one such as you to be, especially alone a defenceless. I think we should move from the Vales edge and talk further as I know that there are things that you wish to tell me." He made a small shuffle

160

towards Elay, she, despite her promise to herself, took a step back. He stopped and sighed heavily, "I have no more times for games Elf, I tried to be civil and polite but you have shown me nothing of the same. Let's move this to the next level." She braced herself ready for the attack that she was sure was coming. The old man did not advance as she believed he would, he simply pursed his lips together and gave the faintest short blow. Immediately her blue magic flickered and then disappeared.

"Now we can talk" he hissed.

CHAPTER
10

Amador made great haste as he left the assembled party as they readied themselves to go off in search for Sam. He had foreseen the safe arrival of Sam at the Vale and even knew of the deception from Elay to her father. Sam would be safe for now, safe until he ventured in to the Vale. Once inside he knew that there was not much that anyone could do for him. This would be his time to stand alone and he prayed inwardly that he would emerge from the Witches domain unscathed. He had to ensure that the events that he had put into motion were not in vein, he needed to make sure that the many sacrifices that would surely have to be made before the end was reached were worth it, no matter how devastating each would be.

He had not intended to leave when he did; he was able to see a lot of what is yet to come to pass, as his use of his magic enabled this, but he could not see everything. He had no insight into the machinations that went on in the world of faerie as this world was closed to all but those who dwelled within, however it was when he was inside the Echenor that he discovered something that unnerved him greatly.

He knew that with the aid of the Orloc in the hands of Sam, it enable them safe passage through, but the Orloc had not flared to life until several minutes after they entered the Echenor mists. Without the magic contained within the orb it should have been impassable for any of them. It was true that Sam had entered Silverdale through the pass created by Tamar on his arrival; however, this is where all the Elves, which ventured out, crossed over. It was the place that the Echenor did not fully reach to and Elven magic still enabled sufficient protection for safe passage. They had traversed through the centre of the Mists; this should not have been possible without the Orloc. There was only one explanation, as much as he wished not to be so, the Echenor was failing. This had only happened a few times before in documented history. It was said that the Echenor would falter should the balance of light and dark in the land of Invetia alter sufficiently enough to tip the scale one way or another. This is why the Echenor existed in the first place. It was a way retaining the evil in the land to keep the balance stable, but also ensured that no harm could be caused as the mists held its captives secure. The only thing that could have caused such a shift in the balance would have been the evil that grew in Varek and the return of Molgoran and the amassing of the armies that he orchestrated. "Unless," he thought," there was even more at Varek that he was yet to learn of." Until Sam could utilise the power of the Orloc, until he could find a way to bring alive the true magic of his father, then the scales would be tipped in darkness's favour. Should the Echenor fail then the whole of the Elven nation would stand within the open jaws of its impending death. With the Elves destroyed, Invetia would soon follow. Without the magic that Elves brought to sustain the land, it would fail disease and rot. Without the Elves the balance would never recover.

He had been a fool; he admonished himself as he ran. He had misjudged the time that they had, misjudged the degree of peril that Invetia faced and his actions would cost many lives.

He liberated a horse from a local farmland that he passed along the way. With the full intention of returning the animal he climbed up and dug in his heels. The horse responded immediately and lurched forward. He ran the horse to near exhaustion for two solid days, only resting when the horse

163

showed signs of collapse. He had to see for himself the army, which must by now have mobilised, and started its long march to Silverdale. He had to find some way of slowing its advance; he had to find a way to buy more time for the races of Men, Dwarves, Elves, Trolls, and every other force, to organise and prepare, in order that they could stand against the might of Molgoran's army. Most of all he needed to ensure that Sam had time to fulfil the destiny that had been set out before him.

The land grew steadily darker the closer he got to Varek. He could already see the mountain peaks in the distance and the permanent storm clouds that clung to the plains like a blanket of death. He was several miles off but could smell the acrid stench of sewage, iron, decay and all manner of other unpleasant smells. He brought his horse to a stop at the bottom of a muddied path that led up to a small rise. "I'll walk from here, take yourself back home" he whispered to his companion. He gave the horse a rough slap on its behind and watched it trudge away until it was out of sight.

He brought up his magic then, just a small amount but enough to make him as one with the colourings of the land around him, just sufficient that he could remain unseen to anyone passing. It would not be a good idea to be spotted out here, alone.

He made short work of the incline and he gained the top quickly. The sight that greeted him caused him to catch his breath. The land below was open fields and grassland that stretched all the way to the Varek Mountains that stood two miles north from his position., but he saw no grassland or fields as he should have, what he saw was a shadow as black as pitch that filled the land as far back as the huge fires that burned at the foot of the mountains ahead; furthermore, this shadow of darkness was moving!

He began to stare harder into the gloom and soon realised that he was looking at rows upon rows of Goblin, Gnome, Kobold and every other imaginable nightmare that had ever walked Invetia's soil. There were bigger monstrosities that he had no name for; some so big they threatened to crush their brethren with each step they took. Most walked on two legs, some

164

walked on four. Onwards they poured, staining the entire plains of Varek with their mass and noise. Howls and shouts echoed across to where he watched. Screams and roars filled the air with a cacophony of rage. All of it heading directly for him. He estimated at least eighty-thousand strong, possibly more. Not the un-organised rabble that Oldair had called them, but an army that marched in rank and file, an army that appeared well drilled and precise.

He tried to see past the seemingly endless lines of bodies, he tried to see for any sign of the puppet master, Molgoran, but nothing appeared. There was not much that he could do here alone. He needed to ensure that the collective armies that would against this foe were prepared for what marched their way. The meeting at Silverdale had finished inconclusively. He knew the Elves would stand ready, they understood the situation better than most. They had the security of the Echenor to stand behind after all, or so they still thought. But he knew that Thealine would send his armies to the East at a moment's notice. Oldair had not been so committed. He still failed to see that any attack would be able to breach the walls of Varon. He had agreed that he would send out scouts to assess the danger but would not agree to any alliance with the Elves in the defence of Invetia. He would "Take stock of the situation and act accordingly" as he had put it. Bannock had been even more aloof. He would ensure that it was brought up at the next Dwarvian high council meeting, which was still a week away. He would send no scouts or commit any of his people. It was only on Greston's insistence that he was permitted to go with Amador's party and only because Bannock wanted to keep a watch on the others. Dwarves were paranoid that the other races would form an alliance against them in their absence, and Bannock was no exception.

Finally the Trolls did what Trolls did. They listened, they considered and they returned home. No committal, no opinion, no emotion. Amador had expected this, Trolls would not be cajoled to act, they would or they wouldn't, simple as that. Kalt was permitted to stay in some reverence to Amador for whom

165

they regarded as highly as one of their own kind. "So, this is what it has come to," he thought darkly to himself.

Time was pressing, he could not wait here any longer and there was nothing that he could do. Sam would be in need of his help and after all, Sam was the one thing that could change the course of the battles ahead. Should he however have succumbed to Graflon's will, then all would be for nothing. He cast the thought from his mind, unwilling to think of failure. He stared at the advancing army below. If he could not fight them on his own he could slow its progress, even for a few hours he thought. He edged back down the muddied path until halfway. He stood as if frozen his face contorted with concentration and focus, his eyes closed. He began to imagine a Scorpion, a black sinister Scorpion with an oversized sting. He imagined how it looked, how it hissed, how its legs would skitter and click as it ran and the speed of its movements. He imagined blood red eyes that reflected danger and certain death. Then, with his image as he wanted, he imagined it to be one-hundred feet tall, massive and destructive. His hands weaved and circled as he built the image for several minutes, his eyes closed and his brow sweating from the exertion of the magic required. Once satisfied he opened his eyes and there it stood towering above him, hissing and clicking as stood awaiting his command. An illusion of course, but real enough to test the resolve of the approaching army below. With a flick of his hand he sent the Scorpion skittering over the hill and down into the plains of Varek. He did not wait to see the result, he was already running before his creation had reached the top of the rise, but he heard the screams and shouts for a long while after and wished that he had had time to stay and watch.

"Do you know who I am?" The voice commanded. Sam couldn't answer even if he wanted to he was still unable to make a sound. "I know who you are, I know all about you Sam Krelyn. I know why you are here, I know where you come from and I know what you carry or should I say carried," the Witch amended.

166

Sam again tried to break the invisible chains that rendered him motionless. Panic swept through him, she had found the Orloc, she had taken the Orloc! Sensing his dread she continued. Her voice soft and steady but edged with steel.

"You did not surely believe I would just allow you to walk into my home, take what you wanted and walk out again did you?" she asked. She was moving as she spoke, he could hear her voice change direction as he lay still. "You also did not think that I would not take advantage of your current.....incapacity to remove that which I found desirable?" She seemed to wait for his response. "Ah forgive me, I have so few visitors these days that I can often forget my manners, you may speak child."

Sam let out an audible gasp as he felt the shackles fall away from his throat. He did not speak, he lay there trying to collect his thoughts and steady his nerves.

"It seems that it was not worth my time to cast you mute as you now have the capacity to speak and yet chose silence. Perhaps I will take your voice away permanently as clearly you have no use for it."

"NO" Sam shouted in response. "Please don't. I need to talk with you." He couldn't hide the fear from his voice, but hoped she would listen.

"Very well, I will let you keep it, until I change my mind that is. What about your sight, do you require my generosity to grant you that back?" She was toying with him now, but he played along.

"Thank you, I would".

His eyes immediately snapped open. Although the Vale was dark and filled with shade, it still took a while for his eyes to adjust to the change. He blinked repeatedly in an attempt to restore his vision. He could see that he was in a clearing. No sky was visible overhead as the tree branches tightly entwined and blocked what little light there was. It had the feel of a tomb, dark cold and dead. He could not see the Witch.

"You may as well feel the full extent of my kindness, after all I do not expect that you will be running off from me," she scoffed. With these words barely out of her mouth Sam was released from his chains and was able to move again.

"Gather your bearings child, I am in no rush." Her voice sounded from behind him, but he was stiff from having lain on the cold earth for so long so could not turn to her. He gingerly began to move fingers and toes and felt the rush of blood to where he was previously numb. He waited a while until he was sure that all was working as it should be then propped himself up on his elbows and finally to a sitting position. He rubbed his legs, partly in an effort to get his circulation going and partly to stall for time. He needed to heed Elay's warning that the Witch would try to trick him and claim him. She was not to be trusted and he must have his wits about him.

"Better?" the voice enquired in mock concern.

Sam did not miss the falseness of the question, "Much, thank you." He thought it best to go along with the Witch.

"Say my name child" She suddenly spat; he was still unable to see where she was speaking from. "I have such few visitors, as I have said and it is nice to hear my name spoken from time to time."

"Graflon, your name is Graflon" he responded. "I am sorry if you are lonely, but I will stay and talk..."

"SILENCE" she screamed, "I dare you to pity me again boy and I will take your life's breath away in an instance!" Sam winced at the rebuke.

"I meant no offence, I apologies if I have caused any." She did not respond for an age. Sam waited for the impending strike that would snuff out his life, but it never came. Finally she spoke again. "Manners Graflon, manners," she scolded herself. "As I have said, sometimes I forget my manners; you must be hungry and thirsty let me satisfy both." With that a loaded plate of meat, cheese and mixed nuts appeared at his side along with an ice cold pitcher of ale and glass. He was hungry, it could have been days since he last ate and although he was on his guard for treachery he grabbed at the food and drink as he found he was suddenly famished.

Throughout the whole time he ate she did not speak nor did she appear to him. Sam had tried to gather in his surroundings as he consumed the fare, looking for any obvious escape routes or

168

clues as to what the Witches intentions were, but he soon realised that it was futile. Graflon, he had been told, was as ancient as the land of Invetia itself. You did not get to live that long without being cunning and smart. He felt, just by his first encounter with her voice that she had both in abundance. He dismissed the chances of escape quickly. This was her domain, she was all powerful within the Vale and she would have no trouble finding him within. He also admitted to himself that he could wander the Skrill for the remainder of his life and never find his way out again. If he were to get through this he would have to be more cunning and smarter than the Witch. He would have to find some chink in her armour and exploit it. He would have to be careful not to underestimate her. Whilst she was sure to have conceitedness as she was the dominant force, she was not stupid either, as he had mused before; you didn't survive as long as her without being smart.

As he picked at the meal before him his thoughts turned to the Orloc. He had checked his pocket where it had been when readjusting his seated position and found it gone. He had no idea where the Witch had placed it or how he was to retrieve it but he would have to find a way soon for without the Orloc there was no point to his being in Invetia. He needed to remain calm and wait for any opportunity that presented itself. He had not imagined for a moment that it would ever have been straight forward; however, he had not expected to have been taken captive and the Orloc stolen from him. Could she even use the Orloc? "Don't panic Sam, listen and be aware but keep calm, an opportunity will come eventually," he repeatedly told himself.

He pushed his plate away satisfied and full. He drained the final drops of ale from his cup and waited.
"Refreshed, I trust?" Came the familiar hushed voice. Sam looked up to find her standing before him. It took him by surprise as he had heard no sound, seen no movement, yet here stood the Witch of the Vale. He stared at her. She was both terrible and beautiful at the same time. Long shining red hair

169

disappeared past her slender shoulders, her face white as ash but unblemished and pure. Her pronounced cheek bones and rose coloured lips all added to her beauty. Her eyes were emerald green that glittered bright and dazzling. She stood six feet tall and her body was lithe and athletic. She wore a figure hugging white dress that hung to the ground and fanned out behind her. She was quite possibly the most beautiful women he had ever seen, and yet there was more. The more he stared at her the more he began to see the hard edges to her features, the iron beneath her silk exterior. It was as if he could sense the lies, corruption and power oozing through her. She was a thing of beauty, that was undeniable but also a thing of deadly intent. It appeared that should she want you dead she would merely think it and it would be so. Sam shivered at thought.

"I have many forms," she continued, "I am rather fond of this one, however, maybe this would be more to your liking?" In an instant she had changed, it was now Anna that stood before Sam. He recoiled in horror. It was Anna's face, Anna's body that he saw, but the eyes were Graflon's. She shifted again. It was Elay this time. She knelt in front of him; cloths tattered and covered in blood. She was cradling a man; he could not see his face and was crying. "Why Sam, why would you allow this to happen she sobbed?" Sam called her name, but in an instant she was gone. The wind began to blow hard through the Vale as the images became faster and faster. It changed again, Jane Fielding from his old life now stood in place looking at him with distain. "You could have had me," she whispered. The eyes still burned emerald green. He was on his and knees now, trying to take in all the appearances that came thick and fast, overloading his mind with images and emotions. People from his past flew at him in a myriad of forms, some recent, some from years ago and some he failed to recognise. Ben appeared to him "You should have kept her safe!" he shouted. "She is my sister!" it screamed at him. He shrunk away from the rebuke. All the time the eyes burned with a green fire. The wind howled in rage as twigs and debris spun around the clearing in dust storms. The dust blew at his face causing him to close his eyes against the barrage of dirt and grit that peppered him. Then in an instant it went still. The wind fell silent and nothing moved. He rubbed at his eyes then opened them to find his mother standing before him! He yelled at the apparition through tears that run down his dirt streaked face. "Stop it Witch, stop it!" But his mother remained. This appearance was different he thought as he squinted through the gloom, her eyes were brown, as they should be, it really was his mother!

He knelt staring at the sight before him, his breath coming in short, heavy pants, unwilling to accept what it was he was staring at. His mother returned his stare. Her face was sorrowful, it was as if she were about to cry, and then, she did. She made no sound, the tears streamed down her face.

"I am so sorry," her voice was barely audible as she spoke the words. "You were always mine. From the day I first I held you in my arms, to the final day when you held me in yours. You were always my son." She wiped away the tears from her face and brushed away a few errant hairs that hung in front of her eyes. "He gave you life and gave me mine back, and you have been loved every second of everyday ever since" He didn't understand the words that he was hearing but he ached at the sadness and at the sincerity that each word evoked within him. "Please understand" she implored him now, "I did what I had to, I did what I thought was right for us both. You were never my compromise, you were my everything." Then the vision of his mother shimmered and grew dim until she had been replaced by the Witch. Sam felt as if the world had opened beneath him, he felt himself falling in a wash of emotion and pain, sadness and grief. At that moment he wished the earth had swallowed him whole.

"Well, wasn't that emotional," she mocked, "You sorrowful little..." He did not let her speak another word; he paid no heed to the danger he would be in, as the anger and rage took over him, he was on his feet in an instance reaching for her throat. At that moment he would have gladly strangled her until dead. But he didn't, he couldn't. With a flick of her hand he was again frozen in place. His outstretched fingers only inches from her neck.

Her laughter filled the Vale. "Such a temper," he heard her spit the words out, "what would your mother say?" He struggled anew, incensed with the Witch. His could feel his face burn with rage, but she held him fast. "Time you had another nap my child; you have had an emotional day." She laughed again and then the world went black.

He slept poorly. It was not a natural sleep from tiredness or exhaustion; it was forced and added none of the usual refreshments a normal sleep did. He awoke to find himself back on the floor of the forest. His body was cramped and cold from his slumber and he stretched to try and relieve its aches. He was thankful that he was able to move and no longer held still by Graflon's magic. He was still in the clearing as before, but candles had been lit around its edges which did little more than cast a sinister glow over the encampment.

He became aware of her sitting in the place where the candle light was weakest. She sat in a rocking chair that creaked with each movement as she slowly swayed, her green eyes studying his every move. He tried to ignore her whilst he brought himself fully awake. The anger and rage that he had felt earlier had abated and he was calm. He had been foolish he knew to react as he did. She might have killed him. He did not think that she would have given it a second thought but he was still alive and that was reason enough to be grateful. He would not allow her to control him like that again, whatever tricks she employed to provoke a reaction. He promised himself that he would not allow her to manipulate a response.

"The child awakes, has its temper rescinded?" She chided from the darkness.

"It has and I am sorry for my earlier actions, it will not happen again Graflon." He did his best to seem sincere.

"Pity, I liked you rather more as an angry child, you were so much more... interesting." She chuckled lightly to herself and rocked the chair anew.

He sat and listened to the period of silence that, other than continuous creak of the chair, ensued. He thought about his next move. He had not been very successful at establishing anything since being taken hostage by the Witch. He was no closer to understanding what he was meant to do or what he was looking for. He didn't even know how long he had been here.

It was then that he remembered the opaque stone that Elay had given him. Upon the third day of passing the stone would glow blue. He wasn't even sure if he still had it upon him, after all, the Witch had taken the Orloc, would she not have taken this as well? He shuffled himself to a sitting position and began to fiddle as if to straighten his clothing. He let his hand drop to his trouser pocket and he felt the smooth outline of the stone tucked within. Graflon watched him with a muted interest as he did so. It appeared the Witch had found the Orloc as she knew he would be carrying it, but didn't bother to check for anything else, after all why should she? She was master of the Vale and nothing that he may also carry would have been of interest to her he surmised.

"Lost something?" the voice from the shadow enquired in feigned concern. He met her gaze square on, "Nope," he nonchalantly replied, "I have all that I need thank you." He could see in her face, for the briefest of moments, the confusion his replied evoked. He knew at this point that maybe he had the forming of a plan.

"Good, then all is as it should be," she quipped.

He let the silence between them carry on for a good while. He sensed that she had expected him to talk. He sensed her growing impatience, but he would hold his tongue until he felt the moment right.

She fumed silently, he should have been begging her to explain the visions he saw yesterday, he should be beside himself with the loss of the yellow Orb, and yet he seemed indifferent to all of it! She had known of his coming for many years, enough time to plan how she would orchestrate his stay. She would make him endure her until she was ready to either kill him or release him. Either way she would never tell of the secrets that she knew, never would she divulge the information that Ceriphan had imparted to her all those many years ago. She would have, once upon a time, she would have done anything for him, but he spurned her, he turned her away and made her feel foolish and she would see that he would suffer the consequence of his actions. He was dead and turned to dust, but she now had his son, his heir. If she could not deliver retribution to him, then his son would be the next best thing. She had savoured the prospect of doing so ever since their final meeting, ever since she begged him to stay within the Vale with her by his side, but he refused. She tried to trick him, she tried to hurt him, but his magic was to strong. He made her take the instructions to pass to Sam. He made her act against her will and she hated him for that. Now she had the boy and she hated him as well. But something was not right; he acted as if he couldn't care less what happened? She could not bear the thought that he was not intimidated by her since he had woken. She sensed no other presence in the Vale; he was alone and at her mercy but showed little concern. She tested for deception but found none. She even felt in her robe for the outline of the strange yellow Orb she had taken from him and found it to be securely in place. "Why then does he act this way, why?" she screamed to herself.

Sam watched her from out of the corner of his eye. She seemed serine and as if she had all the time in world, but he saw deeper than that. She was troubled, troubled by Sam's sudden disinterest in her. This was exactly what he had hoped for. She had been here for as long as Invetia. For all that time she had ruled over the Vale with no challenge to her power. Amador had told him that very few, if any could stand against her within the confines of her home and she knew this. He also knew that she was lonely, she had mentioned it several times that she never got visitors, and no one ever ventured into the Vale for fear of her, for fear of their lives. She exploded when he had mentioned previously that she may be lonely. She had been quick to show her true colours and her rage, but also her vulnerability. Her arrogance at her unequalled power, her years of solitude and her lack of contact with the outside world would be the chink in her armour he was looking for. He had had time to think about how best to exploit it. She was aware that he would be coming to see her for Ceriphan had told her so. She was also charged with imparting information to Sam on his arrival, something he imagined she would be less than happy to do, after all, she was Mistress of the Vale and no one could tell her what to do and therefore it stood to reason that this may be something she now chose not to do, well not intentionally anyway he thought.

She still terrified him but he pushed that emotion down as far as he could. If he was to survive the Vale Witch and get the information he needed he had to be focussed and clear, fear would simply cloud any efforts that he made. So he sat on the ground and waited. His efforts were soon rewarded. The Witch broke the silence first, unable to contain herself any longer; "Are you not curious about the images that I showed you yesterday?" She made the enquiry so matter of fact that he had to try and stop himself from smiling.

"I assumed you would tell me when you so wished Graflon. I assumed you were demonstrating your power to me. Not that I needed the point proven, after all you are the Witch of the Vale, oldest and maybe the most powerful being in Invetia." he responded. She cocked her to one side; "Maybe the strongest?" She questioned trying to keep the annoyance from her voice, "why would you say 'maybe' child do you know of another that could challenge me?"

"No certainly not," he quickly replied. She began to smile, "No one at all that could challenge you within the Vale, but I meant outside of its borders," he kept his gaze firmly on the dirt in front of him, "I meant there are obviously some, or so I have been told that would be your match outside of the Skrill." He saw her lean forward and begin to shake. She gripped the arms of her rocking chair so tight that she was in danger of ripping them off. To her credit she kept her voice steady despite the immense rage that was building within. "Who are these 'some' of whom you speak of? Tell me," she demanded. Sam looked up at her and feigned an apologetic face,

"I know not of their names Graflon, I just heard that there are many Demons that walk the land of Invetia, more now that Molgoran has returned. I was told; clearly incorrectly that there are a few that would be your match as would Molgoran I would guess. Now that he has returned he would be the dominant force in the world, but forgive me Graflon as you know I haven't been here long and am yet to understand the ways of the land." He could almost see the smoke rising of her body; she was incensed and could no longer hide it. Despite everything he had told himself he felt his body cower away from her. She was on her feet now, the chair thrown backwards. She had turned dark with the anger that consumed her. Just her eyes retained their colour and they glowed bright and dangerous. She began to scream so loudly in a language that he didn't understand. He was afraid but did his best to hide it. He watched as she stalked back and forth across the clearing; yellow flames engulfed her hands as she screamed her rage. She sent bolts of flame into the air unable to control her anger.

It was then he heard the voice, quiet at first but growing louder in his mind. *"Use the Orloc."* it said. He looked around, but found no one. Was it Amador, had he arrived as promised? *"All is not as it seems. Pull forth the Orloc and command the Witch as your own."* Confusion gripped him, the Witch still wheeled around the clearing, trees ablaze from her fiery touch and thick smoke filled the air. "Who are you?" he shouted, "She has the Orloc, and I cannot use it."

"All is not as it seems," the voice repeated, *"use it and command the Witch."*

He reached down instinctively to the Opaque stone that Elay had given him and pulled it from his pocket. To his astonishment it glowed bright amber, not blue. He opened his hand and gazed upon the Orloc in his out stretched palm. "How... I don't...." he did not know what was happening. *"You did not think that I would leave you unprotected did you?"* The voice continued. *" I have hold of you know, bring the Witch to bear."*

176

She sensed something was wrong immediately. She did not
wait to find out what. She turned to where Sam sat and sent the
yellow fire burning into his seated shadow. It exploded upon
impact illuminating the entire clearing and sending a shower of
golden embers into the sky. The smoke from her attack hung
heavy in the air. She could not wait for it to clear and with the
slightest blow from her lips it dissipated immediately. What
greeted her was not the ruined from of the boy as she had
expected, but instead he stood facing her, his arm bathed in an
amber glow.

Before she could respond he set the amber fire upon her. It
struck with a speed she did believe possible. She felt herself
rise up several feet in the air and remained aloft encased in an
amber cocoon. She screamed her fury and sent her fire out at
all angles, desperately trying to break free, but nothing broke
the magic's hold. She shifted shape, first making herself ten
times her size in an effort to burst the walls apart. When this
failed she made herself as small as a fly, but again the magic
that held her, changed to match her form. She could see the boy
in the clearing, his arm held out in front of him, commanding
the power that imprisoned her. "Nooooooo", she screamed,
"this is not possible". She had taken the Orb from him when he
entered the Vale. It was impossible that he had stolen it back
from her. She frantically reached into her robe and brought
forth the Orb but to her horror, all she held was a stone that
was glowing blue! She looked again at the boy fixing him with
a stare that would kill a man instantly, but he simply stared
back. It was then she noticed the shadow behind him that held
his shoulders steady and the realisation as to what had
happened flooded over her.

He was riddled with fear but maintained the Orloc's magic. He
still didn't know how he was able to command it or what had
made it answer his call, but it had once again done so in the
time of his greatest need. He stared at the Witch suspended in
her amber prison, but her eyes did not meet his. It was as if she
was staring passed him, behind him. He risked a quick glance

round but saw nothing. Fearing she was attempting to trick him, he swiftly restored his stare upon her.

"She will now tell you all you need to know, she is yours to command," the voice sounded in his head again, *"She is compelled to tell you. I have made it so."* Sam struggled to maintain his concentration on his captive. "Who are you?" he pressed.

"I am but an echo of man that once was, I am a memory left in this place to protect the one that needed it most, and that someone is you Sam. I am the remnants of the magic I once commanded, a magic that is now your legacy to master, I am Ceriphan Krylen. I left my magic here in the hope that one day you would find your path to the Witch, the only place that my instructions were safe, and retrieve them as foretold. I wish I could tell you the instructions myself but the magic does not allow sufficient time for this, but know that although Graflon may speak the words, they are words of my making. I will not speak with you again my son in this life, but my magic will remain to guide and protect you until your time with Graflon has passed. I love you my son."

Then, he was gone, Sam couldn't explain how he knew, he just knew. He didn't know why, but he felt no sadness, he, if anything had found courage rather than sorrow.

He had planned to enrage the Witch to provoke an opportunity to gain the Orloc back, but he had had it all along. Ceriphan had left strands of his magic behind for his protection. It must have happened on his final visit to Graflon he thought, and it lay dormant until today, until the need arose. He remembered back to his thought as he entered the Skrill that this was possibly the first time in his life that he was truly alone and unprotected, he smiled at how little he still knew.

CHAPTER

11

The remainder of their journey passed without incident. The days remained iron clad, but bearable. Anna found that conversation was sparse due in part to the Demon attack and the group being extra cautious at every turn. She could feel the uneasiness that hung over them, not knowing if the next attack was just around the corner. The only one that showed no signs of concern was Kalt. The big Troll remained expressionless. His massive frame covered the ground with ease, never slowing or faltering. When the group rested and took on food and water he did neither. He preferred to stand away from the rest of the party. He would stand almost statuesque and gaze across the land, at what, she did not know.

She asked Evaine about the Trolls aloofness as they sat and ate. He took the time to explain to her, that in Invetia's violent past, Trolls had sided with the forces of darkness. They had stood with the Gnomes and Goblin armies and fought against the Elves and Men. Irrespective of how much time had passed since, it was a dishonour that every Troll still carried with them to this day. The sins of their forefathers passed from father to son and would do so until an opportunity to redeem the wrongs of the past were presented. Kalt did not want to feel a part of the group as he bore the guilt of his people, he did not feel had earned the right to do so. Evaine explained that they were a tribal people that consisted of many communities as oppose to a congregation of people that lived in cities such as Men and Dwarves did. Each community had a leader that in turn was governed by a high command that was made up of the strongest and most respected collective of Trolls from each of the recognised communities. These would resolve disputes and set the laws to ensure that all could coexist as peacefully and productively as possible. He was quick to point out however that the Trolls were by nature a warring people. They lived by hard rules and harder punishments for transgressions. Disputes and fighting between communities was common and death was the way of life, however, they were not a barbaric people as many thought. If threatened the communities were sworn to protect each other. They made formidable warriors as they possessed both huge physical strength and strength in numbers.

The whole of the Westland was populated with scattered communities of thousands of Trolls and they were seldom disturbed. It was only recently that trade agreements had been set up between the Trolls and other races. Their fighting skills were legendary and they had helped train the Dwarvian army. They had also perfected many salves that could cure what even Elven magic struggled to and found that they could trade this with Silverdale. In return the Elves showed them how better to farm and nurture the land, grow food and raise livestock. It was early days, but the Trolls were slowly re-establishing themselves as a vital part of Invetia's future.
"But will they come to aid the races when the need arrives?" Anna asked. He thought about the question before answering. "Despite the strides that they have taken to establish dialogue, the one constant is that they remained unpredictable," he replied solemnly, "if they feel that this is the opportunity to rid them of the dishonour they have carried for so long, then

maybe, however if they feel by getting involved could be detrimental to their race then they will simply stay at home." He sighed. "It is the way of the world, if the risk outweighed the benefit then, whatever was right and whatever was wrong become irrelevant." He looked at her, "Is it different in your world mistress Anna?" he enquired.

"No" she replied. "Half the world is in famine while the other half have so much they discard enough to feed them twice over. We spend more resources on finding better ways of killing each other than we do on medicines and research. We have polluted our world so much that we can see our own extinction and yet we do not stop." She smiled. "Sounds like a barrel of laughs doesn't it?" she joked with him.

"It would appear that we are not that much different, it seems as though the struggles that you face are the same as we face here."

"Maybe," she replied, "but change can come Evaine. It is a slow process, but it can come." She slapped him playfully on his leg as she rose and strode off to refill her empty glass. He stared after her with admiration. Yet again she had proven to be wiser than her years.

They made short work of packing away the remaining provisions and were soon repeating the drudgery that the trek exuded. The rain had made a less than surprising return and the wind, as if not to be outdone, blew colder and harder. Evaine had sent a contingent of Ichbaru ahead to ensure safe passage and Kalt had fallen into his now accustom position of guarding the rear of the group as they slowly but steadily advanced towards the Vale. Anna had begun to notice the subtle differences that the landscape had taken on as they got closer to the domain of the Witch. Things were dead, that's the only way she could describe it. The grasses had browned, the trees stood bereft of colour or leaves, the sporadic bushes that grew along the jutted trail that they traversed were nothing more than a collection of prickles and thorns. They grew in twisted gnarled shapes as if created by some demonic force. The birds did not venture into this part of the world either; the

181

sky was bereft of anything other than the usual grey blanket that permanently hung low and heavy across the colourless landscape. "Well," Anna stated as she took in her surroundings, "if I wasn't depressed before, I certainly am now." No one responded to her comment and so she joined them in their silent vigil.

They walked in silence for several more miles until they crested the rise of a small hill and there, just half a mile off, lay the Vale. Anna knew it be so immediately. It was in a hollow which enabled her to see the size of it. Miles and miles of densely populated, half dead trees encased in darkness. It was like a giant stain upon the world. Smog and mists clung low to the hollow floor which crept and flowed through the forest surround like a silent wraith keeping watch. The stench of death and decay was almost unbearable, even at this distance and Anna covered her face with her sleeve in response. "Was Sam within that tomb?" she thought to herself. She felt afraid for him. Just to look upon the Vale gave her a bad enough feeling, but she could not imagine being within it. Breathing its fouled air and walking is rotted ground. Despite all of that though she prayed that he was inside, if he were, that meant he was still alive. Amador would not allow him to come to any harm, she tried to reassure herself.

Evaine walked back towards her, his head lowered and cloaked pulled tightly around him. She stood where she was and waited his arrival. As she waited she felt the massive frame of Kalt appear beside her.

"We will wait here," Evaine called from a few paces off, "I have sent the guards down to scout the edges of the Vale to look for any signs of our companions. As soon as I have their report we will make our next move. It is not wise to be too close to the Witches home without being invited." he finished.

The three of them waited for Ichbaru to return in silence. Kalt, impassive and staring at the Vale below, Evaine paced restlessly and Anna sat with her back to the smouldering pit, trying to remember to breathe through her mouth to avoid the stench that came at her in waves.

They did not have to wait for long, as suddenly an Elven guard appeared in the distance, sprinting towards them.

"You must come quickly Lord Evaine," he shouted at them as he ran. Evaine was immediately running down towards the Vale in an instant. Kalt was at his side, his massive axe held in front of him as he ran. Anna was on her feet chasing after them, not quite sure what was happening.

"Is it Sam?" She heard Evaine demand of the guardsman as they ran. She held her breath for his response. "No my lord, it is the Princess, it is your sister!"

Evaine ran even quicker now, the confusion and concern etched across his face. It appeared that even Kalt was having trouble keeping pace with Elven Prince as he sprinted at lightning speed. Anna was left trailing, despite her fitness she could not keep up with the charging Evaine. "What on earth was Elay doing here?" she thought to herself as she ran, "and where was Sam?"

The returning guard stayed with her as she ran as a last minute order shouted by Evaine that the girl must be protected. She felt like a burden but was secretly pleased not to have been left alone in this place. They covered the ground in what seemed an instant, criss-crossed through a thicket of trees and skidded into the back of the massive Troll.

"Keep her back!" Evaine screamed, and she was immediately surrounded by five of the Elven guard. Not more than fifty feet ahead, she saw Elay on her knees with her back facing them. Standing in front of her was a dishevelled old man with wicked eyes. Evaine, Kalt and the remaining Ichbaru, stood in a crouch position as if ready to strike, weapons drawn which glinted in the dull half light of the afternoon haze.

"Come no further Elf or she will die," the old man hissed, "as you will never make it to me in time to save her, a single twist of my fingers and you will be carrying home her cold corpse." He grinned wickedly at the Elven Prince.

"If you touch one hair on her head Demon I will follow you to the ends of Invetia until you are dead. I will not stop until you are destroyed. You need to know this before you do anything rash. You cannot stop us all Demon, some of us will die, but not all, and then you will be cut in two and left for the wolves to feast upon." Evaine responded his voice edged with a danger that Anna had never heard before.

As he spoke the words, one of the Elven guards reached to his quiver to draw an arrow. Before he could even pull the arrow clear form its holder the Demon waved his crooked fingers and the guard fell dead in a crumpled heap. The others immediately raised their weapons, but Evaine screamed at them to hold their positions. The Ichbaru did as ordered. Kalt remained impassive, his eyes locked upon the old man, never faltering or blinking as he held its gaze.

"Let's make this more entertaining," the Demon spoke in a hushed dangerous tone. "Don't be rude, greet our guests." With a flick of his fingers Elay lurched up from her kneeling position and hung limp like puppet on a string. She slowly turned to face the group. Her head lolled to one side as she began to turn, her arms hung loose at her side and her legs bowed as she turned. Anna let out a wail, for when fully turned, they could see that her eyes were milky white. She looked as if dead. "She is mine to do as I please with Elven Prince," the Demon spat, "and if you truly want her unharmed you will do as I say, for if you choose not do so, she will die. Lower your weapons and place them on the floor," it demanded. Anna could feel the tension build as nobody moved. Suddenly Elay lurched upwards, her body now gone rigid and stretched. Her face contorted to the pain although she made no sound. "I get bored of waiting, do it now!" the Demon demanded. Evaine gave the order and slowly the Elven Prince and the Ichbaru laid their weapons upon the ground in front of them. Only Kalt remained, still holding his massive axe and not breaking his stare with the old man.

"Come, Kalt son of Kelphus, surely you would not want the death of a Princess to add to your peoples growing list of shame would you? Lower your weapon."

Kalt did not speak, he broke his stare to look briefly at Evaine who simply nodded, and then Kalt allowed the axe to drop from his hand with an audible thud as it hit the dirt.

"You have trained your pet well my Prince," the Demon mocked. "Now we are all getting along so well," the Demon continued, "bring me that girl". He pointed a crooked finger directly at Anna.

"You foul odious wretch, you tricked me! When I break free I will ensure that you die slow. Not slow by your standards but by mine. I will keep you just alive for years but everyday will be painful and unbearable, you will beg me for death but I will not grant it. I will devote the rest of my life to making you suffer and then suffer even more!" The Witch was screaming at him from within the amber glow that held her aloft and imprisoned. She was incensed to the point of hysteria. "I will bring everyone you have ever loved to my Vale and make you watch them die slowly as well. I will turn your insides out, but you will not die, you will feel pain that you cannot imagine." Graflon's once flawless features now gnarled and twisted in utter rage. She sent the green fire careening in all directions, but the magic that held her did not quiver, did not break and did not falter in anyway.

Sam watched her in silence. The Orloc pulsed in his hand and he felt the warmth from the Orb encase his whole body. It made no sound as the shaft of light that emanated from its centre to hold the Witch firm, lit up the clearing. He did not struggle to maintain the magic; it flowed freely from his hand. He had no doubt that the Witch would carry out all of her shouted threats. He had no doubt that she would make his life a life a living hell, but he had no intention of allowing her the opportunity to do so.

"She is yours to command," Ceriphan had told him. "She is compelled to answer all that you ask," he had also instructed. He would ask what he needed answered; he would then command the Witch to get him safely out of the Skrill and back to Elay. He would be quick and not give Graflon the chance to trick or deceive him, but first he would let her rant and rave until she was spent. Quite how long this would take he didn't know. So he sat in the yellow lit clearing and waited. This seemed to enrage her even further!

He did not know how much time had passed, it was difficult to have any gauge of time within the Skrill, but, after what he considered to be several hours, she finally had fallen silent, save for her heavy breathing from her considerable efforts to break free from the Orloc's magic.

He had listened to every possible way that she was going to make him suffer, every way in which she would cause him pain and misery. After a while he had managed to ignore the words that she spat at him and just waited for the Witch to tire. At first he had been unsure as to what he was doing. He often thought that he should abandon the answers that he sought and just run. She was terrifying at first, he watched as she twisted and contorted in an effort to break free and several times he was sure that she would eventually find the key to unlocking the magic that held her captive, but she didn't. She was as much a captive now as she was when the magic first encapsulated her. After a while his fear of the Witch diminished, he almost felt pity for her. She had been alone for all time, and was destined to remain so. None of her kind was left in the world and no one would even notice if she failed to exist. Nevertheless, she was dangerous and conniving and would not hesitate in making all of her threats a reality if he gave her the opportunity. He would need to keep his wits about him.

"Are you ready to talk, Graflon?" His words broke the silence that had ensued. She simply stared at him and curled her lip. "I think we need to get this over with so that I can leave you as I found you. I will not harm you Witch, I simply need answers." She let out a shrill laugh. "You couldn't harm me boy! I am the Witch of the Vale; I am of ancient magic and faerie blood. I gave life to this world and to all of its miscreants." She snarled as she began to feel the rage within her burn anew. "You are a boy, just a pathetic boy who plays with magic, you are nothing but a ..."

"SILENCE!" Sam commanded, suddenly angry. He was not prepared to sit through another of the Witches tantrums. To his surprise she immediately fell quiet.

"Let me ask again, are you ready to talk?"

"Ask," she whispered in response.

It was at this point that he realised that he hadn't actually thought about what to ask. He knew that the Witch had knowledge of what he must now do, where he must go but he also knew the Witch would be as vague as she could whilst answering. He would have to 'think carefully about how and what he asked,' he considered. After a short while he ventured his first question.

"How do I control the magic of the Orloc?" was his first offering.

"Touch magic to bring magic. The magic that you have within is latent and not yet strong enough to call forth its powers on your own." the Witch answered begrudgingly. He stood and considered her response not understanding her. She laughed quietly at seeing his confusion, "We will be here a very long time boy if you cannot even understand my answers, no matter how simple they are." She laughed again and then returned to silence. She was indeed compelled to answer his questions, but as to how she answered them was at her choosing. He knew he had to make his question less broad, less easy to evade with rhetoric or confusing statements.

"How will I gain the sufficient magic to use the Orb?" he pressed.

"By using the Orloc." she replied with a smile.

This was going nowhere. How could he use Ceriphan's magic if the only way to be able to use it was to use it! Confused, he paused again.

"How then do I control the magic now?" He started, "How have I called the magic forth previously if I am not sufficiently qualified?"

187

"Each time you have used the Orloc you have been in physical contact with magic bearers." came her response. He thought back to each time that he had brought forth the magic to command. First was when he was within the Echenor. The magic had come to him to protect and shield him from the spirits that dwelled within. It had flared when they grabbed at him and pulled him of track. Was this the physical connection? He had then used the Orb again when Elay and he had encountered the Demon in the woods. Elay had been holding his arm and Elay had Elven magic at her use. Also within the Skrill, he had been able to use the magic against the Witch as he did now. Ceriphan had come to him and even told him that he had 'hold of him'. This was the obvious physical presence required that had been present at each time he used the magic. He surmised that each time he was able to call forth the magic, the innate ability within him would grow until strong enough for him to use the Orloc unaided or untouched. Happy that he had managed to understand the answer given he pressed on.
"Where is it I need to go to fulfil my destiny?"
"Amongst the dead" came her reply. He thought at first that he had misheard her, but her sardonic smile that met his stare proved that he had heard her perfectly well.

"But beware son of Ceriphan that not all that you have been told is the full truth. The wanderer, Amador, would have you believe that you were sent to save the land of Invetia that you were the promised one, returned to save its people from a terrible evil and yet it is you that will bring the most suffering to its inhabitants. You will be the redeemer of the old world and a curse to the new. You will destroy the Elven nation and be instrumental in their survival."
He could not keep the confusion from his face. He knew the Witch was speaking truths, but he had no idea as to what she meant.
"Explain that," he commanded.
"Little child, I am not at liberty to repeat or explain. Whilst I am compelled to answer the questions truthfully, you cannot command anything more of me. I have fulfilled the

requirements of the question." She began to laugh loudly as she watched him desperately trying to decipher her answer and it took a long time before she had regained her composure and once more fell silent.

He took a while to regain his composure, "This was not as easy as he had thought it was going to be," he told himself. Whilst he believed that the Witch was telling him the truth it was so encased in double meanings and shadow that it was almost impossible to get clarity. He would have to persevere. The Orloc's magic continued to hold her fast and showed no signs of waning, so he could be patient. He had to outsmart the Witch of the Vale, he had to think of a question that she could not wriggle free from and answer without subterfuge, and he just had to think of it.

He remained quiet for a considerable time, considering his next move. Graflon continued to glare at him through the Amber haze that held her. She didn't like the silence and seem to get more agitated as the minutes slipped by. It was then he had an idea. He wouldn't ask about him, he would ask about her. He looked up to meet her gaze, "Do you like being lonely?" he casually enquired.

He saw her expression change as soon as the words had tumbled from his mouth. Her eyes narrowed to slits and she flushed. She held her tongue, but clearly was fighting a battle within to keep from screaming at him.

"I mean it must be awful being the last of your kind, locked away in this place with no one to talk with or command," he continued. "Tell me Graflon, what is it actually like to be lonely, after all you are compelled to answer my questions, so please let me know your answer." She was shaking with rage now, her body trembling with the utter hatred that she felt for him and the impertinence of his questioning. She wanted to kill him outright now. No delay or suffering as she had envisaged before, he needed to die immediately and be gone from her life. "I HATE YOU," she screamed, her breath coming in short, heavy gulps. "You dare to ask me such things; I will tear the tongue from your head. I hate everything about you and I will kill you as soon as I am free."She went on for some considerable time. He sat and watched waiting on the right moment. He waited through several more minutes of her screaming and screeching before raising his own voice to a shouted command.

"I compel you Witch to answer my question and you will do as I command."

"I HATE IT!" came her reply, "I HATE EVERY LIVING MINUTE OF IT. NO ONE TO RULE OVER, NO ONE TO SHARE MY DOMAIN WITH, NO MATE, AND EVERYDAY IS A LIVING HELL." To his immediate surprise she began to sob. Tears ran down her face as she broke down in front of him. She covered her face with her hands and sobbed louder. He suddenly felt sorrow for her. She was dangerous but alone, wicked but sorrowful. She was a paradox of emotions. He pressed her further, he didn't feel comfortable in doing so but he had to if he were to get the answers he needed.

"And when I am gone from this place Graflon, you will be alone again, never to be visited, never to be loved, how does that make you feel?"

"Hollow," came the tear filled reply. He struggled to keep his resolve. She was like a wounded Rattlesnake. If he went to help her, as he wanted to, she would surely bite and kill him for his troubles.

"Why do you torment me so?" she gasped.

"Tell me the answers to my questions and I will leave this place and never return, let me know what I need to do and I will be gone from the Vale forever," he replied, intent now on getting the answers he needed and getting out of the Witches domain as quick as possible. She took a moment to steady herself, then raised her face to meet his stare and replied in a voice laced with venom and warning.

"I will give you the answers you require child, I will tell you everything that I know and I will ensure that nothing is left out. Take what you came here for and then leave my home. But know this; I will then hold you to your word until the day you die. If you so much as ever pass the Vale again in your short lifetime I will kill you. If you ever step one foot in the shadow of the Skrill, I will kill you and if you ever should encounter me again, whether intended or not I will kill you." Her warning sent a chill down his spine and he knew her words to be true. "Agreed, I am listening." Sam felt a twinge of expectation pass through his body, or was it fear? He wasn't quite sure. He had come here for answers to his questions and now that they were about to be laid out before him, he couldn't help feeling that he was not going to like what she had to say.

Graflon's demeanour had changed back to the vision he had first encountered. She was once again a thing of beauty and devilment rolled into one although her appearance remained shadowed and ominous. From behind the amber haze she drew breath and then began to narrate what it was that he had come to learn.

"I will start from the beginning of your sorrowful little life. Whilst I was endowed with the secrets from Ceriphan, I was also given the memories of your life that the mage carried with him. It was not his wish I am sure that I be privy to the history of your existence but rather a useful side effect of the magic employed." Sam listened to her every word and kept his stare fully focussed on the Witch. She, in turn, stared back, never flinching. It was almost an unspoken competition to see who would break the hold first.

"You are not your mother's son, as her son died in childbirth, you were a replacement." The words struck him as if punched; he felt his stomach lurch and the blood drain from his face. He tried to allow the words to settle within him and the emotion to pass, but if anything it got worse as he considered the Witches opening statement. He immediately thought that she was lying, but quickly remembered that she was under the influence of the magic and had to speak the truth, but in contrast to her previous statements, this one was devoid of any double meaning or deception, this was cold and to the point. As he visibly struggled to contain his emotions the Witch of the Vale began to smile. She was going to enjoy this, so she continued.

"The Sario came to her when she returned home, child-less, and gave you to her. She was chosen, not because of her intelligence, beauty or wonderful motherly instincts, quite the opposite actually, she chose her because she was dull, unremarkable and broken. Ruern chose to give you to her because she was a grey life in a grey world, someone that the world would never notice and therefore remain innocuous. Her debility as a person and as a mother brought you together."

He felt his hand close around the Orloc so tightly that his knuckles went white. He, in that instance wanted to kill the Witch. He would squeeze the life out of her wretched form with the power of the Orb and make her pay for the words she spoke. It took every ounce of will power he had to pull himself away from the precipice, to recovery from the madness and the rage that threatened to engulf him and allow her to continue. Graflon watched him fight his silent battle from her prison and laughed quietly, it was getting better and better. Eventually he relaxed his grip on the Orloc and allowed the maelstrom of emotion to rescind. He kept his eyes locked on the ground ahead of him, not trusting himself to meet the Witches stare as he felt that this may tip the balance in madness's favour.

"Shall I continue," she mimicked a child's voice, "or do you want time to cry over mummy?"

"Just get on with it Witch," came his quietened reply.

"So it was that your fake mother took you as her own and lied to the world that you were her son, despite the truth that her real flesh and blood child laid cold, dead and forgotten. She managed to fool everyone with her story by exceptional deception and a little help from the Mage's magic, but she held on to further secrets, for she was told by the Sario that the day would come to pass when she would return to take you away. When the sands of time had expended sufficient grains you would be reclaimed by the life that you were destined to live." She paused sufficiently long enough to ensure that the pain of her words had not passed him by too quickly.

"The rest is as you remember; the Sario brought you into Invetia and your purpose explained. And here you are today, motherless, confused and alone." She gave out shriek of laughter, "Not quite the image one would imagine for the saviour of Invetia are you?"

He held his tongue and did not give the Witch the satisfaction of seeing the utter hopelessness that he felt. It was as if someone had reached inside and pulled out his innards. He knew what she was doing, he knew that she was trying to break him and destroy him. He wanted to know from her the journey ahead and not the history behind but she had seized the opportunity to damage him with the secrets of his past. He allowed the revelations of the Witches narrative to sink in, he allowed them freedom to twist his emotion, fill him with sorrow, then rage, then hopelessness. He did not fight the onset of every possible sentiment. He knew that this was necessary to move on, if in fact he could. He sat for a long time in silence; head bowed and worked through the images that the Witches words had brought to life in his head. Never once though did he feel anger for his mother's deception, never once did he ever consider his mother not to be his mother. In fact, he thought "So what?" What did it matter? He loved his mother as much now as he did before his tale had been told. Never once did he experience that his feelings or love for her diminished in any way at all. The actual realisation of this emotion grew bigger and bigger in his mind. The Witch had used this knowledge and words to break him and destroy him, but actually it began to make him stronger. It began to harden his resolve. Clearly, the role he was sent here to perform was important enough, that the one person he loved more than any other throughout his life specifically nurtured him and grew him into the person he was today in order that he may meet the challenge ahead. She had accepted him as her own despite her terrible loss and given him her love and affection, asking nothing in return. She had carried the burden of truth throughout his whole life but never wavered in her trust and belief in him. He began to feel the determination welling up and burning through him. The Witches words had not broken him as she had intended; they had made him stronger, more determined and prouder of his mother's sacrifice than ever before. To Graflon's utter shock he stood up, faced her square on and smiled at her.

"Thank you Graflon. You have given me the strength and courage to go forward and I am grateful for your words. Now let's talk about what I need to do now."

Her face screwed into a ball of confusion as she now reflected upon his words.

"Tell me about the Orloc and how I am supposed to use it first." he pressed, not allowing her to recover from her failed attack of words. Her eyes narrowed to slits as she considered her response.

"You do not use the Orloc; the Orloc uses you," came her eventual response, "as it is but a part of the magic that the Mage had gathered over his life. He managed to encapsulate this element into the Orb. It has the power to protect and destroy, but can only be wielded by you as you carry the bloodline of Ceriphan. Each time you use the magic it will shape you and become a bigger part of you. Eventually it will transfer all of the magic within into you and the Orloc will disappear altogether. Look at it now, does it appear smaller?"

He looked down towards the pulsing Orb within his hand and to his surprise it was smaller, much smaller. The continued use to hold the Witch incarcerated was speeding up the transfer from stone to user. He was becoming as one with the magic contained within its walls. He felt excited and scared at the thought that he was being changed and shaped, that something that he had never experienced before was soaking into the very fabric of who he was.

He returned his looks towards Graflon,

"You said that I relied upon the connection with other users to call forth its magic, will that be the case once the Orloc's magic has passed into me?"

"No" came her curt reply. His mind was racing now, a thousand questions cried silently to be answered.

"You said that I would both save and destroy the nation of Elves, how can this be?"

"The Orloc, until fully absorbed within your body, draws magic to it so that it may function. It takes a great deal of magic to call forth the powers locked within, more than you posses at present. The resulting effect is that the magic that is

194

entwined within the land of Invetia is depleted each time you use the power of the Orb. Other than me, whom am protected by the Skrill, the next most constant source of ancient magic that exists is the Echenor." He considered her statement for a moment, the Echenor housed the spirits of the Faerie creatures from Invetia's past, and it provided natural protection for Silverdale and the Elves within. If this should be weakened sufficiently then would that mean that the mists would fail and those held within let loose?

"Yes", she rasped, "you see now the dilemma. To save the land you must use the power of the Orloc, but to do so will put at risk the very people that you are trying to save! The mist will fail, those trapped within will scatter to the four corners of the world and be permitted to manifest unchecked. They will then, over the course of time, pose a greater danger to Invetia than has ever been seen before." He felt the revelation push down on him. This was a no win situation, he was doomed whatever he chose to do.

"There... is an alternative however." Her words cut through his thoughts. His head jerked up.

"Tell me Witch," he replied, desperately grabbing at any chance to avoid the paradox of the current choice.

"The Echenor also sustains life outside of its walls. Since it was created it has given the Elves an unnatural longevity, almost immortality as some perverse side effect. The magic that you leech away each time that you call forth the power can be replaced by your magic and Elven magic to rebuild and strengthen the weaknesses you cause; however, the price extracted will be to return the Elven people to a lifespan similar to that of men, maybe a little longer, maybe not," she mused, "I do not know for sure, but nevertheless, you can ensure that Invetia continues to be protected from the Demons of the mists, but the price will be the eventual life of every Elf. You will be the one that is both giver, and taker of lives, you will be the one responsible for the greatest devastation that the Elves have ever faced since the creation of time. You will be more destructive than any Demon that has ever crawled from the pits of the

Void." He felt his resolve weakening at her words, so pushed his immediate rush of emotions to one side as he was desperate now to collect all the information he required and to exit the Skrill as quick as possible. He could then consider the Witches words more rationally.

"How do I kill Molgoran?" he asked, "Will the power of the Orloc be sufficient to destroy him?"

She faltered for a moment, unsure if he were testing her, then her face couldn't mask the realisation that he did not know this either!

"I can tell you where to find Molgoran; I can also tell you that the death of Molgoran alone will not end the danger to Invetia." He studied her, she was not revealing everything, and there was deception in her eyes. "Molgoran possessed power equal to the Mage Ceriphan, but it was used for a very different purpose. It was able to grant him passage through the mists, as it had Ceriphan; however, it was also enable him to remove things from the mist as well. Molgoran was able to choose which of the dwellers within would best suit his plans and place them outside of the mists and into Invetia. The Demons he released were the most suitable to his needs. They have been trickling out for many years. Their numbers, whilst not great, are significant enough to long threaten Invetia after Molgoran's demise. You are simply replacing a problem with another. This is the way of Invetia; this is the way the balance remains. As for killing him, you must travel North East; eventually you will reach the Tillamus River. Follow the river north until you reach its wellspring. Pass through the door that is as rigid as stone but yielding to air and within you will find the one that you are looking for."

Finally he had gleamed all of the information that he was going to require. His head rushed with the amount of revelations that he had been made aware of, but he pushed these aside, as getting free from the Vale was now the most important thing. Rather a spoken thought as oppose to a question he considered

196

if the Elves knew of their potential sacrifice if locking the Echenor was the choice made.

"Some know," she answered his undirected question, "some are aware of the devastation you can bring, but only those of the royal bloodline are permitted such insights."

"Elay," he suddenly exclaimed.

"Ah yes, the Elven Princess that you have deeper feelings for....yes she knows, although she is rather preoccupied at the moment in trying to save her life against the Demon that is intent on killing her as we speak." She gave her familiar shrill laugh at seeing Sam's face turn to panic.

"Take me to her, take me now, I command you to take me to her Witch, I......"

"You cannot command anymore of me boy," she shrieked, "I have fulfilled my duty to answer your pathetic questions so that you may chase your worthless quest, but I am not required to do anymore, I suggest however that you run though as she tires and soon she will meet her demise of that I am convinced."

"Then if I am to go, you are coming with me" he shouted in response, "I will go to her with you imprisoned behind me, I am not ready to release you yet Graflon. I will take you out of the Skrill and to her; I will let the outside world see the fate of the Witch of the Vale."

She inwardly hated this more than he knew; she detested the outside world and only ventured out on rare occasions under a heavy cloak of magic so not to be sighted. The humiliation of being trapped by this pathetic child was too much to even contemplate.

"I hate you boy you know this to be true?" He nodded his response. "However, I will trust your word. I will take you to the edge of the Vale where you will release me from this hold. Once there you will be a scamper away from your beloved Elf Princess. I will not harm you as you leave, but I trust you remember my previous warning should I ever encounter you again?" He nodded again.

"Then think of where you entered my home, will yourself to be there, and it will be so."

He was sure that Graflon could not be trusted but he was out of options. He closed his eyes and remembered the first steps that he made into the Skrill. He wondered how long ago that had been, although the memory still burned fresh in his mind. As he did so he felt an ice cold blast of wind upon his face, when he opened his eyes his was standing just within the Skrill and looking out towards the rays of sunlight that permeated its edge.

"I have done as promised, now for you to return the trust," she spat at him. Despite all of his instincts screaming against it he released the Witch from the hold of the Orloc. He called upon the magic to be recalled into the Orb and it did so immediately. Graflon screamed in delight as she slowly drifted down until her feet touched the earth. Sam was gone by the time she had regained her footing, he had recalled the Orloc's magic and turned to run as hard as he could back towards the light of the world beyond.
"Goodbye son of Ceriphan, I will see you again of that I am sure and when I do, I will kill you!" she whispered after him. She smiled as she allowed herself to imagine the boy lying dead at her feet and then in an instant she had disappeared.

CHAPTER
12

Amador was running now a fast as he was able. He was still a mile from the Skrill, but could already smell the Demon magic thick in the air. Something had happened and he needed to get there as soon as possible. If Sam or any from their party had encountered a Demon that left such a strong stench in the air then they were in trouble. He cursed to himself as he ran; he was supposed to be their protector. For five days now he had been separated from those that left Silverdale with him, "Five days!" he berated himself. He was suppose to have been protecting Sam from his encounter with the Witch and he had failed to do so and now a danger just as ominous had been encountered and he was not there to help. Whilst it couldn't be helped, he considered, as he had to have assessed where and what the threat the armies of Molgoran posed, it had, however, taken him longer than he had allowed. The anger that raged within spurred him on to run even faster, desperate now to reach his destination.

Anna shrank back despite herself as the Demon stared directly at her. The Ichbaru immediately closed rank and blocked any passage that the Demon may have, but she could feel his stare burn through her.

"Bring the girl to me and I will release the Elf," the Demon hissed, his eyes flashing wicked red against the grey of the landscape.

"There will be no trade monster!" Evaine shouted in response, "you are outnumbered Demon, you will release the Princess or you will die," The old man that stood in front of them did not quiver for a moment. With a speed not befitting his guise he flicked his fingers in intricate patterns and sent a bolt of red fire crashing into Anna's protectors. Within the blink of an eye all five of the Ichbaru that had guarded his passage to Anna were engulfed in flame, each fell to the floor screaming before falling silent in smouldering heaps. It happened so fast that no one reacted immediately, no one except for Kalt. Anna watched in horror as the Ichbaru went down in a blaze of screams and red fire, but before the last fell she was aware of a massive black shape rush towards the Demon.

The old man himself only just about saw him in time; he managed to bring the red fire about him to ward off the massive axe blade that arced towards its head. There was a flare of fire as Kalt's axe met the Demons defence followed by a crash as loud as thunder. Kalt's axe recoiled off the protective shield and was catapulted twenty feet across the clearing. The Demon whirled on its attacker, turning the fire from protection to attack. It sent the magic crashing into the back of the giant form of Kalt as his momentum carried him past the Demon from the rush of his assault. Fire and crimson erupted and Kalt was thrown from view into the fringes of the Skrill.

Evaine was running then, running to snatch away Elay as she lay in a crumpled heap, no longer supported by the Demons magic. He did not slow; he scooped her up in his arms and carried on running back to where Anna stood, frozen to the spot in sheer panic. He shouted at her to run but she was not able, she simply stood and watched the advancing Evaine.

200

After dispatching Kalt the old man spun around to see the Elven prince running away from him carrying Elay's body, limp in his arms. The remaining Ichbaru guard had taken the opportunity to load his bow with an arrow and sent it flying towards the Demons head. With no more than a gesture, he twitched his hands, stopped the arrow in mid-air and sent it back at twice the speed from whence it came. It was travelling so fast it went straight through the Ichbaru's head and embedded itself into the trunk of tree fifty feet away.
The smell of burning flesh and burnt grasses had filled the clearing, the smoke of battle hung in the air. The Demon inhaled deeply "Just the troublesome Prince to despatch and then both of the women would be his to take." he thought gleefully. An Elven Princess was good, but there was something that intrigued him about the other, something that excited him even more than the Elf. "This was turning out to be a most productive day," it thought to itself darkly.

Sam heard the crash of battle as he emerged from the shadow of the Skrill, he could smell the unmistakable stench of burned flesh hanging in the air. He pulled the Orloc from his pocket; it was glowing as bright as the sun in response to the danger ahead. Off to his left, flashes of red shot into the sky and immediately caught his attention. He was desperate now on saving Elay, he knew from the Witches warning that this was Demon fire as he sprinted towards the flares as fast as he was able, clinging on to the hope that he was not too late.

Evaine stood with sword drawn facing the oncoming Demon. A veil of blue Elven magic encapsulated him and his two wards. Elay lay unmoving on the ground behind him and Anna stood at his side, short sword drawn and readied. He knew that the crackling blue shield would not last long against the fire of the Demon, but he also knew that running would serve no better escape. He would defend Anna and his sister until his last breath. He had made that promise and was not about to go back on his pledge. He watched the figure of the old man through the smoke that hung low and heavy across the

201

grasslands, swirling at his feet as he made his advance. It walked slowly now, in no rush to finish what it had intended. Evaine raised his sword in response.

The now familiar red fire licked the Demons hands as it continued forward, ready to smash the last defence that the Elves could muster and finish them off. It had not yet decided what it would do with the women, but it had time to think of a suitable use. It would finish this quickly, eager now to take his prize and be gone before more came looking for them as it was certain that they would.

Evaine watched helplessly as the Demon grew closer, the flames that caressed its hands grew brighter and larger, ready to be unleashed into the defensive shield that now stood as the last defence between himself and the Demon. Suddenly Evaine caught sight of a dark streak running towards their direction. It was shadowed and cloaked and was closing in fast. The Demon sensed it as well. It turned to meet this unexpected arrival, just in time to see white fire lance from beneath the black robes of the shadow that streaked towards it. The white fire the attacker unleashed lit up the clearing and his face......"AMADOR!" the Demon screamed in recognition. It didn't have time to raise its own defences as the fire smashed into it, hurling it across the clearing with a thunderous jolt. Amador did not slow; he called upon the fire again and sent it flying towards the place where the Demon had landed. It hammered into the ground however the Demon had rolled free and, masked by the dust and smoke of the fire, disappeared. Amador skidded to halt; sweat and dirt streaked his face from the effort of the attack and his desperate run to reach his comrades in time. Momentarily he had lost sight of the Demon. He scanned the clearing trying to peer through the smoke that hung thick and acrid. He didn't have to wait for long as red fire arced towards him from his left side. He was able to bring up his own fire just in time but was thrown several feet across the ground as the magic's collided in an explosion that shook the earth. He didn't have time to get to his feet as the old man appeared from the smoke, crimson fire raced from his spread fingers. Amador scrambled to avoid the bolts as they exploded around him turning the grass below to smouldering ash heaps. He was trapped, unable to get to his feet; such was the ferocity of the attack. He had to roll and dodge to avoid catching the full force of the Demon fire. If 'he could just get to his feet', he screamed, silently to himself, he would stand a better chance, but no opportunity was forthcoming. He summoned his own fire and sent it towards the Demon, time after time, but none found their mark as the crooked figure danced and twisted away from the incoming assault of Amador. He was tiring now; the exertion of his trek to reach the Skrill was beginning to take its toll, the Demon, by contrast was unscathed, other than its singed and burnt clothes from Amador's initial attack. It was relentless, bolt after bolt of red fire was sent towards Amador, each time getting closer and closer to its target. He could feel the heat as each fire bolt smashed into the earth. Suddenly, as it appeared that the Demon would eventually catch its prey; blue fire shot forth from the haze of the clearing and encased the Demon. It was caught off guard and was momentarily unable to move from the magic that covered it. It was enough time for Amador to get to his feet and send his magic hurtling back at the imprisoned figure. The blue magic of Evaine had served its purpose, the Demon was too strong for the Elf's magic to injure, but it had given Amador back vital seconds. As the white fire exploded around the Demon Evaine's magic dissipated and the old man was free once more, protected from Amador's attack by the very magic that had been cast to ensnare it.

"YOU CANNOT OUTRUN ME FOREVER AMADOR," it hissed at the smoke that surrounded it, "YOU TIRE WHILST I GROW STRONGER, I WILL FIND YOU AND END YOUR LIFE, AND THEN I WILL END THE ELVES. I WILL SAVOUR THE BLOOD AS I...."
The Demon was not sure what happened next, so fast and unexpected the events unfolded. Before it could finish its threats a new attack came out of nowhere. This was different to anything it had ever encountered before. The force of the magic that smashed into its back was shattering. It felt the feeble

203

bones of the body it had taken snap and crack as soon as the strange amber magic hit. The Demon could no longer sustain its upright stance as it seemed that its whole ribcage had collapsed in on itself. But it did not fall to the ground as it should have, it hung suspended just a few inches from the clearing floor, the amber magic holding it aloft and tightly secure.

So shocked that anything existed that could do it such harm, it made no sound, it just watched the boy appear from behind, the light pulsing out from his out stretched hand that held it prisoner. It did not know this boy, but got the same sensation as when it first laid eyes on the girl that walked with the Elves. It then saw the cloaked figure of Amador limping behind the boy with the yellow magic.

"Game over Demon," the strange boy spoke as he withdrew his magic. Before the old man hit the floor Amador sent a crackling mass of white fire directly into its midriff.

The Demon thought it had ripped him in two as the magic struck. It sent him flying backwards for at least fifty feet. He passed from light to dark as he bounced off trees and landed on the forest earth that was decaying and fetid. To his surprise and delight he was still alive. As he tried to haul himself up to repair his broken body he saw her standing in front of him, her white dress blowing gently in the wind and her red hair cascading past her shoulders. He tried to crawl away, desperately grabbing at the stinking soil around him. He knew where he had landed and now wished that he had been claimed by death, wished that he was anywhere else other than here. For the first time in his very long life he was afraid.

"It looks as though I have a companion to play with!" Graflon's voice broke the silence, "and it has brought me magic as its gift" She let out a shrill laugh. She locked eyes with the Demon, "Welcome to your new home!"

The old man let out a scream that echoed through the Skrill for a very long time.

They stood in the clearing for awhile, unmoving. The only sounds that broke the silence, that had now settled over the grassland, was that of their laboured breathing as they tried regain breath after the exertions of battle. After a short while, Amador walked over to Sam and held his gaze for a moment as if seeing something different in the boy since they were last together, then he gave him the slightest of nods,

"Well done my young companion," he eventually spoke through his heavy breathes. He then turned and ran towards the crumpled heap of Elay. Evaine was knelt beside her trying to bring her out of the magic that still had hold from the Demon encounter.

It was Sam that then saw her; unaware that the Elven Princess had been lying behind Evaine. His emotions suddenly flared again as he saw the small form of Elay lying unmoving on the ground. He immediately feared the worst and was soon running towards the stricken girl. He never made it; he was intercepted halfway by Anna. She ran from behind Evaine and launched herself into him, screaming with joy that he was alive and seemingly unharmed. She latched her arms around his neck and hugged him tighter than ever and wouldn't let go.

"I thought you had died," she cried in his ear, "don't you ever do that to me again Sam or you wish you had died." He hugged her back and smiled, it was good to have found her again.

"I will do my best to stay around this time." he managed to tell her. She eventually let go of his neck and stood in front of him as if checking him over for injuries.

"Is she going to be ok?" he ventured, indicating towards Elay who still lay on the ground with Amador and Evaine at her side.

"Yes, I think so; the Demon had her under some sort of reverie. Evaine said that it will take a while for the magic to fully leave her but she should be ok once it does." She watched the concern and compassion etch across his face.

"You care for her a lot, don't you?" she asked him.

"Yes" came his reply. It surprised him just how quickly he had responded. No delay, no need to think through the answer. "I think I love her Anna." Anna studied him for a moment longer then gave him the biggest grin,

"Woohoo! Sam's finally got a girlfriend." She laughed and playfully pinched his cheeks.

"C'mon, let's go see if your girlfriend is ok." She smiled at him again, then grabbed his arm and pulled him over to where Evaine and Amador knelt.

It took almost an hour for Elay to finally break free from the residue of the Demon magic that had held her. Her eyes flickered open and she was greeted by the sight of her brother's face large and concerned close to hers.

"Where is Sam, does he live?" were her first spoken words. Evaine smiled,

"Sam is fine, he is here and we will talk when we have regained our strength. For now little sister you need to rest." Despite his insistence she would not do so, not until she had seen with her own eyes that Sam was safe and unharmed. Evaine beckoned him over to where Elay now sat. On seeing him she began to cry. He ran over and fell at her side and held her tightly until she had stopped shaking.

They looked for Kalt soon after Elay had been reunited with Sam and the others. They scoured the surrounding area looking for any sign of the Troll, but to no avail, he was nowhere to be found.

"I fear that the Witch has claimed him also," Evaine warned, "He had been thrown towards the Skrill and should he have gone down into that pit then I fear that he is lost to us forever." he sombrely added.

"We could go down and look for him" Anna suggested. Sam inwardly grimaced. The thought of returning into the Skrill sent a cold shiver up his back, the Witches warning still ringing in his ears of his certain death if the two were ever to meet again.

"No," came Amador's swift reply, "Kalt knew of the dangers that this journey held and he has given his life to safeguard that of the group. Let us not make his sacrifice for nothing by getting ourselves killed by the Witch of the Vale. We could be looking for him for weeks and never find any trace and the Witch would not permit such an intrusion. I regret that we must

206

push forward and be thankful to Kalt for his bravery that enables us to do so."

Whilst Sam felt a twinge of guilt, he was grateful for the decision not go into the Skrill had been made. They all took refuge under the branches of an old Oak tree and shared the provisions that they carried, each taking time to convey their stories since being separated in the mists. Elay didn't let go of Sam's hand throughout the whole narration. It did not escape the Elven Prince's attention as he looked on.

When the turn fell to Sam to relate his encounter with the Witch, it was Amador that advised him that the words that had been exchanged between Graflon and himself were for his ears only and that they should remain that way, Sam was grateful as he did not know where he would start. He was still wrestling with the revelations that had been imparted to him and he needed to ensure that he was in complete understanding of the choices he would have to make when the time came. Only then would he be ready to share his time with the Witch. As they sat and ate the bread, cheese and nuts that they carried, he wondered if Evaine and Elay already knew the full implications of the choices that he must make.

With the meal finished and stories exchanged, they laid to rest the Ichbaru guards that had fallen in the battle with the Demon. Evaine blessed them with an Elven prayer. It was then agreed that the group should rest before deciding on the next course of action. Sam was both physically and mentally shattered from his encounter with the Witch and Demon, and Elay was still shaking off the remnants of the magic that had held her. Anna, by contrast, insisted that she did not need sleep and felt fine but, shortly after it was agreed that Amador would take first watch, she was asleep and snoring loudly.

The last remains of daylight had faded away and the darkness of night had replaced the familiar grey sky, when the figure approached. Amador had sensed it several moments ago and whilst giving the guise of ignorance, knew exactly where and how far the advancing figure was from the group. He sat with head bowed waiting for the stranger to make its move, the magic he had command over just resting under the surface ready to thwart any attack should it come, but none did. The figure made no attempts to conceal its approach as it stumbled forward in the blackness of the night. It got within twenty feet of their camp before Amador was on his feet and had whirled to meet the shadow in the darkness, his magic readied and lighting up the clearing. Standing in front of him, he was met with the familiar face of Teon. Battered and bloodied but with a mask of defiance there he stood.

"Finally," Teon let out exasperatedly, "I could really do with something to eat and drink". He then smiled a weary smile at Amador.

"Come friend", Amador replied, "Let us get you fixed up." Amador redressed and cleaned Teon's wounds. He strapped his chest with strips of cloth from the spare clothing that the Ichbaru had carried to ease his pain from his broken ribs and gave him food and water.

His arrival did not wake the sleeping group so they talked without interruption. Despite Teon's exhaustion and injuries they talked for several hours recounting their journeys. Amador listened gravely to the tale of Greston's death and the appearance of the Wolves in the forest. All of this gave strength to what he had witnessed in Varek and the advancement of Molgoran's armies. Teon had told him of Neria's departure back to Silverdale to relay the message of Greston's death and return the Dwarfs axe back to Bannock. "Assuming the Elf had made it back safely then both the Elves and Dwarves would be prepared for the onslaught that would surely come." Amador surmised, and whilst he grieved for the fall of Greston, this would ensure action from Bannock and the Dwarves. After each had been brought up to speed on all the events that had transpired and Teon had consumed his meal, Amador sent him for rest. Teon had argued that Amador should wake Evaine to take over his watch but Amador had dismissed him with a wave, promising to do so later. Teon was too exhausted to argue the point. He found a suitable space next to the sleeping form of Anna and was asleep in moments.

When the group finally came awake it was still dark, the sun not yet risen to greet the new day. Amador still remained on watch, silent and still. It was surprising to them all that they had been joined during the night by Teon, Anna especially couldn't hide her delight as she awoke to find him next to her with his arm draped over her body. She lay still for an age, not wanting to disturb him and enjoying the closeness of his touch. After a while he came awake. He took a moment to orientate himself and then, realising his embrace with Anna, pulled away with a hint of apology and embarrassment. She could have sworn she saw him blush in the half light of morning.

 They ate a cold breakfast washed down with some of the water they carried. Again, Teon related the story of his journey to find them and the loss of Greston. The group listened in silence until he had finished.
"Sam," Evaine spoke, "you must now tell us where we go next. I know that the Witch gave you information that is for you and you alone, but we need to know which way we are heading."
Sam began to tell them that they needed to journey North East to find the Tillamus River, but before he could continue, Amador interrupted.
"We will not all be going with Sam." Evaine turned to Amador, the surprise and confusion evident on his face. "We are threatened from all corners. The armies of Molgoran are further travelled into the south than we had expected and will be upon the gates of Silverdale within a few days, after that, Varon and Fenham. Whilst I would hope that Bannock and the Dwarves have begun to march to the aid of the Elves I do not know this to be true. I know not either if Oldair and Varon stand prepared". Teon began to speak but Amador continued. "Without Kalt and no way of contacting the Troll's in the west, we must also assume that they are not alerted or readied to take up arms. The fact is my friends we do not know if any of the races will unite together and come to the defence of Invetia.

209

What we do know is that Silverdale stands at the forefront of the armies march. Silverdale cannot stand alone and if it should be overrun then the southland is for the taking."

"Varon will not allow that," Teon shouted this time to ensure that his words were heard, "besides, Silverdale has the protection of the Echenor mists; it has the security that its borders cannot be breached. It is far more likely that the forces of Molgoran will bypass Silverdale altogether and head straight to Varon to engage with my father's army." Sam immediately felt uncomfortable. He knew that the Echenor was failing, he knew that he was the one that was making it fail and he was also sure that the armies that marched on Silverdale, if as big as Amador described, would be able to smash the defence that the ever weakening Echenor provided. If it were to fail completely then all hell itself would be released. "*Say something,*" he silently urged himself. "*Tell them what the Witch had told you. You have to do something!*" His thoughts made him squirm with indecision. It was Elay that came to resolve his dilemma. "That's not entirely true Price Teon," Elay whispered. Evaine shot her an angry look to indicate that she should hold her tongue. "No brother, it must be said," she answered his glare, "it has been foretold that these days would come, days that saw the return of Ceriphan's son and the battle for Invetia begin anew. It has been documented in the tomes within the private library of Kings at Silverdale the true price that such a war will bring. It has also been told that once again it must be the Elves that stand to lose the most and gain the least, whatever the outcome." Sam felt the words sting him as she spoke, he knew to what she eluded too better than anyone. "As I am sure that Sam knows from his encounter with the Witch, the Echenor fails as it lends its magic to help Sam in that which he is destined to do. No Elf, not even my father can know if the Echenor remains strong enough to repel the forces of darkness. There is every chance that sufficient damage has already been caused and the mists will crumble and allow the Horde to raise Silverdale to the ground. The Elves will fight with honour and bravery, but we have limited magic at our command, certainly not enough to hold the invaders back. There is every chance that Silverdale will fall Prince Teon and then Varon will stand alone should no aid be sent from either Dwarf or Troll."

The silence was deafening, as all but Sam, tried to take on board her revelations.

"Is this true Sam?" Teon finally broke the quiet, "is this what the Witch had advised you?"

"Yes" came his reply. No one spoke for what seemed an eternity. They all understood that it was not just Silverdale falling that would be the catastrophe, but the failing of Echenor would bring forces back into the land of Invetia that would inflict devastation and destruction, without its protective walls the spirits of Faerie that resided within would be free to roam the land as they pleased. This was not a thought that any of them relished.

"Amador is right," Teon finally ventured, "I must return to Varon as quickly as I can to ensure that my father is aware of the dangers that all of the races face. I will make sure that we are ready to stand shoulder to shoulder with our Elven brothers. I fear that without this knowledge the race of Men will be slow to react to the impending danger." Amador silently nodded his approval.

"I suggest Evaine that you also return with me to ensure that the Elves are as prepared as they can be to face whatever it is that comes knocking on the walls of Silverdale. You are the one that the Elven army will look to lead them, should war be upon us." Evaine began to object, "My oath was to protect and see the safe passage for Sam and Anna, and I must see that this is accomplished," he countered.

"You will be doing so by ensuring that they have something to fight for." Amador spoke. "What is the worth of such a quest if all is obliterated before he can succeed in doing whatever is necessary to safeguard Invetia's future? You can fulfil your oath in many ways Elven prince; this is how it has to be."

Evaine knew the words to be correct, he knew that the armies of Elves would be looking for him amongst their ranks, for him to organise and coordinate any defence of the city. He knew that he must go but that didn't make it any easier to hear. He kicked angrily at the ground before walking off to collect his thoughts. Amador watched Evaine stalk away before continuing.

"The remainder of us will accompany you North East Sam, until we find the Tillamus. Once there I will be leaving also." Sam shot him a surprised look, not sure if he had heard correctly. Amador's role in this was that of his protector and yet he was leaving again? Amador did not look at Sam but seemed to sense his concern.

"I will have to get word to Kelphus and the Trolls now that we have lost Kalt. I must ensure that they are convinced to join with the defence of Silverdale, for without them I fear that, even if the Dwarves agree to help we would still be out numbered. You will be safe once we have gained the Tillamus. Besides, you will have the protection of both Anna and Elay." It was Elay's turn to look surprised. She had been fully expecting that she would be made to travel home with Evaine and securely locked away in Silverdale where she would find safety.

"Does my brother know of your intent for me Amador?" she asked. There was a long pause,

"He is just about to." Amador responded before striding off in the direction of the Elven prince.

Sam, Anna and Elay watched from a distance as the now hooded form of Amador spoke with Evaine. Whilst they could not hear the words being spoken, it was evident from Evaine's gesticulations and muffled shouts that he was not in agreement with the plan, however, after several minutes of debate, Evaine turned and began to walk back to the assembled group. It was clear that the anger still raged within him as he called for Elay to walk with him for awhile. He did not wait for her to join him; he continued to walk past Sam and Anna. Once far enough away he stopped and awaited Elay to catch up. They spoke in soft tones, Elay reaching up and placing her hands on Evaine's face as if to sooth him and reassure him. Finally they embraced for a long while before walking back to the group that had now been joined once more by Amador.

212

"It is agreed," Evaine stated, "Elay will accompany you to the Tillamus and beyond, but I place her directly under your protection Sam." He spoke the words softly, but Sam did not miss the streak of iron that ran through each part. Sam was in no doubt that Elay's safe return was what he was charged with. "Amador has convinced me that the power of the Orloc is better protection than can be offered anywhere else in the current times and I have therefore acquiesced to his request." "Then we should be gone," Teon added, "time slips away and we have much to do."

Shortly after that they said their goodbyes. To Anna's surprise Teon gave her an embrace that lasted longer than the others. When holding her close he whispered, "When this is all over I would very much like to show you my city, Varon. Maybe we can arrange that?"

"I would like that too," she replied in a soft voice. Then he kissed her gently on the cheek before turning away to begin the trek home. She felt her face redden.

The remaining four watched the Princes depart, watched until they were obscured by the trees of the forest, then turned and started the long walk in the opposite direction.

Evaine and Teon barely stopped for anything on their journey back to Silverdale, only to take on food and water and to rest when absolutely necessary. Conversation was sparse as each man concentrated on what they would face and would have to do once returned. It was agreed that Teon would accompany Evaine back to Silverdale and once assured that the stories and revelations that they had learnt had been fully explained to the King, he would then depart for Varon and to his father, Oldair. Whilst it was hoped that Neria had already alerted the Elven king to the severity of the dangers faced, they needed to deliver the news themselves to ensure that the true impact of the situation had been fully positioned. Evaine continued to question the decision to have left Elay behind with Sam and Anna. He agreed that Sam had the protection of the Orloc and that any magic strong enough to contain Graflon would be the best defence that could currently be mustered within Invetia, he still felt uneasy at the prospect, especially on hearing the news that Amador would be leaving them before journeys end. This is a decision that he would have to explain to his father and he was not looking forward to that conversation. His thoughts turned to the Elves as he ran. How many would have to give up their lives for the safeguarding of Invetia. If the Echenor had failed, or, was in an advanced stage of failing, how would they overcome such odds? *"Bad enough to have to defend against an aggressor ten times your number"*, he thought, *"but to have to contend with ancient malevolent spirits and Demons as well? That was insurmountable"*. He quickly tried to banish the negative thoughts from his head; he would give the Elves and the people of Invetia the best chance of survival. His soldiers would defend the city and all to the south with a ferociousness never seen before. They would be fast and accurate; they would be silent and resolute in their defence. They would not only out fight the Horde but outthink them as well. It would be hard, and there would be losses, but then wasn't everything that was worth achieving hard? He worried more about the support that the other races would send. He had Teon's word that the armies of men would come to the Elves aid and fight alongside them, but as for the Dwarves he did not know. They were stubborn born. The death of Greston could very well just as equally make them bar their doors and wait out the conflict; it could however be the spark that forced action and involvement. The Dwarves were essential to the defence. They were a hardy race that fought harder and longer than any other. They were skilled in tactics that enable few to hold off many and this was going to be vital in the battle ahead.

Teon faced an even harder job, albeit that his father was a just and wise ruler. He had governed the city of Varon and had been the elected King for all mankind, but he was a cautious man. He did not make decision without proper council and discussion. A decision such as the one that Teon would be asking for was one that caused for an instant response. They could not afford for the matter to be debated or taken before the council, time did not allow this luxury. He knew that Oldair

214

would not be easily swayed to send his armies to their potential deaths without the duties of democracy being invoked. Teon would have to ensure that the case he presented Oldair with was as compelling as he could make it. Teon had run though what that conversation would sound like a thousand times in his mind, but still had not settled on the best approach needed. The days passed without incident and after three days of hard march and run, they finally began to see the landscape change from the familiar muted browns and grey of the grasslands to the rolling green hills that sat around the Elven city. As they got within a few miles of Silverdale, they saw the answer as to whether Neria's message had been delivered. Lines upon lines of Elven archers stood stretched out across the fields ahead. Banners of the Elven king fluttered brightly in the morning breeze. The reflection of hundreds of chain mail clad Ichbaru glinted in the morning sun surrounding the amassed armies in a haze of brilliance. Further forward was a steady line of Elven foot soldiers marching away from the boundaries of Silverdale. They were heading east and towards the Blendon Pass, the route that the approaching armies of the Horde would use. The trail snaked on for what seemed miles and must have been at least five-thousand strong. The marching line was flanked on each side by a regiment of Elven hunters, all on white horseback. Evaine immediately recognised the configuration of the marching army. The riders would be the shock troops that would charge and retreat any enemy. Quick flash attacks and then gone again to confuse and give the impression that their numbers were even greater than they were. It would appear that Thealine had been quick to act upon the report received. Evaine was suddenly filled with a sense of pride. Never before, despite his role as captain and commander had he ever seen the entire Elven army assembled such as this. So great was the impact of the sight before him he began to feel the sting of tears in his eyes.

They watched as a single rider detached itself from the flank of the marching arming and, with two horses tethered behind him, rode out to meet them.

215

"My lords," he bowed as he brought the horse to a standstill just in front of them, "it is good to see you. We feared you were lost to us." Evaine retuned his greeting.

"I need to speak immediately with the King. Teon will be accompanying me but will soon depart for Varon so have supplies and our fastest steed prepared."

The Ichbaru nodded his understanding and passed the reigns of the tethered horses to Evaine and Teon. They both mounted and were galloping towards Silverdale in an instance.

As they neared the mass of trees and hickories that Silverdale stood behind, the Elven soldiers began to turn and look upon the two approaching horsemen. Cheers began to erupt throughout the assemble army.

"The captain has returned!" was the shout. Soon the crescendo of shouts, cheers and swords being banged against shields filled the whole air, replacing the weight of war with the lightness of determination and joy. Evaine smiled and saluted the rows of men as he passed by. He felt his resolve tighten and his optimism grew anew.

They passed through the opening in the Hickories that entwined with the Echenor mists and there was Silverdale, spread out before them in all its beauty. The smell of the tended flowerbeds coupled with fresh grasses and the spring water from the numerous waterways that meandered through the open fields rushed to greet them. The city stood ahead, from its gleaming white towers of the palace to the brightly decorated cottages on its outskirts, it shone a welcoming glow. Evaine felt his heart lift. He would never get bored of this place; it was going to take a huge sacrifice to keep it in the world, but in that instance he believed it worth it.

They rode as fast as their horses would carry them across the open fields and then into the dusty rutted roads that led to the city centre. People watched and cheered as they rode past throwing up a dust trail in their wake.

They passed the assembled personal guard of the king that stood at the front of the royal palace, their numbers had swelled

216

fivefold. They watched the Prince swing off his horse and race up the palace steps closely followed Teon. Once inside and out of view they returned to their silent vigil.

"My lord Evaine, Silverdale welcomes you home." An older Elf stood in front of him and bowed low. Indra had been the king's personal assistant for as long as anyone could remember and always welcomed Evaine with the same words whether he had returned from a two day hunting trip or had been gone for weeks.

"Greetings Indra, will you please take us immediately to my father."

Indra gave Teon a quick look, nodded, and then turned away and began to stride down the hallway, "Follow me my lords." They followed Indra down the wide corridor of the Palace. Evaine kept his gaze firmly ahead whilst Teon noted the colourful tapestries and paintings that hung on the walls. They passed numerous doors that led into different parts of the royal home, until finally arriving at a set of heavy double oak doors on the left.

"I will just alert the King to your arrival my Lord" Indra informed Evaine. He then knocked softly and entered the room, closing the doors behind him. They did not have to wait long as almost as soon as Indra had entered the room he was back out informing them that King would see them immediately and that they were to go through. Indra bowed to them in turn and then strode back down the corridor and out of sight.

Evaine gave a single knock on the door then pushed it open and stepped inside. He was not expecting the sight that he was greeted with. Thealine sat in a high backed chair in an alcove of floor to ceiling windows. He turned slightly to acknowledge their entrance and Evaine almost stepped back in dismay. His father stared back at him with sunken eyes, his skin spotted with brown marks that hung loosely from his almost skeletal frame. When Evaine had left for the Vale his father had been fit and healthy and whilst he had been old for as long as Evaine could remember, he had retained the look of youth and fitness. That now was gone and in its place sat a man that was bent and crippled with age, a man that looked as if he could break at anytime.

"It's alright my son," Thealine spoke in a cracked voice noticing his shock, "come sit with me and we will exchange our tales." Teon hung back, he too seeing the transformation that Thealine had undergone in the short weeks that they had been gone.

"You too son of Oldair, pull up a chair and sit for a while." Thealine indicated with a wave of his brittle arm to the chair opposite from where he sat.

"I like this time of day, the sun is at its warmest and it soothes the aches of an old man." Evaine and Teon sat where intended, neither taking their eyes off of the King.

"I will tell you my tale first as I am sure that I have less to impart than you." Thealine looked at his son. Evaine nodded for the King to continue.

"The Echenor fails as we have known it would. The Elven histories are correct in their teachings and it has happened as foretold. I, along with others have patched it as best we could from the magic that we still posses but the toll extracted has been great." He allowed his eyes to wander to the windows as he spoke, letting the sun's rays warm his lined face. "We have also known that when the mists fail a choice must be made by the chosen, to either allow its demise or seek a way to restore its hold on the spirits that dwell within. The fact that Sam continues with his quest, the fact that he seeks the destruction of Molgoran and the forces that move against us, means that the decision has been made and the die has been cast." His eyes returned to meet Evaine's. "You see my son there really was never a choice for the Elves to make. Allow the Echenor to fail completely and the Elves would perish at the hands of those within, decide to replace the magic that has been lost from the mists and re-establish the protection and the changes required to the magic would not sustain our longevity." He sighed wearily as he once again returned his stare to the gardens that sat outside of the window.

"We have enjoyed the benefit of the Echenor since records began. The Elves above all others know that everything must end, everything must readjust to survive. We will continue on, we will just have to work harder to achieve things in a shorter lifetime that is all." He smiled a tired smile and relaxed back into his chair.

"Neria performed his duty well," he finally restarted, "he advised us of the Demon Wolves you and he encountered, he advised me of the sad death of Greston. I of course sent an envoy to Bannock to advise him of the news of his son along with his axe that Neria had returned with. I had taken the precaution shortly after you had left for the journey to the Vale to send out my own scouts to better understand the threat that we face. Of the three I sent, just the one returned. He gave us a description of the battle that lies ahead and the dark days that are sure to come. The army that has massed and is marching, number about one hundred thousand." Teon took a loud intake of breath at the news. Thealine did not slow. "They will be at our borders within two to three days and at the Echenor within three to four if we do not delay them. It was with this in mind that I summoned the captains of each regiment of Elven guard and told them what was needed and how quickly we needed to mobilize. I now handover that responsibility to you my son, they are your army to command and I have every trust in your decision and ability to serve the Elves well," He leant forward and patted Evaine gentle on his knee, "but I ask that you take two pieces of advice from an old man. Our role here is to defend and slow the advancing army, we cannot hope to stand against a force of this size and win. We will slow the advance thus giving Varon and Fenham time to send reinforcements. I have sent my two most senior advisors to Varon to speak directly to Oldair and bring him up to speed on the happenings, but I am sure, Lord Teon, that the story coming from you will be enough to convince Oldair of what must be done." Teon gave a light nod to indicate he had heard. He had also not missed the expectation that the Elven King had just placed on his shoulders. "Bannock will either act or not, there will be no swaying the Dwarves on this decision. We will wait and see on the Trolls. The second piece of advice is that you take extra care as you lead the Elves to war. My time left is surely measured in days not months or even weeks. You will soon be King," Evaine winced at the words," and you will be the one that has to restore the damage that inevitably will be served on the Elves, I deeply regret that this burden will fall in your reign, but a King they must have. You are no use to the Elves as a dead hero." He sat back in his chair, finished now in his narration, clearly tired from the exertion of his speech, and now eager to hear the news from Evaine.

"So, tell me what it is that you have learnt."

It was at this point that Teon took his leave. He still had several days journey ahead of him to reach Varon and was eager to do so as quickly as he were able. Evaine embraced him and wished him good luck and good speed. The provisions requested by Evaine were strapped to the saddle of brilliant white stallion that had been brought to the Palace steps. Teon climbed aboard, and dug his heels into the animal's flanks. In no time at all he was leaving the city of Silverdale and heading towards the open plains of the South.

It did not take Evaine long to advise Thealine of his journey and findings, he saw that his father was tired from his earlier discussion so he explained with brevity all that had happened. When he had finished they both sat in silence for several minutes, each man lost within their own thoughts. Finally it was Thealine that broke the silence.

"Where is Elay?" Evaine sighed, then drew breath, and began to tell his father the tale.

CHAPTER
13

They stood and watched until Evaine and Teon were out of sight then; they gathered up their belongings and headed in the opposite direction. Amador felt sure that they could reach the banks of the Tillamus within three days if all went well. As for the journey to the wellspring, this was maybe a further four days march through difficult and dangerous terrain. He had advised that the further North East they head, the more mountainous and rocky the landscape became. The Tillamus started somewhere deep within the Sentinel Mountains, so called as their peaks were the tallest in all of Invetia and looked out over the whole of the land. Sam asked Amador if he had ever seen the wellspring from which the Tillamus flowed.

"I have looked for it on occasions but never found its source." he curtly replied. It was then that Sam remembered what Graflon had said, *"Pass through a door that was as rigid as stone, but yielding to air,"* she had told him. He asked Amador and Elay if this meant anything to either of them. Elay was quick to state that she had never heard of such a thing, Amador too was adamant that he knew not of what the Witch referred, but something told Sam otherwise, his eyes flickered a split second of realisation upon hearing the description and then it was gone as quick as it had come. Sam did not pursue the matter; Amador was complicated at the best of times.

They walked for several miles, Amador taking the lead with Anna behind, Sam and Elay followed. Sam had noticed that Elay had not spoken to him much since her ordeal with the Demon at the Skrill. She had recovered physically quickly after the remnants of magic that had held her captive had finally left her body, but she now seemed a little withdrawn. A few times he had turned and smiled at her to check she was alright but she had kept her gaze directed on the path ahead. He had tried to hold her hand as they walked but she kept them inside her cloak and made no attempt to accept his advances. He put it down to her needing time to mentally recover from her ordeal and, other than having his ego a little bruised, left the matter alone. Anna, by contrast was being Anna. She had been effervescent since Evaine and Teon had departed. She had flitted between Sam and Amador, buzzing with a thousand questions for each of them. She had made Sam narrate the encounter with Graflon several times; needing to know every event or word that was spoken. She was then around Amador, quizzing him about how he would get the support of the Trolls and what he would say. To Sam's amusement she was even telling Amador how best to approach the situation. Amador did not seem to enjoy being told how best to handle the liaisons, but the more irate he got the more it spurred Anna on, so much so that even Elay gave out a small laugh as Amador's patience was continuously tested.
"I assure you Mistress Anna that I am sufficiently well versed in how best to practice diplomacy." Sam heard him respond angrily to a comment that Anna had made.
"Well I assure you Amador that if you knocked on my door with that high and mighty attitude I would slam it shut in your face!" she had replied. And so it continued for many more miles until Amador brought them to rest. Sam was sure that this was as much an opportunity to get away from the incessant

lecturing that he was receiving from Anna as it was to take on sustenance. Sam, Anna and Elay took on food and water without the company of Amador who had left them to eat as he made sure that the way ahead was clear of danger. After a short while, Amador, returned telling them that he found nothing to suggest that there was danger present and that they could continue onwards.

Footsore and weary; they packed up their belongings and were on their way again. Amador walked them for several more hours. With each step the surrounding landscape began to change. The long grasses had now been left far behind and the ground underfoot became drier, dusty and strewn with small rocks and stones. It was not long until all the trees had disappeared from view and a colourless, barren wasteland spread out before them in all directions. In the distance they could now see the peaks of mountains, the tops shrouded in cloud. Amador informed them that this was the destination that the three must make for; this was the Solitude Mountains and the birthplace of the Tillamus. They stopped again as the land began to darken as the first touches of the evening sky began to take hold. As the land slipped into darkness, the air turned cold and they huddled together in an effort to ward off the chill from the wind that blew across the exposed landscape. There was no shelter to find here, so they relied on the light blankets that they carried and tried as best they could to find sleeps embrace. It was Amador that stood watch, Sam couldn't remember the last time that Amador had slept, and in fact he couldn't remember him ever doing so. They rose at dawn after a broken, restless sleep, consumed a cold breakfast of dried meat and resumed their journey onwards. The cold morning soon gave way to the blistering heat of the sun.

"Too cold to sleep, too hot to walk," Anna bemoaned as they trekked forward. It was not long before they had to stop again such was the need to take on water and recover their breath from the extremes of the march. Elay still remained aloof and did not talk much. Sam continued to walk by her side, just happy to be in her company. Even the usually talkative Anna

223

had fallen silent, the efforts of the journey were taking its toll on all of them, all of them except Amador who never slowed or tired, never slept or complained. He just kept pushing them forward with a pace that they were barely able to maintain. The second day passed much as the first. They encountered no one else on their travels and the land remained silent and still. The distant Mountains loomed ever closer but still remained considerably further away than they would have liked. The rocks that were strewn across the barren expanse of the land became bigger, the further they advanced, big enough that they were able to find some shelter from the familiar wind and cold that seemed to accompany the fall of night. They found a huge boulder that jutted out from the earth like a massive spearhead. There was enough shelter to start a fire and they sat huddled around, each trying to take whatever warmth they could. There was little wood to be found and it was not long before the fire had burned itself out and they returned to the cold darkness of the evening. It was then that Amador spoke to them.

"We are being followed," he stated. There was no emotion in his voice, nothing to suggest panic or surprise. The others snapped their heads up at his remarks. Elay instinctively grasped Sam's hand and he felt her body tremble. "Whatever stalks us has been doing so for the past two days. I think that it is still some way off, but it will catch us eventually if we continue to rest and slow as we have been. Tonight we will sleep for a few hours, but then must resume our trek under the cover of nightfall. We will make the Tillamus by midday; I will then ensure that it is I that our stalker follows when we part. Your tracks will be hidden, I will see to that."

"Do you know what it is Amador?" Anna asked.

"I am unsure, on our first day, when we took rest, I skirted back the way we had come to see if I could catch sight of them, see if I could distinguish the tracks that they had made but I could not. My magic sensed its presence, but I am unable to ascertain more than that at present. I am however confident that we will keep ahead if you follow my instructions."

"Is it another... Demon?" Elay spoke. Her voice frail and dry with the fear she was immediately feeling.

224

"I am unsure, but I do not believe it is." Amador replied. Sam couldn't tell if he spoke the truth, but either way, he felt Elay's relief on hearing his response. He put his arm around her and hugged her gently. She looked to him and smiled.

"Go, sleep now," Amador instructed, "I will wake you all in a few hours."

"Great!" Anna muttered as she huffed and moaned before rolling herself into her blanket and promptly fell asleep. Sam, by contrast, did not. Try as he may sleep would not find him this night. He lay still, feeling the rise and fall of Elay's chest as she lay sleeping next to him. He gazed up at the night sky and wondered again how his life had changed so dramatically. It seemed as if he had merely dreamt the life he once lived as it felt so very long ago. He couldn't imagine being back there, going back to the 'normality' that his life once was. He tried to remember the sounds and smells of his old life, tried to remember the faces of all the people that he had ever known or met. Apart from a few he found it increasingly difficult to do so. This was his life now, no matter how it panned out, this was reality and his early life was fast becoming a distant memory. To his surprise he didn't seem to mind. He had fitted into the life he now led with a swiftness that he would never had imagined. He then thought of Anna and wondered if she felt the same? She, after all, had a family that would be worried as to where she was, she had people that would notice her not being there, and she had had a life that was full and purposeful. He wondered if she ever regretted the decision she made all that time ago in his flat to accompany him on this journey. He felt increasingly responsible for her being here. She hadn't given him any choice of course and she wouldn't have allowed any different outcome to that what had transpired, but it didn't stop the mounting guilt that he was feeling. He wondered as he lay and listened to the quiet of the night, what would happen when they reached journeys end? What would happen when this was all over? He had made his decision long ago, this was where he belonged and as hard as it would be to say goodbye, this was not where Anna's future was, she would have to go back, but could she? Could one simply return through whatever it was that brought them here and resume where they had left off? Would time have passed at the same rate? In his world, would they have been gone for but a few hours and no one would even have realised that they had in fact gone anywhere or would years and years have passed? What if decades had passed and Anna was returning to a world where everyone and everything had changed? He sighed at the amount of questions that he had no answer for. He decided that he would ask Amador about it before they parted tomorrow, not that he was sure that he would know the answer or even if Sam really wanted to hear the answer, but nevertheless, ask he would. As he lay, mulling over the questions that raced through his mind he felt a hand shake him lightly on his shoulder, it was Amador,

"It's time to leave Master Sam, come awake." Sam nodded his response and gently roused the sleeping Elay.

The darkness still had a tight grip on the land as they began anew their journey. Breakfast was a meagre affair as they had almost depleted the last of the food that they carried and they drained the last of their water. Amador had informed them that they would be able to replenish their ale skins once they reached the Tillamus. Its waters evidently ran crystal clear and were pure and safe.

The walk was difficult under the blanket of darkness, the land had changed again and was becoming increasingly rock strewn and no discernible path was evident. Often they found that they needed to scramble over massive boulders that littered their path as no other route around was possible. The going was slow and they had not ventured far before the orange glow of the Sun in the distance signalled mornings arrival. Amador did not relent, pushing them every step of the way, reminding them of their need for urgency to reach the Tillamus by midday. Sam was not sure if this indicated that their pursuer grew closer but all seemed to accept the challenge and they maintained a reasonable speed over the terrain.

Sam waited until there was a break in the rocks ahead and let go of Elay's hand and quickened his pace to catch up with the tall cloaked form of Amador. He fell into step with him and walked by his side for several minutes before Amador turned to him.

"You have questions of me?" He was not asking Sam, he was more telling him.

"Yes, I have questions." Sam responded.

"Then ask and I will see if I am able to meet them with answers that will satisfy."

Sam then relayed all of his thoughts from the previous evening when he lay awake. He asked about Anna's possible return when all of this was over, he asked about the time that had passed and if both worlds shared a same speed of passing.

"The way that brought you to Invetia is closed," Amador started, "that was how the magic worked, a one way journey that cannot be opened again for it no longer exists. Remember Sam, there was never an expectation that a return journey would be required. You were always going to have stayed. As for the possibility of Anna's return, I am unsure. There may be tomes within the Elven library that give an idea as to if this can be achieved; however, I feel it is likely that there is not. Mistress Anna's destiny was tied as much to Invetia as yours was on the day she agreed to travel with the Sario and you. I fear that her future destiny is equally as committed to Invetia as yours is." Sam felt his heart sink at the revelation. He was sure that there would be a way to return her.

"Do not ponder on it to much Sam," Amador continued, "there are far more pressing issues that require your attention. Anna's safe passage back is mute unless you can fulfil your destiny to end Molgoran's life. I suggest that this be the only thought that you harbour at this given time." Sam felt his blood boil at the rebuke.

"Let me tell you this Amador," Sam was unable to hide the anger from his voice, " I have been told from the day that I set foot in Invetia of my destiny, my purpose, the sheer level of expectation that has been placed on my shoulders. There is not a waking moment that passes without me thinking on it and I do not need you to be reminding me for the umpteenth time. What I do need to know is that what I am doing is worth it.

What I am doing will ensure that my friend can get her life back. She chose to accompany me but she has done so at great sacrifice to her life, to her safety and to her wellbeing. She has no affinity to Invetia, she neither owes it anything or it her. She came to help in a common goal. I therefore do not feel that I am unreasonable in trying to see her safely returned." Once he finished he was immediately aware that they had stopped walking and Anna and Elay had heard every word. He suddenly felt very awkward. He could feel the icy glare that Amador gave him from beneath his cowl. The big man grabbed him by the arm and pulled him away from the confused Anna and Elay. Once out of earshot he turned to Sam, his anger now evident.

"You have been told everyday of the importance that has been placed on your shoulders because when this is over thousands will lay dead," his words came at Sam like daggers, each one causing him to wince as they found their mark,
"thousands that will have given their lives to ensure that you succeed in your quest. As we speak and waste time now, men die, evil grows and the very existence of Invetia hangs in the balance. Should you fail in the destiny that has been handed to you then life itself will eventually fail and everything will die, everything!" He was enraged. "I understand your concern for the girl but she is but one person, one small piece of the tapestry that Invetia weaves. She will have her part to play in its survival as I am sure we all will. If you succeed, if we succeed and the land again can be safe, then that is the time to worry about anything else. Until that time comes, until you can walk the meadows and towns without the fear of the dark, until the stain upon this earth has been banished and contained then nothing else matters, not me, her, the Elven Princess, nothing!" He let go of Sam's arm and the two stared at each other in the silence that had now ensued. They stood for several minutes before Amador spoke again, this time composed and steady. "Sam, I know that this has not been easy, I wish that the burden had fallen to me to carry for you, but fate cannot be changed no matter how much you wish it to be otherwise." He was stooping down to meet Sam's gaze square on, his shadowed

eyes now reflecting nothing of the anger that burned before, but now there was almost sorrow and compassion. "I give you my promise that should we prevail, should we see the light of day where we are no longer at such terrible risk, I will do all I can to see Anna's safe return. She follows a path that is written, a path that cannot be deviated from, should this path lead her to where she is supposed to be then I will do all I can to make sure that she arrives safely. Until then, let us see this out." Sam was no longer angry; he felt it slip away, leaving him resolved to the task ahead. Amador's words were right, if he did not succeed in doing what was expected of him then none of it would matter anyway. He nodded in response to Amador's words. The big man smiled from within his hood, gave him a pat on the arm. He called Anna and Elay to follow and resumed his walk towards to the Tillamus. Anna came to Sam's side. "We will talk later" he advised her and then turned to follow the tall shadow of Amador.

It was not long before they were back into familiar landscape; jagged stones split the land they walked upon. They rose up on each side of them, tall and imposing creating small passageways that could only be passed in single file. They often had to resort going down on all fours to enable passage over the massive slabs of rock that stood in their path. There was no greenery here, nothing grew, just stone, rock and granite. Occasionally they would pass under massive overhangs of rock that dripped down ice cold water in silvery streams. Each one looking like it could collapse on them at any moment. The sounds of their footsteps echoed through the stone walls that encased them, making the journey feel even more disconcerting than it already was. Despite the shade of the passageways it was humid and hot, the air stale and unmoving. This clearly was not a path travelled by many; in fact it was not hard to imagine they could be the first to have ever passed through. The claustrophobia of the small passages and imposing rock walls seemed to go on forever, every step they took had to be precise due the looseness of the rubble underfoot. Often one of them would stumble and fall. Each time another would help them up to carry on.

So intent were they on watching where the next step should be placed, none noticed the massive black shape detach its self from the shadow of the rocks. It watched them pass before coming at them from the rear. Amador, who was several yards ahead, sensed it at the last moment. He spun around, white magic already forming in his hands, just in time to see the huge black shape of a mountain bear lunging for the un-expecting Anna that trailed behind. There was no clear line to send his magic to her aid as Sam and Elay stood directly in front of him. He screamed in warning to Anna with the lunging bear inches from her head, jaws opening. Anna cried in horror as she turned to see the monstrous form behind her. The bear snapped at her exposed head, ready to claim its prize when suddenly there came an almighty thud. Anna was instantly covered in a shower of thick, crimson blood. Sam screamed in horror as he turned to see Anna fall to the floor covered in red. Then the bear slumped to the ground, unmoving. The massive axe that protruded from the rear of its skull had almost taken its head clean off. Anna lay on the floor not sure what had happened, she had no pain? As she looked back at the slumped broken form of the bear, she caught sight of the massive frame of Kalt lumbering towards her.

"It appears we now know who has been following us." Amador shouted loudly to the others. His voice continued to reverberate down the passageway for several moments.

Kalt slowed to retrieve his axe and then walked straight to Amador. He was limping; an after effect of the fight with the Demon Sam surmised. Other than that and being streaked with dirt and sweat from his journey, he seemed unharmed. Amador greeted him with his arm over his chest and Kalt replicated. They then began to talk in Kalt's language so no one understood what was being said. Sam, Anna and Elay looked on as the strange guttural sounds of the dialect of Troll punctuated the quiet. When finished, Amador came over and spoke to Elay. It appeared that the big Troll's leg was injured to a greater extent than had been first thought and Amador asked if she would look at the wound and tend it with the sparse provisions that she carried. Elay was happy to help and made her way over to the now seated Troll.

"He was thrown into the Vale of Graflon during his fight with the Demon as we feared; this is why we could not find him." Amador reported to Sam and Anna. "It was only by luck that the Witch was more interested in the arrival of the Demon that he was able to crawl free. He then tracked us to this point. His leg is ripped open from thigh to shin and needs to be healed, Elay has the Elven skills to tend the wound as a temporary measure, but I need to get him back to his people and Kelphus as quick as I

am able before infection sets in."

"You still intend to leave us then Amador?" Anna enquired.

"I do, and I am thankful for Kalt's arrival as it has just made the negotiation easier as the Trolls will now have no doubt of the danger we collectively face upon hearing it from the son of Kelphus."

"You intend to leave now, don't you?" Sam interjected.

"Yes Sam, Kalt needs my assistance and will not be able to make the journey unaided and, as I have already advised you, I cannot make the journey to the Wellspring with you. This is your journey Sam. I will be waiting for you when you know where it is that you need to be, rest assured I will know when the time is right. The Tillamus is found not more than three miles from here. Follow the passage down as far you can go. You will then descend through much of the same terrain as we have been travelling and you will come to the banks of the river. There is only one river so you cannot miss it. Follow the river against its flow until you can see no more and this will be where the Wellspring is located. I am unable to provide you with exact directions as I have said, I have never found the source, but you will, I know you will." Amador concluded.

"And what am I to do once I find it, if I find it?" Sam asked, almost with a hint of desperation.

"You will know. The three of you will know what needs to be done."

231

He sat with Sam and Anna on an outcropping of rock as Elay continued to tend Kalt's injuries.

"I have faith in you both," he spoke in a hushed tone, "I made a promise a very long time ago to a friend that I would not allow harm to come to you. I would not be leaving now if I were in any doubt that your safety was at risk, besides, you command a magic far greater than anything I can muster, you have the Orloc." Sam immediately felt to his pocket for the reassuring shape of the Orb and found it to be safely tucked away.

"May I see it Sam?" Amador asked. Sam reached into his pocket and pulled it free. To his surprise it had gotten smaller still, now little bigger than an Acorn.

"It is nearly complete Sam," Amador told him, "the Orloc's magic has almost passed from stone to user as was foretold. Once within you it will stay with you for life, yours to command as you see fit. It will be as much a part of you as your heart." Sam stared at the small glowing Orb one final time before stuffing it back into his pocket. Anna listened on, not quite sure if she had understood correctly, but for once, she chose to hold her tongue.

"Invetia is lucky to have you on her side Sam, keep safe and alert and I will see you when the time demands it." With these words Amador rose, he gave Sam a nod of assurance and to Anna's surprise he bent down to give her a parting hug. As he held her in his arms he whispered, *"Your being here was no accident Mistress Anna, you were foretold also. Do not consider yourself as not important, who knows, you may yet turn out to be the most important one of all."* He kissed her gently on her cheek, then turned and headed towards Kalt and the waiting Elay. After a short conversation with the Elven princess, he nodded to Kalt and they both headed off back down the passageway and out of sight. Once again Sam felt very exposed and alone.

They rested for a while and finished the last few strips of meat and the few berries that they had left. They had no water to wash it down so it was a quick affair. Then, with Amador's instructions still fresh in their minds, they turned and began the long walk down the rocky passage. After a few hours of walking, and scrambling over the obstacles in their path, they began to descend. The high rock walls of the passage fell away and the land began to open up. It was a welcome relief to be free from the stale air of the enclosed passageways and they appreciated the warm breeze that greeted them as they emerged. All three walked in silence, each lost within their individual thoughts, each trying to forget just how thirsty and hungry they had become. Despite the deafening silence, Sam and Anna missed the faint sound in the distance; it was Elay that heard it first.

"Listen!" she told them. They stopped and listened to the silence of the world, and then they all heard the most welcome sound, running water! With a new found burst of energy they almost ran down the last few hundred yards of the descent. They collectively passed the last few boulders and then were greeted with a mass of bright colours of a meadow. Green lush grass swayed in the breeze and bushes loaded with multi-coloured fruits grew in large patches, and there, just beyond the colours of the meadow, the Tillamus flowed, fast and full. For the first time since they departed Silverdale, they forgot their situation, forgot the aches and pains and the journey ahead still to undertake. They ran through the meadows and jumped into the crystal waters, fully clothed and laughed and splashed like children on an outing. The cool water of the Tillamus, just for that moment, washed away the stresses and worries that they carried, cleaned them, not only physically but mentally too and replenished some of the strength that they had lost on the way. They felt as if they were free of everything that had troubled them as they played and swam in the sparkling flow of the river and Sam wished that they could stay like this forever.

Thealine, King of the Elves died the following morning. Indra had gone to wake the King as he had done every morning since being appointed to his role all those years ago, to find that he had passed away sometime during the night. He immediately went to Evaine's quarters to inform him of the news. It took Evaine several minutes to understand Indra as he was sobbing so hard the words would not form. Once Evaine had understood the message he immediately went to the Kings bedside. He stayed with Thealine, alone for the better part of an hour. He stroked the Kings hand and told him of his sorrow for his passing and the joy he experienced as having him as a father. He softly sang an old Elven prayer to inform the dead that a King was soon to join them and to care for him in death as the living had done for him in life, as was tradition.

He then leant over and kissed him softly on his forehead and left the room. Upon exiting he was greeted with by the heartbroken Indra and a contingent of six of the Palaces Ichbaru guard. They bowed deeply at his approach, a sentiment that he had always felt rather uncomfortable with. He had always preferred to treat all that he met the same, be they Kings, Ministers or even the washerwomen that worked in the city; after all they were all people. Just because he was of royal blood he breathed the same air as they did, loved his family as they did and laughed and joked as they did. He saw them as equals, as individuals and not subjects. This was the reason he was held in such high regard by the Elves of Silverdale, they loved him for it. Then it dawned on him, he was no longer Prince Evaine, son of Thealine, he was King Evaine, King of the Elven nation. The realisation hit him unexpectedly, he suddenly felt unsure of himself, and doubts rushed his mind that he was the one to lead the Nation of Elves. The enormity of the void his father had left was not going to be easily filled. He would have to lead his people through their darkest times. 'Fate and destiny could be wicked mistresses' he thought as he stood in the corridor, momentarily paralysed by the fear that now gripped him.

It was Indra that came to his side, his face streaked with the tears that had run down his face but now resolved and steadied.
"Are you alright Sire?" he whispered softly.
"I am not sure," Evaine responded, "I am not sure that I am up to the task that is demanded of me."
"You are most eminently qualified, my King" came the quiet, confident response from Indra.

"I am not my father Indra." Evaine immediately regretted the tone in which he delivered the words, but Indra smiled softly back at him.

"No you are not; you are Evaine, King of the Elves of Silverdale and Invetia. You are the King that the people will look to lead them out of the darkness that awaits us, you are the King that will stand shoulder to shoulder with the Elves and defend what is right and what is just. You are the King that will see us through whatever is thrown at us and will rebuild that which breaks. You are the King that Invetia has been waiting for. It's time to step out from the shadow of Thealine and embrace the destiny that awaits you for it cannot be escaped or sidestepped. You will be the King remembered in legend as the one that saved a Nation. I stand ready to serve you King Evaine."

Indra's words chased the doubt from his mind and the aches from his heart. He was right; there was no escaping destiny even if he wanted to. He would fight against the Horde, he would stand beside his soldiers and they would win whether the other races chose to help or not. Silverdale and the Elves would persevere, of that he promised himself. He embraced Indra and thanked him for his counsel and friendship and asked that the preparations for the Kings burial be prepared. He also asked that the news was not yet to be broken to the Elves; there was no sense in sending a nation to war with heavy hearts. He ordered the Ichbaru to summon his Commanders and to meet him in the Kings study. If the Elves stood alone, then they would be prepared.

He briefed his Commanders that the King had been taken down by an infection and would not be able to leave his room for several days. As Commander of the Armies of Silverdale, he would be formulating the defence of the City and the southland beyond. They accepted this freely and discussions began. They argued back and forth for most of the morning as how best to achieve the goal of stopping the advancing army of Molgoran, whilst suffering the lowest cost to Elven lives. Each

Commander had his own view as to how each of the units under their command could be best utilised.

"Let my cavalry run them through, split their attack into smaller units for the foot soldiers to engage in more manageable numbers." Commander Eflen argued.

"No, engage them at distance," argued Commander Litten, "my Archers can thin their numbers from afar; the bodies of the fallen will slow their advance which will break the Horde into separated groups that your horsemen can cut down."

Then it was the Generals that commanded the foot soldiers that had a different take on the matter, believing they should be used to create a wall of soldiers that would stop the approach whilst Horsemen and Archers attacked the flanks. The arguments, all of which were feasible, went back and forth for several hours. Evaine listened to each and weighed its merits against the next, he wished that Tamar were here, he would know instinctively which to implement. After several more debates and raised voices, Evaine had heard enough.

"My Lords," he commanded and all fell silent, "I thank you for the wisdom that you have collectively brought to the table this morning and I am now in a position to know what needs to be done. We will continue with the march to the Blendon Pass, this is where we will set our defences. The pass will give us a natural advantage as it will funnel the approaching army into no more than one hundred men across. Commander Litten, you will assemble your lines of Archers atop the cliff face so that we can rain down arrows on the Horde below, but be hard targets to hit. General Eflen, your cavalry will circumvent the pass and attack from the sides. Quick flash attacks, in and out, then regroup and start again. This will confuse the attackers as to our size and position. Once they realise our strategy you will order you men back to cover the access points so that the enemy cannot get in behind us. If that were to happen we will be trapped in the pass and the Horde will crush us from the fore and the rear." The assembled Generals did not speak each visualising Evaine's plan. He seized the silence to continue.

"Our fallback position will be the Telishan Forest. This lies directly in line with the Blendon Pass and is but three miles back. This will enable our armies to move back in a straight line swiftly and unencumbered. We will then repeat the tactic except we will use the trees as our cover instead of the rock of Blendon. The Telishan will not be easy for an army the size of which descends upon us to negotiate; it will slow and fragment them. We will use this to our advantage. A smaller fighting force will have the upper hand. After that my friends Silverdale will be our final stand so let us hope that it does not come to that. The Echenor will not protect us from the advancing darkness, it will slow them, but it will no longer hold them. Rest assured there are other plans in place to remedy this, but we have to face the possibility that we will have to fight, for the first time in recorded Elven history, within the borders of Silverdale itself. Let us do all we can to ensure this never happens." The room stayed silent, the thought of an enemy breaching the Echenor was unthinkable and this thought alone was enough to inspire the army to fight harder and longer. It was a short while before anyone broke the hush that had descended across the room; it was Commander Litten that spoke.

"My Lord Evaine, we will carry out your command as discussed. You will have an army that fights with a ferocious honour for Silverdale and its King. We are all agreed on what each of us must do. We fight for Silverdale, to honour the memory of King Thealine and to mark the ascension of King Evaine!"

Indra smiled as he heard the words through the door at which he listened. Most of the time Kings were right in their decisions, but heavy hearts would not be taken to the battle at news of Thealine's passing, steely resolve, pride, passion and strength would be the result. Sometimes new Kings just needed a little nudge in the right direction.

The room cleared quickly after the plans had been agreed, each of the Generals eager to get their respective units organised and moving. All left by individually pledging their support and allegiance to the new King as they filed past. Before he knew it Evaine sat alone at the empty table in the empty room. What type of King would history record him as? Would he be the King that led his proud Elven people to victory against overwhelming odds or would he be remembered as the fool that saw the annihilation of the Elves from Invetia? He thought about it for a moment longer then rose from his seat and strode out the room. History, whatever the outcome, would remember him as the King that did all that a ruler could have done for the welfare of his charges. He marched down the steps of the Palace with a purpose and intent, climbed aboard his waiting steed and galloped out of the Palace grounds heading for the Blendon Pass as quick as his horse would carry him.

CHAPTER

14

Evaine raced onwards, pushing his horse as hard as he could in order that he could reach the Blendon Pass in time to ensure that the defensive lines that the Elves had planned were in place and ready to meet the massive army that marched towards them. Cheers went up as he streaked past the lines of foot soldiers making their way to the pass; they called his name and waved the banners of Silverdale in response to his passing. He wondered as he rode, how many of these men would lay dead before the day was out, he wondered how many would not be returning to see their family, he wondered if any of them would again.

He continued onwards at pace, his mind a blur of a thousand things to do and organise. He had instructed his Generals and

they would carry out his orders to the very letter, but he wanted
to see it for himself, he wanted to be sure that the Elves of
Silverdale and in fact the whole of Invetia had been given the
very best chance of life, the very best chance of survival. He
brought his horse to a stop only once on his journey to the pass.
He had seen one of the unit commanders talking to a scout that
had recently returned from his order of finding the enemy and
reporting as to its size and movement. The scout was on his
way to give the news to Thealine but Evaine had told him that
the news of his mission needed to be relayed to him instead. It
was not good as Evaine's worst fears had been realised. The
Army of Molgoran was huge, bigger than anything the scout
had ever seen before. He estimated it one hundred thousand
strong. It moved swiftly and without rest. He described it as a
black roiling sea that stretched as far as he could see that came
in wave after wave. Goblins, Gnomes, Kobolds and countless
other forms that he had never seen before made up its vast
numbers. Some were small, that moved with a swift furtive
movement, with teeth that flashed wickedly in the light; others
massive, as big as the trees of the Telishan, which lumbered
along, threatening to step on the ones in front. A fog of steam
and stench hung over the army as the mass of bodies jostled for
position and breathing space. It came for them screaming and
maddened on the promise of battle. The whole army crushed
forward in attempt to reach their destination as quickly as they
could. The ones that couldn't keep up or fell were simply
trampled to death by the others behind. There seemed no
consciousness to the Horde, no emotion other than hate and
destruction. They were a tide of claws and teeth and they were
intent on breaking whatever or whoever was in their path.
The scout described the creatures with the red eyes that seemed
to cajole and entice the army as it marched into frenzy. They
were ever present, some at the forefront, some at the sides and
back, but always there, always talking and shouting across the
roar of the army. He could not tell how many there were but
they were easy to spot. They walked with a control that the rest
of the assembled did not. They walked with a silent authority,

upright and bold. The sight of these had sent a shiver down the spine of the Elven scout.

"Demons" Evaine whispered.

"Yes my Lord, I believe they were, but how, where...?"

Evaine ignored the scout's question. "You have served the Elven Nation well, what is your name?" Evaine enquired.

"Tumlus my Lord," the Elf replied.

"Go on back to Silverdale Tumlus; go back to your family and friends. You have earned that privilege."

With that, Tumlus bowed briefly and was gone. Evaine remounted his horse and was racing forward anew.

It took a further two hours of hard riding before the Blendon came into sight; the road began to narrow as the rocks on either side began to close in. A shaft of bright light greeted him as the sun's rays were funnelled through the gap ahead. As he rode he could already see the Elven archers atop the cliff face. Hundreds had taken up position as agreed earlier that day. His Generals had done well and the defence of Silverdale was already well underway. He saw no sign of the cavalry, but surmised that these had already started to tackle the long journey around the Blendon to take up their position of concealment to attack the exposed flanks of the approaching army. The pass itself was beginning to fill with the foot soldiers of Silverdale. The white's and gold's of the soldiers dress shone a haze of colours as the brilliance of the sun danced from soldier to soldier. The air was still and despite the number of soldiers gathered, there was a silence that hung upon all. They knew what they were here to do, they knew that the battle ahead would be fierce and bloody but there they stood, resolute and determined. It made Evaine grit his teeth in defiance. Silverdale would not fall this day, nor would it the next, every Elf would defend it until they drove all of the armies of Molgoran from this land or all of them lay dead.

It was then, in the hush of the afternoon when they first heard the soft booming. Barely audible it sounded off in the distance. There was a faint murmuring that went around the gathered Elven defence, looks exchanged to echo the confusion as to what the sound was. It was then that Evaine realised that it was war drums. The approaching army was beating out its advancement. Each boom resonated quietly through the Pass of Blendon, but he knew that with each boom sounded the army grew closer and closer. So massive was the force that advanced upon them that they made no effort to hide their arrival, confident that nothing would be able to stand against the force amassed. Evaine sat still atop his horse and listened to the advancement as General Litten came up to his side.

"So it begins my Lord. I worry that so few need to stand against so many. There has been no word from Oldair or Bannock? Will the race of Men and Dwarf not stand with us, fight with us as brothers in Invetia's hour of need?"

"I do not know General Litten, what I do know however is that it will take more than a few drums to break the spirit of a Nation. It will take more than an army, no matter how big in numbers, that fights with no purpose or honour, to prevail against one that, no matter how small, fights for survival, for all that is right and just and with a belief in what it fights for. Every Elf stands with a passion and desire to protect and defend a loved one, a home, a way of life. What do those that advance on us stand for General? I will tell you that when a man has nothing to fight for the appetite for battle is lost very quickly, and that is how we will stand against the Horde, that is why we will defeat whatever they throw at us, irrespective as to whether Men, Dwarf or Troll stand by our side. Because every man and woman here today fights for something or someone General!" They both sat on their steeds in silence for a while listening to the booms in the distance, then General Litten gave him the slightest of nods and steered his horse away to continue to organise the defence leaving Evaine alone with his thoughts once more.

The Elven army of Silverdale continued to fill the pass for the remainder of the day. They had streamed in and taken up position as directed. The pass itself was now completely full of heavily armed Elven guards; they numbered about three thousand, one hundred across and thirty rows deep. There was enough room for each row to move up, and the front row to move back so that when they were defending the pass the army would rotate and every row would eventually take on the front position allowing the retreating row to fall to the back before repeating the cycle. This way the Elves could remain fresh and strong at the fighting front. The Elven commanders had also made it possible for the second and third rows to reach over the first with long pikes and spears if the frontline showed signs of buckling to support and repel the attacking force. Evaine was happy with the planning; the defence looked as strong as it could. With archers raining down arrows on to the advancing Demon led army, this would add a further attacking force. The army they faced was so large that it would not be able to retreat even if they wanted for the sheer numbers behind would crush them forward, so as the dead mounted higher and higher this would make it even harder to get to the Elven defenders. The Elves had the entire road behind them in which to retreat into and therefore numbers did not matter in the equation. The soldiers that had lined up on the roads behind the Blendon had to ensure that if any enemy lines came around then they would be dealt with as the Elves could not afford to be trapped in the Pass by the Horde. If this were to happen then all within the Pass would have no escape and would be killed very quickly. It was a calculated risk, but the assembled cavalry was watching the flanks to stop this happening. Evaine was satisfied that as much as possible had been done to ward off the possibility. The last of the warming sunshine had now left the land as it began to slip into the darkness of night. Fires were lit to illuminate the pass and the Elven guard huddled around each in an effort to ward off the chill that now came on the evening breeze. All the time the booming of the distant drums continued, never stopping but growing louder with each passing minute.

The fires continued to burn bright against the now black of the night. The war drums echoed now through the pass, a constant drone that never relented. They were loud now as if the enemy stood at the mouth of the pass. Elven scouts had returned and advised Evaine that the amassed army of Molgoran stood not more than two miles from the defensive lines of the Elves. Evaine knew that an attack could now come at any moment. He called on his commanders to ready their troops for battle and be prepared for anything. The hours slipped by and they waited, but nothing happened, no attack came. An uneasy quiet had descended across the Elven defenders, each man thinking of the battle ahead, each man silently praying that they would see the sunrise of another day, when suddenly, the drums that beat the advance of the enemy stopped. There was a deathly hush throughout the Pass and surrounding land. The Elves held their position and stood ready, but confused as to what this meant, Evaine, by contrast, knew exactly what this meant. The advancing army of Molgoran had arrived, but still no attack came.

Suddenly a cry went up from behind the amassed troops within the Blendon Pass, Evaine immediately feared the one thing that he had dreaded the most had come to fruition, the enemy had somehow had got in behind them and were going to trap them inside the Pass. He immediately began running from his position issuing orders as he ran at break neck speed to reach the source of the cries.

"My Lord Evaine", came a shout, and a breathless Commander Eflen ran to his side. "Oldair has sent his Son and his army" Evaine's fear turned instantly to joy and could not hide his elation.

"Where are they Eflen?"

"My scouts have seen them about two miles back, heading past the Telishan."

"How many Men?" Evaine pressed

"About two thousand strong my Lord."

Evaine's elation slipped a little from his face. The city of Varon and Fenham combined had an army of twenty thousand strong, why had they only sent two thousand to aid the Elves? He quickly cast the thought from his mind, he had believed the Elves to be alone in this fight and two thousand extra warriors were better than none. Varon and Fenham needed to be guarded, he surmised, in case the Elves could not hold the

Horde. If that were to happen Oldair could not leave his city nor Fenham undefended against the tide of Molgoran's army that would wash over them, would he have done the same had the situation been reversed?

He turned to Eflen. "Seek out Prince Teon and have him join me. See that our comrades are well fed and watered should they require it, but be on your guard Eflen as I fear that we are not far from the commencement of war."

Commander Eflen acknowledged his orders and disappeared into the night, shouting orders as he went.

Evaine returned to his post. He had taken up position on the right side of the rock face so that he could see over the massed army that stretched before him into the Blendon, but reach its floor in an instance if he needed to. His father's words had resonated in his mind, *Take extra care of yourself, you are no use to the Elves as a dead hero. A king they must have."* He would remember the warning, but if the fight came to him he would not turn his back.

Evaine didn't have to wait long until the familiar figure of Teon, making his way through the assemble Elven defences, came into view. He was not the bloodied, dirt streaked and broken bodied man that Evaine had last seen, he now walked as a Prince, head held aloft and an expression that exuded intensity and focus. Silver chain mail adorned his body and he wore a bright red tunic with the crest of Varon emblazoned on the front. A heavy sword lay strapped across his back and a shorter sword hung at his waist.

He immediately spotted Evaine and his expression changed to a broad smile that he could not stifle.

"You decided to join us then?" Evaine shouted over to him.

"Well I had nothing better to do old friend, plus I couldn't let the Elves claim all of the glory now could I?"

Evaine returned the smile and leapt down to greet the Prince with clasp of hands.

"I am glad you came Teon, you have my thanks, come, we have much to discuss."

Evaine led Teon to his lofty position and filled the Prince in on the detail and the enemy they faced. He advised him of the strategy that they had agreed upon and Teon nodded his agreement with the plan.

"I just wish I could have brought more men," Teon stated, "my father is eager to support the Elves and all of Invetia in the struggles ahead, but felt that he needed to ensure that the cities of Men be protected should Silverdale fall. It will then be up to the Men of Varon and Fenham to be the last stand, the fallback position if you like, for the whole of Invetia and that needs strength of arms to defend."

"You have nothing to apologise for my friend. I had given up hope of any coming to our aid, your presence, no matter how big or small is most welcomed. But I warn you Prince Teon, your Men will have to work hard to keep up with the Elves when battle comes." They looked at each other and laughed, not knowing that this would be the last time they would do so for a long time.

"No news from Bannock or Kelphus?" Teon enquired.

"None" came Evaine's short response.

Evaine advised Teon of the death of Thealine and that he now stood as the uncrowned king of Silverdale. Teon passed on his condolences and those on behalf of his father.

"I fear that he will not be the last of the Elves to die in the coming days, such is the force that we stand against." Evaine informed him in a whisper.

"Then we will die defending our lands, our people and our liberty." Teon replied and shot him a determined smile. "What of Sam and Anna? What of your Sister? Has there been any news?"

"None, we can just pray that they travel fast and true and play their part in the writings of history." Evaine solemnly replied.

"Then we will ensure that we give them enough time to make all of this worthwhile." Teon responded with an edge to his voice.

Evaine was glad Teon was here, he somehow felt that the burden of leadership had been slightly relieved; he had someone to share his thoughts and fears with as he could no other. Teon was a good man to have by his side.

It was just before the break of dawn that the attack came. As predicted, the Horde came at the Elven defenders with full force, thousands strong surging forward in a wave of snarls and edges. Goblins made up the frontline of the attacking force, gnarled yellow wiry bodies were everywhere. They screamed and howled as they threw themselves against the Elven blockers. Such was the force and numbers that rushed forward, the Elves found that they were being pushed deeper into the Blendon from the pressure applied. The first row of Elves were overrun and broke apart within minutes of the attack and many lay dead or screaming in agony from the horrific injuries sustained from the pikes and razor sharp long swords that the Gnomes waved around. The attackers killed many of their own from the indiscriminate swings and lunges that they made, but this did not stop them, if anything the howls of delight grew louder and the attack more ferocious. It took moments for the Elves to rally to the attack, but in a battle at close quarters, moments lost meant countless lay dead or dying. It was the Elven bowmen that finally began to slow the attack. As Evaine had hoped, the bowmen had clear sight of the enemy. They rained down a blanket of arrows into the mass of screaming Gnomes. Each arrow finding its mark, sending the yellow gaunt forms falling to the ground oozing thick brown blood from the wounds inflicted. The enemy did not stop to clear its dead; they simple clambered over the fallen and began to attack anew. By this time the Elven foot soldiers had prepared for the next onslaught and met the rush head on, Elven blades cutting and slashing the barely armoured Gnomes, cutting them down in great swathes with each swing of their swords. Blood exploded skywards as each sword met with the flesh of the Gnomes. Arrows continued to rain down on the enemy and they fell with each twang of the bowstrings. After a while the frontline of Elves retreated and the second row stepped up to take their place, fresher and prepared, they were able to continue the defence of the Pass. Fewer Elves fell now and the grass beneath their feet had soon turned into a mass of sticky brown blood that seeped from the bodies of the fallen. Slipping underfoot the Elves began to push the Horde back. Inch by inch they fought to win back the ground lost; minute by minute they managed to advance further and further until the Elves themselves had to manoeuvre over the fallen Gnome and Elven soldiers. Every few minutes the frontline would fall back and the next row would step up to the task. The Gnomes were maddened and tiring, the Elves calm and fresh.

Evaine watched with Teon from his position further back and felt the slightest twinges of hope, "*It was working*" he thought as he watched the Gnome Horde slowly being edged from the Pass. Eventually they had retaken all the ground they had lost from the original attack and Elven soldiers again stood at the mouth of the Blendon. Their losses had been 'many but not catastrophic,' Evaine considered, 'maybe two hundred' and although he felt pain and anguish for each of the fallen, it was a good start to the defence of Silverdale. The Gnomes began to retreat back to the ranks from which they came, until all had left. A cheer began to resound around the Pass from the victorious Elves of Silverdale, they had thwarted the first attack and had stood strong, and they had won this first engagement. Amid the shouts and cheers, Teon lent into Evaine, as the Elven king had joined in with the cheering and shouting.

"My Lord, that was a victory for the defenders of the light, but I fear this was nothing more than a test of our resolve and strength. I fear that we have yet to see the real army that Molgoran commands. The next attack will be more of a test of that I am sure. We need to clear the dead and make ready for the next wave for I fear it will be here all too soon." Evaine hated hearing the words from Teon, not because his words were false or inappropriate, but because they were true. He knew that the army that stood beyond the mouth of the Blendon was massive and ferocious, he knew that the forces that made up its numbers were from the darkest pits of Invetia, and he knew that it was only a matter of time before the next wave of horrors crashed upon the small collection of Elves and Men. He turned to Teon and gave him a resolute nod.

"I know this too my friend, but let them have this moment, let them have these briefest moments of joy and relief for I know that soon we may have neither again for a very long time."
Before Teon was able to respond Commander Eflen was at his side.
"My Lord, I have ordered my horsemen to commence their attacks, I feel that this is the time to start to harass and confuse the blackhearts. Let us take the fight to them for a while and plant the seed of doubt within them, let them know that we are not for the taking, that we are a fighting force that they will not run roughshod over. Do I have your blessing my Lord?"
Evaine was not sure, he didn't want to alert the Horde as to his plans too early, but they would have to be called into battle eventually, maybe it was an opportune time to do so.
"The Cavalry are yours to command Eflen, just make sure they do us proud," came his eventual response.
"They will do so my Lord, of that you have my word."
Within seconds Commander Eflen was atop his horse, bellowing orders and disappearing into the distance.

They waited, waited until the sun had fully risen and the warmth of its touch began to warm the land, but no attack came. The army of Molgoran was obscured by the high cliffs of the Blendon and Evaine had given the order that no man was to venture forward. He had feared that the sight of the endless rows of blackened snarling attackers that stretched as far as the eye could see would achieve nothing other than to feed hopelessness, 'no, it was better that they remained an enigma' he had decided. They would fight each wave that attacked and stay focussed on the duty and job at hand, nothing more was needed. He had still sent scouts forward to watch for movement of mobilisation within the Horde ranks, but these reported directly to him or Prince Teon and no one else. So they simply stood and waited. The men within the Pass began to clear a path through the bodies that lay broken and lifeless in front of them. They carried the wounded from the battlefield and sent them back to Silverdale for nursing. They had no time to deal with the Elven dead. They would have to wait until they could offer them a burial in keeping with the Elven tradition, but for now they moved them to the edges of the Pass with as much care and respect as could be given. They stacked the dead bodies of the Gnomes directly at the mouth of the Blendon, stacked them so the enemy would see them first when the next attack came, maybe this would distract them from battle. Evaine could hear no sound from ahead, no sound of the Elven Cavalry's flash attacks and foray's that Commander Eflen had gone to deliver. The cliffs muted everything. He would wait for the next report.

It was well into morning before the shout went up from the front of the defences, something was happening.

They sat on the banks of the Tillamus and allowed the sun to dry off their clothes. Anna and Elay and gone to find food and returned with armfuls of assorted fruits which grew all around the lush banks of the river. Elay had also found some wild mushrooms and nuts which she loaded into her pack. They sat and ate their fare, the Tillamus had replenished their depleted water supply and they drank until full from the crystal waters that gurgled and splashed passed them. Sam lay on his back after consuming his food and gazed up at the blue cloudless sky. He felt the warmth of the sun on his face and the cool breeze in his hair, he wished again that they could stay here forever, he wished that the world would forget them and they could disappear from memory and live here for all time, but he realised that no amount of wishing would change the task at hand, he had to succeed in doing what he was destined to do or Invetia would be plunged into everlasting darkness and misery. "What will you do when all of this is over?" Anna asked Elay. "Return to my people and help my father govern the land, also to my teachings. I help with schooling in Silverdale for the younger Elves; teach them about the land and how to care for it and about what it truly means to be born of Elven blood, at least that is my hope Anna, so long as there is a Silverdale to return too." Sam watched Elay look at Anna and he knew the question was coming but couldn't stop her from asking, part of him wanted to hear the answer.

"What about you Anna, what will you do once all of this is finished?"

There it was, she asked what he had feared, and he waited silently on the response. Anna considered the question for some time before answering.

"I don't belong here Elay, not like Sam. I have a home and a family in my world that will be missing me and worrying no doubt. As hard as it will be I guess I will return when the time is right. If I get back and find that I wasn't missed then maybe I will come back to stay." She laughed and threw herself back to lie on the soft grasses and soak up the sun's warmth.

"And you Sam, what will you do?" Elay asked.

The question caught him by surprise; he didn't expect her to have asked him.

"Well...I....I" He couldn't find the words.

"Sam will stay here Elay," Anna interjected, casually and relaxed as she continued to lay staring at the sun, "Sam has a different situation back home and I would guess that, whilst he never knew it, he has been searching for Invetia for the whole of his life"

Elay flashed a quick smile at the response, Sam flushed slightly at Anna's appraisal.

"Thank you Anna, I am quite capable of answering my own questions, anyhow it's time we got going, and we have a long journey still to complete."

He got up and threw his bag over his shoulder and waited for the girls to respond. As they gathered their belongings Sam allowed himself a quick grin, Elay smiled when Anna had said he was staying, she wanted him to stay! As they left their place of rest and had walked for a few miles along the river bank he found that he was still grinning to himself.

They walked for the remainder of the day, enjoying the surroundings and the sounds of the Tillamus as it rushed past them in flashes of silver and gold as the sun reflected off its clear surface. They rested occasionally and briefly, to quench their thirst and rest sore feet. The mood was good as they talked about how different their lives had become and how

251

different they were to be after they had reached journeys end, whatever that may be. The conversation of Anna leaving still hung heavy in Sam's mind but the subject was not brought up again and he was content to let it alone. Gradually the sun began to shrink into the horizon and the long shadows of the approaching night began to form. The peaks of the Solitude Mountains loomed ever closer now; they stood massive and forbidding ahead of them, like huge leviathans at rest. Tomorrow they would pass from the greenery of the meadows and trees and into the foothills of the Mountains. They knew that tomorrow would bring harder travel and difficult terrain, so they ensured that they fully rested and enjoyed their current surroundings. They made camp near the riverbank. Elay and Sam set about preparing the meal. They started a small fire and cooked the mushrooms and nuts that Elay had foraged earlier, Anna went for another swim in the Tillamus under the half light of the now full moon. Once finished she joined them and they sat and ate together. Conversation was sparse as each of them drank in the last remnants of the tranquillity that the land offered. Sam sat with his back against a tree and Elay sat next to him, her head on his shoulder as they began to drift off to sleep. For the countless time, Sam found himself wishing that time would stop and leave them as they were for eternity.

Morning came all too soon and they were packed and heading for the Solitude Mountains as the sun rose to signal that start of another new day. Whilst the sun tried as hard as it could to break free from the grip of night, the sky remained grey and heavy that morning, the air now taken on a colder chill that had been absent the day before. As they neared the Mountains it grew colder still. It wasn't long before the lush grasses had been replaced by shingle, stones and small rocks as they pushed forward. The Tillamus continued to gurgle past them but the water now ran uneven as it began to cascade down mini waterfalls and splash against bigger rocks that jutted out from its riverbed. They had walked for several hours and now stood almost at the base of the Mountains. The river had begun to narrow as it was squeezed between the now huge rocks and boulders that rose up on each side. It ran shallower also, and soon they found that they often needed to wade through its waters to ensure that they were able to follow its path. The day remained overcast, the landscape mute of colour and sounds and the chill of the wind began to bite. They had passed into a wide canyon which funnelled the air directly at them which made it feel colder still.

"Where are we going?" Anna asked no one in particular, "I mean we have been told to follow the river, but to where? When will we know when we have arrived at where we should be?"

"I guess we will just know." Sam responded, not sounding entirely confident in his response.

"Ah yes", Anna replied, "when we have reached the door that is as hard as stone and as yielding as air!" she exclaimed with a heavy dose of annoyance. "I mean, what the hell does that even mean, Amador did not know, although I suspect that he knew more than he was letting on, Elay doesn't know, so what chance do we really stand of finding it?"

Sam began to try and answer her when he noticed Elay staring at him with a look of dread.

"Danger!" she hissed whilst pointing at Sam's pocket. He immediately looked down and noticed the amber glow emanating from beneath his clothing. He stuffed his hand into his pocket and brought forth the Orloc. It instantly flashed into life; amber magic fell about them all and pulled both Anna and Elay close to him. It had a different feel to it than before, it was more of him that felt the magic and less of the Orb. It had never acted on its own like this before, he had simply pulled it free and it had responded to his touch, acting on its own accord. He felt the exhilaration of the magic coursing through his body as the Orloc glowed bright and dazzling. Every part of him tingled as the magic wove its intricate web around him, through him and out into his surroundings.

He stared in awe at the magic that held him cocooned within, lost momentarily to its wonder and beauty, when suddenly his attention was immediately diverted to a huge shadow that detached itself from behind a boulder ahead. Elay cried out at its appearance, but Sam was already facing the giant as it lumbered towards them. It stood well over nine feet tall and was shrouded in darkness. Its yellowed eyes locked unblinking on them from beneath its hood as it approached. Although cloaked and hooded, Sam could see the blaze of its eyes piercing into them. It rasped as it walked towards them, menacing and slow. He felt Anna come up to his side, short sword drawn and ready. She was breathing heavy and he saw her sword shaking as she held it in front of her protectively. Sam, much to his surprise, felt no fear such was the euphoria and security that the Orloc emanated. He stood and watched as the massive form continued its slow advance. He knew the power was there to command if required, he now understood that he was becoming more and more at one with the magic as Graflon had told him would happen. He didn't fight it he let it wash over him and fill his senses with the feeling of excitement that the Orloc brought.

"This is the path of the dead that you walk upon," it whispered to them as it advanced. It was not a sound that it spoke aloud, it was sounding in his mind and he could see from their reactions that Elay and Anna heard it too.

"This way is closed to the living. You will find nothing here but death and sorrow. Are you prepared to sacrifice that which you hold most dear? For if you wish to pass this is the toll you must pay."

"We have to pass. We have to reach where we are destined to be." Sam responded, his voice steady and confident.

"You seek passage where stone, both prohibits and permits. I know of where you seek, I know of your coming, I have known for an age, and yet you know little of what is to behold. Your ignorance will not serve you well, however, knowledge will not have saved you either. The magic of Krelyn will not aid you once you have passed through, you will be alone."

"Who are you?" Sam shouted at the creature as it stood now not more than forty yards ahead. It did not respond it just kept its gaze fixed on the group. Anna shifted her position to move back to stand with Elay. The creature immediately shifted its gaze to follow.

254

"I am the watcher, I am the guardian of the pass, and I am the servant of the dead that lay within. I am the keeper of their eternal rest."

"Then let us pass Watcher, let us fulfil the duty that has fallen upon us to deliver." Sam demanded.

The creature stood in silence as if weighing up the words and considering its decision. Sam watched didn't take his eyes off it for a moment. It was almost ethereal; it seemed almost as if it were made up from smoke as its cloak wafted in the breeze of the pass. After several moments of silence it spoke again.

"The dead will be waiting; they have awoken from their slumber. The price is agreed, the passage is clear for you to travel."

"About time," came Anna's voice behind Sam.

"About time what?" Sam whispered back at her, his eyes never leaving the apparition ahead. As he continued to stare the Watcher, it suddenly disappeared and was gone.

They stood for a while unsure as to what had happened, then the magic of the Orloc shimmered and died away indicating that the danger had passed. Sam went to place the Orloc back into his pocket and was immediately shocked; the Orloc had disappeared, it was no longer in his hand and yet he felt its presence, he felt the familiar warmth that it radiated. It was then he realised the transition was complete, the magic of the Orloc was now his, now enshrined within him and no longer within the Orb, his to command forever. It was now as much as part of him as the blood that flowed through his veins. He had not disbelieved Graflon when she had told him that it would be so, it was just that he did not expect it so soon. He stood for a moment longer, feeling the magic flow through his body and trying to acclimatise himself to its feel. Anna and Elay were then at his side.

"Is everything okay Sam, are you alright?" Elay asked, the worry she felt evident in her voice.

"Yes Elay, I am fine, look." He showed them his empty hands.

"So it has come to pass, the magic of father passes to son." Elay spoke, her voice now filled with wonderment and awe.

255

"What the hell was that thing?" Anna asked, getting back to moment, "it scared the crap out of me!"

"It said it was the Watcher" Elay replied. "I have heard that the Solitude Mountains contain the passages to the dead. For that reason no one ever ventures here. Even the trackers and tradesmen that have to pass this way avoid the Mountain passes. They would rather make the week long trek around rather than enter. We will have to be careful as they say you can wander the Mountains forever if lost."

"I hope the price agreed is worth it then." Anna added. Sam looked at her, his head still not clear from the loss of the Orloc and the transition that had ensued, then collected his bag from the floor and began the trek forward. They walked deeper into the Mountains, the Tillamus still flowing alongside them as their ever present companion. It was much narrower now; it had the appearance of a stream more than a river. The land was also becoming far more difficult to pass now, huge boulders and cliff faces appeared at each twist and turn. A few times they were forced to divert away from the river just so that they could find a passable route. Climbing rocky slopes and hauling each other over the boulders that they could not go around was becoming the norm. Each of them ached from the exertion of the trek, yet still the Tillamus flowed, steady and constant down the Mountain passes. They were stopping more often now to take on water. The day had remained dull and overcast but, as before, the passages and proximity of the Mountains made the air stale and stifling. Cuts and bruises covered their arms and legs from the continuous clambering over sharp jagged rocks, but the route showed no sign of levelling. As they looked ahead all they could see was an endless wall of rock and stone.

Night came quickly in the Solitude Mountains, the sky going from day to night in, what seemed the blink of any eye. They found a suitable spot, as level as they could find, ate a cold meal and rolled into their blankets and were asleep within moments.

They were awoken in the middle of the night by torrential rain pouring from the sky. Thunder echoed through the canyons and passageways and streaks of lightning flashed across the sky casting a silvery glow to the landscape. They were soaked through before they could gather up their belongings and find some cramped shelter under an overhang of rocks. Too wet and too noisy to sleep, they huddled together with knees drawn up against their chests in an effort to keep warm and watched the storm rage across the sky. Sam and Anna had never seen a storm as violent as this. The wind howled in rage and the thunder threatened to rip the sky apart. Small stones and rubble fell from the overhang like waterfalls as the thunder shook the earth. There was to be no more rest this night. They sat and watched the rain cascade down the rocky paths until the first hints of the approaching morning were in sight as the muted orange of the Sun came slowly into view. The thunder and lightning had passed but, whilst lighter, the rain persisted and showed no signs of relenting.

Wearily they began the slog forward.

"What I wouldn't do for just one more day like the day we found the Tillamus." Anna shouted through the rain, wind and gloom. Both Sam and Elay nodded in agreement, too weary to answer. Nearly the entire journey ahead now was ascending. The river flowed down from somewhere ahead. In some parts it cascaded in waterfalls that collected in pools that then fed the tributary of the main river. The rocks were now slick and glistening with the rain which made traversing them even harder, coupled with their lack of sleep; often someone would slip and add to their collection of cuts and bruises. The going was slow and ponderous, and it required all their concentration and energy just to stay upright. It had been three days now since Amador's departure with Kalt. He had told them that he believed the wellspring to be four days walk, but this was not allowing for the weather and slow pace that they were now forced to adopt. Onwards they went, deeper into the Solitude range, ever watching for the river's start point, ever hoping that the next boulder they climbed would signal journeys end. The Tillamus was now little more than a weak stream, so narrow that it could be stepped over in one big stride and the current was little more than a trickle, but still it went on.

"We must be close now," Sam called back to the girls as he scrambled over a particularly big rock that stood in their path, "the river is barely running"

"I hope we are," Anna called back; "we are exhausted!"

Sam waited atop the climb and reached down to help haul both Anna and Elay up the slippery surface. Once all up they walked over to start down again the other side when they all caught their breath. From the vantage point that the rock offered they could see for several hundred yards down the canyon that stretched away on the other side. The trickle of the Tillamus ran the length of the passage and then disappeared into a wall of rock that closed the passage off at the other end. This was the birthplace of the river; this was the Wellspring they had been searching for.

CHAPTER

15

The shout from the frontline of the defenders indicated that something was approaching the Blendon Pass. Evaine immediately clambered to his position on the cliff face to see if he were able to have sight of the new threat that the Elves would face. Just past the mouth of the pass where the Elven defenders waited was an incline and beyond that the land opened up into wilderness and scrubland, this is where the armies of Molgoran had massed. It was not visible from the mouth of the pass, however, the passage that led to it was. At the opposite end from where the Elves waited mist and smog hung low obscuring anything beyond. It was not until the enemy set foot on the passage between their camp and the Elves that anything was visible. He watched with intensity.

He felt his stomach tense as he fought down a mixture of fear, excitement and dread. He watched and waited. Finally, the mists began to swirl and a solitary figure came into view, its dark form silhouetted against the backdrop of steam and fog. From his viewpoint it looked like a man, hooded and cloaked and walked with the aid of a staff. It did not hurry, it walked towards the encampment of Elves as if out for stroll in the afternoon sun.

"Demon!" Evaine immediately thought. He was scrambling down the cliff face then, pushing his way through the collection of Elven warriors in an attempt to reach the frontline. Teon had seen him run forward and given chase. Several of his Ichbaru guards also followed on, anxious that the King be kept safe at all costs.

Evaine was hurrying now, he knew that this single figure was more dangerous than the thousands of Gnomes that had attacked previously, and he knew that a false move from an archer's bow or a soldier's sword would see hundreds die from this single figure alone.

"HOLD YOUR POSITION AND YOUR FIRE!" he screamed as he ran forward through the ranks of surprised and confused defenders. "DO NOT ENGAGE THIS ENEMY BY ORDER OF THE KING" he shouted anew, desperate to avoid the inevitable bloodshed should anyone fail to heed his orders. He was three rows from the front of the Elven guard now when the approaching figure stopped. It stood, head bowed and waited.

No one moved it was as if time itself froze, such was the stillness and the silence. Except for the rushing figure of Evaine, Teon and the Ichbaru, the land and its peoples stood motionless. As they raced forward and finally broke through the frontline of the defence, they too then stopped, one hundred yards from the statuesque figure in the distance. The minutes slipped by and no movement or sound was made. Mist swirled around the figure in the distance as if he was smouldering from some unseen flames, but this was all that showed movement for several minutes more. Evaine could feel his heart beating hard as if it were going to burst free from his chest. He shot a quick look at Teon who stood by his side; he didn't notice the King's stare, as his eyes were transfixed on the figure in the distance. Eventually the hooded figure raised its head slowly and broke the silence.

"Elvesssss," it hissed, *"little Elvesss. Why do you fight the inevitability of your demise? Why do you offer yourselves so freely to death when I can offer you life? Listen to my words and save yourselves from annihilation. Surrender the Echenor to me and I will see to it that you live, stand against me and I will see to it that you die. But know thisss, death will not come to your women and children this day as it will you should you stand against us, oh no, they shall live, live to serve usss, they will serve our will and answer our bidding, they will live a life of torture and misery, they will live a life of eternal pain and suffering, death will be the dream that they desire. Little Elvesssss, do not make them pay the price for your stubbornnesssss."*

"DEMON" Evaine called out to the cloaked figure. The hood of which lifted to the sound of his voice.

"There is not an Elf alive today that would lay down his arms for such a foul twisted being as you. There is not an Elf alive today, whether man or woman, boy or girl, old or young that would not take up arms against you. You will be destroyed should you march against the Echenor, against Silverdale, for there is more than Elves that stand against you today. Men, Dwarf and Troll stand with us shoulder to shoulder along with the rest of Invetia. Do not fool yourself to think us weak, we are stronger than you can possibly imagine for we fight for what we hold most dear, we fight for life, we fight for an end to tyranny and we fight for Invetia. We will see that your actions, whatever you decide on this day, are met with an overwhelming response. If it is war that you choose Demon, then the people of Invetia will see your demise. I suggest you tell you're Master to choose carefully." Evaine was shaking with the anger from his words and fire that raced through his veins. The land fell absolutely silent as they waited on the Demon's response. It was a long while before it spoke again.

261

"Foolisssh Elvessss. We answer to no Master; we are masters of all we choose. You speak of Molgoran as if he walks among us, Molgoran is long dead, but his magic remains, his magic helped release us from the Echenor, his magic made us strong once more. You ask me if I choose war, YOU chose war when we were imprisoned centuries ago. Your ancestors brought this day upon you." Evaine felt the Demon's eyes burn into him from beneath the cowl. *"Do not think that the son of Ceriphan will save you either."* The Elven King felt his blood run cold. *"Yessss, we know of him, we know of his journey to seek audience with the dead. But we also know that he cannot remove the magic of Molgoran, he cannot stop its heartbeat. He will die as will you all. This day will be remembered Evaine, son to the dead Thealine, as the day you allowed the annihilation of the Elves from Invetia. I know that the Dwarves have not come, I know that the Trolls have ignored you and I know that the pathetic race of Men have barely answered your call. You stand alone and you will die alone."*

The Demon began to turn away and walk back down the path, when it stopped and turned back to face them. It reached inside its cloak,

"You might want to keep this as a memento of our time together." He pulled an object from his cloak and tossed it high into the air. It landed and rolled to within feet of Evaine's boots. There, looking up at Evaine was the severed head of Commander Eflen.

"I broke your little horssssess." the Demon let out bloodcurdling laugh as it turned and walked back into the mists, its laughter left echoing in the air.

It was within the hour that the next attack came. There was no restraint on numbers as before. The mists broke apart at the far end of the passage and were filled instantly with thousands upon thousands of clawing and screaming shadowed bodies. They rushed heedlessly forward in a tide of darkness, climbing over each other in the rush to get to the Elven defenders. They came in all shapes and sizes from the smallest that skittered

262

along in a blur of speed and teeth chattering and snapping, to the biggest that lumbered forward in mighty strides. Every manner of creature crushed together, maddened and wild. Gnomes with their wiry yellowed bodies squashed against a tide of Kobolds that snapped and bit with their razor sharp teeth, Goblins that carried jagged edge swords and oversized bows run the risk of being trampled on by Ogres that lumbered forward wielding spiked chains and crossbows. Things that flew followed, ghostly and malformed, they rose up through the steam and dust of the clambering Horde. In the midst of the nightmare that descended on the Elves were the Demons, just a few, but they stood out instantly, their red eyes burning hatred and malevolence. The creatures that fought for them gave them a wide birth, none wanting to get to close. On occasions when they did, they burst into orange flame and turned to dust in an instant.

Evaine watched on, the sight of the advancing horror began to leech away the confidence and belief that he had carried. He watched the distant landscape fill to capacity with the terrors of Molgoran's army and he knew that, behind those which he saw, there were ten times more waiting for their chance to rip the Elves apart.

"Evaine" came the familiar voice of Teon. "We need to have our Pike-men at the front; we need to keep the enemy off long enough for the archers to find their mark."

Evaine allowed the doubt and terror a moment more before snapping back to the moment.

"Agreed, give the order Teon; I will see to it that the archers stand ready."

"My Lord" Teon interjected, "That's not your role Evaine, you have Commander Litten to see to the archers." Evaine shot him a dark look, but Teon continued, "You have Commanders and Generals that all know their roles, they all know what to do." He was having to shout now as the uproar from the advancing enemy grew loud in their ears and the war drums restarted, booming through the pass. "You are the King, you are the one that has to endure, and you must lead your people whatever the outcome!"

263

"What would you have me do Teon?" he shouted back at him, unable to hide the anger from his voice, "Would you have me scurry away and hide? Would you have me take refuge behind the walls? Well I will not do that Teon; I will not run from this battle whilst my men die. My place is here."

Teon stared at him for a short while, then smiled and grabbed his hand.

"Then we die together brother."

Both men drew their swords and made their way down from the cliff face.

The enemy had now reached the frontline. Elven soldiers stood with long Pikes held forward to meet the surge of the Horde. They did not slow as they approached, launching themselves at the Elven army. The crunching of bone against metal resonated even louder than the incessant booming of the war drums. Screams rose as hundreds of invaders either ran at or were pushed onto the extended bladed poles of the defenders. Bodies ripped apart as the razor sharp blades cut into the exposed flesh of the enemy. Blood sprayed in all directions as bodies were sliced open and the ground underfoot turned reddish-brown as the attackers fell in heaps, but the enemy numbered far too many for this to slow the attack, onward they poured, crushing forward in a blind rage. The Elves could not swing their weapons quick enough to meet the number that pressed forward and eventually their line started to buckle. Commander Litten had given the order for the archer's to concentrate all fire upon the massive figures of the Ogres that stood in the midst of the attack force. Fifteen foot tall goliaths that could crush anything that got to close. He ordered that the arrows be dipped in buckets of pitch that had been carried to the cliff face, lit, and fired into the approaching giants, but upon seeing the frontline of the defence starting to sag under the pressure from the number of attackers, he switched targets and started to try and give the Elves time for the rows to fall back and regain strength. Hundreds of arrows zipped over the heads of the bulk of the Elven army, leaving the air filled with the smoke trails of their flight, each one striking with a deadly accuracy and finding their intended target. Screams rose as the arrows found their marks and for the briefest of moments the attack faltered as the first entire line of attackers fell dead. Immediately the Elves seized the opportunity and the front row fell back to allow the next row to step up, but almost as soon as the last man had taken his place the attack came again. They clawed and screamed in fury, ripping and tearing the Elves that stood in front of them. Hundreds of Elven soldiers were dead, each one ripped apart with the ferocity of the Kobolds claws or the Goblin's swords. Evaine saw that his army was being pushed back, deeper into the pass as the advancing Horde pressed ever forward. The archers reigned down their arrows again and again but this now barely slowed the maddened attackers. He gave the order then for the remainder of the pitch to be poured across the whole of the pass behind the third line of defenders. The battle was not going well, hundreds of Elves lay dead or dying and they needed time to regroup and reorganise. If they could pull back the frontline and ignite the pitch it would give them sufficient time to rest the soldiers and arrange a better defence. He knew it was a risk, Commander Eflen's death and the destruction of the cavalry that kept watch over the routes in behind the Elven army meant that they were now largely unguarded. If the enemy got in behind them they would be trapped, but he was running out of alternatives, they were losing the battle and would be overrun completely if he did nothing. With torches standing at the ready, the front three rows gave as hard a push forward as they could; archers reigned down arrows as fast as they could load them. The long pikes from the Elves further back jabbed and stabbed at the attackers from between the gaps of the soldiers in front. It took every ounce of strength that they could muster. The screaming bodies of Molgoran's army were so tightly pressed into the pass that there was no room for them to be pushed back into; such was the crush from behind pushing them forward. Each time an attacker fell another two crammed forward, slashing and screaming.

It was then that Evaine made the hardest decision of his short reign. With two rows of Elven defenders ahead of the pitch line he gave the order for the fire to be lit. Two hundred Elves stood trapped between fire and the enemy but he had to safeguard the lives of the thousands of Elves and Men that stood behind. He shouted warning and all of those that could get back behind the line did so, but many did not, could not. The line of pitch blazed immediately from the touch of the torches in flames ten feet high. A wash of the sudden intense heat seared their faces as it crackled to life. For an instant there was no sound other than the roar of the fire, and then the screams began and the smell of burning flesh filled the air. Evaine could bear no more and stalked away, unwilling to let his men see the tears that now ran down his face.

Anna immediately grabbed Sam's arm on seeing the wall of rock ahead of them. The passage was completely closed off and there was nowhere else that the Tillamus could run too, this had to be the spot.
"Are you alright?" she asked him as he stood atop the boulder and just stared into the distance at the rock face ahead.
"I think so, it's just, it's just that it has taken us so long to reach here, cost us so much, it kind of feels weird to have finally found it. I am not sure I can yet believe it." he replied.
"Well let's go check it out, let's make sure that it is what we think it is. I think you should go first Sam," Anna stated. He looked at her and nodded.
He climbed down the other side of the boulder and waited at the bottom to help both Anna and Elay down and then the three of them started forward, all staring ahead at the trickle of the Tillamus disappearing into the wall of rock, each almost expecting it all to disappear before reaching it, but it didn't. They reached the rock face after the short walk, Sam in the lead. They had now momentarily forgotten their aching bones, sores and blisters, cuts and bruises. In that moment they were filled with an excitement and expectation that blotted out all other emotion and feeling.

He arrived at the end of the passage and, sure enough, looked down to see the small stream of water that was the Tillamus disappear into the stone. He ran his hand over the smooth surface of the rock. It felt almost warm to touch and was as flawless as silk. No rutting or jagged edges could be seen, it was as if it were carved marble. Anna and Elay joined him and watched as Sam ran his hands over the whole surface, watched as he knelt down to look as to where the water disappeared, and then repeated the whole process.

"Anything?" Anna asked impatiently. Sam turned to her, his face full of confusion.

"No, nothing."

"Well what now then?" Anna's euphoria at finding the Wellspring was now rapidly turning to impatience. "Can you not summon the magic to let us in?"

Sam stepped back and called on the magic that he now housed within. He felt it stir to his call, felt it rise within him as commanded, then....nothing. He felt it at his fingertips as if it was trying to break free, but nothing happened.

Sam shot Anna and Elay an exasperated look.

"I guess we will have to wait, for something or someone."

"Aaaaarrrghhhh", Anna shouted. "I have not trekked all this way to just sit around and wait. I am going back up the other end of the passage to check we didn't miss anything, any levers or whatever." She stormed off back the way they had just come mumbling and cursing. Sam was content to let her go, she needed to let off steam and he rather her do it alone. He took the time along with Elay to check the every inch of the stone before them. It was definitely different to any that they encountered anywhere else in the Solitudes, but there was nothing. The surface smooth and warm to the touch, but no niches, ruts, handles anything. He thought back to what Graflon had said, *"Pass through a door that was as rigid as stone but yielding to air."* He looked again the smooth surface in front of him, "This was surely it," he surmised yet it made no sense. He put his back against the rock and pushed as hard as he was able, but nothing, nothing moved, clicked or showed any sign that this was exactly as it appeared, a block of stone.

He let his body slide down the stone until he sat at its base, defeated and frustrated by it all.

"We will work it out Sam, we have to be patient and the answer will come." Elay soothed his temper as she sat next to him. She leant over and kissed him deeply on the mouth. He was not expecting it and it sent his emotions cart wheeling in all directions.

"What was that for?" he asked when she finally pulled her lips away from his.

"Because I believe in you and because I love you."

He didn't know who seemed the most shocked him on hearing it or Elay on saying it aloud. He stared at her, she was impossibly beautiful. She giggled and buried her head in his shoulder.

"I love you too." he whispered and hugged her close. They sat and watched together the distant figure of Anna grow ever closer as she scanned every inch of the passage looking for any clue as to gaining access to the wellspring. She was in a considerable funk. At one point she cursed loudly as a sharp stone dug into her foot. She balanced on one leg as she pulled off her boot and hurled it across the canyon in her temper before rubbing her foot clear of debris. She then realised that she was now going to have to retrieve it by either hopping across to where it lay or risking further pain from the stones on her barefoot. She chose the hopping option. Both Elay and Sam, despite their weariness and frustration, broke out into fits of laughter that did nothing to ease Anna's temperament. Eventually she gave up and came to sit in front of them cross-legged and sighed in her defeat.

"Can we eat now?" she asked in a pathetic voice.

"C'mon Elay, let's get the bags, wouldn't want her highness to hurt her foot again now would we." They laughed as they rose and, hand in hand, walked over to retrieve their backpacks.

"Laugh as much as you want," Anna scorned under her breath, "seems I am the only one taking this seriously. Well you won't be laughing when you get back as I am taking the comfy spot against the rock." She rose gingerly and allowed the numbness of her legs to depart then moved over to where Sam and Elay had sat. She let herself almost fall down onto her behind and then leaned back against the smooth stone. As she was leaning back to rest she thought that she must make contact with the stone soon, she wasn't that far from it when she sat, then suddenly, before she knew it she was tumbling head over heels backwards and into darkness.

Sam and Elay retrieved the bags from where they had dumped them still laughing at the mood of Anna as they did so.
"Do you want me to rub your feet for you Anna?" Sam called out jokingly. He turned to see Anna's reaction but she was nowhere to be seen!
"Very funny Anna but if you want to eat I suggest you come out before it's all gone." Sam called out. He looked at Elay for support but found the Elven Princess not laughing or smiling. Her face was full of worry and anguish.
"She's just playing one of her pranks, don't worry Elay," he tried to reassure her.
"Look around Sam, where could she possibly be hiding?" she replied.
Sam did so, the passage was clear of any places to hide, it was a straight line from the smooth stone that they stood in front of to the boulder and rock that they had climbed down to get in at the other end. Anna could not have made it the hundred yards to the rock and got over it without help in the seconds that their backs were turned. There was nowhere else to hide, no other rocks or boulders, no crevices to crawl within, nothing! Elay was right and Sam now began to panic.
"She was right here," he said, "right here sitting on the ground. Where the hell could she have gone, there's no way out of here apart from where we came in."
"We know that there is a door Sam, a door that we haven't yet found." Elay mentioned ominously. Sam felt the blood drain from his face.
"ANNA, ANNA!" he yelled as loud as his lungs would permit, but all he got back was the echo of his call.

She fell for some time, it was impossible to tell how long as she tumbled over and over into complete darkness until finally coming to a juddering stop as she hit the ground with a thump. She lay on her back, the wind momentarily knocked from her body. She gasped short breathes as she tried to catch her breath. Eventually she began to gain control of her breathing. She lay perfectly still, disorientated and confused. *"What the hell just happened?"* she thought to herself as she lay in the dark. *"I was sitting down against the rock and....."* Then it hit her, the rock, she had somehow managed to unlock the door that they had been searching for. Somehow she had triggered something that had allowed her to enter albeit unsuspectingly. She began to feel the fear well up inside of her, what if Sam and Elay could not find the mechanism to release the lock as she had what if they never did and she was here alone forever. "SAM" she yelled, nothing. "ELAY" still nothing, no sound permeated here; it was tomblike, dark cold and silent.

"Get a grip," she told herself as she still laid flat on her back. She began to wiggle her toes and fingers to check for any breaks, she felt no pain but needed to be sure. Then she moved her arms and legs to find all was as it should be. She had some pain in her back and head, but apart from that she was unharmed, which she considered to be a miracle based on how far she thought she had fallen. She slowly rose to sitting position and tried to orientate herself. As her eyes became more accustom to the dark she was able to make out the rough outline of the walls. She was in what appeared to be a narrow tunnel. Gingerly she got to her feet and found that there was enough height for her to stand upright, she could also touch each of the side walls with outstretched arms. She could see no further than an arm's length in front of her, such was the blackness, so she had no way of knowing which way the correct direction was, or if there even was one, to start walking towards. Staying put however was not an option though, she reasoned that if you could get in here you must be able to get out and staying where she was would not help her find the exit. She decided to head down the tunnel to her right and started off with arms outstretched to use the walls as guidance. She didn't know if she was shaking because of the cold or because of the fear that she was now feeling. She had not been without Sam or a guide during her whole time in Invetia and now she had neither. She was alone, cold and lost. There was water down here that ran down the middle of the tunnel. She was not able to see it, but she could hear it splash against her boots as she made her way slowly, following the path of the walls. She was thirsty but she didn't want to risk the water, she could be drinking anything such was the darkness and she decided that she would not take any until she absolutely had too.

She soon realised that time was immeasurable down here in the dark. She did not know if she had walked for twenty minutes or several hours, she did not know if she had covered several miles or not yet one, she found it very disconcerting.

"HELLO" she shouted periodically into the dark but no response came, not even an echo, everything remained muffled and muted. She had no food with her and she was hungry but tried not to think on it and just concentrated on putting one foot in front of the other. On and on the passageway ran, never deviating from the straight path it seemed to follow. Anna couldn't remember if she had walked around a corner or even a slight bend, it just seemed to go on dead straight forever. She trudged on wearily, each step she took she felt as if she was slipping further and further away from Sam and salvation, her fear and self doubt growing with each passing minute. She was about to stop, her feet sore and soaked from the long walk when she saw something in the distance, a pin prick of light shone directly ahead. It was so small she had to stare for an age to check that it wasn't her eyes playing tricks on her, but the more she looked the more she saw it. It was a light!

Buoyed by the sight she doubled her efforts and began to move towards this tiny piece of salvation at a greater pace. Each step brought her closer to the object in the distance. As she got closer it began to take shape, it began to stretch out into a thin shaft of light that ran from ceiling to floor. She was almost running now, stumbling forward, desperate to reach the source. After several minutes of running in the dark, she had reached the light and was standing in front of it. The brightness radiated from the left hand side of the tunnel. She groped blindly in the dark and found that the tunnel had come to end at this point. She desperately spread her hands against the tunnel end and felt around, almost immediately she felt the cold metal of what felt like a ring handle, it was then she realised it was a door, the light she saw was seeping through from the other side of a closed door! She grabbed the handle with both hands, silently offered some prayer that it be unlocked and twisted. It groaned in response, and then slowly began to turn. She applied all the limited strength that she could muster and twisted it as hard she could. The handle groaned a final time then turned completely round. The door opened inwards and she was blinded by a rush of the light that exploded forth into the darkness of the tunnel. "*Welcome*" came a whispered voice from within.

Sam slumped down next to Elay after checking the stone again. She had lost count of the amount of times that he had done so and still he had found nothing that could have triggered entry or any mechanism that could have enabled Anna to disappear from sight. He had even walked to the far end of the passage to make sure that Anna had not gone back over the boulder, but found that it was not possible for a single person to have scaled the boulder from this side, the height of any grab holes were too high for him and he was taller than Anna. It would have required a second person to have lifted the first to reach. So it was that he came back confused, dejected and increasingly worried as to the whereabouts of the missing Anna.
"There is nowhere else that she could have gone," he told Elay, "nowhere other than through that rock."
He was at the end of his patience, he had even tried to force his magic to react, to somehow find the missing girl but, as before, it had failed to answer his call. He didn't know what else to do.
"I am sure that she is safe," Elay tried, "time will return her to us Sam."
She tried to sound assured and convincing; however, it was difficult when she didn't fully believe her own words.

They ate a little food and took on water and remained seated for the remainder of the day. Sam had told her that they were not going to leave the passage until they had discovered Anna's fate, no matter how long it took. Elay had suggested trying to find the Watcher, try to find him and ask him as to Anna's whereabouts. It was an option, but not yet, not until he had no others. He was not ready to leave yet, not wanting to go from where Anna had last been, if she returned and found them to have gone she would panic, she would need them and he wanted to be here for her. It was decided that they would stay the night and make a decision in the morning. He didn't like the idea but there was nothing more that could be done this night other than to wait. They unpacked the blankets and draped them over their shoulders, neither attempted to try and sleep for they knew that it would not have come, so that sat and watched the light of the day slowly fade away until replaced by darkness.

She was immediately blinded by the brightness that stabbed at her eyes like shards of broken glass. Anna clenched them shut in response feeling the heat of the glow radiate off her face. Slowly, after a while, she began to prise them open, little by little allowing her senses to adjust to the new environment. Eventually she was able to open her eyes fully and found that she was starring at a door that was now half open. She could not see beyond, such was the brightness of the radiance that emanated from within. She stood and waited, had she really heard a voice or was her tired mind playing tricks on her? Then she heard it again, but this time it was joined by other voices that floated towards her from within the room.
"Why does she wait?"
"What is it doing, why has it not entered as was foretold?"
"Where is she, let me look upon its face, let me see the messenger."
The voices cascaded out of the room and into the tunnel. They washed over her as they went, hundreds of voices falling over one another, speaking all at once, jostling for attention. They became faster then; rising and falling in tone, questioning and

answering all at the same time, louder they grew, faster they came, each one rushed to greet her and with a force that made her dizzy. Faster and faster they went until she was unable to understand what was being said, all of the voices melded into a single shrill sound that drilled into her and caused her to put her hands over her ears in attempt to block out the noise. It didn't work, they rose louder, accusing, shouting, whispering, demanding, questioning, all of them at once, all of them jabbing and poking her at the same time, the sound was deafening. She turned her body away in response, trying to make the voices stop trying to escape the cacophony of noise that attacked her, but louder they rose in reply, faster they grew again, whirling around her head, filling her senses with noise, suffocating her with each spoken attack, each one smashing into her with increasing force. She began to feel unsteady on her feet, she began to feel her head cloud over and her limbs go heavy, until the last thing she remembered was falling towards the floor and then blackness.

She didn't know how long she been unconscious but she came awake to a voice that carried to her softly and calmly in her mind.

"Time to wake my child, time to wake."

Her head was still spinning and felt bruised from the incessant barrage that it had been subjected to, but this voice was different, this voice spoke alone and without the accompaniment of others. This voice soothed the pains that she felt and made her feel safe and warm, it wrapped her up in its silk and cradled her until recovered.

"My child, it will soon be time for you and your destiny to meet. You have travelled far and have endured much but it is nearly over, you have arrived where you were always destined to be. There is but a few more rivers to cross, but your journeys end stands almost before you."

She fought the heaviness that she felt and forced her eyes to open. She was lying on the ground, the light was more of a glow than the harshness that she had seen before and it was not abrasive, it was as comforting and soothing as the voice that spoke to her. She could not see too much of her surroundings as her eyes were sore and blurred from her recent awakening, but she could just make out what seemed to be a huge cavern that spread out before her. Then the voice sounded again.

"Allow my voice to heal your pains, hear me Anna and me alone."

Anna's eyes snapped open wide, she knew this voice!

"Ruern?" she called out.

"I am here my child, and I will stay with you for as long as I am permitted."

Anna was confused and scared, she wanted to get up, she wanted to get back to Sam and Elay she wanted to run and run and run, but she couldn't, her body still felt heavy and her mind was not yet fully clear.

"Where am I Ruern, where is Sam, how is it that you are here?" She spoke out to the emptiness of the cavern. There came no reply. She closed her eyes again and lay on her back trying to allow the heaviness to fade from her limbs and for some feeling to return to her numb body. It took a long while until she felt that she would be able to move to a sitting position. She opened her eyes and found that she was starring at a high ceiling of what looked like a cave. Stalactites hung massive from the rock above and finished in sharp points, they were many and looked as if they could come crashing down at any moment. She began to gently shift her body to lie on her side and then propped herself up on her elbows and looked into the cavern that spread out before her. It was indeed a cave but massive in scale, so large that she was unable to see across to the other side. Water ran down the slick walls and formed large pools, each dark and murky, that glistened in the soft glow that bathed the cavern. Huge pillars of stone lifted from the floor and joined with the ceiling above, they stood like Giants, frozen by time, ancient and forgotten. Anna could not see the door that she had passed through to gain entry and there was no sign of any other life down here. It was cold and filled with the echoes of the dripping water that ran down from the walls and dripped from the ceiling above. Apart from that it was silent and still, nothing moved.

275

"Ruern," she whispered harshly and waited, but again, no response came. She moved herself then to a kneeling position and finally she rocked back and stood up. She felt a little unsteady on her feet but the numbness had left her legs and she was beginning to feel the blood begin to flow, restoring her strength and balance. Slowly she began to walk towards the centre of the cavern; each of her footsteps echoing around the cave as she went. There was a larger pool of water that sat at what she believed to be the middle of the room, all the other pools of water that had collected across the cavern floor seemed to flow into this one, she wondered if she was looking at the birthplace of the Tillamus, the Wellspring that they had been searching for. She got within twenty feet of the pool when a voice rang out from within.

"You have crossed to the land of the dead, you have come to the place that we rest and your arrival is as foretold." Anna stopped immediately and felt a shiver of fear run through her body.

"You stand before us to fulfil that which you were destined to do, but there is much to discuss before the empty pages of your life can be inked upon forever."

She did not understand as to what the voice was referring too and she felt exposed and small in the presence of the tone that spoke to her within the cavern.

"Who are you?" she managed to shout out to the emptiness.

"I am many that speaks with one voice, I am the voice of the dead," came the reply.

Anna was beginning to feel herself shake such was the fear that had welled inside, but she fought to keep her composure.

"What is it that you require of me? I am not the one to face Molgoran; I am not the bearer of the magic of the Orloc. I am Anna not Sam," she shouted defiantly. There was a long pause as the voice seemed to consider her statement.

"We know exactly who you are and you are here to fulfil the role that you were born to fulfil. The door of stone would not admit anyone but the heir, and here you stand."

She stood and waited for the voice to speak again, but the room had fallen silent other than the constant dripping of the water.

She dug her nails into the palm of hands in frustration at her inability to understand what was going on, angry that none of this made any sense. Sam was the son of Ceriphan, Sam now possessed the magic of the Orloc and Sam was the one to destroy Molgoran, they had been told nothing else since arriving, even Graflon had told him so, and then, suddenly, she went cold as the realisation began to sink in. Graflon had told Sam that he would face a door that was as rigid as stone but yielding to heir, not air! She felt her heart racing in her chest, but this was not right, Sam was the heir, Sam was the one to destroy the evil from the land with his magic.

"I DO NOT UNDERSTAND!" she cried out and slumped to her knees crying freely, as much in fear as in frustration.

"Child," came the voice of Ruern, soft and calming, *"do not cry, and do not be sad. You cannot change the path that has lead you to the here and the now, those pages have been written and cannot be altered. Look upon the pool now my child and see what it is that is asked of you. Look and you will understand what must be done. I will stand beside you; the dead have permitted it to be so."*

Anna opened her eyes and lifted them to the dark pool of water that lay before her. She kept her eyes focussed on the middle looking for anything that would help her understand the role that she was being asked to play. She stared for a long time until eventually a small glimmer appeared at its centre. The light grew into a dull pulse as it grew bigger. It began to change from a pure white colour to a purple glow. She watched as it seemed to float across the water's surface until it hung not five feet from her kneeling position. She stared hard into the heart of the purple light that floated before her and there in the middle she saw an egg shaped Orb. She then realised that she was staring at an Orloc.

"Let me tell you what it is you need to do." Ruern's voice spoke to her softly from within as the Orloc flashed into life and engulfed her in its purple haze.

CHAPTER
16

They stood for a while and watched the flames of the fire raise high into the afternoon sky. Each man leaning heavily on their weapon trying to recapture their breath such was the intensity of the defence of the pass. Some sat and simply stared off into the distance as if trying to decide if this was all really happening and not some waking nightmare. They tried to ignore the screams that rang out from behind the fire, tried to ignore the stench of seared and burning flesh that filled the air and hung heavy, trapped within the confines of the Blendon. They tried to block out the horrors of watching their brothers trapped and burning within the pass. They knew that Evaine had been left with little option but it still did not change the sorrow and heartache that each felt.

After a short while orders rang out from within the ranks for them to start to fall back away from the fires. They would hold the Horde for a while but not much longer. They had to reassemble, regroup and re-forge the defensive lines that stood between the attackers and the gateway to Silverdale. Evaine stood with Teon deep in conversation about the best way to try and halt the advance. They spoke of the options available to them and it seemed that they would soon have to give up the Blendon Pass altogether and start the second phase of the plan. They would start to pull the Men and Elves back to the Telishan. They would hold the pass for as long as they could but they would not wait for too long before falling back. Evaine gritted his teeth, he did not want to give an inch to the Demon's but he knew that if they were to delay the advancement then the Telishan was the best place. They looked at each other as they spoke, both men's eyes now missing the optimism that had existed before, both looked tired and anguished and both knew deep down that they would not be able to hold the Telishan for long, such was the force that pushed against them. Soon they would be back to Echenor and Silverdale, after that, they would be destroyed.

"It's about giving Sam enough time my friend; it was never about you or me, never about the survival of Elves or Men but the survival of Invetia." Teon spoke as if reading Evaine's thoughts.

"I know, just doesn't seem fair," came his quiet reply.

"That's because it isn't my friend." Teon patted him on the back and walked off to find his horse. Evaine stood alone for a moment longer and watched his Elven soldiers, dirty battered and bleeding as they began to walk to the other end of the Blendon Pass. He watched the flames crackle and dance and he listened to the roar of the army that waited beyond, an army so massive and strong that the Elves could never have hoped to have stood against it. He watched wearily as Commander

Litten approached, he too covered in cuts and slash marks, his clothes ripped and stained with his blood.

"We await your order my Lord," he called out as he grew close. Evaine closed his eyes against the smoke and dust that swirled around the Pass.

"Get the men to fallback Commander; amass at the far end of the Pass. Bar the way with anything that you can find, pikes, fire, wood, bodies of the dead, anything. We will slow them here whilst the rest of the army retreats into the Telishan as planned. We will make our stand there." Commander Litten hesitated,

"Are you...okay my Lord?" Evaine met his stare.

"I am not sure Commander, I guess time will tell." With that he walked away leaving the Commander to consider his response. The first of the attackers broke through the diminishing flames shortly after the Elves had fallen back to the far end of the passage as ordered. They came in a flurry of screams and howls as they raced towards the barrier that stretched across the Blendon. They tore at it with fury and rage and were through in the blink of an eye. Wood, mud and bodies were tossed aside as they crashed through and into view of the waiting Elven army. They were immediately met with a volley of arrows that cut down the foremost in their ranks but, as before, they did not slow, they kicked aside the dead before them and continued their rush forward, jaws snapping and blades glinting as they came on. The pass where the Elves once stood was now overrun with a tide of blackened twisted bodies as they crammed forward. Another volley of arrows raced to meet their charge, many fell but still they came until they stood within striking distance of the Elven line. Swords met flesh as the two armies clashed. Screams once again filled the air as blood and rendered flesh exploded from the meeting of the opposing armies.

The vast bulk of the Elven army had fallen back and was starting the three mile march back to the Telishan. The plan was that the small contingent of Elves that held the Blendon bought as much time as possible for the retreating men to reach the safety of the forest. They would hold for as long as they were able, and then break away into the foothills allowing the army of Molgoran through. Evaine had ordered them to find somewhere safe to regroup and then rejoin the Elves in the Telishan but all knew that the last defenders of the pass would most likely not live to see the sunset on this day.

As the battle raged behind a stream of several thousand Elves and men hurried along the dusty path to reach the Telishan. Evaine sat atop a white stallion as he headed the retreating army with Teon at his side. The sounds of the struggle that raged behind them soon began to fade to silence as they marched further away from the Pass. They had been marching for thirty minutes, the trees of the Telishan beginning to come into view when a young Elf ran from the marching army and to the side of Evaine's steed.

"My Lord," he panted, "they have found us, they have come around the Pass my Lord and they flank us on both sides, look!"

Evaine cast his eyes to the direction in which the young Elf was pointing, and there cresting the ridgeline, was a line of shadow, a line that was moving towards them at speed. He spun around to look in the opposite direction to find the same image mirrored. The forces of Molgoran had them trapped. Evaine's worst fear had come to be; the Horde had found a way around the Blendon Pass as he had feared. The destruction of Commander Eflen's cavalry had meant the route was lightly guarded and easy for the Horde to traverse. He cursed in rage; the Elves left behind had been left to the slaughter with no need. The Demon's had thrown them a distraction, they had committed just enough attackers to give the impression that the Pass was where they would come at them, but all the time they had been streaming through the side passages that circumvented the Blendon. They were now trapped, they had the enemy on both sides of them whilst they lay spread thin and exposed on the road. They could make a bolt for the Telishan but this would serve no purpose, there would be no time to set defences and to get the Elves to safety, the opportunity was gone. Now they would be slaughtered on the road and

Silverdale and the Echenor would be for the taking. He roared in anger and frustration at the sky.

"THIS IS NOT FAIR! THIS WAS NOT HOW IT WAS MEANT TO BE, FATHER HELP ME!!" He felt Teon grab his arm as he began to regain control over his emotions. So few were brave enough to stand against so many and their reward was to be slaughtered on a dusty road, left to rot and turn to ash, left until time forgot that they had even existed. All of this and it was under his command and under his kingship that these days had come to pass. The Elves of Silverdale had come to a stop behind their King. They looked on bemused, tired and battle worn. Evaine turned to face them, now aware that the sounds of an army marching had ceased and silence had descended over the land. Teon leant over and whispered in his ear.

"Your people need you more than ever now Evaine, they need a King that will inspire them to fight harder and longer, they need a leader to remind them as to what it is they are fighting for. If Silverdale falls, if Varon and Fenham succumb to the Horde then let us give our people time to get away, let us give them at least a chance to rebuild that what we once had. Do not rollover and let the Demon Horde run us down, if we die today we die defending what we hold most dear. They need to hear this Evaine, it is time to be the King that you were destined to be."

Evaine turned and faced Teon from atop his horse and smiled a sad, weary smile, "Thank you my friend, you are right, maybe I just needed to hear it."

Evaine turned back to his people that stretched out before him their faces lifted up at him in expectation; he drew in a long deep breath, then in a voice edged with steel, shouted across the rows of soldiers that stood before him.

"Brothers and friends, we stand at a point in time where history will judge each and every one of us. What that judgement is will depend on our actions we take before the sun sets this very day. We stand united against a force which outnumbers us ten to one, a force that is intent on wiping our existence from the histories of Invetia. Whether we live or die today is not important, what is important is how we lived and how we died, what we lived for and what we died for. It must be that we defended to our last breath, our last man and with our last ounce of strength that we could have mustered. The race of Elves and Men will survive for we will give them that chance today, we will give them a chance to rebuild that which we may lose, a chance to rise again when the time is right. We will give them that chance so that it is our descendants that take forth the charge against the Demon kind in our names. I know that history will remember us as the ones that gave our Nation a future. I need you all to stand with me as we write our own chapter in Invetia's history. I need you to stand for the Elven Nation and for the race of Mankind. I also ask of you that, on this day, that you stand with me as a brother and as a friend. Will you stand with me?"

There was a rumble that arose from the ranks of assembled soldiers, a thundering of swords clashed upon shields, boots stomping on the dust below their feet and roars of defiance from the assembled. A voice boomed out from the army.

"For Silverdale and the King!" The cheers erupted and it was as if the torment and exhaustion from the past battle had washed away leaving just ironclad resolve and determination. Evaine felt the hair on the back of his neck stand up such was the outpouring of emotion that washed over him. If he had been looking he would have seen the approaching Horde hesitate for a moment as the crescendo of noise erupted into them like a tidal wave.

The outburst was brought to a sudden halt when a cry of warning went up from the men in front of Evaine.

"My Lords look!" They were looking and pointing back towards the road that led to Silverdale. Evaine swung himself round in his saddle to see rows upon rows of shadowed figures approaching them from the direction of Silverdale.

"How could this be?" Evaine exclaimed. "How is it that the enemy has got behind us without us seeing?" He was shouting out orders, mobilizing the men into defensive positions.

"If they come at us from there, what has befallen Silverdale?" Commander Litten cried. "Is it already lost to us?"

Evaine felt the bottom begin to fall out of his world; after all of his courage and words spoken to inspire his army, this was a hammer blow like none that he had ever had to deal with before. If the enemy marched on them from Silverdale's borders then the city would have been raised to the ground. If that was so then what was the point of fighting if the one thing they sought to protect was lost to them? He looked about in desperation as men ran in all directions preparing for the onslaught. It was just Teon that sat unmoving atop his horse, staring at the approaching army. He sat for sometime before he screamed so loudly that all seemed to stop what they were doing and looked at him.

"LOOK!" he cried, "LOOK CLOSER AND SEE."

Evaine squinted at the sun streaked horizon at the advancing Horde, but these were different, they wore armour that caught the sun's rays and blazed in splendour. They were shorter, stocky. He suddenly caught himself as he realised what he was looking at.

"THE DWARVES!" he cried, "BANNOCK HAS ANSWERED OUR CALL!"

He immediately dug his heels into his horse's flanks and started charging towards the Dwarvian army.

As he got closer he could now see the banners of the Dwarf army fluttering on the breeze as its numbers advanced on him. Almost as soon as he was able to make the faces in the distance, a loud booming voice sounded out from the Dwarf that marched at the front.

"I HEARD YOU MIGHT NEED SOME EXTRA HANDS, AFTERALL, YOU ARE ONLY ELVES." This was followed by Bannock's irrepressible laughter as it filled the air. Evaine brought his horse to a stop and jumped out of his saddle and ran to the Dwarf Lord as he advanced. When close enough he stopped and held out his hand in greeting to the Dwarf.

"Greetings Bannock Lord of the Dwarves, you are a most welcome sight. I offer my thanks for your arrival and my respects for the loss of Greston; he was a fierce warrior that was a credit to you as a father and the Dwarves as a nation. He died with honour."

"Well" Bannock roared, "I couldn't let the Elves soak up all of the glory. My son was indeed a brave and strong warrior and I grieve his loss, but how better than to honour his memory by smashing some skulls." He roared again with laughter.

"I bring twenty-thousand of the best fighters that Invetia can muster, let us stand together once more and do some killing!" Evaine once again felt that slight glimmer of hope, despite his efforts to keep it repressed. Twenty-thousand Dwarves was more than he could ever had wished for, enough that that glimmer of hope pushed its way to the surface and made him smile.

He walked with the Dwarf lord back to the army of Elves and Men that stood awaiting their arrival. He brought Bannock up to speed on the size and location of the Demon Horde, the losses that they had suffered and the death of his father. Bannock had told him that they would honour both Thealine and Greston by the stand that they took, shoulder to shoulder against the might of Molgoran's army. The battle would be dedicated to the memory of those lost.

"What of the boy?" Bannock asked.

"Nothing as yet, but we live in hope that he has arrived safely and is soon to finish the quest given to him." Evaine replied. As they arrived at the waiting Teon, a ripple of excitement went through the standing army having seen the sheer size of numbers that the Dwarves had brought.

Molgoran's army was closer now; they would be within striking distance within the hour. Accompanied by their Commanders, Evaine, Bannock and Teon sat down to formulate a plan that they would employ when the attack came. After several minutes of talking they agreed that a part of the combined armies would continue to the Telishan and make ready the defences required should they need to fall back. Whilst they had been bolstered by the Dwarves the enemy still out numbered them four to one and they also had the Demon's to consider. They did not know how many walked among the Horde but even a handful would be a match for hundreds of men alone. The battle would be hard fought and it was likely that falling back would be a necessity. There would be no other plan than that, they were flanked and had nowhere to go, no shelter to seek. They would engage the enemy at distance for as long as was possible with Archers, once the enemy was too close they would fight hand to hand against whatever came at them.

"Sometimes my Lords the simplest of plans are the most effective." Teon had offered.

"Agreed" Bannock spoke in his gruff voice, "but then again, sometimes you haven't got any choice in the matter."

Once agreed they rejoined their men and awaited the signal for the Archers to begin their assault.

They awoke to the sun already risen and burning off the morning haze that had settled across the Mountains. Both Sam and Elay had had a restless night, neither of them slept for any real length of time and found that they had dozed the majority of the night, unwilling to give up their vigil to Anna, but morning had come around and still Anna had not returned. They set about eating a breakfast of the berries that they had managed to pick in the days before by the banks of the Tillamus. Sam sat and stared at the food, reminded of just how wonderful that day had been and how different things were now. He had managed to lose the one thing that he had responsibility for, the one person that he had sworn to protect throughout their whole time in Invetia. Anna was not even meant to be a part of this and if something had happened to her he would never be able to forgive himself. Elay returned from collecting water from the waters that ran down the passage and offered him the skin to drink from.

"What are we going to do Elay?" he asked, "how long do we wait for something to happen? What if it never does, what if she is lost to us forever?"

Elay stroked his hand as she sat back down next to him.

"We will do whatever we have to, to find her Sam and we will find her. I will not leave your side as I share the blame for her disappearing, I feel the pain you feel and I know just how much she means to you. We will find her together." He looked at her, tears forming in his eyes and smiled,

"Thank you." he managed.

They sat and ate their breakfast in silence huddled close to each other not wanting to let each other out of their sight. Elay laid her head against Sam's shoulder and they sat and watched until the sun was fully raised in the morning sky. Elay watched the slow rise and fall of Sam's chest as they sat; she felt his head droop down and felt his body go limp as he drifted back to sleep. She remained still as she did not want to rouse him from his slumber. She looked up at the cloudless sky and sighed and wondered where they were to go from here and where this would all end. She thought back to Silverdale and the armies that marched upon it. Was it still there or was it lost? Had the Echenor retained enough magic to keep out Molgoran and his Demons or had it failed altogether? She closed her eyes against the questions, not wanting to have them crowding her mind. She opened them again to look down the passage and there, lying on the floor by the boulder at the other end was Anna. She blinked several times to make sure that her eyes were not playing tricks on her, but each time she opened them, there she was, laying on the ground unmoving.

"Sam!" she cried out. Sam immediately startled awake.

"What's happened? What's wrong?" Then he saw her too, laying not more than fifty feet away from him. He didn't wait for Elay to rise; he was on his feet in an instance racing towards the body of Anna. He reached her and found her to be breathing. He felt her face and found it to be warm to the touch.

"Anna," he called out softly, "Anna can you hear me?" he pressed. He watched as her eyes began to flicker slightly then, opened to meet his stare.

"Hello Sam," she whispered. "Miss me?"

She lay still for sometime allowing her body to regain its feeling, eventually she rose and managed to walk back, with the support of Sam's arm, to the blankets and food where Sam and Elay had kept their vigil the previous night. She took on a little water and food and rested with her back against smooth stone which stayed firmly closed this time. Sam wanted to ask her a thousand questions but bit his lip and allowed her to fully recover before he would ask them of her, but it was Anna that broke the silence first.

"I know what you are going to ask Sam," she said suddenly, "I know that you want to understand what happened, where I went, if I am okay and so on, I know this as I would want to have known it of you had our roles been reversed, but I need you not to ask me, at least not yet."

He stared at her blankly not fully understanding what she was saying. Anna pressed on.

"I am fine and unharmed, I have been given information as to the final part of our

Journey Sam and I ask that you trust me as I will tell you when the time is right." Sam began to shake his head, she was telling him that she had been gone for the best part of a day, disappeared to god knows where and now expected him to ask no questions! This didn't make any sense. He was suddenly angry, angry that he had travelled all this way, nearly lost his life on more occasions than he could count and now he was being told by the person that he trusted more than anyone else in world that he couldn't ask any questions, that she wasn't going to tell him what the hell just happened!

"Anna, what is going on? I need to know what happened, I have told you everything from the outset, I have shared every secret with you from the beginning I have..."

"SAM!" she screamed at him. "Let it go will you! I am asking you to trust me on this; I need you to just do as I ask. I know it's difficult but please, just this once will you accept this?"

"You know it's difficult!" he shouted back, then immediately stopped as he saw the tears streaming down her face. Elay was at her side and placed her arm around her as she sobbed into her shoulder. Elay shot Sam a stern look.

"Aaarrgggh," he screamed in exasperation and kicked out at the loose stones on the ground suddenly feeling very awkward with the whole situation.

They stood in silence for some moments until Anna had regained her composure. Sam looked on suddenly filled with regret and remorse from his outburst. It was Anna that finally broke the awkward silence that had ensued.

"I know where we need to go and I know how we get there." She spoke whilst looking at Sam. "I wish I could tell you everything Sam but I cannot, not yet. I promise that I will tell it all to you when the time is right and that time is not too far away, but please try to understand just how difficult this is for me. I don't like having secrets, I never have, but I seem to be the one that has to be burdened with them. It was same with your mother and what she told me before she died, I never asked for it but it was given to me to keep and I did so, not because I wanted to but because I had to. It's the same now Sam, it's not fair and I don't want it but I have no choice." Sam smiled at her as best he could. He didn't understand what was happening and he was frustrated by the whole situation, but still he smiled at her.

"I know Anna and I am sorry for shouting. I would trust you with my life and I know that you would not have it this way unless there was a very good reason. You said you know where we need to go and how we get there? Well come on then, tell us so we can get as far away from this place as possible." Anna returned his smile.

"We have to go back and find the Guardian of the Pass."

They came at them from both sides at once. The Horde screaming and frenzied as they ran towards the tightly formed ranks of the Elves, Men and Dwarves. They howled as they came, savage and wild, intent on crushing this final resistance that stood before them, but Evaine's army stood ready, buoyed by the arrival of the Dwarves and filled with a new sense of hope and possibility. The snap of a thousand Archers bows rang out from around Evaine's ears as the sky filled with arrows that flew in all directions. Hundreds fell as the enemy rushed forward, but as before, where a hundred fell two hundred replaced them. Again and again the longbows snapped as they unleashed their deadly bolts, hundreds fell and hundreds more swarmed to take their place. Still a mile away the advancing army continued its thunderous advance. The ground shook to signal the march and the size of the numbers that descended upon them. Evaine had already given the order for several thousand of his army to continue forward to the Telishan and prepare defences. He knew that even with the arrival of the Dwarves they were still massively outnumbered and would have to fall back at some stage of the battle, he just hoped that they could gain sufficient time for the defences to be readied in time.

Bannock growled in response to the enemy's advance, eager to engage the servants of Molgoran.

"I can wait no longer Evaine," he roared, "I will not stand and await their arrival; the Dwarves will take the battle to the evil that advances."

"Bannock, we must hold our ground, we are stronger as one unit rather than fractured ones," he shouted back, "stand with us and fight by our side." But the Dwarf Lord had already made up his mind and nothing Evaine could do or say was going to change his need for vengeance. Bannock roared, his voice transcending the rumble of the advancing Horde.

"DWARVES TODAY WE AVENGE GRESTON, TODAY WE SPILL THE BLOOD OF THOSE THAT TOOK HIM FROM US! STAND READY AND WAIT MY MARK."

Bannock gave the order to Rotrim who had joined him at his side to take half the amassed Dwarf army to the invaders on the right and he would lead the charge to the left. The Elves would support the attack from a distance with their longbows.

He turned to Evaine and Teon as they stood and watched as the Dwarf unstrapped the axe of Greston from his back.

"I wish you good fortune and sharp blades my friends."

"And to you," Teon replied.

With that, Bannock gave the order and ten thousand Dwarves detached themselves from the group of Elves and Men and fell in behind the Dwarf Lord, axes and swords drawn they roared at the advancing army. Rotrim shouted orders to his command and then they began their march out to meet them. The Elven

Archers came to the fore and another volley of arrows zipped out towards the Horde. But this time there came a response from within the ranks of Molgoran's army, winged beasts lifted from amongst their midst and headed straight for the Elves. Immediately Evaine and Teon were shouting commands to focus all bowmen to bring them down. Hideously twisted things and black as the night, they came at them with speed and frightening size. Huge leathery wings beat out a rhythm as they advanced. Massive horned heads with blood red eyes stared at the ever nearing Elven ranks. Their maws split wide as they gave out terrifying screams as they came in low and fast. The Archers responded firing hundreds of bolts at the winged demons, but nothing seemed to slow them. They were on top of the army within seconds, massive claws raking at the men below. Screams went up as those caught in their path were torn to shreds and fell in pieces to the ground. Others were snatched up in the massive claws and dropped back onto their comrades from a great height. As the Elves of Silverdale defended against this new threat the Dwarves had engaged with the bulk of the dark army that they had been marching towards. The Horde screamed their delight as they charged at the advancing Dwarves, in response the Dwarves cried out in rage as they swung their massive axes and spiked maces at the faces of the Horde ahead. They met with a bone crunching crash. The Dwarves were fierce warriors that hacked and slashed with a force that momentarily halted the enemy advance. They fought with tireless strength and ferocity as they smashed the enemy frontline and pushed deeper into the Horde ranks, but the sheer size of the opposing force eventually brought them to a standstill. They soon had to fight where they stood, strong and resolute but greatly outnumbered. They had halted the Horde's advance, but were now taking casualties themselves as more of the gnarled twisted forms surged mindlessly forward. The line of Dwarves began to buckle, but, above all of the screams and noise of battle, Bannock's voice rang out in a rallying call. "FOR GRESTON AND THE DWARVES OF INVETIA, FOR MY SON!"

The sound of the words seemed to strengthen the resolve of each to fight even harder and stronger. They bolstered their lines and repelled the force where it was showing signs of breaking through the defence, but Bannock knew that it was not sustainable, they would eventually tire and the enemy would run right over them. He called for the Dwarf lines to tighten, for second and third rows to form behind the frontline. This reduced the width of the defenders but made it a harder core to break apart.

Evaine watched as the Dwarves fought bravely, he watched as the winged horrors made pass after pass over the heads of his army stealing away and destroying more and more men on each pass. The Elves had managed to bring a few down but there were still at least ten that remained overhead, tearing and ripping at the Elven defenders. Such was the effect of the attacks that the Elves barely noticed in time that a large portion of the marching armies of Molgoran had managed to bypass the Dwarves now that they were fighting in a narrower configuration and were beginning to engage the flanks of the Elves and Men. Evaine's army was beseeched on all sides and from above.

"Be ready to move Evaine, be ready to start the retreat to the Telishan," Teon shouted across.

"No, we have to hold them longer!" came his angered response. They had barely been fighting for an hour, they had to give the defenders in the Telishan more time to have prepared, after all, if the Telishan fell then nothing stood between Molgoran and the Echenor and then Silverdale. Another winged beast was downed, he watched as is plummeted towards the earth punctured by several hundred arrows.

"All that time and all these soldiers just to down one," he thought darkly, "at this rate they would be wiped out before the bulk of Molgoran's army even reached them!"

He began to pray for a miracle.

They started back the way that they had come with Anna in the lead. They climbed the boulder at the end of the pass and were greeted with the familiar rocky landscape that they had left just a few days before. Sam trudged wearily alongside Elay watching the Tillamus grow wider and faster with each passing step. He had no idea where they were heading and had given up considering asking Anna again thinking that this was best left alone until she wanted to tell them. His spirits were slightly lifted when he considered that they may pass back by the spot where they first discovered the Tillamus, that day was wonderful as they bathed in its waters and rested in the warmth of the sun along its grassy banks. It seemed so long ago now that that had happened and he wondered if there would ever be another day such as that. They all seemed to have changed since then. Anna was now quiet and drawn into herself, whatever had happened to her was obviously still taking its toll, and he was changed also, the Orloc now a living breathing part of him, no longer a separate object to be kept in his pocket but something that now flowed through his veins as naturally as his own blood. He still hadn't got used to how it felt. He would, on occasions, forget that it was there, but on other times he would feel the butterflies in his stomach and the thrill of the feeling as it coursed through him. He could feel it now just resting below the surface ready to spring forth should the need arise. It had been this way since the re-emergence of Anna and he had put it down to the fact that she now more than ever needed his protection.

The land began to take on its familiar challenge to negotiate as they headed away from the peaks of the Solitude Mountains. The huge boulders and rocks that they had been so eager to clamber over now once again stood between them and wherever it was that they were heading.

The day was beginning to draw to a close and the skies darken when they arrived at the spot where they had camped just a few nights before under the overhang of rocks.

"I think we should rest for the night," Anna turned and spoke. Both Elay and Sam simply nodded their agreement.

After another cold meal of berries and nuts washed down with water from the ever present Tillamus, they unpacked their blankets and rolled into them to ward off the chill. Elay lay close to Sam, sharing the warmth of their bodies, Anna settled down a few yards away. Soon Elay was asleep and Sam turned to find Anna in the near dark.

"Are you asleep?" he whispered.

"No, trying but not happening," came her reply.

"Are you okay Anna? You seem distant. Is there anything I can do to make whatever is bothering you better?"

"No Sam, I am just tired and well a little scared." she replied in a frail voice.

"Do you think it will turn out alright Anna?" he continued, "I mean do you think we will be okay? Once we finish this what then, what will happen with us? After all, whilst I have heritage here it's as much a strange world to me as it is to you, maybe we don't belong here. There is so much that we don't know or haven't seen, in fact outside of the Elven world we know next to nothing about Invetia. What if it has no further need of me once I have done what I am supposed to do, what then?"

"I am sure that Invetia and its people will have need of you Sam Meredith once this is all over. I am sure that the people will make you their own."

"I am not sure Anna; in fact, can I tell you a secret?"

Sam then divulged his conversation that he had had with Graflon no longer seeing that its secrecy was needed. He explained that by saving the Elves and the Echenor from destruction he would also bring mortality back to the Elves and therefore be responsible for more deaths than could be measured. He told her of the dichotomy that he faced.

"I have to destroy Molgoran, I have to ensure that the Echenor is restored, even now it is depleted and who knows what has either passed through or broken free, but to do this I must ultimately be responsible for every Elf's eventual death. How am I supposed to live with that?" he asked. Anna remained silent for a while, he wondered whether she had fallen asleep, but then she replied.

"Nothing is without its price Sam," she spoke, "in making the Elves mortal you are not responsible for their dying you are responsible for their living. If the Echenor is not restored, if Molgoran is not destroyed, then they would live an immortal life of torture and sorrow. You are sparing them this existence, giving them a chance to live again free from tyranny and threat, and yes, they may have a normal lifespan but imagine how much more rewarding and fulfilling that life will be in comparison to the alternative. The way I see it is that you never really had a choice to make, it was always going to be obvious which one to choose." She stopped momentarily to catch her breath, "You will have saved them Sam, and you will have saved Invetia."

He lay there staring into the darkness of the night considering her words.

"Thank you Anna," he finally responded.

"For what?"

"For being with me throughout this, and for making it all okay. I don't think I could have come this far without you, you know, and once again you have been the voice of reason. Now get some sleep or you will be moody in the morning," he joked. He then rolled over and went quiet.

She lay awake for some considerable time after that. Sam never heard her crying as she lay in the darkness. After a long while she reached over and stroked his blanket.

"Goodnight Sam, I love you," she whispered, then rolled over and started to silently cry anew.

They came awake early the next morning, the dark of the night still not fully replaced by the rise of the sun. They ate a little, for that was all they had left, took on water and resumed the walk back through the difficult terrain. They knew that they were heading away from the mountain peaks as the Tillamus was much bigger here, back to resembling a river and not a stream as it had been further back in their journey. The day remained overcast much to their relief as it was again tough going climbing over the many obstacles that littered their path. As before they were often forced to stray away from the river's edge in order to traverse the landscape as some routes were simply impassable, but once around or over whatever blocked their path they were back on the banks of the Tillamus. It had become their ever present companion.

They walked for the remainder of that morning, Anna leading as she had been since leaving for the return journey. The pace had been slowed by the constant changing of direction and stoppages to take on water and capture their breath when faced with a particularly difficult climb. It was approaching early afternoon when Anna turned and stopped to face them.

"We have arrived, this is where we have to wait for the appearance of the Watcher," she spoke in a hushed tone. Sam and Elay looked at her then around at their surroundings and vaguely remembered it from a few nights ago, but nothing stirred, nothing alerted them to anyone else's presence apart from their own. Sam tested the air with his magic trying to send out feelers as to anything that may lay close by but nothing was apparent to him other than the constant uneasiness that the magic had been causing since their departure from the Wellspring.

"Are you sure this is the right place Anna?" Sam enquired.

"I am sure," came her short reply.

With that Sam and Elay pulled the blankets from their packs and folded them to sit upon and slumped to the ground to wait for whatever was going to happen. Anna by contrast remained standing and looking off into the distance.

Sam turned to Elay as Anna continued to look off towards the horizon. "Do you have any idea as to what is going on and where we are going?" he whispered.

"No Sam, I am not able to see the next step that we must take. Since leaving Silverdale to come and find you I have been unable to see anything past the now, I do not know what it is that we are intended to do but feel sure that whatever it is its time soon approaches."

Sam slunk back and watched as Anna paced up and down waiting for the next step to be revealed. It took several hours of sitting and waiting before finally something began to happen.

Sam was idly sitting, Elay had drifted off to sleep with her head resting on his shoulder, and even Anna had sat down not too far from his position, still staring off as if waiting, when suddenly she saw him, the Watcher, the Guardian of the Pass. As before his ethereal presence just lifted out of the landscape and stood not more than one hundred yards in front of her. Anna was on her feet immediately looking directly at the apparition. Sam jerked his head up, aware that something had caught Anna's attention. She was starring off into the distance as before but this time her gaze seemed to stop short of where the landscape ran away too, but try as he may to stare into the openness before her, he saw nothing there.

"Anna?" he spoke to her, but she ignored his voice, "Anna, what is it, what's wrong?"

"Sshhh, do you not see him?" she replied.

"See who?

"The Watcher, he is here, he is just there in front of me. I am going to speak to him; he has come to take us where we need to be going Sam be ready to go as soon as I am back." With that she strode off in the direction of her stares.

"ANNA!" he shouted, but she again ignored him and continued walking.

"What's happening?" Elay enquired, brought awake by the movement and shouting.

"Its Anna, I don't know what is wrong with her but she says that the Watcher is here, that he has come to take us to wherever it is that we are going. I am done playing games," he allowed the frustration he suddenly felt to be evident in his tone; "I am going after her!" Sam rose and began to run after the diminishing figure of Anna in the distance. As soon as he had gotten within twenty feet of her his magic brought him to a stop as it flared to life within him with an intensity that he had never felt before. It almost knocked the wind from his body and he was suddenly unable to move as if immobilised, he then realised that, whilst he could actually move, he just could not move forward, not towards the direction in which Anna walked. It was as if a barrier had been raised blocking his passage and barring him access. Try as he might he was unable

297

to break through. He summoned the magic within but each time it was unable to break that which blocked his path. Then he heard the voice resonating in his head. *"This is not your time Son of Ceriphan, not all words that need to be spoken need to be spoken to you. I will see that she is returned to you very soon, she is in no danger. Go back and await her return, your way is barred."*

Then silence. Frantically he tried again and again to summon the magic to break down the invisible wall but each time nothing happened. He banged against its invisible edges with his fists until they hurt, but nothing, he was locked out. He stood and watched as Anna walked a short distance further then she stopped and raised her head as if looking at something or someone, then she started talking words that he could not hear. He heard Elay running to catch him up from behind. She stopped by his side breathing heavily and watched Anna in the distance talking to what appeared to be nothing but air.

"The Watcher is talking with her," Sam said, "I heard his voice in my head telling me that the words were for her only. We will have to wait for her to finish as the path ahead is blocked to us."

Elay tentatively held out her hand and immediately retracted it as if burnt.

"There is a powerful magic here, an ancient magic that cannot be broken," she said. "Come Sam let us wait for her to return, I am sure that no harm will befall her whilst she is with the Watcher." She slipped her hand into his and they stood and watched.

"You hear my voice and you have come to my call?" the voice sounded in Anna's head.

"Yes" she replied to the shade that stood before her. "Why can my friends not hear your words or see your presence?" she asked.

"As the dead have told you already, this page of your combined destinies relates solely to you and you alone. Once the page is turned then they will find their chapter. Did they

298

explain what must be done; did they tell you all that you wished to know?"

"They did and I am ready to do what must be done," she replied trying to remain calm and collected in her response.

"Then the journey for you all is almost complete, but before I return you to your companions I must ask again that the price is agreed?

"It is"

"I will then grant you passage to that which you seek, I will see that you and your companions are safely transported to where you need to be; you simply have to tell me when you are ready. The path lays set."

"We are ready now Guardian of the Pass, we need to be on our way." Her hands were shaking and she felt her legs buckle such was the fear and emotion that coursed through every fibre of her body, but she held her ground and stayed on her feet.

"Very well," the Watcher replied, *"as the Orloc of Ceriphan and the Orloc of Molgoran are both present I will be able to take you to where it is that you must travel, the Elf girl of course may not enter when we arrive, she must remain outside. Rejoin your friends and I will make the arrangements to transport you to inside the Echenor mists!"*

CHAPTER
17

The Dwarves were failing. The crush of the Horde was pushing them further and further back towards the besieged Elven army. They fought with a ferocious pride and tireless effort but that simply wasn't enough to contain the numbers that poured forward at them. The dead of Molgoran's army lay like a black stain on the landscape, thousands killed at the hands of the Dwarves but still they came; still they threw themselves at the defenders with mindless insanity. Bannock's voice rose above the cries of battle urging his men to fight harder and longer. He was in the thick of it, swinging his axe at everything that launched at him. The enemy were trying to bring him down knowing that if they could kill Bannock then the Dwarf resolve would be tested to the limit, so it was that every Gnome and Goblin pushed forward in a maddened attempt to reach him. Several almost succeeded, they had him surrounded ready to silence his voice before a rush of Bannock's guards cut them down just in time, but it was more down to luck that he still breathed.

The Elves were also in trouble, a huge contingent of Kobolds and Ogres had bypassed the Dwarf frontline and were engaged in hand to hand fighting with the flanks of the gathered Elves and Men. As with the rest of Molgoran's army there appeared to be no concern as to whether they lived or died as they tore and raked at the Elves before them. Massive Ogres with barbed chains swung heedlessly at the tightly formed ranks of Men that blocked their path. They were slow and cumbersome and many were cut down before they could fully bring to bear their destructive weapon, but when the chain did find it mark it took the lives of many Men in an instant.

Evaine stood back to back with Teon as they cut down the attackers that stood in front of them, each sprayed with the black sticky tar like blood of the aggressors, yet still they came.

"WE HAVE TO FALL BACK!" Teon cried.

"WE CANNOT, WE NEED MORE TIME!" Evaine shouted back, his face contorted with the strain of battle.

"EVAINE, WE MUST..." Teon didn't finish the sentence as something immediately drew his attention. Evaine had stopped fighting, his attention also captured by what he was seeing. Red fire lanced out from the mass of the Horde and smashed into the Dwarves led by Rotrim. It crackled across the battlefield at a frightening speed and lit up the day in a red hue. As it crashed into the front ranks of Dwarves it boomed as if thunder and a whole phalanx of fifty Dwarves were launched skywards. Blown to pieces, their body parts rained down on the Dwarf army. Screams of defiance went up from the Dwarves but this was met with another bolt, then another. Each time the fire hissed and crackled as it raced out from the darkness of Molgoran's army and each time it exploded into the Dwarf's showering the soldiers in blood and gore.

"DEMONS!" Evaine screamed as he watched the massacre unfold.

Dwarves were sent scurrying in all directions as the fire danced across the landscape. Further shouts went up from behind, Evaine turned to see that Bannock's contingent of Dwarves were facing a similar attack as red fire spewed forward burning and destroying anything that was in its path. The sight of this

301

seemed to send the twisted forms of Molgoran's army into an even greater frenzy. They screamed and howled in madness and charged with blind abandonment, slashing and hacking at anything in their path, even their own kind.

It was clear to Evaine as he watched the horror unfold that it was the Demon's that had control over the Gnomes, Goblins, Kobolds, ogres and every other dark twisted being that they stood against. The Demons held them under their control twisting their minds and making them hate filled, making them act with no regard to their own lives or each others. They were nothing more than puppets being manipulated by each pull of the string that the Demons held. Teon had seen this also.

"Evaine," he called, "we must bring them down, the Demons control the Horde, we must kill them."

"How?" came the reply to which Teon had no answer.

The world seemed to stop at that point for Evaine as he watched the systematic annihilation of the defenders of Silverdale; time seemed to slow as he saw the countless bodies of the dead lying broken and ruined across the land. He saw the streams of blood that formed into shallow pools as the land could absorb no more. He heard the screams as they sounded from all around. The battle was lost and he felt something inside of him break, he then realised it was his hope.

"EVAINE!" Teon screamed trying to rouse the Elven King from his stupor. "We must fall back to the Telishan we cannot hold this ground anymore."

Evaine turned and found Teon's gaze, "No my friend," he said with tears in his eyes, "there is nowhere for us to run too where these things will not hunt us, there is no protection from which these things will not break. We make our stand here, we take our last breathes here. Send runners to call the men back from the Telishan, let us flood these plains with all the force we can muster for there is nowhere left to run. Go Teon, return to Varon and inform Oldair as to what he faces for once Silverdale is raised to dust it will be your home next."

Teon starred at him for a moment longer before responding.

"I will send the runners but my place is here, we will fight together until we can do no more." Evaine smiled despite the sorrow that was crushing him.

"Then let's get on with it." came his resolute response.

Bannock gave the order for the dwarves to fall back. He was brave and proud, and the decision had not been easy one to make, however, even he saw the destruction that was being wrought on his men. He knew that it was now about the survival of his race and not the winning of the battle that mattered any more. Slowly the lines of Dwarves began to rejoin the Elves and Men that were gathered in the centre of the battlefield. Orders had been sent to Rotrim to do likewise as the retreat was started. To their confusion and amazement the Demons allowed this to happen, the attack from the collected dark forces stopped. The winged horrors withdrew and returned to the darkness of their gathered army and the attackers that had engaged the Elves in hand to hand combat withdrew to their own. An unnatural silence fell about the land, save for the sounds of boots on ground of the retreating Dwarves.

After a while the combined armies of Elf, Men and Dwarf stood together, their numbers depleted and the soldiers bloodied and torn. Breathing heavily and exhausted they awaited the next onslaught, but it didn't come. The armies that now stood on both sides of them remained five hundred yards off. They stood in close ranks snarling and spitting at the Elves, hissing and shrieking their intent but none advanced. It was if an invisible line held them back. Evaine had a feeling that this reprieve, as welcome as it was, was the start of something far worse. He drew a deep breath and waited for it.

An hour passed with no signs of any change. His men had taken on water and they began to tend to the injured. They cleaned themselves off as best they could and removed the flesh that still clung to their weapons from battle, but still nothing happened. They watched as the steam rose off their attackers in the distance, they listened to the continuous snarls and rasps from the blackened forms, but there was no movement to be seen.

Another hour passed and Evaine stood with Bannock and Teon looking out at the encampment of the Horde.

"What is it that they are waiting for?" Teon asked.

"It's a game lad, they want us to be afraid, and they want us to know that we are still alive because they let us not because of anything else. Well my axe will tell them differently!" Bannock responded.

"I don't think so Bannock," Evaine interrupted, "they are waiting for something to happen." Almost before the final words had left Evaine's lips a murmur went around their encampment, and a scout ran up to Evaine's side.

"My Lord, one approaches, look." They turned in the direction of where the young Elf was pointing and, sure enough, through the light drizzle that had now started to fall a solitary figure had detached itself from the group. It walked slowly and purposefully towards them, cloaked and hooded and leaning on a staff.

"Demon," Evaine hissed. "The same one as came to us before at the Blendon Pass I am willing to bet. He comes to negotiate our surrender."

Evaine, Teon and Bannock made their way through the assembled soldiers and to the frontline to meet the approaching stranger. A detachment of Ichbaru immediately fell in behind them but Evaine ushered them away.

"If they wanted to have us dead then they would have done so by now," he said as he watched the guards reluctantly retreat back in with the rest of the awaiting soldiers.

The trio moved out some fifty feet from the throng of bodies and stood to await the arrival of the approaching figure. They watched as it meticulously picked its way forward, stepping over the ruined bodies that now littered the plains between them. Although hooded each could feel the eyes of the stranger boring into them from beneath its cowl. They watched as it edged ever closer. Bannock shifted the weight of his axe from hand to hand as he grew impatient at the approaching figure.

"I could kill it from here," he mentioned under his breath.

"Do not do anything rash Dwarf," Teon whispered, "remember what we are dealing with here." Bannock growled in response but held his ground and his tongue. Evaine by contrast said nothing, his eyes locked firmly on the Demon.

It got within twenty yards of where they stood before it came to a stop. It simply stood and stared at them for some considerable time as if assessing each of the men before it. Eventually it was Evaine that broke the silence that had ensued.

"You came to speak to Demon, so I suggest that you start speaking." His voice rang out in the relative silence of the plains. "Tell us what it is that you want, but be warned that whilst I do not doubt your power, I have one thousand arrows aimed directly at you, should anything happen to any of us then my Archers will ensure that your ability to stop a thousand arrows is put to the test."

The Demon reached up and pulled the cowl from its head in a slow and fluid motion. Its face was that of a man, an old man as before with blood red eyes. Its lips curled as it let out a slow mocking laugh.

"Such anger little Elvesss, especially when I have spared your lives so that we may talk, but I will forgive your indiscretion on this occasion."

The Demons eyes remained staring and unblinking at Evaine as it continued.

"You must have the clarity of vision that the war that ravages your troops is not one that you can prevail, you must be aware that death and destruction are not avoidable outcomes but an absolute definite. Little Elvesss have fought bravely and I am offering you life as I did before. Lay down your weapons and we will let you live, choose to fight and you will be cast into the pages of history until even time forgets who you were. I will see to it that all I promised you before comes to passss; your loved ones will be at the mercy of our will. I have been generous to make such an offer, not once, but now twice, I will not ask again."

Evaine struggled to keep the anger from driving him to do something he would regret. It took every ounce of resolve that he had not to have rushed at the Demon to kill it where it stood, but he knew that this would not be possible. He allowed himself a few moments to compose himself before answering. "I ought to cleave its foul head from its rotten body!" Bannock growled.

"Stay calm Dwarf; let us not be foolish in how we act." Teon quietly advised.

"And what would you do with us once we had surrendered to your will Demon? What would become of the races then once you controlled Invetia?" Evaine demanded of the Demon.

"You will serve us, you will be at our mercy, and your sole purpose will be to attend to our every wish. Your days will be long and punishing and your life will be an abject misery." the Demon responded. *"But at least you will survive as a people; you will be a part of Invetia. The alternative is that the land will go on without ever remembering that you once existed. Make your choice Elvessss, but make it a wise one this time."*

This was more than Bannock could stand and he had heard enough. He suddenly flew at the Demon, axe held above his head screaming in his rage. Teon made a grab for him, to try and stop him and pull him back but the Dwarf was too strong and enraged to be stopped. The Demon watched impassively as the Dwarf bore down on him. Bannock made it to five yards in front of the old man when red fire exploded from beneath the cloak of the old man and caught Bannock squarely in the chest. His body exploded in a crimson eruption as he fell to the ground in several pieces. A roar went up from the dark creatures of the Demon army as they watched the Dwarf lord fall dead upon the earth. Teon screamed his anger and hatred and it was down to Evaine to restrain him from making a charge himself.

"I am waiting for your response Elvesss. I assume that you will show more sense than your friend did." With that the Demon kicked out at the lifeless form of Bannock to further cheers and screams from the Horde.

306

"I will need to hold council as I cannot speak for the nation of men; I need time to discuss your offer with Teon." Evaine remained calm in his response. He was hoping to buy sufficient time to try and formulate the best way in which they could inflict damage on the Demons and their army. He knew that this was a futile battle; he knew that fate had chosen them to die this day and he was not afraid, he just wanted to ensure that he found the best way to take as many of the Demon Horde with them, especially the Demon that they faced, he wanted to make him pay for the death of Bannock more than anything.

"You have five minutes Elvesss," came the response.

"I cannot hold council on such an issue in five minutes Demon, I need more time."

"You have four and a half minutes." the Demon replied softly.

Evaine turned his back to the Demon and faced Teon so that it could not see what was being said.

"Teon, is there any way that you can make a signal to the Archers to fire at a secret signal without the Demon seeing? I no longer care that we will die this day but I need to see this foul creature dead before I am claimed."

"Yes, I believe that I could, but what then, we will be struck down by one of the others as soon as the arrows have left the bows."

"Then the army of Men and Elves will fight until dead, for death is a better alternative than living under Demonic rule, besides, we know not of Sam, for all we know he could be putting plans into place as we speak that will bring an end to the Demon Horde. We have to remain hopeful that Amador has steered him to the right path and done what needed doing. Whether we live to see it or not is not relevant, our races must persevere."

"One minute Elvesss," the Demon hissed.

Evaine smiled at Teon, "It was an honour to fight at your side Teon. It is a shame that we will not see the union that Men and Elves could have forged, that would have been something." He then turned and faced the Demon head on.

307

"I have your answer Demon." The old man smiled a wicked smile as he watched the lines of torment grow ever deeper on the Elven Kings face.

"*And.....?*" it said gleefully.

"After consultation we have decided that it should be you that surrenders your arms, it is you that should be returned to the Echenor for as long as time itself, for you and your kind are abhorrent to the land of Invetia. You are a side effect of magic, a cast off that has been thrown away and allowed to grow untended. You have no people, no history and you have no home. You are a sickness that needs to be cut out from Invetia before it can poison anything more. It is now your time to chose Demon, but you will give me your answer NOW!"

The Demon screamed in rage. It expected that the Elf would not have acquiesced to his demands, but to have the arrogance to ask for his surrender, to have the guile to speak to him like that was not what it had been expecting. The Demon immediately brought forth the red fire and held it in its hands in front of him.

"*You disgusting stupid Elvesss, I have your answer here!*" it spat the words as it looked at its hands ablaze with the life taking flames. Teon placed his hand behind his back, ready to summon that every bowman send forth their arrows into the Demon spawn. Evaine knew what was coming, he did not feel fear for himself, but he felt sorrow for the ones that would not die. He closed his eyes and stood ready for the burning blast of the Demon fire. He heard the magic crackle and snap; he heard the sound as it rushed to greet him, rushed to steal his life away. He felt the heat on his face as it raced towards him, then....nothing. For that split second there was no pain, no burning as there should have been. Then the screaming began.

He opened his eyes to see the Demon burning before him; white fire engulfed it from head to toe. It burned white hot as it began to turn to ash. It screamed a final gut wrenching scream that filled the plains with noise, and then disappeared into a pile of smoking ash. There was a moment of complete confusion as no one knew what had just happened. Then the

Demon army were moving in all directions screaming and shouting as they ran around confused. Teon grabbed Evaine's arm and spun him around, "I think that miracle you prayed for has just come true, look." Teon pointed off to beyond the Demon Horde. Evaine looked to see an advancing army of massive size, at least forty thousand strong. Each soldier a walking giant and as dark as the Horde army that they now marched into, and leading them into battle was a cloaked man that sent white fire hammering into the Demons that now stood confused and shocked.

"The Trolls!" Evaine exclaimed, "Kalt has come and Amador with him!"

The collective army of Elves, Men and Dwarves gave a thunderous cheer and then charged to join in the assault. Before he knew what he was doing Evaine was running towards the battle screaming and swinging his sword in front of him.

Sam and Elay watched as Anna began slowly walking back to where they stood. She managed to get halfway before collapsing on the ground. Sam was at her side in an instant.

"I am okay Sam," she managed, "but I could really do with some water."

He kneeled down by her side and cradled her head in his lap as she took sips from her flask. She had turned a ghostly white in colour and her body trembled. Sam sat with her for some time without speaking, gently stroking her hair and, after a while, watched the colour slowly return to her face and her shaking pass.

"I am okay now," she told him, "I guess I am pretty exhausted from the walk." she stated.

"And the meeting with the Watcher" he added. "It's been a tough day, perhaps we should rest a bit before we continue," Sam went on, "maybe we could head back to the banks of the Tillamus to where we first discovered it, do you remember that day Anna?" He said. "The sun was beating down and the breeze was cooling as we bathed and laughed, maybe we could do that again." He then stopped suddenly as he saw that her face did not return his smile that the memories evoked and he knew without a single word spoken that they would not be going that way. In that very instance he realised that they would never have a day like that again, the journey and the revelations that they had both been told had changed them from the people they were. Life had suddenly gotten complicated and serious and he didn't like it.

"We are not going back to the Tillamus are we?" He said it more as a statement than a question. Anna simply shook her head and looked sad. She thought that she was going to cry but she held back the tears, 'she had had too many of them recently,' she thought to herself.

"Then tell me Anna, where are we going?" he pressed. She held his gaze for a moment longer then softly replied, "The Echenor Sam, we are going to the Echenor."

White fire erupted throughout the Demon army's ranks and was met with screams of anger and pain as it burned all that it touched. Several of the winged horrors lifted off the ground to take flight away from this new threat, but were instantly burned into ash that fluttered down like snow from above. The Gnomes and Goblins rushed the advancing Trolls, screaming their hatred but they were brushed aside by the massive axe's that the Trolls swung with terrible force. Demons appeared and sent their red fire lancing towards the lumbering Trolls killing several instantly but the Troll's kept coming, shrugging off the slashes of the Kobolds blades as they advanced. Both sides of the enemy forces were being attacked by the advancing Troll army and they were in disarray. The Elves, Men and Dwarves were then in the thick of it, attacking the exposed rear and flanks as Molgoran's army turned to face the new threat that had arrived. Each time a Demon fire erupted it was immediately met with the white fire of Amador that burnt the Demon to nothingness. They screamed in their anger and sent fire lancing towards his position, but he was faster, he was prepared for the response and danced away retaliating with fire of his own. Thick acrid smoke began to form over the battlefield as the war raged, the army of Evaine had taken casualties, many lay dead or dying, but the army of Molgoran had fared worse. Thousands lay twisted and dead all across the plains, but their numbers were so great that there were thousands more that fought with blind rage, corrupted by the Demons that drove them to the point of frenzy.

Evaine then caught sight of Kalt swinging his massive axe into the small forms of the Goblins that stood before him, sweeping them away with a bone crunching snap as each of their bodies met his axe. Evaine ran to try and reach the Troll but momentarily lost him from sight as the gnarled yellow forms seemed to overwhelm the massive frame of the Troll At least thirty Goblins swarmed over and around him hacking with their swords. Evaine feared the worst until Kalt erupted from their centre sending bodies flying into the air. He was cut all over his body and in some places deep enough to see bone yet he did not falter or slow. His immense strength was brought to bear upon the Goblins, and soon they were nothing more than a bloodied pulp that stained the grasses below.

Kalt looked up to see the advancing Evaine and stood and awaited his arrival. As he did so, he failed to notice the huge form of the Ogre that loomed up behind him. Evaine saw the danger immediately and yelled at the Troll in warning but his words were lost in the screams of the battle. The Ogre brought up its huge mace over its head ready to smash the Troll into the ground when three arrows zipped out from the smoke and dust of the battlefield and embedded themselves into the Ogre's skull. It was killed instantly and fell to the ground with a crash. Kalt turned to see the dead beast at his feet and turned back to see Evaine almost at his side carrying an ash bow.

"Your debt is repaid." Kalt spoke as Evaine stood before him. "No Kalt, I could never repay the debt that we owe the Trolls, Kelphus or you. Thank you my friend, thank you for giving us a chance."

Kalt didn't respond, he looked at Evaine briefly then continued his attack on the Horde.

Sam's face turned ashen white, the place he feared the most was to be their destination. He thought at first that he must have misheard her that she must have still been confused and disorientated, but then he saw the look on her face and realised that he had heard her perfectly well. He stood for a long moment; her words had struck him mute. He was unable to find anything to say in response to her revelation. As he stood staring at Anna he felt Elay come up to his side.

"Are you able yet to tell us why we go to the Echenor Mists Anna?" She asked.

"No, not yet Elay, but soon I promise," she replied.

"Do we have to trek back as it will take many days and I fear that any threat that has either begun or about to begin to Silverdale will lay directly in our path. How are we to get there when faced with such danger?"

"The Watcher will take us; we will be safely transported there as soon as I tell him that we are ready to leave. I do not know how he will accomplish this, he did not say, just that it will be so."

Elay pressed her hand into Sam's as he continued to try to take on the words of Anna.

"Then we will go together and finish this that we have started." Elay said defiantly as she gave Sam's hand a tight squeeze.

Anna gave her a nod and looked away, not wanting the Elven Princess to see the sadness in her face as she knew that Elay would not be going in with them.

"EVAINE!" A cry sounded across the battlefield. He looked towards the voice and found Amador closing in on his position. He held his ground and continued to cut the Goblins and Gnomes to pieces that charged at him from all angles. White fire erupted all around him and they were gone, just smoke and ash remained as Amador reached his side.

"Evaine, it is up to you now," he shouted over the sounds of war that resonated around him, "I have done all that I can to give you a chance in this war. I have to leave; I have other things that must be attended too."

"You cannot leave us now Amador" he screamed, "we need your magic, the Demons are not all dead and they will be too much for us alone. What can be more pressing than this?"

Amador spun around to burn the advancing Demon that Evaine

had not even seen. He whirled back on Evaine, his face fierce and filled with rage.

"Do not think that I would abandon you. Trust me when I say that if I do not leave now the few Demons that remain will soon have a few thousand more join them. Invetia's future hangs in the balance and I have yet to play my part in its outcome!"

His face then softened as he met Evaine's stare. "Strength and good fortune to you Evaine, King of the Elves."

He then embraced him and was gone into the smoke.

"Strength and good fortune to you Amador, may fate and luck be on your side." he shouted after him.

Amador cloaked himself in his magic and left the battlefield unseen. He ran back past the ranks of Elven defenders bloodied and exhausted, past the attackers of Molgoran, screaming and full of hate and back onto the road that lead to the Telishan and ultimately to Silverdale and the Echenor mists. He ran with his cloak billowing behind him as he picked up speed to reach his destination. He never knew how he would know when it was time, he had often wondered how he would feel or what if he missed the signs but now he had the answer. There was no great light that descended upon him to guide him, no booming voice from above telling him to go, he just knew. He had gone from fighting in the thick of the battle to feeling the slightest twinge in his magic, the lightest of changes that alerted him to the fact that now was the time to depart and make for the Echenor.

He pushed himself even harder now, desperate to reach his goal and see this quest completed. He knew that he was going to die; he had always known that the arrival of the son of Ceriphan would mark the nearing of the end of his life, Ceriphan himself had warned him so, but he was not scared, he had had a lifetime to prepare for this moment, for this day, and he guessed that he had just grown accustomed to the idea. It was the way that it had to be and nothing that he could do would change his destiny that now raced towards him. He watched as the landscape passed him by in a blur as he ran ever

313

faster towards the Echenor. He was soon approaching the Telishan and saw the determined faces of the Elves that had started the march back to the fight upon Evaine's orders. 'He had given them a chance', he thought to himself; he had delivered the Troll army that would aid them in the fight with all that was evil within Invetia. He did not know what the outcome would be, even his magic didn't allow him to see that future, but at least he had given them a chance. He had also managed to see that the races of Invetia once again stood shoulder to shoulder against the rise of the darkness. He knew that it was no guarantee that the new alliances would hold for long after the threat of Molgoran had passed, if they survived the Demon attack at all, but he had done all that he could to try and unite Invetia as it had once been.

As he ran he thought back on his life, he had lived for a very long time and he had witnessed many changes to the people and to the world in which they lived. Every action that he had ever taken, every word he had ever spoken and every footstep that he had ever made had ultimately led him to this point in time, this here and now. He tried to remember all of the places that he had been and the people that he had met. He tried to recall the moments of his own life that held the most significance. Some he remembered, Ceriphan he remembered and the friendship that he had formed, his only true friendship that he had ever had, but for most of his memories, they were both cloudy and vague like a half remembered dream or they had faded away over the years of his life until forgotten completely. His life was nothing more than a patchwork of memories that hung loosely bound together with frayed thread, never quite fitting as they should have. And so it was that now he raced towards the most significant moment of all, the moment that his jumbled tapestry of life had led him to, and he embraced its coming. His life had been a mystery to most, cloaked in myth and legend, no one ever really knowing the man behind the stories. His life had also been based on half truths and subterfuge. He had never quite been able to divulge the whole story or the full outcome to those that he needed help from. He considered once that it was both powerful and desirable to know most of what was going to happen when he was younger, that somehow he held the upper hand in knowing just that little extra something, which gave him a fuller insight. But as he aged he realised that it was in fact a curse as it had always led to mistrust and suspicion of him. He, in return, had never been able to trust anyone since the passing of Ceriphan; he had never had the love and companionship of a woman. He had lived a solitary life, a life devoted to Invetia and nothing more, he now prayed that his sacrifice was not in vein and that Invetia would reward him for the services that he had given so freely and for so long.

The sounds of the battle diminished the further he ran and soon they had been completely left behind as he ran in the stillness and quiet of the day. It was as if time itself had stopped to witness his final act as he ran ever closer to his destiny.

"Are you ready Sam?" Anna asked as she now turned to face him. His face was contorted that gave off so many emotions; fear, confusion and shock were the most visible.

"There is no other way?" he asked, "no other place that we can travel to but the mists?" He asked.

"No Sam, the Echenor is where we must travel to see this thing through." She replied.

"And what will happen when we get there? What will be waiting for us within the mists and how will know what has to be done?" He continued.

"I do not know," she lied, "I just know that we will be instructed on what is to happen and how it should happen. As to anymore than that, I know no more than you." She lied again.

"So how will this Watcher get us there; I mean am I to click my heels together three times or something?" He was desperate now seeing that there was to be no other choice presented. The Echenor was where they would be heading and although every fibre of his body wanted to resist, wanted to run and hide, he knew inwardly that it was inescapable, it was destiny. Anna kept her voice as calm and as steady as she could muster.

315

"As soon as we are ready I simply tell the Watcher and it will happen, we will go."

Sam looked at Elay hoping that she could offer an alternative; hoping to find anything that she could say or do that would alter the need to go back to that place he feared so much, but she didn't need to speak as her eyes portrayed the inevitability of the journey required. After a short while Sam drew in a large breath and turned back to Anna.

"Call the Watcher." He said quietly.

He turned to Elay and held her in front of him, gripping tightly to both of hands as he heard Anna call out to the Watcher. As before he neither saw nor heard the Watcher as it approached.

"I love you." He mouthed silently to Elay as he held her hands ever tighter.

"I love you too." She replied, then there was a flash of brilliant light and the world around him melted away.

He felt as if he was falling, down and down he plummeted and faster and faster he fell. He kept his eyes clamped shut as the sensation washed over him. He did not know how long he fell for, but it felt an age, until, abruptly, it stopped. He felt his feet on solid ground again and the icy air hitting his sweat streaked face. When he finally gained the courage to open his eyes he was standing within a mist of greyness that stretched away in all directions and he felt his body begin to tremble at the realisation of where he was; he was within the Echenor mists. Anna stood in front of him, her face mirroring the fear that coursed through his body. It was then that he suddenly realised that Elay had disappeared. Frantically he looked around as far as was possible in the thick swirling mists in a blind panic for the missing Princess but she was nowhere to be seen. He was about to call her name when he suddenly froze to the spot, unable to move or speak, the voices that had called to him and almost claimed him on his last visit began their calling once again.

Elay closed her eyes as she felt herself falling through the air as she held onto Sam's hands as best she could, she felt her body get buffeted and shook from side to side so violently that she momentarily lost her grip on Sam. When she opened them to find Sam's touch she was back in her bedchamber in Silverdale, alone.

It took a few moments to get her bearings and realise just what had happened. Somehow they had been separated and she had gone to Silverdale whilst Sam and Anna had presumably been transported to the Echenor as foretold. She panicked and began running towards the door of her room. She had barely reached out to turn the handle when the door flew inwards and contingent of Ichbaru guards rushed in.

"My lady?" The foremost spoke in his surprise. "Are you unharmed? We heard a scream and feared the worst." He looked at her standing there, her clothes dirty and torn her face streaked with dirt, sweat and tears, confusion etched across his face.

"I am fine, now stand aside as I must get to the mists," she demanded.

"We cannot allow that," came a familiar voice from behind the Ichbaru, "Amador was quite specific in his instructions Princess Elay." the voice continued.

"Indra, I demand that you step aside I need to speak with my father."

Indra pushed his way through the guards and stood before her, his face emanating a kind but saddened smile. "Princess, can we sit for a moment, there is something that I need to tell you." He quietly stated.

CHAPTER

18

Sam stood facing Anna and listened to the voices resonate around him, trying to find some way to stop the sound from tearing him apart as they called incessantly at him. Over and over the voices called his name, urging him to join them forever within the mists, to take his rightful place with those that dwelled within.

He concentrated on the image of Anna ahead, not allowing the voices to break his stare and concentration, and, after what seemed to be some considerable time they began to quieten and the mists began to return to silence. The voices had either decided to wait and see what would happen next or the concentration that he had exerted was working and he was just failing to hear their calls anymore, either way, he now stood in silence and faced Anna.

"I am scared Anna, where is Elay?" He managed to speak, his voice trembling as he did so.

"She is safe Sam and I know that you are scared Sam, so am I," she replied.

"What happens now?" He asked in the still of the Echenor. His voice echoing through the emptiness as the mists swirled around him, caressing his body and soothing his aches from the long journey that had brought him to this moment in time.

"We wait Sam, we wait for another to arrive, I know not who, but I have been told that another will join us to ensure that what needs to be completed is done. So we just await their arrival."

"Are you now able to tell me what secrets you were told Anna? Why we have returned to the Echenor and why it is that you are here with me?"

She stared at him through the mists and half light that hung in the space between them, her face no longer able to mask the pain and sorrow that she was feeling.

"Soon Sam, soon all will be revealed and this nightmare will be over, soon we will be free of the dangers that we face and can return to the feeling of wonder that we felt when we first arrived within Invetia. It seems so long ago now, it seems as if our lives before are nothing more than a half forgotten dream, this now feels like home more than anything else I have ever felt." She continued to hold his stare despite the tears that now run freely down her face. "You asked me a long time ago Sam what I intended to do once this was all over, do you remember?"

He nodded in response to her words, thinking again that it did indeed seem a long-time ago that these words were spoken.

"Well I have decided Sam; I have decided that I am staying here in Silverdale, staying here in Invetia with you."

She watched as the words reached him, watched as his face reflected the unmistakable joy that they evoked and she cried some more.

"What about Ben, your Mum and Dad, your family, wont you miss them and wont they be missing you?" he asked, "There is nothing more that I would love than you to stay with me Anna but you have a life, you have a family to return to, are you sure that this will be the right decision to make?"

"I am sure," she responded quietly.

He stood for a while longer and listened to her quietly sobbing in the greyness of the mists, before stepping towards to her to embrace her and hold her. He had got halfway when a new voice called to him on the swirl of the mists.

"Sam, you cannot. You must not touch her now that you stand within the Echenor."

Sam spun around to find Amador standing behind him. His cowl was now lowered and Sam saw his face, now lined with age, sadness and pain. Sam looked at him confused as to why he had to hold his ground.

"It is time that you are now told as to how this is going to end my young Sam," Amador spoke, "as there has been much kept from you, much that had to be kept from you to ensure that the journey you made was completed, that the path that you had to tread was walked. It was never my intention that so much would have to be kept concealed; however it was necessary to do so. It is also true of Anna that she has also had to be kept blinded to the truth until recently, for she perhaps is to play the greatest role in the conclusion of our adventure."

Sam stared, even more confused now than he had been before, "Amador I do not understand," his words tumbled out, "I have always known that it was required of me to kill Molgoran and rid Invetia of the darkness, that it was the legacy left to me by

320

my father to carry the magic that would see an end to his threat. Now that we have been brought back to the Echenor I thought that this is where I will finally fulfil that destiny, I assumed that this where Molgoran will await me and my father's magic will destroy him. I do not see how Anna fits in with this; in fact I am unsure why you are now here? Please tell me what I have misunderstood about all of this?" His voice failing to hide the raw emotions that now raced through his body.

Amador stared a little longer; heaviness seemed to weigh him down as he considered the next words that he would speak in response.

"I was chosen too Sam," Anna suddenly spoke in a soft calming voice.

Sam turned slowly to the statuesque figure of Anna, feeling a cold shiver grab hold of his whole body. He felt his whole being begin to shake at its touch fearing the words that would follow. Anna continued,

"I did not know it to be so until I passed into the halls of the dead and spoke with those that dwell within." The tears continued to run freely down the pale skin of her face, but she did not falter in her words, "I spoke to Ruern Sam! She kept me safe within and stood by me as I was told the secrets of my past. She argued that I be allowed to take from the cavern that which had been sealed there for eternity." Slowly she reached into her cloak and pulled free a small purple Orb that pulsed dimly in the greyness of the Echenor. Sam immediately felt his magic respond to the sight of the purple light and flared up within him.

"Anna! What is that?"

"Do you not recognise it Sam?" she responded shaking her head, "it's an Orloc, its Molgoran's Orloc Sam, the same as Ceriphan's that you once had. Like yours, mine was once bigger but has grown smaller the longer that I have held it, like yours it is becoming one with me!" Sam screamed at her upon hearing the words,

"ANNA, NO, HOW CAN THIS BE?" he cried. He knew why the Orloc would grow smaller, he knew that to do so it meant that the magic within had leeched into the one that possessed it. He knew that Anna now stood before him with the magic of Molgoran coursing through her veins as Ceriphan's coursed through his.

She ignored his cries as best she could and continued to tell him of the events that had been kept from him.

"At the time of Ceriphan coming to your mother through Ruern, I was also chosen to play my part in the survival of Invetia. I was not born of magic as you had been, I was simply selected by Ceriphan's instructions, at some point near my birth, as to be the one to carry the seed of Molgoran from the caverns of the dead and bring it here for you to banish it from the lands. No one, other than Amador knew of this and it has been kept secret until now from all others. You see Sam, you cannot touch the magic contained within, to do so would destroy you and Molgoran knew this, the Demons knew this and this is why they did not fear your arrival. The Orloc was locked away and none could carry it without being destroyed, none that is apart from the one that had been given the magic to do so, that one was me."

Sam continued to listen in silence, the horror and realisation growing within him with each word spoken.

"So it was", she continued, "That I was given a part of Invetia's magic, just enough that, along with the presence of your magic, I would be able to pass through the door to the dead as the rightful heir to the magic. Just enough that would enable me to carry the Orloc from its resting place to the only site in Invetia that it could be destroyed, the Echenor. Once here, once destroyed it will remain locked within, unable to corrupt or enslave any more to its call. The mix of magic's,

322

Ceriphan's and Molgoran's will seal the Echenor once more. The magic of Ceriphan that you have however will not be sufficient to do so alone, the balance of light and dark makes it this way, neither can control the other, so another will be needed, Amador's will be needed. His magic is balanced by the Demons that walk the land and drive the armies of Molgoran forward. Once his has passed from Invetia the Demons will pass also, restoring the balance of magic's within the land."

Sam felt his body being crushed with the revelations that pushed down on him, unable to think straight and disorientated. Every emotion that he was capable of feeling rushed at him at once, each one demanding to be felt, to be answered. His body felt numb and lifeless as he stood and listened to the words that Anna spoke stab at him like daggers, each one leaving a scar upon him.

"What then happens once the magic of Molgoran is destroyed, what happens to the magic that is within me?" he asked.

"That too will be destroyed Sam," Amador responded. "Ceriphan's magic cannot survive without Molgoran's."

Sam stood still unsure as to what he was being told. "So what is to become of Anna, and what of me? What happens once the magic has been destroyed?"

"You will be free to leave the Echenor Sam, you will forever carry the remnants of that which you once carried, but it will be small in part. Ceriphan's magic will remain within to heal the Echenor, to once again make it strong, strong enough to house the evil of Molgoran. The Elves will return to a mortal life as the land will be changed forever, the magic changed forever. The memories that you have inherited will remain with you for as long as you live. How you then chose to live the remainder of your days will be for you to decide, but the path back to your previous life will be closed, Invetia will be your home for always now."

"Then Anna can leave with me?" Sam responded, "Once the magic of Molgoran has been destroyed she will be free to leave and live within Invetia too like me?"

There passed a long silence, a silence that Anna finally broke.

"My dearest Sam, I am to remain within the Echenor mists. I cannot leave with you for the magic contained within me is to be destroyed. I will forever be a part of the mists, forever be a part of Invetia. I wish there was another way but there is not, trust me, I have asked that question a thousand times. I know now that this was always to be my destiny Sam. I am so sorry Sam but there is no other way."

Sam broke down in front of her, unable to keep his emotions from pouring out. He fell to his knees and cried aloud into his hands that covered his face. This journey had cost him so much already, he had given up all that he knew and been thrown into a world that he neither understood nor had known, a world that he was born into without ever knowing so. He had lost people that he had come to love and trust, he had found and lost his father in his time here, but none of this compared to the loss of Anna. Never had he ever imagined that he would lose her, she was his rock she was the best friend he had ever had. Losing her was unbearable; he would trade his life for hers in a heartbeat. The thought that he would go through the rest of his life never again speaking to her, laughing with her, crying with her, tore him apart inside.

It took a long time before he had recovered enough composure to speak. He wiped away the tears from his eyes and looked up at Anna who now stood not more than ten yards in front of him.

"You said that you would stay here, with me, here in Invetia. You said that you would be with me forever." He sobbed the words as he began to breakdown again.

"I will Sam; I will be here within the Echenor. I will speak to you whenever you feel the need. I will be here for all of eternity. Once you have done wondrous things and lived your life, long after you have departed this world I will remain. The magic that you keep will enable you to walk the mists as and when you wish. You only have to call for me and I will be here, always. I am your friend Sam and always will be, and nothing that happens today will ever change that. I love you more than anything that I have ever loved and I am glad that I will be with you for all time."

"Master Sam" Amador spoke, "I will be here with her also as my path leads alongside Anna's. I will keep her safe within the mists; I will be here to accompany her through the times ahead. Ruern will be here also, she will not be alone, but time is pressing Master Sam, the grains of sand have almost run dry on our time together. The purpose for which we are gathered here today must be done soon. The Echenor grows weaker by every passing minute and cannot hold out for much longer."

"I am not sure that I can do this," Sam uttered, as much to himself as is was to Anna and Amador.

"Sometimes we all have to do what is right and not just what is easy." Amador replied, "You have strength that you have yet to realise."

Amador reached down and gently held Sam's arm. Slowly he began to get back to his feet helped by Amador. His legs had gone hollow and he felt weak and frail despite the magic that now rushed through him with renewed vibrancy as it sensed its master's summons would be made soon.

"Tell me what I must do Amador," he whispered.

Elay listened as Indra advised her of the Kings death. He told her of Evaine's departure to the Blendon Pass to meet the army of Molgoran head on and his plans to block the enemy's advance. He told her of Teon's departure, back to the kingdom of Varon and the mission to enlist the Men of the cities of the south to join with the battle ahead. She wept for the death of her father and promised Indra that he would be mourned properly by the Elves of Silverdale, but that Silverdale had to survive first. She had asked him how he knew that she would be returned to her bedchamber and Indra had advised her that Amador had been at the palace not five minutes before her arrival and that he had subsequently left for the Echenor. On hearing these words she ran from Indra, down the hallway and into the courtyard. She found a horse and was racing towards the Echenor mists at full speed. Indra called after her to stay and that she could do nothing once there but his words went unheard as she steered her horse through the streets and into the farmlands and beyond at full speed.

Evaine swung his sword into the mass of yellowed bodies that closed in around him, thick brown blood spattered across his face as his blade met the flesh of the attackers. His army had inflicted significant casualties to the Horde, but still they poured forward maddened by the Demons magic that held them captive. The arrival of the Trolls had evened the numbers greatly and the fighting prowess that they had brought significantly slowed the advancement of Molgoran's army, but since Amador had left the battle they were finding that they were still being pushed back by the swarms of attackers that came at them again and again. The Demons that drove the Horde forward had now appeared in the thick of the fighting, explosions of red fire rang out across the battlefield as they sent their magic smashing into the ranks of Evaine's army. The Trolls had managed to bring down a few of the Demons but each attack that the crimson eyed monsters launched claimed fifty or more men at a time such was their power and there was still too many of them left to take down quickly despite the Elves efforts. Evaine quietly prayed that they could hold out long enough for Amador to finish whatever it was that he had left to start. His warning that thousands more Demons could join the battle if he did not succeed meant complete annihilation, of not just the Elves but, all of Invetia's inhabitants as nothing could stand against an army of Demons that size. As he fought he caught site of Teon go down under a mass of attackers. He screamed his rage in response and swung harder and faster in an attempt to reach the Prince, but his way was cut off by a swarm of Goblins as they came for him with swords raised and madness in their eyes.

Amador stood behind Sam as they faced Anna in the mists of the Echenor. She stood still holding the purple Orloc before her. Sam could see that even in the short time that they had been within the mists it had diminished even further. It was now almost gone, almost absorbed completely into the girl that stood before him. When fully absorbed she would hold the power and the memories of Molgoran. Amador had advised him that once that came to pass she would no longer be the Anna that he had known and loved, she would be at the mercy of Molgoran's power. She would not hesitate to try and destroy them; she would leave the Echenor and take the evil that was housed within with her. Molgoran would be reborn through her and the land would fall into shadow. The power of the Orloc had to be destroyed through their combined magic. Once it was done the essence of Molgoran would have no escape from the restored Echenor and it would be incarcerated for all time. The price however would be high; it would take the life of Amador and Anna too. She would pass over to the world of shades and the voices that were housed within. He had asked again if there were any alternative anything else that could be done that would see her unharmed, but he already knew the answer before Amador had spoken.

"Sam," Anna called, "You must now act, I can feel the magic within me, and I can feel the stirring of his soul awakening.

The Orloc is almost gone, you must stop it Sam. I know that it is difficult but know that I want you to do so, you must Sam. Don't forget me; I will be here waiting for you. I love you Sam Meredith." She smiled at him, yet she did not cry but looked upon him with pride burning bright in her eyes.

He began to bring his hands up slowly from his side, never taking his eyes off Anna as he did so. He felt his magic stir and react to the movement. He watched as she nodded her approval. She stood now with her arms stretched out from her sides and tilted her head back and waited.

Sam's arms were now fully extended before him, his eyes again filled with tears as he did so. His body was almost convulsing from the shock and fear that was clawing at him. He felt Amador touch him lightly on the shoulder.

"It is time Sam. I thank you for what you have done for Invetia and I thank you for making my purpose in life fulfilled. I am sure that your road goes on for a very long time and I am sure that it will be filled with wonders and joys that you cannot yet imagine. The hurt of today will eventually pass, the scars will eventually heal and, over time, you will once again be the man that you are destined to be. Luck and life to you, Son of Ceriphan."

With those final words he unleashed a bolt of white fire that shot towards the standing figure of Anna and encased her in flame. She made no sound as it engulfed her. Before he could react to the sight before him, the amber light of his magic exploded forward into the figure of Anna. He didn't send it, he didn't think that even now he could of; the magic simply could not be contained any longer and acted upon itself.

He screamed as it unleashed itself into the now blurred image of the girl that stood before them. He cried out to her,

"I AM SO SORRY, ANNA, I LOVE YOU, I LOVE YOU PLEASE STAY WITH ME, I AM SORRY!" But there came no reply, no sound. The purple glow that had pulsed from the Orloc began to dim. Once or twice it briefly crackled as it struggled to cling on to life, desperately trying to thwart the attack from both Amador's and Sam's magic, but it could not stand against the combination and eventually it dimmed to nothingness. Still the magic exploded from him, growing brighter and hotter as it did so, even if he had tried to stop its flow he could not have, the magic was no longer at his command. He then saw the white fire of Amador begin to falter as it spluttered then died. He saw Amador fall to his knees, then onto his back and lay unmoving on the Echenor ground. His own magic then was beginning to fade, he felt it rather than saw it, it was leaving his body, being absorbed into the mists that swirled thicker and faster as it did so, he felt it drain from him as if being pulled from his very essence until the last remnants left him. He dropped to one knee, crying, exhausted, and bereft of any feeling other than desperation and grief. His head dropped as he felt as if he would pass out from the exertion of the magic, but he didn't, he managed to steady himself as his breathed in fast heavy gulps. His body felt strangely light and empty, he then realised it was the missing magic that was causing the sensation. The mists were quiet again, nothing stirred, nothing called, and it was as if it were just him alone in the thick greyness that now layered everything around him. He hesitated in lifting his head, he did not want to look, he did not want to see what lay before him, but he knew he must. Slowly he raised his head and looked first for Amador, he found nothing, nothing to suggest that the man had ever even been here beside him. With his body still trembling, grief stricken and with an overwhelming feeling of guilt, he looked for Anna. His eyes came to rest on the place that she had stood not a few moments before, he pictured her standing waiting for his magic to strike, her arms wide open, her head tilted back in readiness, but as with Amador there was nothing; she was gone.

He stayed on the Echenor ground for a long while after that, he curled himself up on the ground as if a child and wept aloud.

He saw the memories of his time with her throughout his life come into his mind as if thumbing through a photo album, he remembered her laugh, her smile, her sarcasm, he remembered her resolve and her kindness, he remembered her friendship and her companionship, he remembered everything that was good about her and then realised that it wasn't just the missing magic that had left him feeling light and empty, in fact the magic was just a tiny part of it, it was Anna. She was what was missing, she was what had made him whole and now, without her, he was hollow. He didn't know how he could go on without ever seeing her again; in fact he wasn't sure that he even wanted to try. He coiled himself up tighter and cried until he eventually succumb to his exhaustion and fell into sleep's embrace.

Elay brought her horse to skidded halt as she reached the Echenor mists. She arrived just in time to see the now transparent mists roil and twist, reacting to some event that was happening from within. She screamed as loud as she could for Sam, but there came no response. She watched as the mists began to thicken and take on the form that they had resembled in her years as a child, dense, foreboding and impenetrable. She felt a small change in her as they did so, unbeknown to her, so did every Elf. She walked along the perimeter of the mists for a short while until she finally came to a spot that drew her attention, her insights suddenly returned to her and she knew instinctively that this would be the place where Sam would emerge from. She returned to her horse and retrieved her blanket from its saddle pack, wrapped it around her shoulders and walked back to the spot where she sat herself down and stared into the mists. She would wait for him, she would wait if it was an hour or a year; she would wait for as long as was required for the man she loved to return.

Evaine desperately tried to reach Teon. He cut and slashed at the bodies that blocked his way forward. He was halfway through when he felt the change in him. He immediately knew what this was, he didn't know how, he just knew. Sam had managed to reach journeys end, he had managed to do what he had returned to Invetia to do and Molgoran was dead. The Horde army seemed to feel it too, in that same instance they hesitated as if not sure what was happening, and then the screams began to ring out across the plains. Tortured, painful screams, which filled the air, and flooded the land with its agonising sound. Evaine looked back and saw the Demons clutching at their heads, tearing at their own bodies in agony. They twisted and turned trying to escape the source of the pain as they began to fall upon the earth. He watched in disbelief as each of them began to get dragged across the ground by some unseen force. They screamed and tore at the earth trying to stop from being pulled away, but it was to no avail. They began being pulled back at a faster rate, back towards Silverdale. Then Evaine realised, back towards the Echenor! Then in blink of an eye they were gone and all that remained was the claw marks in the dust that was the only indication that they had ever existed. In that moment the Horde army broke apart. The magic that had held them captive for so long was no more, the spell broken and gone. The collectives of Gnome, Goblin, Kobold and every other fouled creature that stood against the races of Elves, Men, Dwarves and Troll began retreating at an immense rate. No longer held captive by the fouled touch of the Demons, they were leaderless and confused. The Elves pursued them for a short while, but when it was apparent that they had no intention of returning they called off the pursuit and let them leave. Evaine stared in shock at the battleground. Soaked with the blood of thousands upon thousands of dead, it now stood empty of all, except for the armies of those that had stood against Molgoran. As he looked he felt a firm slap on his back and a familiar voice.

"Told you it would be easy my old friend!"

He turned to find Teon beside him, bloodied and cut but alive. They stared at each other for the briefest of moments before erupting into laughter and embracing each other and then all of the soldiers that stood around them. The Elves, Men and Dwarves broke into cheers and laughter as they realised the battle was won. Only the Trolls remained impassive to it all. Evaine saw Kalt standing several hundred yards off in the distance. He watched as the giant Troll caught sight of him looking. Kalt made no attempt to come over to Evaine; he simply stood and watched for a while before placing his right arm over his chest in salute to Evaine. Evaine copied the Trolls gesture in response, and then the mighty Kalt turned and began walking off in the opposite direction with the remainder of the Troll army following.

Elay waited throughout the night for Sam to emerge from the Echenor, she didn't sleep nor did she take on water or food, she just sat and waited for him. It was at sunrise that she finally was rewarded for her vigilance. She could just about make out the outline of his body as he neared the edge of the mists before breaking free into the chill of the morning air. She stood to greet him as he shuffled along, dirty and pale; he did not see her at first, his head bent low. She watched him approach and noticed that no one followed him out, he was alone. She considered that maybe Anna had been taken somewhere else as she had. He walked a little further before raising his head and seeing her for the first time. The pain and weariness seemed to lift instantly from his tired face. Then he ran to her, it took every ounce of effort that he could muster but he was determined to reach her, determined that he would not fall or falter. He needed her more now than he had ever needed anyone in his life before. As he ran he felt the shackles of despair lift and drop away, he felt that maybe there was something worth living for; he felt the first tiny twinges of recovery begin. She ran towards him, tears in her eyes and threw herself at him. They stood there silhouetted against the morning sunlight and held each other for what seemed an eternity, neither wanting to let the other one in go in case they should lose each other again. Eventually Elay spoke softly in his ear,

"I can carry us on my horse, will anyone else be coming?" she asked as she cast her looks to the Echenor.

"No Elay, it's just us," he replied quietly.

She led him to where her horse was tethered and helped him atop. She then swung herself astride the saddle and slowly began a slow trot back to Silverdale.

Exactly three weeks after the battle for Silverdale had ended, Evaine's coronation was held. Thealine had been laid to rest and the Elves had seen the customary two weeks of mourning that followed a monarchs passing.

The battlefields had been cleared of the dead and the Elves of Silverdale that had given their lives were remembered and mourned along with their King. Five thousand Elven soldiers had left to defend the city and less than two thousand had returned.

Rotrim had visited to collect the body of Bannock and had promised that once the Dwarves had installed a new Lord then alliances and trade would be opened up with the Nations of Elves and Men. Teon had stayed on until the coronation. His wounds now fully healed, he too now bid farewell to Evaine and the Elves. He had told Sam of his great sorrow for the loss of Anna and had wished that he had been given the chance to have spent more time with her. He had told Sam that he would return soon as his friendship with Evaine had now been firmly forged.

Within these few weeks Silverdale had almost returned to life as it had been before the war. The Elves now had a mortal life and everyone seemed intent on living every minute to the full. Sam had been welcomed back a hero, despite Graflon's warnings that he would be the destroyer of the Elven nation. Evaine, at his coronation speech, spoke of Sam's sacrifice and great losses that he endured. He had also ensured that the Elves knew of Anna's bravery and the pain and suffering that she endured to see that peace and security was returned, not only to the Elves, but to all of Invetia peoples.

Evaine had also given his blessing for Sam and Elay to be united in marriage under his rule. Not that there was a rush for this to happen as Sam was still not recovered from the events that had transpired. Each day he grew a little stronger and healed inside a little more, but it would not be a quick process.

As the weeks passed, Sam would often walk out to the edges of Silverdale with Elay. They would stroll hand in hand in the warmth of the summer sun to where the Echenor mists bordered the fields of Silverdale. He wasn't ready yet to venture in. The magic that had remained within him allowed him passage, he would not be at risk of harm or any danger, but he did not yet feel that he would be strong enough to once again hear Anna's voice.

"Maybe next time" he would say to Elay when she asked if he would like some time alone to go in. She would smile and let him decide when the time was right.

As they walked past, Anna would watch their shadows pass hopeful that this would be the day that he would chose to stop and enter.

"Maybe next time," she would tell Ruern.

It was on a morning much like any other that they walked along the Echenor edge, the summer was coming to an end and the leaves were beginning to brown and fall from the trees. They laughed as they walked hand in hand and talked about their wedding that was fast approaching.

"How about today Sam?" Elay asked her usual question, "Would you like some time alone today?"

"Actually I think I would," he replied to her complete surprise.

She released his now sweating hand and felt his slight tremble as she did so.

"It will be alright," she whispered. "I will wait by the Ash tree for your return." She leant in and kissed him gently on the cheek. "Say hello from me," she called back as she made her way to the tree.

He stood before the mists and took a deep breath to try and compose himself. He felt strangely nervous, not of the mists, but of what he may find inside. It had been a long time since he had heard her voice or seen her face, longer than it should have been and, whilst he yearned to see her again he felt as if he was about to meet her for the first time in his life. He took another steadying breath before finally stepping into the gloom. He stood for a while, his eyes closed, not yet ready to open them until he felt his composure return. When he did he saw nothing other than the familiar greyness of the Echenor. Then suddenly he was aware of a shadow approaching, he then heard the voice,

"Hello Sam, took you long enough, thought you'd forgotten all about me."

Upon hearing her voice all of his inhibitions and nerves fell away, he felt a rush of joy and a feeling of excitement course through him, he felt almost whole again.

"Hello Anna," he replied to the shadow.

Elay smiled as she sat under the tree, she was pleased that Sam had finally found the courage and had healed sufficiently to make the trip into the mists. It seemed to her that everything was now well on its way to be mended.

As she sat beneath the canopy of the tree, she lifted her face to the sun and felt its warming touch radiate through her and she felt at peace. She may, however, have felt differently if she had cast her eyes down to where the Echenor met the border of Silverdale and seen the small crack that had appeared at the bottom of the wall of mist.